Also by Lynne Hugo

*The Book of CarolSue*
*The Testament of Harold's Wife*
*Remember My Beauties*
*A Matter of Mercy*
*Where The Trail Grows Faint: A Year in the Life of a Therapy Dog*
*Team*
*Last Rights*
*The Unspoken Years*
*Graceland*
*Baby's Breath*
*Swimming Lessons*

# PRAISE FOR LYNNE HUGO'S WORK

"*The Language of Kin* takes something we all possess—our ability to communicate with others—and has us examine that gift with new eyes. Hugo's words are beautiful, but this riveting story shows us how words can often fail, and forces us to see the many others ways we communicate, sometimes even unintentionally. This novel is an emotional read full of page-turning highs and cathartic sorrows. I fell in love with this complicated, compelling cast, both human and otherwise."
—Katrina Kittle, author of *Morning In This Broken World*

"A timeless and emersive story exploring the complexities of human engagement and the lengths we will go for those we love."
—Donna Everhart, USA Today bestselling author of *The Education of Dixie Dupree*

"Filled with empathy for all and a plot that will keep you flipping pages as fast as you can."
—Audrey Schulman, Author of Philip K Dick award-winning *Theory of Bastards*

"Brilliant, fascinating and deeply moving...gracefully written, this is a book that astonishes, even as it shows the way to cross divides...Full of science, love and drama, I couldn't love this book more if I tried."
—Caroline Leavitt, The New York Times bestselling author of *With Or Without You*

"Hugo takes a compelling look at the ethical issues and connections between humans and our fellow animals. *The Language of Kin* offers a well-researched, unbiased perspective into this multifaceted issue through a well-written, captivating story,"
—Samantha Russak, Ph.D., Primatologist

Hugo's writing might remind some readers of Annie Proulx, although her ear for dialog is closer to Larry McMurtry's ...Hugo offers convincing three-dimensional characters with convincing psychic wounds." —Ben Steelman, *Wilmington (NC) Star News*

"The kind of novel one longs to read...beautifully written, full of crooked fates, terrible loss and hard-won second chances." —Laura Harrington, bestselling author of *Alice Bliss*

"I lost hours of sleep as I raced to finish this extraordinary novel." —Randy Susan Meyers, bestselling author of *Waisted*

"Sparkling prose, wry humor, relevant themes abound." —Donna Everhart, *USA Today* bestselling author of *The Saints of Swallow Hill*

"Hugo's latest is a sweet, sad, funny, meditation on the nature of aging and grief...This is a novel that would fit right in on the shelf next to novels like A Man Called Ove and similar books that balance humor and heartbreak." —*Booklist*

"A widower takes up her late husband's mission to get revenge on the man who killed their grandson in the gripping latest from Hugo." —*Publishers Weekly*

"A winning and wonderful novel, with a unique and distinctive storyline, there is a little bit of magic for everyone within the pages of this book." —*The New York Journal of Books*

"Hugo writes about loss and redemption in a way that makes you laugh out loud one minutes and tear up the next." —Diane Chamberlain, *New York Times* bestselling author

"A richly told tale that explores the human/animal connection and the journey to get past tragedy... a tender hymn of hope and rebirth that stays with you long after the last page." —Kim Michele Richardson, *New York Times* bestselling author of *The BookWoman of Troublesome Creek*

"Full of intrigue and heart, as gritty as the inside of a clamshell and tender as a beach sunset."
—Jenna Blum, *New York Times* & internationally bestselling author of *Those Who Save Us*

"A profound and heartfelt book...Hugo is a tender and wise guide to the realities of aging, and Hannah, her chocolate Labrador retriever, who brings love and life to residents of a Midwest nursing home, is a true charmer. Where The Trail Grows Faint charts the territory with a rare spirit of hope."
—Floyd Skloot, author of *In the Shadow of Memory*

# THE
# LANGUAGE
# OF KIN

A NOVEL

# THE LANGUAGE OF KIN

## A NOVEL

*Lynne Hugo*

# LYNNE HUGO

Blank Slate Press | St. Louis, MO

Blank Slate Press
Saint Louis, MO 63116
Copyright © 2023 Lynne Hugo
All rights reserved.

For information, contact:
Blank Slate Press
4168 Hartford Street
Saint Louis, MO 63116

www.amphoraepublishing.com
*Blank Slate Press is an imprint of*
*Amphorae Publishing Group, LLC*
www.amphoraepublishing.com

Manufactured in the United States of America
Cover Design by Kristina Blank Makansi
Cover art: Kristina Blank Makansi
Set in Adobe Caslon Pro, Acumin Variable

Library of Congress Control Number: 2022948577
ISBN: 9781943075775

This one is for my beloved Ciera, Andrew, and Alyssa:
May you do better than we before you when you
inherit this beautiful, wounded earth.

...The moon looked down
between disintegrating clouds. I said
aloud: "You see, we have done harm."

— Jane Kenyon, an excerpt from "While We Were Arguing"
in *Let Evening Come*

...to be understood
            to be more than pure light
    that burns
            where no one is...

—Mary Oliver, an excerpt from "Poem" in *Dream Work*

# Eve

IT WAS THE BABIES they were after. Not that there wasn't a market for adults. Bushmeat sold well in the village.

The men were excellent trackers, silent as big cats on the hunt as they made their way through the hot dense green of western Uganda in search of mothers nursing their babies together.

Eve had been nursing while her mother groomed one of the other mothers. Mothers did that, groomed each other, taking turns. Had the birds ruffled a warning along the treetops? Eve didn't know. But in the deep rainforest where sounds were liquid, ape, cat, reptile, insect, bird, breeze, it was sudden when the green quiet exploded. A mother chimp fell from her rock and the barks, hoots, shrieks, screams of the others rose. Mothers scattered, made for the trees. The ear-hurting noise cut through the air again, again. Eve clung to her mother's back through the panicked scramble amid the *hu* and *waa* of alarm, fiery blasts again, again, bodies dropping. Blood, hair, shattered limbs. Blood, bone, pain. Tumbling from trunks and branches, spilling bits and pieces of themselves, mothers fell like heavy fruit, babies holding on to their chests or backs, babies holding on, holding on, falling, falling, falling through green, red, brown, falling hard to the ground.

The men were very good shots.

Two mothers did not reach the trees and they went down neatly, like the end of a dance, one breaking her newborn's neck when she went down on top of the infant cradled to her chest. None of the eight mothers in the nursing party lived; the sticks that exhaled death reached them whether on ground or in the trees, and even the one mother who ran farthest, she went down too, her baby beside her, knocked loose by the blast, too dazed to scream until her eyes, ears, and nose woke and she joined the panicked mayhem of the surviving babies.

Eve's mother had jerked and grunted, crashed through the leafy green and brown of the tree she'd climbed, tipped to fall face-first. Still Eve clung to her back, though her mother's blood streamed in her eyes and her ears were stuffed with noise and terror.

Rough hands pried her, screeching, off her mother. A small metal cage, just her alone, other babies in other cages. Heavy cloth tossed over the cage.

Her mother's blood and her own fear-feces matting her hair, Eve curled, shrieking, under the covering. The movement rough as when she'd clung to her mother, knuckle-running for the false safety of the tree. Now Eve's body, locked in airless darkness, banged the bottom of her cage again and again, as the underbrush was thrashed aside and broke under the heavy movement, careless, loud as the other babies' terror cries now.

The poachers were pleased. The capture was done, and they would not be caught. Money to ensure their escape had changed hands. They'd gotten five babies. They'd hoped for more, but three died with the mothers. Middlemen waited at the marketplace for as many babies as could be had.

The brilliant light blinded when the cover was removed, the cage surrounded by noise and swirling figures, tall, loud animals that were bright as parrots. Eve cowered, trembling. A different stick was pointed at her, and she screamed as a sharp pain entered her thigh. Her muscles turned soft as mud, and the world dissolved as a starless, moonless night crept over her eyes covering the last she'd know of good—sky, forest, fruit, comfort—for eight years. Then something would wake a memory, small as the ants her mother used to catch. Mother.

# Chapter 1

MY EYES ALWAYS THREATEN to spill tears when I'm really frustrated. Back when she had words, my mother used to warn me that women's faces get red and ugly if they cry when they don't get their way. She had me pegged all wrong though. What upsets me to that point is seeing my own failure. Like now, when it's clear I've failed to sway Marco Lopez.

"Dammit, Marc. No. Captivity is just wrong." My face was probably a crimson flag.

He answered in his low-key, unruffled way. No wonder he was so good with the great apes. "But the alternative is that inevitably some species just go extinct. Is that acceptable?"

How could a man as smart and kind as Marc, a man who'd been a primate keeper for seven years, still believe zoos were ethical or moral? He couldn't think they were for the chimps, anyway, not after all he'd learned about their minds and hearts; I'd trained him to work with our primates myself. Before we hired him, he'd been a top-notch vet tech whose references had blown us all away, but he had zero experience with gorillas or chimpanzees.

And now, we were arguing in the zoo's break room, the last people at the table. He had that earnest look he'd worn so often as he sat by my desk in his pressed open-collar shirt, clean shaved, and dark hair clean cut, even his heavy dark eyebrows not straggly. I'd heard he lived with his mother and wondered why a good-looking guy well into his thirties would want to do that. Contrasting his life choice with my own made me feel bitchy, but then he'd say or do something that elicited something better in me, and when I looked at him, I'd wish I'd combed my hair and tucked my shirt in, too, instead of letting it wander around untethered from my waist like a lost child. I couldn't help liking his aftershave if I leaned over his computer to show him something. He'd get up to make space for me, and I'd notice again how he moved like one of zoo's big cats, at ease with his strength. Every woman on staff, even the well-married ones had noticed his good build. A couple had even made jokes about our individual supervisory meetings being nice and private. Hadn't they read the code of ethics? I was his supervisor for god's sake.

Or I had been until Thurston, the zoo's Executive Director, took that job away from me, showed me that my career was made of flimsy toothpicks when he said that I wouldn't be considered for the new Research Director job I wanted so badly. With my experience on top of my doctorate, I was ideally qualified for the position, but Thurston had gotten wind that I wasn't committed to the zoo's essential mission, as he'd put it. At first, I thought he was letting me go, but instead, he'd put me in charge of creating the new habitat for our primates—with no staff reporting to me, no one to contaminate with my heresy.

Marc went on now, animated and sincere, but not upset like me, though I was trying to hide it. "They're taking down the rainforests, the corporations," he said. "Logging. Farming. On industrial scales. How can the apes live with no habitat? They're on their way to extinction. I'm not saying anything you don't know better than I do. Do you think I don't love them as much as you? We're their last line of defense." It was Marc's pragmatic logic. And it put him right in Robert Thurston's camp.

He must have known exactly what I'd say—again—before I jumped in with, "We have to put a stop to the clearcutting, act against the poachers. Bushmeat has to be illegal in the countries where it's sold. We've got to supply incentives in countries that don't have endangered species laws. Stop the problem where it starts. Because the chimps will die out sooner or later in zoos, for god's sake. Zoos are a finger in the extinction dyke." My voice was going up with the heat of my certainty. The tingle behind my eyes meant tears were about to embarrass me, but I couldn't stop. Every chimp I'd known had become a dear individual to me.

Linda Marchers, who was the Primate Curator and my boss— and now Marc were the only people with whom I'd had discussions like this. Linda wasn't unsympathetic and I'd thought I was in line for her job when she eventually left, since I was her assistant curator. Well, I'd thought a lot of things I doubted now.

"You really think we can stop human greed? That's what's at the heart of habitat destruction." Marc shook his head. "Not gonna happen."

I brushed my hand across my cheek pretending I was moving a wayward strand of hair instead of keeping a tear from spilling. "You're saying we just give up? Catch a bunch of them, breed them in cages, send 'em off to different zoos?" A deliberate exaggeration on my part, but I didn't care.

Marc started to answer, but right then, Thurston came in the door. I'd heard others mock the director behind his back for his flattop hair and nineteen sixties black-framed glasses, true-enough descriptors, but I noticed something strange in his footfall, as if one foot had a slight drag. He carried himself with a barely discernable lean to the left. Was it his hip or his knee that bothered him? Strange how paying attention to the bones of the great apes sensitized me to those of homo sapiens.

Marc and I made eye contact and understood each other, as usual: time to get going. Each of us picked up our cups and napkins and pushed back our chairs before Thurston could turn in our direction. Marc was sensitive that way, something I really liked about him, especially since we both knew Thurston would have jumped on his side.

"Are you serious?" Marc yanked his attention away from the lunch remnant stuck in one of his teeth and turned in his chair to look at Linda, his eyebrows up and eyes wide. "We're getting another chimp? How'd you pull that off?"

They were in the staff lunch area and Linda had just told him that the first new chimpanzee since Marc started at the zoo would be coming soon. He'd been hired just after Lolly's arrival and was too inexperienced with primates then to be involved in socializing her. Lolly, who was now seven, had been an orphaned baby the zoo acquired after some idiot realized it had been a terrible decision to buy a chimp as a pet.

During his initial orientation, Linda had gone on an extended rant about it. "Maybe people don't know that chimps nurse their babies for five years, or that the only way to get a baby chimp away from its mother is to kill the mother, and that's exactly what the poachers do to feed the pet trade," she'd said. "They damn well *ought* to know." She'd been showing Marc the correct way to offer the chimps a new toy, which Kate would teach him at least three more times before letting him do it himself. "It's called failure to thrive, and it's just like what happens to human babies when their worlds fall apart. Or maybe people do know, and buy them anyway, dress them up in those ridiculous outfits and put diapers on them, thinking they can raise a chimp like a human child in their family. Well, that lasts until they get tired of the whole thing, or the chimp gets too big and too strong to manage. But baby Lolly must have been too sad and needy and sick to have even started out cute."

The zoo had taken Lolly for lack of a better alternative, tried pairing her with Jasmine, and bless that chimp's good heart, she'd taken to mothering. Jasmine had had enough time with her own mother that she'd had a model. She'd remembered. "You should have seen it," Linda told Marc back then. "She was great. Carried Lolly around like she'd given birth herself until Lolly caught on and could ride on Jas's back, groomed her, you know, the whole nine yards."

The whole nine yards was Linda's favorite expression and it always meant something extraordinarily good or bad. Linda had an unguarded, straight-on honest gaze beneath a mane of untamed, helter-skelter curls that were dark as the cafeteria's late day coffee. Her brows, just as dark, were narrow as pencil lines on her fair skin, and her nose was thin and centered. She was a kind woman and attractive, Marc thought, though he tended to fall for women like Kate who didn't show the slightest interest in him. It was a tendency that didn't lend itself to long-term relationships. It didn't matter, though. He knew what was appropriate in the workplace.

"So, what's the deal?" he said now, leaning over the table and squinting as if trying to figure something out. "Is this because we'll have room? I mean, once we have the new habitat?" He paused and when she didn't answer right away, cleared his expression. "Anyway, it's great. I want in."

Linda ignored the question about timing. "That's why I'm telling you." Sitting next to one another, they were nearly the last people in the staff area. "This may be tough," she said, "but I'm giving you the lead in transitioning her. I know you haven't done it before, but no one else has either—Lolly was a different set of issues—and it's going to require a lot of time and patience."

"You got it. Tell me…" Marc said, while his mind stuck on Linda not assigning Kate. She'd been lead with Lolly.

"She's coming from a medical lab," Linda said, animated, angry. She'd put her glasses on top of her head and now they slipped down toward her forehead. They had tortoise shell frames and Marc had wondered if that was a statement one way or another. As she grabbed to catch them, her elbow hit the edge of her tray, and her bottle of iced tea rocked. Marc stuck his hand out and braced it before it tipped over.

He let go of her bottle and closed his eyes. "Shit."

"Exactly." She shoved the glasses back on her head and sighed. "How bad?"

"Don't know exactly. Do we know of any that are good?"

"How much do we know about her background?"

Linda sighed. "Some of it's expectable. She's *Pan troglodytes verus*—western African origin like most lab chimps. Wild caught when she was maybe three, three and a half. Still nursing." Linda paused to shake her head. "Breaks my heart over and over. Have you heard Kate's spiel about what those poachers do to capture them, the whole nine yards about how they're treated?"

"Not that part."

"Well, Kate's witnessed the aftermath in the field, so I shouldn't call it a spiel. You'll likely hear it when we get the new chimp. Kate's ideas drive Thurston up a wall. But we're damned lucky to have her, especially with her reputation in the field. Thurston's not exactly an expert on primates," she added, rolling her eyes, "and Kate wrote the book on them."

Linda had never spoken of another staff member to Marc, and he wasn't sure how to respond. Was this some kind of defacto promotion? A test? Was that tea spiked?

Marc nodded. "Yeah, she really is great." Was that a safe thing to say?

Linda nodded and took a long drink. "Oh, and her name's Eve. The chimp. So, anyway, Eve got to be with her mother for three years, not near enough time, but not quite as bad as a lot of what the bastards do taking the tiny babies away," she said.

"And now the lab is dumping her because?"

"They weren't the first lab to have her. They got her from another one. The first lab failed to get their grant renewed, I guess it was pretty soon after they started chimp experiments. Don't know why. The usual, I imagine. Inadequate safety protocols for their workers. It wouldn't have been failure to protect the apes, that's for sure. Probably used for hepatitis or AIDS research. We'll be sure if she's got the scars like here," she looked down and pointed to a spot high on her own abdomen, "you know, over her liver, from multiple biopsies. Anyway, that lab, couldn't go on because of, you know, Endangered Species Act. Can't do what they want anymore, too many limits, too expensive to feed and house chimps, even in their tiny cages—well, be grateful for that much because at least then they go looking for a zoo to take 'em. You know."

"Yeah." He did know. He'd been wondering if there was something other than the usual. Apparently not.

"So...Eve, huh?" He grinned. "She socialized at all?"

"Nope. Caged. Alone."

No grin now. "How old?"

"Eleven. I mean as best they know. No menses yet, so probably accurate."

"Uhhh." Marc blew it out through pursed lips. "What's the word on personality?"

"Nothing helpful. Not that a lab paid a lot of attention to that. No mention of aggression, though." Linda leaned forward over the lunch table now, shoved her tray aside. "Look, it's going to be a steep learning curve, but it's a pretty good time for us to get her, since we're building the new habitat. Maybe she'll be able to be integrated into the social group about the time that's ready. We can aim for that, right? Coordinate with Kate on the timing. And you can consult with her too, about integrating Eve, if she's got the time."

On his way back to the primate area after lunch, Marc let himself be really excited. Tuition reimbursement, his zoo salary, and the help with his mother from the hired graduate students had gone a long way toward transforming his life. He'd hoped that the comfort in the wider world and deaf culture of a few audiology students with their own hearing issues would encourage his mother not to be so dependent on him, even start venturing out. That hadn't happened, but still, Marc was thinking about going on for a Ph.D. He could probably do his dissertation research at the zoo. Why not? The other keepers had become good work friends, happy to trade schedules when any of them had a conflict. His life—other than living with his mother and her dependency on him—had settled toward normal, like earth neither flooded nor parched. And now this! Being the lead with the new chimp. He flipped through his mental files searching for what he knew about socializing a new chimp into a troop. He'd ask Kate for help if that wouldn't be too weird now.

He did have a bit of a thing for Kate McKinsey. Maybe her looks put him in mind of Dr. Duff, the first vet who'd mentored him, or maybe he just liked blondes with that nice eyebrows and streaky hair thing, and the same way of carelessly tying it back or sticking it behind their ears. It was almost like Kate couldn't really be bothered with fixing herself up much because she was too busy fixing things for the apes. Not that she needed to fix herself up. When she smiled, which he wanted her to do more, he could see she had nice straight teeth, so why not? He got it, though. All the supervisors kept a distance; the zoo ethical rules were strict, and the big departments operated separately. It had to be lonely. He liked trying to make Kate laugh. And she was so smart. That's what first drew him to her, that and her passion for the apes.

After all this time learning from her, all he really knew was her devotion to the apes and to leaving yellow sticky notes on staff desks with little reminders. And if someone proposed something she thought would be bad for the primates, she'd say, "Over my cold dead body," he knew that, too, and had taken pride in not provoking that response. But there wasn't anything she didn't know about great apes, and she was generous with explanations in the way the best teachers are. She hid it, but he guessed it must drive her crazy to tiptoe around Thurston, who was all about publicity, fundraising, getting the next tax levy passed. Marc let himself off the hook for noticing her breasts when she wore that one light green shirt with the sort-of low neck; there wasn't a straight male alive who wouldn't notice. He'd have tried to get to know her as a person, but he wasn't an idiot. She was his supervisor.

Until she wasn't. Not anymore.

But his wasn't the time to be distracted by what was under Kate's green shirt even though they were peers now. The truth was, he didn't know a damn thing about socializing a chimp coming from a medical lab. From what Linda said, he was going to know virtually nothing about her history. What hell had she been through for the last eight years, an orphaned, unmothered baby coming into adolescence and now coming to his care?

# Eve

THE TRACKERS RECEIVED ten dollars each, the middlemen many times that. Two of the babies were sold to private collectors, pets for wealthy people, a European and an American who would put them in diapers and baby clothes, raise them like toddlers until they were about five, large and heavy enough to assert their wills and bite their human caregivers. One infant was sold to a circus to be trained to perform. She'd wear a collar attached to a leash, rewarded with treats when she did the tricks, punished with an electric prod when she failed. One baby went to a medical test laboratory in eastern Europe where she died of a viral infection four months later. The experimental treatment did not work.

Eve was sold to a medical laboratory in the United States. Injected on a schedule to ensure she would remain sedated, she was moved by truck to the airport, transferred to another metal cage, and flown overseas to New York and then to Chicago's Midway airport in the cargo hold of a transport plane. Two lab technicians picked the three-year-old up there, where they hosed the urine and feces from the cage with her in it and, because she was stirring, one of them used an air pistol to shoot her with another sedative dart, in order to transport her to the medical testing facility. Seven other chimpanzees were already there, each in a separate, bare metal cage. The cages were stacked in twos, a line of four, so that the chimps could hear but not see each other.

When she woke, Eve tried to hide herself by cowering in the corner of her cage. The monkey chow was hard, strange, and there was no fruit, the cage cold, barren, the noise of a few older chimps shrieking protest or pain terrifying, though some had stopped and gone silent as they picked at their own bodies, slowly removing a patch of hair here, another patch of hair there. Eve started to rock, sometimes hitting her head on the solid back wall.

Too soon Eve knew what it meant when she got no food and her water was taken away. A big animal with little hair and covered in white would come with a gun to shoot her leg, unless he missed and hit another place that was worse, like the time it was her neck. She'd scream and curl away. One of them would make sounds, "Time to knock you down," and narrow his eyes as he'd aim, but the others made no sounds, just shot. There would be the pain, hot and searing, and then the blackness spreading over her eyes. When she woke up, her body would hurt.

Hurt where it had been cut.

Hurt all over.

Hurt.

# Chapter 2

ONE DAMN DELAY after another with the new habitat. First, waiting on the grant money to be deposited. I'd been able to argue for more space for the chimps, but that required moving the smaller enclosures for the lemurs, which would involve the sacrifice of one of the zoo's flower gardens, which meant moving some water lines.

Patience doesn't come naturally to me. But what's natural is the whole point, as in let the chimps live as naturally as possible for captive great apes. Give them space to climb, material to nest, a way to retreat. Let them have their family bonds, let them give birth if they've mated—don't inseminate the females, though we're not a breeding zoo, thank heaven. But let infants be nurtured and raised by their own mothers. A habitat richly green with branches, water, rocks, privacy. Leave them alone. Give them indoor space for protection in winter, outdoor space the rest of the time, and let them be!

It was that last part, leave them alone, that made Thurston batshit crazy, of course.

He wanted the animals in full, glorious display. The public didn't like coming to the chimp—or any other animal—exhibit and not seeing them. If the chimps could hide, well, they might well do it, and how would that exhibit be meaningful to the patrons?

It was complicated, for sure. I had a decent budget for consultation. What I wanted was cutting edge: overhead trails for the great apes with an extra benefit—the big cats could use them in winter when apes have to be indoors. I wanted the zoo to have our own version of what the Philadelphia Zoo already had underway: ZOO 360, started in 2012, a whole treetop animal trail system that had let them create functional spaces spread all over the property for food, water, dens, and rest. It had been the Australian zoological park designer John Coe's brilliant concept. Big trails for great apes shared by the big cats; medium and small trails shared, at different times, by other species. It was revolutionary, a real effort to replicate how their apes live in the wild, with those kinds of trail-connected areas used at different times of day.

And the Philadelphia Zoo visitors loved it. I'd seen how they stopped to stare, riveted on the pathways between exhibits because an animal might be making its way in a mesh-covered "trail" overhead. It was magical and all it required was millions and millions of dollars, a visionary director, and keepers who shared that vision and believed in it passionately. Three critical requirements.

Linda would support it. I was sure about our keepers, too. I loved them. They'd see the benefit for the apes, and I could train them in the new protocols. And the big cat curator had to want it, too; curators and keepers always want more space for their animals. I'd need Thurston on board. He was the budget man.

I did my homework. I had sketches and figures when I brought it up to Thurston, a specific proposal, and the design consultant I wanted to hire.

"We can't do that, Kate," he said, his voice flat, no apology in it. I'd mentioned the success of the Philadelphia Zoo. "Do you know the difference between Dayton, Ohio, and Philadelphia? Think about potatoes, will you? Fingerlings versus Idaho baking."

I must have had a baffled look on my face because he added, "Relatively speaking, one is small potatoes. And do you get that we're in a hurry? The new chimp is coming, we don't know exactly when..."

Another chimp was all the more reason. I kept trying different approaches. "Couldn't we—"

"It would involve an overall redesign of the zoo. Isn't that obvious? Find a designer to work with who gets what's possible here. We don't have that kind of money."

"But if we did it for just the big cats and the chimps, the shared trail thing, different times for each, couldn't that work? See, that's what I've proposed, not the whole zoo." I tried to filter frustration from my voice. I'd already told him that. "Or what about just the chimps? I can put a rush on everything. Of course, I understand about the new chimp. She's a huge concern for me. We weren't expecting to acquire—but can we look at some overhead trails between foraging and sleep areas just for the chimps, maybe we could—" I was casting, trying to salvage something of how they'd live if they could.

Thurston sighed and looked around the office as if there might be a hidden source of strength. He left enough silence to tell me he was annoyed but didn't let his expression show it. He managed to keep it out of his tone, too. He shoved his glasses back up on his nose with a forefinger and said, "I'm sorry, Kate. I'm not sure what figures you're working with, but they don't seem to be the ones I gave you. Maybe we should go over the budget again, or would you like for someone else to head this up? Linda could—"

"No, thanks. I understand. I'll work with the space specs. I just thought we could use the treetop area and maybe—"

"As I said, I'm sorry. Too big a picture."

I'd known it would require not only extra money but a progressive director. We didn't have either. It had been too much to hope for.

Back at my desk in the primate area when I was alone and with was no chance of being seen, I ran a search on for job opening at the big sanctuaries. Just to see if anything came up, which nothing at my level did. But really, I had something else in a secret mind-pocket: to go back for another stint in Western Africa, the Ugandan home I found when I did two years of field work there after grad school. My heart never left the place where I'd learned to love and respect the chimps.

The work with an endangered species in an endangered habitat had saved me, which is ironic. Some nights even now I dream I'm sleeping again in that tent in the rainforest and it's not my own voice that wakens me, but the thrum of insects and wildlife calling in the dark stealth. I was fearless there, and it had been so easy to make friends. The director was as hands-on as the rest of us, without the power hierarchy and constant focus on everyone doing what would raise money. Not that we didn't need it, for sure. But it was all about the work. I still talked often with Becky, my tent mate who'd become a dear friend. She was now Assistant Primate Curator at the Seattle Zoo. Our cohort was scattered in random states and Europe, but we had reunions. In a year and a half, I'd be hosting in Dayton. Those who'd remained in Africa came in on Skype, too. We'd all developed the same mindset from seeing what was happening live and up close. I needed some Becky time and advice now; maybe I should take some vacation and go out there, see what she thought about my going back.

But of course, I couldn't. The thought of going back to Africa, working to stop poaching and clear cutting, actions that really would save the chimpanzees—the notion was nothing but a gossamer wing that had brushed over my eyes, iridescent and lovely. I blinked and when I opened my eyes again it was gone. At the same time, my cell phone rang.

Sycamore Community, the screen said. My mother's assisted living center. At the time, I thought, yes, this is how it is: offer up a bad day to the universe and the universe will hand it back worse.

"We'd like you to attend the next team meeting when Dorothy's care is discussed," the director said. "Thursday at ten. We need you present since Dorothy can't speak for herself."

A masterpiece of understatement that was. Even though Mom shouldn't be the only one who can't speak her mind, it was doubtless a good thing that I managed not to spout what I wanted to: Oh thanks, but I have a luncheon date with a great ape, so I'll skip the meeting since I already know what you're going to say and damn, I do not want to hear it.

Even a long weekend out west with Becky would be out of the question.

I made a face at the phone and exhaled so my head wouldn't explode. Then I dragged up a polite voice and agreed to be there at ten on Thursday. I even said thank you. Mom would be so proud.

But if Mom could have been proud, it would mean she could have made sense of what was being said, and I could have gone to Seattle or to work in Africa, and the earth wouldn't have been slowing, tipping over on its axis until it fell and spun off, irretrievable.

What they were going to tell me was entirely predictable. I could already see the bony, pinch-nosed director patiently trying to make it clear to the resident's clueless daughter: *your mother isn't understanding what anyone says to her at all, and she can't tell the staff what she wants or needs. It's not safe. What if there's a fire? It's a safety issue. Really, she needs to be moved over to skilled nursing where there are other residents who need close attention. It's entirely for her own safety.*

The woman would never say that it was too time-consuming to ferret out pictures of anything my mother might need. Or to figure out what she might be feeling, for god's sake. In other words, she'd be saying she needed to be where there's a better cage and more keepers.

The director's ace would be "What if there's a fire?" In assisted living, residents had to be able to understand evacuation instructions. Pictures weren't possible to use in case of fire, the director would explain with elaborate patience. She'd be dressed better than I , to remind me who held the power here, and power would be why she'd overcome my arguments, even though I'd whip out some polysyllabic words that just meant, *hey, I'm educated too. I'm trying to tell you my mother is in there and I'm trying to save her. It's words she's lost, not her mind.*

The skilled nursing building would mean another diminishment. I'd have to move the furniture I'd hauled here—with help, of course—from the big old house, gone now, to her two-room unit with its kitchenette and her own table and chairs in the dining alcove, the drop-leap walnut table we'd had all my life. I'd salvaged that for her, along with placemats and personal things that Mom had saved from her own mother. Well, those and a lot of other junk I waded through, wondering if everyone's parents saved so much crap or if I was just exceptionally lucky.

My idea was that Mom's friends could come see her there, have a simple lunch with her in her own little apartment. There'd be a vase with a few red, yellow and orange dahlias on the table in summer, and the favorite pictures, also from the house—Monet prints—that I hung around the living area.

But Mom still had some language when she'd moved into assisted living. Labor-intensive for her to birth them, but words were still there. And she'd been slow to comprehend what was said, but if a person took the time to try a couple of different ways, the right combination of words would click into place in her mind like tumblers unlocking meaning. Not anymore. Friends slowly stopped coming until there were none, and I almost didn't hold it against them.

Except I did. I understood how helpless they felt, but did they understand that I felt helpless too—and alone on top of that? My closest friends were scattered around the country. Zoo rules about boundaries—to make sure supervision wasn't compromised and safety for animals, guests, and staff were always the focus—had limited my socializing with the people I really cared about. I rarely talked with my father, and certainly not about Mom. He was wrapped around his new family, Candy's family. I didn't fit into that package.

The next time I moved my mother, it would be to one room. One small room that would put me in mind of a cage. A bed, a night table. A chair. A bathroom. Oh, it wasn't difficult to see what was coming. I could see it just fine. I just didn't know how to bear it.

# Chapter 3

SOME DAYS LATER, after brooding about the upcoming meeting, I wiped my face with the back of my hand. No. Not yet. I couldn't face it quite yet. I needed a little time. Just a little breathing room.

"Marc," I said. He was at his desk, two away from mine in the primate department office. "I need to make a personal call if anyone's looking for me. I'll be outside. Back in a little bit. Will you keep Bruce company if he takes his break?"

Marc looked up and smiled. "Of course."

"Thanks," I said and meant it. He didn't have to do any favors for me now. Not only that, Linda had taken over as field supervisor for his master's project, which was almost complete anyway. She'd just check a few details for his thesis and be present for his orals. He'd graduate next month. The announcement had come by memo from Thurston. It used to be my job to sign off on academic research done in the primate area, and I'd always liked keeping my hand in. Maybe it was just as well, though since I disagreed with Marc's thesis statement. He was a wonderful keeper, one of the rare ones with a natural gift, a quick-study pleasure to train when he'd joined the staff after graduating from a two-year vet-tech program. I couldn't help wondering why it had taken him so many years to finish his undergraduate work and that program; his academic transcript was damn near perfect. He'd sure sped up since then. But, not my ponies, not my rodeo. I didn't ask personal questions when I supervised.

I took my cell phone all the way out to the employee parking lot and got in my car, which was incredibly inconvenient but the only way I could be sure of complete privacy. I inhaled, exhaled long, steadied myself and pushed the number in my contacts list.

When I was put through to the director, I led with the biggest lie. "I'm terribly sorry," I said. "I won't be able to make that team meeting on Thursday. It turns out I'm needed at work. Could we reschedule for next week, or the week after next?"

The director hesitated. "We're very concerned…this is about comprehension and safety issues."

But I was sure it was about what made it easier for the staff. And all right, for me it's about guilt, the weight of sorrow, postponing hopelessness. "I'm so sorry, I'm just not able. This weekend I can bring in more magazines with pictures and cut more of them out, maybe put more on posters so she can point to more…objects." It sounded weak, but I wasn't going to give up. I forced energy and resolution into my voice. "I think that will help." Yet another lie; I didn't really believe it would help. That terrible difference, sometimes, between what we wish were true and truly believe. But I have a whole special skillset for avoidance. I couldn't stand the thought of failing my mother.

There was silence from the director's end, and I thought I heard her sign, before she said, "If you wish to do that, fine, but we still need you to join us as Dorothy's medical and legal power of attorney. If you can't make it this week, then next week, our team meeting for Dorothy will be on…let me check…Wednesday. Ten o'clock again."

"All right. Thank you."

"We'll see you next Wednesday at ten, Kate." Was there an unnecessary emphasis on the day and time, or was I imagining it? A serration on the warm edge of the director's voice?

"Certainly. I've got it down."

I didn't have it down. I'd end up having to call back in a couple of days to ask her assistant when the appointment was. I wished I had some water, then I tried to clean up some smeary mascara mess under my eyes in the rear-view mirror. The day was bright enough to make me squint as I sat in the driver's seat going nowhere.

*You look terrible*, I said out loud to my reflection. *Just breathe.* I looked away. *You don't have to think about it right now.* The grounds crew had done a brilliant job with the flowers, like troops of dancing color everywhere, and I hadn't told any of the workers how gorgeous and welcome it all was again this spring. It was like I hadn't even noticed.

Agonizing about my mother wasn't the only thing eating at me that week, either. Linda put Marc in charge of transitioning the new chimp we were getting. It stung. I'd been the one to transition Lolly seven years ago. It had been my idea to pair her with Jasmine and when it worked, I'd rejoiced at Jasmine nurturing her, so mother-like. Now when I wondered if we did any good that justified the zoo's existence, I looked at the bonds between our chimps and thought, *there's a small something that's right.*

The new chimp's name is Eve. She was coming from a medical laboratory, and doubtless whatever we'd eventually learn of her history—and there'd be a lot we'd never know—would break our hearts again. I love our great apes and repeatedly reminded myself that the habitat redesign and implementation had to be the most important job. It was up to me to make sure that it be as close to what they'd have in the wild as possible. Hard to do given captivity as a constraint.

Still, I couldn't fool myself. Maybe I'd only make something that was all wrong look better, doing nothing more than helping the wrong side, like building a nicer prison to house the innocent.

I was awash in ambivalence. It was a dreary day, too, a grudging sky rumbling about more rain that we didn't need or want. Thunder meant that a lot of the animals would be kept in their indoor enclosures, which always bothered me: less space, cement floors, no open air. Linda stepped into the primate keepers' shared office area while I struggled with modifications to the habitat redesign, her arms cradling display materials like heavy babies she was in a hurry to put down, which meant there wasn't going to be any discussion about whatever she said. I knew that signal, and it wasn't a favorite of mine. "I'm going to have Bruce put in some time with your crew so he learns more skills. Okay by you," she called. It wasn't a question.

"Sure," I said to Linda's back. Pointless. I could hear her low heels clicking down the hallway. Bruce would require extra supervision mainly because of the number of questions he'd have. He was a quiet nineteen-year-old, mid-level on the autism spectrum, working as part of a city-wide initiative in which the zoo was participating to hire people with various mental, emotional, or physical challenges. I liked him a lot and was slowly drawing smiles out of him as he became less afraid of making a mistake. A predictable set of rules and procedures that didn't vary was what he needed, and as long as he had it and knew exactly how to do each task, he was fine.

We'd been warned by the offsite placement manager that change agitated Bruce and he needed to learn to adapt to new tasks. We were working with that, and he had, lately, seemed to try to meet my eyes, one of his manager's goals for him. It was fleeting, but it had happened. His were a blue as bright as the head of a painted bunting. His coloring put me in mind of prairie and sky, with his sandy gold hair and those startling eyes. Lately, he was not as reticent about answering when I asked how he was feeling, though there was a discomfort in his gawky stance as if he didn't quite know what to do with his arms and hands, or where exactly to put his feet.

Having him on the habitat construction team meant everything would be new to him. The team wouldn't take on the job of explaining everything in painstaking detail; I'd need to do that. And we'd have to come up with certain job routines that he could learn thoroughly and relax into. I wanted him to succeed, to make it. Really, all of us did.

If Linda had stuck around, I'd have told her I had to go to my mother's care meeting tomorrow morning. I didn't have to report to her; I punched no clock. It was just a courtesy. But I wasn't feeling courteous enough to chase her down. Not even enough to send her an email. I'd tell Bruce was what I'd do. I didn't want anything to throw him off.

As it happened, though, I told Marc too. Because he came in later to ask me for help. That was rich, the person in charge coming to me—who should have been in charge—to ask what to do. He owned that part of it, though, which was good of him.

"Kate, I know you've got the whole habitat redesign on you, and you're probably buried, but I—"

"What can I do for you?"

His tone was apologetic. "I know you transitioned Lolly and you're the expert here. Linda only put me on this because Thurston gave you the redesign. She said that if you had time, maybe you could give me some consultation. Have you possibly got anything free tomorrow morning?"

Dust mites floated in the sun shaft from the windows. Maybe I was blinded; I sniffed at what he'd said for flattery. "Marc. Come on. You're not exactly new at this. And you've essentially finished your master's in anthro. Good lord, you've specialized in primatology. You don't need me."

"Thanks, but every chimp I've worked with has been here. In a social group. Not isolated, not coming from a lab, very likely traumatized. I want to do right by her. I want—I mean, I'd really appreciate it if you would."

I picked up my coffee mug and started to get up, as if I were headed out to fill it. He'd done that thing that made me ashamed, eyes coming to mine straight on like good earth, unguarded. Told a quiet truth, no scrollwork. Eve was coming this week whether I said yes or no. Nothing had stopped the horrors she'd already lived. But deep down—or not so deep down—I didn't want to help him do what he believed in because he'd be good at it, and it would help him rise professionally in a world in which I was convinced the standards for success were fundamentally wrong.

Still, Marc was a caring, kind human being who'd be good to Eve. I told myself I really didn't have much choice.

"Of course, if I can help. But I can't meet tomorrow morning because I have to be at a meeting offsite. About my mom."

It was unlike me to have added that last part. Funny how one sentence can change a life.

Every time I made the drive to Sycamore Retirement Community, I was aware again that it was too late, too late to fix things between me and my mother in a meaningful way. Oh, I did what I could, like picking the west side of the city for an assisted living condo, to avoid the Dayton Airport, and Wright Patterson Air Force Base to the northeast, where there was another excellent facility closer to me. I worried that the air traffic noise would bother my mother the way it would bother me, and I couldn't ask her if it would.

Back when there was still time, when it counted, I'd asked her nothing, only talked to her in the most cursory way. Dad had even warned me. "Ease off your mom," Dad said before he moved out, not that he mentioned the moving out part then. That lovely surprise was just ahead. "She loves you." I was seventeen.

"Well, I hate her," I told him. Matter-of fact. Teenage snotty. Dad was easy.

"No you don't, Katie girl," he said, touching my shoulder with his big hand. It was warm, soft as a lawyer's, the only calluses on the pads where his golf clubs rubbed. "You just haven't caught on to yourself yet. But she's going to need you and I hope you'll do right."

"Right, Dad. Uh huh."

The primary progressive aphasia that had started with a slow loss of speech had been first misdiagnosed as depression. Next it was mistaken for the effect of a transient ischemic attack, a mini stroke—robbing her of words, even written words, as a blank silence crept in like a doom. It hadn't mattered in the end. There's no effective treatment. It had taken us so long to be able to talk to one another, and now words were so many dead leaves carried off in a dry wind and dropped somewhere at random. Somewhere out of reach.

Regret was a weight on my chest crushing the words I'd denied her for years. I couldn't tell her I was sorry, so sorry. What was my mother's mind without words? And yet—the MRI showed no Alzheimer's disease, no dementia. My mother's mind was still there. She was there. Gestures worked when I could get them right, and so did showing her pictures, so I knew my mother was still there. Caged, but there.

When the announcement about the habitat redesign was first made, Marc had figured Kate must be ecstatic about overseeing it and had congratulated her warmly. She'd always said their habitat was detrimental to their apes and had lobbied hard for major changes. But now, he wondered if she was upset that she wasn't in charge of transitioning Eve after all the work she'd done with Lolly.

Getting up after Kate stood so abruptly, Marc knew something wasn't going down right with her. Maybe he shouldn't have tried to talk to her right then, but how could he have guessed that? He hoped it wasn't personal, that she'd been his supervisor and now she wasn't, but that wasn't his doing, unless building up his credentials and experience and his being ready was something she held against him. Or worse, Thurston or Linda was using him to hurt Kate. That whole idea made him feel complicit, something he never sought, never wanted.

He thanked her and started to head back to his own desk, but then turned around to say one more thing and saw that she wasn't on her way to get coffee. She'd sat back down. She was looking at her screen, tucking errant strands of blonde hair from her ponytail behind her ear.

"I hope things are okay with your mother," he said, aware that her telling him about tomorrow's appointment was the most personal thing he remembered her saying. "I, well, I know what it's like to worry about your mom. I hope it's okay, is all."

She looked startled. Or maybe embarrassed. "It'll be fine."

Marc had spent his life reading faces, body language, nonverbal signals. If they'd been friends, he'd have called her on the bullshit, but he just said, "I'll make sure Bruce is okay while you're out." She hadn't asked him to, but he thought it would take one thing off her mind.

"Thanks. That'd be good," she said. Marc threw a wave over his shoulder and got out of her sight.

It made no sense, really, the administration moving Kate away from daily interaction with the primates and putting her on habitat design. She knew as much as anyone in the country about how chimps lived in the wild; she was always talking about their needs. Marc hoped that at least the time he'd spent in grad school studying the role of zoos in conservation of species brought something to the table. He was well aware she was a renowned primatologist, and he was just finishing his masters, but shouldn't their shared interests give them something to at least have a normal conversation about?

He wondered if Kate had a dog, or ever had. Or a cat or gerbil or something. They both wanted to save animals, even if what drove him hadn't begun with a love of zoos or primatology but rather in the heart place where children save indelible memories.

Marc's course had been shaped by a golden retriever named Goldie and his grandmother, who'd given him the dog. There wasn't one without the other. And together they'd saved him, a boy whose first language wasn't English, or even the Spanish of his grandfather, but the American Sign Language of his mother.

Speech hadn't come easily to a child with no hearing adult available except from Friday afternoon to Monday dawn when his grandmother came for the weekends and chatted about anything and everything. When she talked, her words made pictures that flew in front of his eyes like birds, and then there were sounds like songs, too. Songs coming at him from every direction. Especially when he started school.

*Talk, talk, talk*, people said to him. *What did you say? I didn't understand. Tell me again.*

He'd stuttered in his half-day kindergarten, pressured to use his words if he accidentally signed. And then in first grade, there were reading groups. Marc was in the Purples. Reds were the best readers. Blues were good, too. Next were the Greens, but they were not as bad as the Purples, the worst. Marc knew all the words and could read them to himself perfectly and fast, but when it was his turn to read out loud, he couldn't help thinking how to sign it. Then he'd have to close his eyes to think of the noise, to make it come out of his throat, over his tongue, shape his lips around it. That made his stomach hurt because he knew it all. Then some sounds would get afraid, stuck, like they tripped on something in the dark on the way out. Signing them out in the light would have been fluid as pouring water.

He knew he could have been in the Reds. Should have been in the Reds. Just as he knew that those indelible memories and the unshakable convictions that rose from those years continued to shape his life.

They'd been sitting around the dining room table, a vase of daffodils in the center, fancy for Sunday dinner. His grandmother had made *pollo rojo* because Thursday had been his grandfather's birthday, so she did it in his memory. The air was different when she made the foods she'd made for his grandfather, and he wondered what the word sound was for that smell. He wanted to sign the question, but his mother or Gram would just tell him to say it, and that would be too hard because he didn't know the word, so he skipped the whole stupid thing.

"You're in grade two, and you need to practice talking like other hearing people," his mother complained when he signed to Gram without talking. "And it will help your reading. Mrs. Dalton says you need to practice your reading out loud." The school had sent an interpreter to sign for his mother at the parent-teacher conference. That made Marc mad. He could have done it and then he'd have known exactly what was said.

"It's fine, Ria," Marc saw his Gram sign to his mother after dinner. "Let it go, we'll work this out."

It was in June, right after school got out, that his grandmother showed up with Goldie on a red leash. "She needs lots of exercise and attention," she told him. "Are you up to that much responsibility?"

"I can have her?" he signed, carefully speaking it also to his grandmother.

"Your mom already said yes, as long as she was housebroken. But here's the thing. She's used to my reading to her before I go to bed. Hearing me read helps her settle down and feel safe. You're good at helping your mom stay safe, but do you think you can make Goldie feel safe if she sleeps in your room? If that's too much..."

She bent from the waist and put her face against the puppy's, kissed the black nose. The puppy licked his Gram's mouth. She laughed and rubbed the dog's long ears, one hand on each side, as she lifted her own chin inviting more kisses. (His mother's hands exploded where his Gram couldn't see them. Don't let me catch *you* doing that, they warned.) "...she's such a sweetheart. I'd love to keep her myself. So just tell me if you don't want to. Read to her, I mean."

"Only me to just her?"

"Just you two. Out loud. She doesn't know sign."

Then Marc's face was buried in the dog's neck, a skinny arm looped around her back as the golden retriever tried to climb on him, her back feet scrabbling for purchase, nails clicking on the hardwood, tail flagging delight.

"I promise," Marc said, speaking it to please his Gram even as he signed to his mother.

His mother shrugged. "We'll see," she signed.

Gram soothed, hands calm as a lullaby. "Ria, he says he'll read to her."

Those first weeks with Goldie lengthened into what Marc would later think of as his golden summer. He and Gram took the puppy to first one obedience class, then, when Goldie proved herself a quick study, another one. They practiced skills in the park during stretched-out mellow twilights. His grandmother sat back on a bench and watched, interfering no more than the quiet white clouds overhead. There would be long slices of peach and watermelon spilled across the western horizon before they went home to supper, faintly sweaty and good-mood happy, the tired puppy lapping water from her silver bowl and flopping on her bed with a sigh.

His grandmother spent extra nights to take them to the classes because she was off work for the summer. *Teachers have it easy,* he'd seen his mother sign. *That's hilarious,* his gram had signed back. His mother did her famous shrug then. Gram didn't smile, but she didn't say anything back.

"Do you think you might like to have me listen while you read to Goldie?" Gram asked one night. "You might not get nervous when you go back to school if you got a little practice for the people part." It had started to get dark earlier, and she'd turned on the lamp. It reflected in her glasses and her blue eyes disappeared behind them. She used one finger to touch his hand lightly. "Up to you, honey."

Marc buried his fingers in Goldie's thick undercoat all the way to her skin, scratching it the way she liked. Goldie curled next to him, nose nestled on paws, feathery tail occasionally breaking from the circle of her body to thump approval of Marc's caress then wrapping it back around herself. "Maybe for one page." Those words caught, but on the idea, not in his throat.

When he read, he didn't tell her to leave because the words were coming out whole.

When third grade started, he didn't get put in the bad reader group, but one up from that. In the winter, he was in the next to highest group. He finished the year in the best reader group.

The next summer, he and Gram took Goldie through her Canine Good Citizen class and started advanced obedience training. Another summer, they did two more rounds of advanced training.

They'd been doing agility classes and starting to compete at the trials when Gram was first getting sick. That summer, she could still go to watch. By then, they won more times than not.

The absence in the viewing stand was a chasm after Gram died both too slowly and too fast, Marc frantic, full of regret when he came to believe it could really happen . For a while he couldn't bear to show Goldie, couldn't do much of anything. But finally, there was nothing else to do with what he felt except what the three of them had done together. Goldie rescued him again, their communication deep, perfect, wordless and complete when there was nothing to say. But nothing needed to be said; they each knew the other without words.

# Chapter 4

I'D BOUGHT AND CUT pictures out of six different magazines before the team meeting, organizing and gluing them to posters for the staff: kitchen implements and common foods, bathroom supplies, bedroom needs, pictures of facial expressions to denote feelings, all the components of daily living I could think of that my mother might be able to point to or the staff could use to ask her a question. I tried it all out on my mother again, over that weekend.

It worked. Sometimes. "Try, Mom. I'll make us lunch. Would you like this? Or this?" I said, having waited past noon so she'd be hungry, and pointing meaningfully to first the picture of a bowl of tomato soup—which she loved—and then to one of a ham sandwich, another favorite. I raised my eyebrows to my hairline, hoping maybe that would give her the idea there was a question involved here. She stared out the window. I finally gave up and made her a sandwich. Later that day, she pointed at grapes, strawberries and spaghetti. Progress, I thought, and brought out grapes as a snack.

I hadn't done my laundry. My bedroom floor was starting to look like a yard waiting to be raked, so much had spilled from the hamper, and the apartment needed to be vacuumed and dusted. There were crusted dishes in the sink. If I didn't get to the grocery store, I'd be eating at the zoo cafeteria all week again. But it was warm outside, everything newly green as hope, and I couldn't let go of possibility. I led my mother outside for a walk through the gardens where daffodils, jonquils, and blue hyacinths nodded, thinking maybe it would stimulate a different sensory area. I knew she was in there. She bent from the waist and touched one with her forefinger. That was all, but it was enough. I found big cluster of dwarf grape hyacinths and picked one for her. There were so many it wouldn't be missed. Who had ever really looked at this single one but her? Who would know what was missing?

I sniffed it—the fragrance lovely, heady—and gave it to her. She held it in her hand and walked on. Unsure what that meant, I waited a couple of seconds until I realized I wasn't going to know, and then scurried to catch up with her.

At the team meeting, I argued for more time.

The pinch-nosed director's name badge said Marjorie Wilcox, R.N. She had narrow hips, but her boobs hung like overripe fruit. She'd said to call her Marjorie. In my mind, I started calling her Majority during that meeting because she kept referring to The Majority, meaning the various staff aides, which unreasonably angered me, because I was outvoted by some anonymous group I couldn't reason with, who weren't even present.

The "team meeting" consisted of the social worker, the director of occupational therapy in the nursing home division, and the director of skilled nursing. In other words, the decision had been made. I'd either agree to move my mother to the skilled nursing section or I could move her out. This meeting was to arrange the change. They assumed I'd have no option, and of course, they were right about that much.

"It's a safety issue," said Majority again. "We're in agreement." We sat around a table in the conference room, and she peered over her glasses at me, ignoring the strand of peppered hair on her forehead, escaped from the helmet she'd sprayed in place. "We applaud your efforts with the pictures, of course, and you can continue to work on a way to communicate—the staff will cooperate with that—but surely you can see that in an emergency, staff could not communicate effectively or quickly with Dorothy. We have to place her where the protocol is entirely different. As it is in the skilled nursing section. Quite different from assisted living. And, frankly, staffing levels are higher. We know you want the best possible care for her...if she's to stay at Sycamore Community."

There it was, the threat, like a loaded dart pistol pointed at me. Guaranteed to knock down the wild beast daughter. Majority took a drink from her bottle of water. Satisfied with their stance.

Any other assisted living facility I might try to move my mother to would talk to Sycamore, as well want her medical records. I knew what they'd say. Assisted living was no longer an option.

I don't know if I was successful in stuffing down my frustration. I knew enough to realize that I couldn't afford to alienate these people; they subtly helped the families they liked and were rigid as bones with those they didn't, no matter how much they liked the resident. Even if charm—sucking up—wasn't one of my talents, I did try. But they knew I didn't think my mother belonged in a nursing home. She was still *there*, I believed that. I just needed to find how she could communicate without words—and a way for the staff to communicate with her. I needed more time.

"How long will you give me before she needs to be moved from assisted living?" I said. "I'm really swamped at work, and I'll need to rent a truck and get some help with retrieving the furniture, and..." Angling for more time.

"This weekend will be fine," Majority said.

"This weekend? I don't think I can even find a place to put the furniture. I brought it here when we sold the family house, and I don't have—"

"A storage unit may be your best choice."

"If I could please have one extra week. I know this will sound strange, but we're getting a new chimpanzee at the zoo, and building a new habitat. It's a huge undertaking, and I just have too much going on to accomplish packing my mother up in the next three or four days."

The social worker looked at Majority then and spoke for the first time since we'd started. I guessed she was near retirement age—gray roots showed before her hair turned dark blonde, and wrinkles formed parentheses around her mouth while lines like loose flower petals extended from the outer edge of each eye. She reached across the table and covered my hand with her own. The gesture was kind. So was her voice. "Would the extra week truly make a significant difference in practical terms, or are you hoping that something will change?"

That was what undid me. My eyes were wet when I said, "I don't like this, and I don't agree, but I'll do it because I have to. Thank you for asking that, and yes, another week would truly make a significant practical difference."

The social worker moved her gaze to Majority then and said, "Can we make that happen, Marjorie? I think it will go better."

Majority sighed. As if she were making a momentous sacrifice. "All right. Ten days. A week from Saturday. Tina has new papers for you to sign if you'll stop at the business office."

The meeting was over.

I went directly to work afterward. I had a headache, and neither the heart nor stomach to see my mother, especially since I hadn't thought to ask the social worker if I was supposed to try to communicate the move to her, or if someone there would. I needed ibuprofen, water, silence, space to breathe, to think, to develop a plan. The work of packing Mom's belongings and storing—or disposing of—most of them would be mine. How was she going to feel comfortable or safe in another new place, wordless, surrounded by strangers? My eyes and forehead tingled with the pressure of held-back tears.

I'd have to rent a small truck again. Get boxes and packing material. Figure out what Mom would most cherish and could keep, how to make a small space as homey as I could. And learn exactly how much space she'd have. I had to get over there and take a close look, something I'd been encouraged to do when she first moved to assisted living, but I'd skipped that step.

I was distracted by all this jumbled together and fast forwarding through my mind when I got to the primate area. Sticky notes flagged me down, light pink as the palms of our primates, as I approached my computer screen, messages stuck there by Linda and Marc who knew I don't always check email right away. They were probably retaliating for all the yellow ones I stick on their screens.

Eve was being transferred to us on Friday of this week. Linda wanted me to know she was asking everyone to swap schedules around so there would be extra weekend coverage in the primate area. Could I please be available? Marc wanted to confer with me as soon as I had time available. And a phone message from the habitat design consultant that had routed to Linda instead of me: a death in his immediate family. He apologized, but he would not be working for the next several weeks and needed to delay his last site visits.

That meant we were getting Eve early and the new habitat construction would have a delay in completion. We could work with the second part, but I'd have to think through what it meant for integrating Eve. The mess of tasks and worries had spread like weeds in an untended garden. I put my head down on my desk. A few tears leaked. I wasn't letting go or making noise, but I hadn't had time to get hold my myself or wipe my face when Marc came in, heading for his area. He caught me with my head down.

"Hey, you okay?"

I was startled and jerked upright. "Just a headache."

"Huh," he said. "Okay. Want me to get you something to drink from the cafeteria?"

"No, it's okay. I'm all right." I forced a smile and pretended to look at my monitor.

Marc turned away from his desk and headed back toward the hall. "Actually, I'm just going to go get you an iced tea. If you don't drink it, no problem. But you look like you might need something."

If Linda had said that I'd have wondered if she were being critical. I didn't then, though, and it helped that Marc didn't wait for an answer. Still, I was embarrassed. I couldn't let this happen again.

When he came back with a large iced tea, I'd spit into a tissue to clean up my smeary-mascara eyes —which, with the bloodshot teary residue, looked not only raccoon-like, but slightly rabid at that—added some fresh lipstick, and refastened my ponytail.

"Bad meeting?" he said.

"What?"

"Your mother? Is she ok?"

"Oh. Yes. Fine. Thanks very much for the tea. I've just got a headache is all. So, I've got your note here. You want to get together about Eve, right? Before Friday, I take it."

He grimaced. Dark brows knit, cheeks rising, eyes squinting, slight head shake added as he said the rest. "I heard from Linda about the design consultant. But hadn't he finished most of the work? How much more…how much delay?"

"We're still trying to work out a way to use more overhead space—within what we're allotted—and create something like trails between areas. The Philadelphia 360 thing on a grossly reduced, Thurston-proof scale." I sighed and shrugged. "Two weeks."

"Well, that's a pain. But Eve needs to be isolated anyway until we get a sense of how long it will take to introduce her, so…I know you've got a lot going on but I'm hoping you might have some time before she comes?"

"I'll make time." Did I sound pissed off? Maybe. It wasn't his fault, none of it. He stood there, all clean as a spring morning. I wondered if he knew any swear words, which these days comprised most of the private lexicon in my head. He had been as respectful and nice as he was good looking, but if he was trying to subtly point out that I wasn't his supervisor any more by acting all chummy, I didn't appreciate it. That wasn't fair of me, and I knew it.

"What's a good time for you? I'll make anything work," he said, standing there in his pressed shirt, blue plaid this time, tucked into khaki pants with a brown belt. Obviously not doing any of the grunt work this morning, or he'd have been in coveralls.

I couldn't suppress a sigh as I pulled my calendar up on my computer screen. "I can do tomorrow afternoon at two."

"That would be great," he said. "I know you're busy and I really appreciate it."

He seemed young. Not in looks—he was my age if I recalled correctly—but doubtless, I thought that because he lived with his mother. I knew that sometimes he went home for lunch, and I found that strange. But maybe I was the one who was strange—I felt cynical and world-weary. With reason.

I bought moving boxes and reserved a U-Haul truck for the weekend I had to move my mother out of assisted living. I still had to decide what I might shoehorn into my own apartment. It couldn't be a lot more, but the things in my mother's apartment now were what remained after I'd already winnowed out everything I could and carefully curated what she—and I—most cared about. What she had was precious. Was I just supposed to stick what I didn't have room for in some sad, rented storage unit forever? Would I ever have space for it myself? I'd already taken as much as I could. Or would I grow tired of the drain of the monthly rental, want to store less and less, be more and more orphaned as I slowly gave up on preserving our history, until I had no parents to ground me and even my mother's possessions were as gone as her words?

Making a list, usually a comfort, didn't work its tranquilizing magic. I didn't have even an illusion of control. Mom's single room in the skilled nursing section had vertical blinds on the window. Nice enough, but could I also hang the curtain from her apartment, the one with the hand-tatted lace that had been her mother's? I'd made it work in her assisted living. Would they let me put up a rod? And what about the spread? The facility had a plain white cotton get-up on the bed, probably because it was frequently changed. She'd want the quilt she had now, splashy red and yellow flowers linked by trailing greenery.

I gave up on a list and started to write questions to ask when I went over to measure the room. That was because the first item on my list was to draw a floor plan, to see how much I could cram in there before they called it a safety hazard.

Part of me knew the futility of all this. How had I not ever grasped the unspeakable pain of losing a mother?

Ever since he'd started at the zoo, Marc had consciously continued to learn from Kate and Linda's expertise, dovetailing observation with graduate study in anthropology and primatology. He'd made friends with the long-experienced assistant keepers, Sandy and Tom, and picked up practical tips from them. Even more, he'd connected with the chimps—though he'd be hesitant to say it that way aloud—and recognized that he'd earned their comfort and their trust much as he'd earned Goldie's.

"You're gonna be okay," Kate had said once after he'd worked under her for a year, and it had meant as much to him as Linda's enthusiastic, "You've got the gift, Marc."

This, though. This was different. The lead could make his career. Logically, that meant it could also break it. But no pressure, Linda said. Right. He couldn't allow anxiety to gnaw on his confidence; Eve would likely be traumatized just by the move even if nothing else—that was a decent guess—and if he allowed himself nerves instead of approaching her with relaxed ease, she could misread it. He hadn't been there when any of the resident chimps had arrived, so he was missing a lived model and would have to rely on instinct and advice.

A new chimp. Didn't matter what Linda said: it was *pressure*. Like compression chamber pressure. They weren't just getting a new chimp. For god's sake, they were getting a lab chimp. Who knew what she'd been through? He could assume a caged life without stimulation and companionship, the cruel consequence of the types of medical experimentation performed on chimps because of their close match to human DNA. Which led Marc to a specific question: exactly what experiments had been done on her for the past eight years? How much fear and suffering had she endured? Marc had to close his eyes when he thought about that.

He'd been observing Lolly and Jasmine especially closely since Linda told him about Eve; Lolly because Kate had socialized her so well, and Jasmine because he'd noticed that she gestured a lot, and he'd been reading about chimp communications. He'd swear that Reece used some of the same gestures. Those two had been together the longest, of course. But what did it mean? He tried mirroring the gesture to Jasmine and was rewarded with a show of teeth. What did *that* mean? "You telling me something big girl? or just laughing at me," he said. "Talk to me, huh?" By way of response, Jasmine inspected two of her toes before heading to the Lixit for water.

He was pulling on coveralls to get the isolation unit ready for Eve's arrival when Linda showed up, Bruce trailing her, flapping both hands like small pale flags. Marc caught Linda's eye and flicked his own toward Bruce as a signal that Bruce was worked up.

"Hey, Buddy," he said quietly. "How's it going?"

"My name is Bruce."

Marc chuckled. "Yep. I know. Remember? That's how I tell you I'm your friend. Buddies are friends."

"Okay."

Marc put up his hand for Bruce to high five it but had to drop it back to his side when he got no response. *Stupid*, he chastised himself.

"Bruce is going to learn some construction skills with the new habitat team, but I thought today he could just give you a hand with the isolation unit. Moving the heavy stuff, bring in the wood wool, that stuff. I know you've got a lot to do," Linda said, covering, filling in the air where Marc's hand had just been.

Marc looked toward Bruce, who was looking into the middle distance to Marc's left. "Yeah, for sure. Bruce, I've got to move bales of wood wool into the enclosure and spread it," he said, speaking to the side of Bruce's face. "See, the new habitat will be so much better, but we'll have to introduce Eve to another chimp first. Get her into the group slowly. She's been alone a lot of years, at a lab doing medical experiments, maybe surgeries, on her."

Marc abruptly stopped himself, thinking that was too much for Bruce to know. "Anyway, we'll try Lolly first, on the other side of bars, for short times, well, I'll show you, but not until Eve's used to me, sort of settled in—and I want her to have something to climb right away, and to give her a little space to be private. A boulder to hide behind. Toys. So, yeah, I really could use an extra pair of hands setting up."

Bruce flapped his hands. "You can't take them off."

"No, sorry, I can really use your help," Marc said, and heard his voice, too hearty. Back off, he told himself. Go quieter. Talking to Bruce in front of Linda was throwing him off. "Can you look at me, Buddy?"

Bruce glanced at Marc's face before he looked away again.

"Good job. I'll show you what to do." Better.

"My name is Bruce. Okay."

"Those pencils that are all different sizes—they're messed up again. Would you like to put them in order first?"

"Okay."

Marc looked at Linda. "Let me go get them. Won't take two minutes. Can you wait?"

"Sure," she said, glancing at her watch. "I'm already late. What's another two minutes."

She wore a dark business suit and low navy heels. Her hair was pinned up or down in some arrangement that Marc couldn't identify; it wasn't buzzing around her head like a swarm of bees the way it usually was. She must be headed to some meeting.

Marc went through the heavy doors and crossed the walkways to the primate keepers' area. He'd gathered as many old pencils as he could find around people's cubicles and bought a box of new wooden ones that he'd broken off to random lengths when he learned from Bruce's case manager that Bruce liked lining up objects in a particular order. Carol Davidson never expected anyone to make up activities like that, but Marc thought it was an easy way to calm Bruce when he was agitated and that it might help him adjust to transitions. What job wouldn't involve changes, new tasks sometimes? Maybe over time he could help Bruce learn small ways to calm himself down rather than flapping his hands, a behavior that was problematic around some of the animals.

Carol Davidson had been skeptical about Marc's idea when she explained what flapping meant for Bruce. "Hand flapping is like other repetitive behaviors—it's called stimming, and it releases intense stress—you know, like rocking, humming, rubbing or bouncing. We all know someone who taps their feet or bounces their knee when they're nervous, right? Stimming is like that." Then she'd said, "But if his hands are a deal breaker because it freaks the animals, I can move him to another placement."

"No, we'll make it work," Linda told her, speaking as department head. Maybe it was Bruce's guilelessness that made them protective. And he *was* a good worker.

"Vulnerable…he's really vulnerable is the thing," Carol had answered. "But let me know if it's too much." She shrugged and nodded, eyes narrowed, lips pressed over her teeth. "Could be." Carol had hesitated then before she added. "Bruce has trouble expressing himself, but don't confuse that with not having a rich inner life, feelings, and opinions."

"It's fine," Marc said now as he returned with the pencils. He put both palms out, as if to stop Linda's thought. "I can do it."

# Eve

ONE TIME ONLY, after many years, Eve was put with another great ape. The lab was dismantling the chimp area, sending the chimps to whatever place would take them. Like the rest, Eve had always been caged alone, often unable to see the others. Sometimes she could hear them, though the sounds they made were not the comforting ones she'd been born to, but those of alarm, panic, or pain. But the lab was repurposing space, and so for a brief time, until one of them had a new place to go, Eve was moved in with a larger male chimp who had not shown himself to be aggressive. She could be caged with a male because she had not had her first menses, being too young.

Eve liked him because sometimes they groomed each other and even played chase as best they could in the small space. He would bite her to show he was her boss, but not too often. One time he began to hit his knuckles on the bottom of the cage after he'd groomed her for quite a while, and then he did it again, again, and Eve thought she remembered what the females in the rainforest had done when the alpha male banged that way. She presented her backside to him, and that was what he'd wanted.

Soon after that, a pale animal with little hair came with the gun and this time it was the male who was shot with the dart, though both of them had screamed when they saw it and tried to hide. The male was taken away, and Eve was the last of her kind left there. No one came to hurt her. No one came at all except one with her food twice a day. Eve rocked alone and pulled hair off her arms and legs.

The pale animal with little hair came at her cage. No food. She stopped rocking when she saw what he held, screamed and cowered against the other side, the bars pressing into her back. The dart came hard into her upper thigh, spreading the sear of pain that sent muscles into slack, eyes into the slow black.

The man waited only a moment, to be sure it had been enough, and left the room.

Some time passed, and two men came. One unlocked the cage and pulled the dart from Eve's thigh. She did not move. He locked the cage again, and the two men slid the cage onto a cart that rolled. It was very heavy and difficult to move, but they were experienced, and Eve was underweight.

The cage briefly passed though sun and open air, which would have been the first time Eve would have seen trees or sky in eight years had she been awake. It was expensive for a lab to keep chimps that it could no longer use for medical experimentation and could not kill because they are an endangered species. The administrator had finally found a zoo that would accept this last one. The cage holding the unconscious body was taken up a ramp, put onto an animal transport truck and sent on its way.

# Chapter 5

ON FRIDAY, when Eve was to arrive, my mind was scattered like dandelion seeds into the rising wind of my mother's life. I stepped outside just because I couldn't stand to miss the official hand off and because Linda had asked me to sign the paperwork. Technically, I was still her Assistant Curator. I'd not been nearly enough help to Marc, but he was already there, waiting for the truck that would bring her, his face lit with anticipation

"You ready for this?" I asked. "I'm sorry there was only time to meet once. But I'm around, and you can call on me. I really mean that."

"Thanks. I hope I won't have to bother you much."

"You just...waiting?"

He blushed, a peony pink rising up from his neck. "Yeah. Not really getting anything done anyway, and I wanted to be outside just in case she's waking up when..."

"Hey, I get it. The sedation will probably be heavy. They do that, y'know. For transport. Damn labs. It's pretty disorienting, remember, so don't..."

"...don't be discouraged if she seems either aggressive or too passive or dumb as dirt. I know what you said. Immune function will be down. She'll have lost a pound or two. It'll be the drug. Can't really assess squat for days. Transport is trauma. Give Eve time." He grinned. "Right?"

I'd have taken offense, but his tone wasn't dismissive or snotty. He was letting me know he'd remember what I'd warned him about. "And it's nerve-wracking, hard to be patient and let her get comfortable with you just…being there. She probably has good reason to be suspicious of humans, and I don't mean just from when she was caught."

"Yeah." He let out a long sigh.

"When I think of what she was taken from—and what's been done to her—and even now, you know, it'll be better, but it's nothing like what she was born to, what she should have in the wild. Her mother. That life."

Marc started to say something but didn't. Instead, he squinted down the zoo's service road as it snaked between the big cat area and the lemurs, then down toward the reptile house and the birds of prey, the areas between them punctuated by ice cream and beverage concessions and bright masses of blooming flowers, mainly tulips now.

"You started to say something…go ahead."

"Nah, it's nothing. Thought the truck might be coming, but I don't see it."

"Marc. Go ahead, say it."

He sighed again, still gazing down the road. "It's not like she could ever be returned to the wild—"

"Of course not. The point is, she never should have been taken from the wild in the first place." Then, when Marc didn't say more, only nodded, a moment later, I couldn't keep myself from tacking on what he must have known, "Remember to stay calm. If she's at all awake, keep it low key. No agitation. Calm is key."

Marc turned his head to look at me with a grin. "Thanks," he said. "It's okay. I know." Then, we saw it at the same time. "Oh, here she comes now!" he said, nowhere near calm about it, either.

We watched the truck crawl along the service road until it pulled up to the loading dock where we stood. The engine stopped and a short, burly driver stepped out; a second attendant, a very tall, skinny man with an unfortunately long nose, got out of the passenger side. "Mutt and Jeff," I said sotto voce, as they approached us, and Marc stifled a laugh.

The tall skinny one introduced himself as Jeffrey something, and I risked a glimpse at Marc, who I noticed would not look at me right then, but a smile flickered. Jeffrey Something had the papers for me to sign. Marc could have done it, and I wondered why Linda wanted me there. A cop to make sure he did everything correctly?

After I checked the paperwork and signed in three places, Mutt opened the back and Jeff pulled down the ramp, and both went up and in. Marc moved quickly to assist as the large metal cage emerged from the darkness.

Eve arrived still heavily sedated, and Christine Meade, the zoo vet, took advantage of that. Doing her initial evaluation while Eve was still under meant one less time the chimp would be sedated to be weighed, examined, have blood drawn. Most important to Marc, though, was that Christine would compare her lab test results against the ones the medical test facility had sent. It would give them a fix on how well—or badly—she'd reacted physically to the transfer. Most often it wasn't pretty. It could take months for a chimp to fully acclimate and recover.

"I shoulda gone to regular med school. Just for the primates. Ninety-eight percent plus the same DNA as us…" Christine said. Again. She blew her hair off her forehead and drew the blood from Eve, who was strapped to the table in case she started to wake.

Marc had lost count—they all had—of how many times Christine had marveled at that basic fact. She wasn't a specialist, of course. The zoo used specialists as needed. The budget for that was astronomical. Right now he didn't care to hear Christine rhapsodize at how closely related chimps and humans are; he needed her to rush, which she was doing anyway, because he wanted Eve to at least be in her isolation enclosure, where she could be on the soft wood wool bedding he and Bruce had put down, where he had set up a ladder and toys and a rock—even if it wasn't the size he'd asked for—to hide behind, not strapped to a cold metal table with white lights glaring down at her. How would that begin to build trust? The sooner she trusted him, the sooner he might be able to start having Lolly come into the other side of the enclosure, where a glass wall would separate them. He couldn't risk only bars between them. Not at first.

"Her vitals are good, and so's her membrane color. She feels dehydrated, though," Christine said, kneading Eve's shoulder and forearm above the strap. "Look." She lifted hairy skin away from the bone. "I hope that's what it is. How long did they fast her before sedation?"

"Paperwork says twelve hours. I'll watch carefully, make sure she's using the Lixit."

"I'm noting it, so we keep track. Nothing by mouth until she's fully conscious, though."

Marc suppressed annoyance. "Yeah, I know that, and I'd watch anyway." Did she think he wouldn't monitor water intake? Or food? Find out what Eve liked, what she didn't? What kind of a keeper—a primatologist—did she think he was?

"All right, of course. Looks pretty thin, poor thing, belly slightly distended and rigid. I bet she'll be a beauty when we get her healthy." Christine was placating now, practically batting those grayish eyes at him. Not interested. The female getting his attention had a brown, hairy body with longer arms and shorter legs than his. He hadn't seen her eyes yet, but they'd be brown. And intelligent. And Kate had said, likely to reveal something akin to human PTSD. "So, what do I need to know?"

Christine got his point. "Okay, noting multiple surgical scars abdomen, upper left quadrant, chest upper left. Right shoulder. Poor color. Hair loss. Some evidence of possible self-mutilation, left thigh, forearm. Probable malnutrition. She's been through a lot. Ordering vitamins and high calorie diet."

"Got it," Marc said. "Thanks."

# Eve

SHE CAME INTO a slow wakening, like climbing through blackness, through the roar in her head to the place where it hurt, to opening her eyes to confusion, then a new terror. *Move legs knuckles ground look move where move move hide—hide!*

# Chapter 6

"IT'S GOING TO BE SLOW, so you need to be very patient."

Both Kate and Linda had admonished Marc that a sedated chimp wouldn't be herself—whatever that was—for several days, and that, added to the strange people and surroundings, could create difficult behaviors that might or might not last. Kate reminded him that they knew nothing about her personality anyway, and it didn't augur well that the lab hadn't appeared to pay any attention one way or another.

What Marc knew at the end of the first four days was that Eve didn't know what to do with a ball or a swing and was initially confused by mesh wire on the walls—*a chimpanzee who didn't remember climbing!*—but either remembered or figured it out because she used it to get to the high perch Marc had built. That's where, either by memory or instinct, she used wood wool to improvise a sleeping nest.

"Do you remember sleeping in nests your mother made in trees?" Marc said to her the first time he saw what she'd done. "I hope so, girl. I hope so. That was the idea." She used the wooden spools, pushed together, to create an inadequate hiding place, where she hid and rocked. The temporary isolation enclosure was a bit crowded with stimulating equipment for Eve, but since it would need to do for two, and possibly even three chimps at once as Eve was slowly introduced into the group, Linda had given him the largest space available to work with. Not enough—it never was—but Marc had taken full advantage.

"Whew!" Linda had whistled when she first saw what he'd done. "Impressive. Wow."

Marc brushed the compliment aside. "I had a lot of help. The spools were Kate's idea. Actually, a lot of it was Kate's idea. She suggested the lumber yard. Oh, and when we finally move Eve into the new habitat, the spools can go with her. And thanks for loaning me Bruce. It went a lot faster than it would have, and you were right, Kate's crew was fine with not having him for a couple days."

"Well, it's the most I've ever seen anyone do with an isolation enclosure. Really great job," she'd said then, nodding her enthusiasm as she spoke, which made her glasses slide off the top of her head and bounce off her face. Marc shot his hand out and caught them before they hit the floor.

"Thanks. Geez, you maybe think I should quit putting them on my head?" She laughed and shook her head. "No, see, it's a test of staff reflexes I've devised. Don't tell the others." She was good about making fun of herself like that.

"Oh, don't stop." He handed the glasses to her, allowing himself the smallest suggestion of an eye roll before he smiled. "I like passing your stupid tests."

He was pleased by Linda's recognition. How could he not be? The Primate Curator herself. She was his boss, her opinion the one that counted. So why did it eat at him that Kate, who had helped him with ideas, had only checked in on the enclosure's progress to see how Bruce was doing. Wasn't that a little insulting, as if Marc couldn't or wouldn't watch out for Bruce? But more than that, all she'd said to Marc was, "Looks good in here." That was the best she could manage? He wanted her to rhapsodize.

Whatever. It didn't matter.

Now Marc was spending as much time as he could with Eve, from the other side of the glass. Talking to her so she'd come to associate him and his voice with the papaya he put through the food service drawer. But every time he approached the enclosure, Eve got as far from him as she could.

"She hides from me, even when I'm putting treats in the food tray. She waits until I'm out of sight, dashes up to snatch them, and takes them back behind the spools to eat. What did they *do* to her?" The question, posed to Kate as she was sitting alone scrolling through her phone, was rhetorical.

It was late and the lunchroom was nearly empty, the few staff on break were using one of the picnic tables on the patio. He knew Kate rarely socialized with colleagues, but he'd decided to take the opportunity to approach her just to talk. A risky move. Marc put down the brown bag that held his cheese sandwich and apple but didn't open it because there was no evidence as to whether or not Kate was eating.

She didn't look up. Outside, the last redbuds and dogwood were still blooming though the grounds crew had already started switching out the spring bulbs for summer annuals: the petunias, marigolds, zinnias, impatiens, all the bright cheer that would line the walkways all season. The earth was a song, alive and vibrant. If Marc hadn't wanted to catch Kate for a word, he'd have been outside too.

Kate shook her head. "Well, it's obviously not just the sedative now. Let's hope that some of it is still the trauma of being moved. But Christine noted surgical scars, right?"

"Yeah. Multiple."

"So, there's pain and trauma associated with humans coming at her. And she's been in more than one lab, so who knows what else has been done to her, how she was housed, how much deprivation and pain as well as isolation she's been through. That's what the rocking is about. This could take a lot of time and patience. And sometimes, it never..."

Marc wasn't going to hear that. "I can do it. I just want to ask you about shaping behavior if I can't elicit change. I'm not getting any approximations toward the goal. No behavioral alterations."

"Try letting her just hear Lolly. See if she shows any interest. Maybe she'll remember unstressed chimp sounds? It's possible. You can reinforce that. But it's been over eight years, so I don't know. You could also try some pant-hoots yourself."

"Huh. Okay. What I wanted to ask you, though. Am I rewarding her for hiding?"

"No, you're letting her know she can feel safe with you around. Just keep with it. Remember, though, the goal is to socialize her to other chimps. Not to humanize her. That's not...natural for her." She looked back down at her phone. "The company of chimps is. Their own language is." Kate had left her hair down today and in the afternoon light from the patio door, it shone like something ephemeral. Marc was uncomfortably aware of how pretty she was. He wanted to touch her hair.

Just then she looked up. "What are you looking at?" she said.

"Uh, nothing. Your hair looks nice. Down like that." He made a small gesture toward her shoulders with one hand.

"I said to try some pant-hoots. If you start trying to groom me, I'll slap you silly," she said, deadpan.

Marc could feel the heat rising from his neck up his cheeks. "I didn't mean anything. Sorry."

"No, I was kidding. Thanks."

*Oh, didn't that go well.* A silence, then he cast for anything to recover. "Uh, you gonna eat?"

"No, I'm just taking fifteen minutes to sit away from the computer. I'm leaving early today. Gotta...just gotta take care of stuff for my mother."

"Everything okay?"

"Sure. And I've gotta get back to work now. Hang in there." She leaned over as she rose from her chair. A thin gold chain swung out from above her cleavage, which was the color of the inside of an apple. Marc averted his gaze.

"Will do. Thanks for the help," he said, aiming his glance as if there were something fascinating happening three empty tables away.

After Kate left, Marc took his lunch and went outside where Tom, one of the other primate keepers, was at a sunny table talking to one of the grounds crew. Marc joined them. His sandwich rather than his foot would go into his mouth, the guys would be easy to talk to, and nothing to look at.

That afternoon, Marc recorded Lolly pant-hooting, trying to isolate her vocalization from the other chimps. That took a big chunk of time. He didn't play it for Eve that day, wanting to spend the time just being with her, wanting her to bond with him first. He kept talking to her, now pant-hooting, too, hoping that, paired with fresh fruit and a new toy put into the enclosure, would slowly, slowly, bring her around. Still, Eve hid and rocked.

# Chapter 7

KEEP. DONATE. DISCARD. Another winnowing, another diminishment of a life. My living room carpet was piled with the empty boxes and packing material I'd collected from grocery and liquor stores, all ready to pack my mother's apartment, all over and in the way, ready to hold what she held dear. I was chipping away more and more pieces of her until the day she would be utterly gone.

But I couldn't think about that now. Tears wouldn't help me get through this. I'd live with this mess a few more days, pick up the truck I'd rented, steel myself, and get the job done. Meanwhile, I'd take boxes over to Sycamore in the car each day after work and get the packing done as much as I could in advance of Saturday.

I scanned the room, trying to calculate what of her furniture I could bring here. I hoped they'd let me put up the Monet prints, his garden at Givenchy, and the water lilies. She loved those. If they wouldn't let me hang them, I'd put them up here; they'd always make me think of her. Maybe I could get rid of one of my end tables, and keep hers? It was solid cherry, and mine was some wood I couldn't identify. That was probably a good plan. Maybe I could donate her kitchen table and two chairs to an incoming Sycamore resident, and they'd let me leave them in place. I still didn't know whether I could fit her good teal recliner into her new room in the skilled nursing unit, and even if I could, how I could get it there. It was much nicer than the chairs they provided for patients. Which is what they were called over there. Not residents. Patients.

The decisions were harder than I thought they should be, like some sort of end game I did not want to play in my mother's name.

It was still daylight beyond my window, each day now stretching its legs farther into a long-shadowed dusk. I wished I had a dog again, one like Taffy, and could go for a hike with her. How I loved that dog, and the comfort of her body against mine. When I thought of her, it was strange how I couldn't hold back tears.

I shook my head. Enough.

I got up off the couch, headed for the kitchen, poured myself a glass of chardonnay, held the glass up to the buttery light in the window, the color of Taffy's tawny hair. *I love you*, I whispered. I'm sure I did tell my mother that too, but not soon enough, not often enough. I spent wasted years being angry with her. She was the wrong target.

"Wake up, Kate, he's *not coming back*. Your father has a *girlfriend*," I remember Mom yelling one late night, her mouth stretching big and toothy. It was a month after he left. She and I were fighting in the kitchen where copper pots hung over the center island. Dad never liked those because every now and then he'd hit his head on one. But he'd made me laugh, pretend to stagger, mugging that he was going to pass out.

Mom had waited up—said she couldn't sleep, but I was sure she'd just stepped up her surveillance since Dad wasn't there to calm her down. She'd caught me sneaking in, gotten in my face to smell my yeasty breath for alcohol, her face looming too close. She was right, of course.

That was how I found out about Candy, a girl barely out of diapers. For god's sake, Dad's sideburns were going grey. I wanted to call him and insist that he at least find a girlfriend with a dignified name, say Emily or Stephanie, if he was going to wreck my life. Better yet, a Joyce or a Donna within shouting distance of his age.

"I don't blame him," I shouted. "She probably doesn't boss him around all the time."

Mom pulled a tissue out of her pocket and blew her nose. She carried them around and put them back in her pocket after she used them.

"I don't understand why you won't talk to me," Mom was crying then, which made me feel guilty, and then I got mad because Taffy, my big sweet yellow Lab, stirred herself off the floor to go nose Mom, and Mom leaned over to kiss her, laid her cheek against my dog's face.

I gestured to Taffy to come to me, and she did. "You don't understand anything," I said then. How strange and cruel it is that she really can't now, when I'd tell her anything.

"I want to be close to my daughter. Can we just…talk?"

"There's nothing to talk about. Come, Taff," I said, and left the room, Taffy at heel, my obedient shadow. Fifteen minutes later I went back to the kitchen for a soda, thinking Mom would have gone to her room. But she was still sitting there, teary. Ginger, my cat, was curled up in her lap running her purr-engine while Mom stroked her orange fur and whispered some secret tenderness I couldn't hear.

The assisted living units allowed cats. Should I get my mother a kitten now?

It wasn't like I could ask her if she'd like one. She'd nod at a picture, but I wouldn't know what she understood or meant.

I went back to the couch carrying my glass of wine and switched on the television in search of a story I could bear tonight.

It was afternoon the next day before I had time at work to catch up with myself. Marc came into our office area briefly, in search of Bruce's pencils, because one of the construction crew had gotten impatient with him and Bruce was agitated. "I need to get back to Eve," he said. "But I'm not willing for Bruce to be worked up. Could you talk to your guys and ask them to back off? They just have to break instructions into clear steps and he's fine. And he can be helpful."

"I told them that. But yes, I'll tell them again. Should I reassure Bruce?"

"I think I've got him covered," Marc said.

"Hey, Marc, your hair…um…it's sort of standing straight up. You okay? You look like you've been in a wind tunnel." Normally, I wouldn't say anything, but his near-black, somewhat wavy hair looked like it had been brushed in the wrong direction. Even his heavy brows looked somehow disheveled.

He laughed, put both hands on his head and fingered his hair in the general direction of his usual side part. "Yeah, I forgot. No wonder the construction crew looked scared."

I side-eyed him.

"I thought maybe if I looked the part, and was making chimp sounds, Eve might…oh never mind."

"Did it work?"

"Well, she *looked* at me."

"Probably thinks you're either batshit crazy or dangerous. I wouldn't go out in public like that." I didn't say it, of course, but weird as he looked, I felt something soft for him then, that he would care so much, and think of doing that for Eve.

"Or anywhere, doubtless. But hey, since I'm here, I have a huge favor to ask. The person I have scheduled to be with my mother on Saturday can't make it, and I'm trying to be really consistent with Eve, so I was planning to be in. Is there any chance that you could cover for me with her for part of the day? There's no one else with your experience and I thought maybe if you work with her some…"

I was shaking my head before he finished. "No way. I'm sorry. I have to move my mother this weekend. I already don't know how I'm going to manage that. I can't take on one more thing."

"Okay. I just felt like I was maybe starting... Well, thanks anyway." He turned and walked toward the doorway to the hall, but before he got there, he turned back. "Hope everything goes okay for you."

I looked up from my computer screen. "Thanks," I said, and looked back down.

"Where you moving your mother to?" Marc said, a casual question as he approached the door.

I sighed before answering. "From assisted living into the nursing home section of her retirement community. Over in Sycamore." My eyes burned and I blinked back the start of tears.

Marc came back into the office then. It wasn't a large room shared by the primate keepers; only Linda has her own space, but we were lucky to even have desks and computers, walls to put color posters of primate anatomy and maps of the countries our chimps and gorillas would be found in the wild, were they so lucky. Marc's desk wasn't next to mine; Tom's and Sandy's were. His was across the room. He pulled his own chair out and slid it toward me, straddled it with his chest against the back. "Oh, god. Kate. I didn't know. I'm so sorry. That's so hard. How can I help?"

His voice was so caring it undid me. I couldn't stop my eyes from watering, and then my nose started to run. I yanked some tissue from the box on my desk and fought to pull myself together. "I'm just tired," I said. "I'll be okay."

"I'm sure you'll be okay, but that doesn't mean it's not extra hard. And you've got the redesign on you at the same time. How are you doing the move?"

I shrugged. "What do you mean? With a truck. I've got to get most of her stuff out of her apartment and move what will fit into the room in skilled nursing. Bring the rest back to my place. Or Goodwill. Or a storage unit. And it has to be this weekend. Otherwise, I'd work with Eve for you. I'm really sorry I can't."

"Do you have family helping?"

"There's just me."

He shook his head, letting out a long sigh through puffed cheeks. "Yeah. I know that story."

"Seriously?"

He nodded. "Seriously." We were both quiet a moment, then he added, "It's hard."

I tried to shake off emotion, change the subject. "Listen, I don't think you need to worry about leaving Eve this weekend. You don't have to rush this. I'm guessing from her behavior that she spent years in isolation. Half days here and there aren't going to be a big deal. You've given her a lot of stimulation in the enclosure—that's already a huge change. The new habitat is behind schedule, and if we move the others in before Eve is ready, well, then we do."

Marc just looked at me for a minute, like he was taking it in, and my eyes met his as I tried to decide if it sounded like I was trying to tell him what to do. "Hey, I didn't mean to come off like some know-it-all. I realize I'm not in charge of this," I said.

I was just too tired, too lonely, too in need. When Marc slid his chair closer, reached his hand over and briefly covered the one of mine that was resting on my desk, I didn't pull it away. "I'm not like that, Kate," he said. "I didn't take it that way. Can we just be friends now?" He had a good, baritone voice, on the quiet side.

There was real kindness in the deep brown of his eyes. I saw him differently than I had, though it wasn't the first time his good looks registered. His beard would have come in dark and heavy if he weren't always close-shaved. His nose was straight, almost chiseled, and his lips full around good teeth. I saw all this new then, but what moved me in that first touch was the comfort.

He moved his hand as soon as I nodded.

"Good," he said. "That's settled. I'm going to head out to find Linda, okay?"

"Sure," I said. "Thanks."

"Thank *you*," he said, and put his chair back in place.

After Marc left, I took two more ibuprofen for what was becoming a chronic headache and turned to clear my email. There was a confirmation for the truck I'd rented buried in there; it had come, I saw, two days ago. I was behind rather badly, but I had the credit card receipt anyway. I clicked on it and pushed print. The shared printer was in another office, but we all did that and picked up our stuff when we were ready. Then I went to check on the habitat construction team—and Bruce.

"The boy doesn't have a great future in construction," Mike, the crew boss said when I got there. Burly, with porcupine haircut and tomato face, he pulled a dirty cloth from his overalls pocket and mopped his face and neck. "Keeps wanting all the tools lined up according to size. Doesn't work that way on the job. Once I get him doing a task, it's okay, but he worries too much."

I sighed. "I do understand, but Bruce is a good worker. Explain his tasks, demonstrate, and then let him try. He doesn't need hovering. We appreciate your teaching him. When do you think you can get to the skylight?"

"That mother is enormous. Never done any that big here."

"That's for sure. It's all new. But do you know the height of trees in the rainforest?"

"Can't say that I vacation there much."

"Great apes need to climb."

"Whatever you say. Do you know the rest of the layout yet, what's going in?"

"Still working on final design details," I said. "You've got the worst of it underway, ripping out the old space. I'm grateful."

I was finishing up early so I could get over to my mother's. I'd just shut down my computer when Marc came in with a piece of paper, extending it to me.

"Hey, Kate. This was in the printer feed. I could see it's yours, so I brought it down."

"Sheesh, I forgot to go get it. Thanks. It's just my truck confirmation for Friday." I looked down at what he'd handed me. "Oh no, no, no. This is all wrong. I can't do this."

"What?"

"This is way bigger…I don't want… Oh wait—shit! It's standard shift. I don't drive standard shift." I was blathering, panicky.

"Did you specify automatic?"

"I specified the size, same size I got when I moved her in, and that was automatic, so I didn't think… I've gotta call them right now and get this switched."

"Yeah. I'll be in with Eve if…I'll be in with Eve. I hope they don't give you a hard time."

"It'll be fine," I said. And I thought it would be.

An hour later, I was still at my desk and desperate. No, they didn't have another truck available Friday evening or Saturday or anytime this weekend, and no, I hadn't specified automatic shift. University students were moving out of dorms this weekend, and all their smaller trucks were booked. They could give me one next weekend, no problem. Or Tuesday. I was doing a search on the computer, calling around to car rental places to see if any also rented small trucks.

When Marc came back to the office, he tossed a question in my direction as he got to his desk and sat, ready to close his computer.

"Got the truck you need?" he said, assuming I had, more a statement than a question.

Dust motes swirled like tiny lazy insects in a shaft of late afternoon sun that slanted between us, and I was grateful knowing he couldn't see me clearly. I just shook my head. Marc rolled his chair sideways with a question on his face. When I still didn't answer, he said, "Well?" Maybe I looked as upset as I felt. This was all my fault, of course. I'd stretched out moving my mother until the last possible time.

"There's not another one. I'm calling all over trying to find something now."

"You don't need to do that," he said, "I was thinking about it anyway. I can help you do the move. And…" here he raised his eyebrows in a joking way "…as an added attraction, I happen to drive a stick shift."

"I can't accept that."

"You absolutely can. Look, you help me out with Eve, okay? I'd like some more tutoring on socialization. Not my specialty, and you've done it before. Consider it a trade."

I hesitated, wanted to give a final refusal and stopped myself. What was I going to do? I hadn't factored in the University of Dayton or Wright State. They must have had spring finals at about the same time. I should have done this last weekend. I should have been more prepared.

"Okay. Thank you. Really." I was both relieved and terribly uneasy. It was so unlike me to be this exposed. I felt as if he were accidently seeing me naked. Only he wasn't going to be embarrassed and stammering an apology. This mistake was all on me.

"Hey, it's no problem. Happy to do it. I'll be getting the good end of the deal."

Marc wondered if Kate really knew what she'd agreed to. For sure, he'd gotten the better deal. He'd never seen her so stressed. She was the one who was always in charge of herself as well as the people she'd supervised, cool as a mountain stream in high summer. It had moved him to see her need help, but more—it surprised him when she said yes. A whole different side of her, human and vulnerable. He'd sensed her discomfort with it, a bit like a cornered

animal with no fight left, and admonished himself, *don't overstep.*
The next day, he didn't even mention it, just let the plan lie where it
was, settled and known to the two of them.

Friday morning, he said, "So, do I pick up the truck tonight?
Or tomorrow morning? And I'll need the name and address of the
place."

"Is there a chance you can get it tonight? Would that be
convenient? Like after work? If you have time."

"Sure, no problem. I just need to run home first, and let my
mother know—"

"Maybe you could just call her?"

"Can't do that. Gotta go. But then I'll—"

"How come?" The direct question, Kate making herself vulnerable again by asking something personal. Something he could rebuff.

They were in the hallway, outside the office. He was so sick of
explaining what no outsider would ever get. He'd given up. Not
because he was a reticent sort, but because there was just too much
to it.

Some secrets hadn't ever been erased from his mother's mind
and Marc wasn't about to get into explaining all that old history. It
wasn't subject to reason now, no more it had been when Dr. Duff,
his vet tech program advisor, pushed him to go full time, saying
he could handle that plus his job at the clinic. His undergraduate
advisor would be the next to try that, pushing him to accelerate.
Marc had only said to both advisors that he couldn't, he had to get
home during the day to check on his mother.

"Marc, good Lord, son, is your mother not part of the Deaf
community at all? I did a little reading to educate myself. It's a
whole thing. Deaf culture, it's called." Dr. Hardy had started in on
Marc when he stopped by the office after his Ethnobotany class.

Marc looked at Dr. Hardy, taken back by the *son* moniker. He'd
swallowed, blinked, and dissembled. "She prefers to keep to herself,"
he said finally. "Ran in her family."

"Maybe a change could help you both. There's help available—think about it, will you?"

"Okay" Marc said, knowing it was hopeless.

Dr. Hardy picked a couple of leaflets from his desk and handed them to Marc. "Take a look at these. I picked them up from the Health and Wellness office. Maybe show them to your mother," Dr. Hardy said.

"I will, sir," Marc had lied. "Thank you very much."

Later, in the icy parking lot where a few March-bare scrawny trees scratched at the sky looking for a way to escape the drear, Marc had shoved the flyers in a zip compartment of his backpack simply because there was no trash can nearby. He'd only needed to glance at the address of the Speech, Hearing, and Deaf Center of Greater Montgomery County. Just as he'd thought: the place was forty-five minutes away. It really didn't matter what Life Skills Class they offered for deaf adults, or what social groups were available, did it? Even if his mother would consider it—an absurd idea anyway—who was supposed to take her there, wait, and bring her home? The class was during the daytime, and on Monday, Wednesday and Friday, no less. Right when Marc had his own classes. The social support program was on Tuesday and Thursday with a lunch gathering included. Great. He worked in the clinic on Tuesday, Thursday, and Saturday. Plus, his mother was afraid about leaving the house. That fear hadn't ever lessened.

A black hole had opened inside Marc during and after that conversation, as black as the magnolia blossoms killed by the last night's unreasonable spring snow. Hidden in that darkness was fury. At the sky: even damn flowers didn't get a fair chance. At his Gram for swallowing antacids instead of seeing a doctor. At Goldie for getting too old to go on. At Dr. Hardy for showing, no, for *proving* what Marc knew his mother wouldn't or couldn't do. At his deaf mother. At himself, failing. At everything and everyone he hadn't saved.

And still now, all these years later, when Kate asked him why he couldn't just call his mother to say he wasn't coming home after work (and why should a grown man in his mid-thirties have to tell his mother if he was or wasn't coming home after work anyway), his voice took on an angry, defensive edge that he hated. "Jesus, Kate, she's deaf. And mute."

And then he was both grateful and annoyed that Kate did not know enough about deaf people to wonder why his mother wasn't using technology.

Kate had been subdued after that. "I'm so sorry, Marc. That was incredibly dumb of me. I just...forgot. I mean, you never talk about it, not that you should, and—"

"No, no." He wiped a hand over his hair. "I'm the one who's sorry. I didn't mean to sound like that. It's a reasonable question, and of course it's not part of other people's realms."

"Oh no, it's fine, I'm just sorry. It was stupid." A faint redness had crept up her neck and reached her face and her eyes were glittery.

Marc realized they were falling over each other apologizing and shook his head. "Let it go." He willed himself to relax and smile. "Where and when do I get the truck and where do I take it? Shall we get one load tonight? Like the stuff that's going to your place?"

Changing the subject was a good call. She jumped on it, grateful. "Really? I do have that ready. It's some of the furniture and a couple boxes. I don't have room for much more than I took when we sold the big house." And damnit, that loss still stung: its buttercream paint, black shutters, front porch and mature trees, sedate on two thirds of an acre in Centerville. Might as well be another country now.

They went into the primate keepers' area, walking together from the hallway as they talked, and Kate said, "Here, I've got you the address of the truck place and—do you possibly know where Sycamore Retirement Community is?"

"Heard of it. Over on the west side? Should I get on I-75 or use surface roads?"

"That's it. Depends on the traffic. I usually use surface roads but I'm not a fan of the interstate. You'd want the downtown exit onto Salem, keep to the right there, and then you've still got ten minutes before you're even in Westwood. It's a pain. Go to N. Riverview, and then take Hoover. Once you're at Sycamore, take the second left. It's confusing and way too much to remember. Here's my cell phone number, and her apartment address for your GPS, anyway. I can meet you there." Kate had the information already written out on a yellow sticky note.

Marc slapped it on his forehead. "What I always do with your notes. My forehead never gets sunburned."

"I'm thrilled you find them useful."

"See you later," he said, lifting his hand in a wave as he started to leave. Kate grabbed his arm to stop him.

"Wait. About my mother. She'll be there—"

"I figured as much," he said. Airy. It wasn't like he didn't have a mother himself. This was no big deal. "Don't worry. I'll be nice."

"Marc. She's got something called progressive primary aphasia. She's lost the ability to understand words, meaning she doesn't talk or understand what you say. But she doesn't have dementia. It's... very hard to grasp. But the point is, if you talk to her, she won't understand what you say. And she can't talk herself."

Marc narrowed his eyes, thinking. "Huh. So...she's mute."

Kate hesitated. "Well, yes, but not deaf. I just wanted you to know ahead so..." She closed her eyes as if the right words might be written on the inside of her lids. They weren't. "It can be awkward. It's why they're making me move her to skilled nursing."

"Okay. Got it. Thanks."

As he walked outside into the waning afternoon to his car, Marc mused about what Kate had said. Mute but not deaf. Still, unable to understand words so might as well be deaf, really. And

Kate with no tool to deal with it. Maybe there *was* no tool to deal with it. She'd said she had no family to help. Marc knew what that was like, the loneliness of the only child.

# Eve

NOW EVE WOKE UP each day in the new place that was bigger. She didn't know what had happened or what was coming. There was something high above her head, and some soft stuff, almost like something faintly remembered, but she wrinkled her nose and smelled nothing she knew. Afraid, she found a place to hide and waited for the animals with little hair who would come again with food or the sticks that hurt her.

# Chapter 8

WHEN MARC SHOWED UP at my mother's apartment, I was ready for him. The boxes to go to my apartment were by the door, and I'd gotten the couple pieces of furniture moved there, too, though it would have been easier to wait and have his help with that. I thought it was going to be awkward, Marc and Mom clumsy and uncomfortable as people who speak different languages without a translator—except my mother's native language is buried in some dark inaccessible silence, so even a translator would be useless.

I thought this because it's so often awkward and difficult for me, so although I had no idea what my mother might feel, I assumed it would be for Marc, too. I was wrong. When he came in, he went over to where she sat in her beloved blue recliner, the one I was determined to move with her even if it made her room tight as a fist closing around her. He picked up her hand and gave her a warm smile, then reached his other hand over to rub her shoulder. He put her hand down then and did something with his hands and arms that looked like a hugging motion while he said, "Hello, Mrs. McKinsey." He pointed to himself and said, "I'm Marc," pointed to me, "Kate's friend," then did something else with his hands too.

My mother smiled. That's all, but she smiled. It doesn't sound like much, but it doesn't happen a lot.

Marc turned to me and said, "So is that the stuff to go to the truck?"

I was somewhat stunned, still standing by the stuff near the door like some kind of a mannequin posed to just stare. "Uh huh," I said, stupid-sounding. "I'll start loading now."

"No way. You stay with your mom and keep her company. It looks like only that one table would be safest with two people taking it down the front stairs. The rest is no sweat."

"Were you doing sign language to her just then? She...doesn't know sign language."

"Oh, yeah. It's just automatic for me to do with anyone who's mute. Sorry. Didn't seem to bother her, did it?"

"No, I didn't mean that. Just wanted you to know she doesn't... um...speak...doesn't know how to do it."

"You can just say she doesn't sign. It's ASL, American Sign Language that I was using, because it's what my mother uses. There are other versions of sign, but my grandmother taught mom, so it's what I grew up with." He laughed and rolled his eyes. "Okay, Marco, that's TMI."

"No, it's good. Thanks for telling me."

"Thanks for tolerating my auto-signing." He laughed. "When I was a kid, I signed before I could talk. It's like my first language."

"That's actually really neat."

Marc kept talking while he moved boxes closer to the door, testing their weight and deciding how to stack them, I guessed. "Well, I had some hard times learning to talk without signing...I still remember that." He shrugged. "School. Anyway, I'm going to get this stuff to the truck now. And you were right. That mother fuc... uh, that *darn truck* is way too big. What the hell were you thinking?"

"Don't start with me," I said with a huff of disgruntled laughter. I picked up a box and started out the door.

"Nope, you stay put. I load, remember. Stay with your mother. This might be upsetting for her." He nodded over her direction, where she was still sitting, docile as a frightened child in the recliner. If anything, she looked faintly confused. Dusk had crept through the windows while I wasn't paying attention, and I hadn't turned on any lights. Perhaps she was having trouble seeing, I thought, and I switched on the floor lamp as I answered.

"I can't tell. But okay, I'll stay. Thank you."

I hadn't asked if I could bring her floor lamp to the nursing home, but I decided to bring it over and hope they'd let it stay. The more light the better, surely.

It was strange and different, sitting with my mother while Marc made the trips loading the truck. Fortunately, it didn't take him long. I didn't have all that much to go to my apartment, and I didn't want to empty my mother's apartment of the items I was putting in a storage unit, not until the next day, after we moved her. I didn't want her in such a stripped-down place that night when I suspected she had no idea what was going on. But if I could have explained it to her, none of it would be necessary. It wouldn't be happening at all. How many times did I remind myself of that?

Each time Marc came back in, he brought some funny observation about one of Mom's neighbors, enacting a comparison to one of the animals at the zoo. It was my job to guess which neighbor, he said, by pointing to where the apartment was. Marc was so good at this, I had no trouble. The unfriendly heavy-set white-haired woman two apartments away was a polar bear. Marc put Mom's white pillowcase over his hair, the pillow under his shirt, and copied Betty's walk by hunching over and lumbering. He accompanied that with a damn near perfect imitation of her facial expression, sticking his jaw out and growling. When I laughed and pointed, indicating an apartment down the hallway to the left, my mother actually grinned, clapped her hands twice.

It was the most I thought she'd understood in months. And Marc had accomplished it without a word.

"All ready," he said, when everything he'd piled by the door, like so much deconstructed habitat material, had disappeared. It would have, for sure, taken me much longer. "Shall we head over to your place and unload before it's totally dark?"

"Good idea."

He was the first to go to my mother. "Good night, Mrs. McKinsey. It was a pleasure to meet you," he said. He pressed his palms and tilted his head sideways on them. Then he did that hugging motion again and waved as he walked away from her chair. I pulled the signal line that would ask an aide to come assist my mother with getting to bed and said goodnight to her myself with a kiss to her cheek and a quick hug, as I always did. What I saw then was another shock: it was Marc she watched as we left, and she waved to him as she sat in the amber circle of light from the floor lamp, her lips parted in a smile. In that forgiving light, she wasn't the bare-faced woman gone gray and slumped; she looked as she had during the brief years after the divorce pain had healed, and she and I had forgiven each other our trespasses, before her aphasia started, the brief years when she was lively, vibrant as spring again, happy.

Marc followed me to my apartment. We each carried things from the truck and the unloading went quickly. "How about some wine? I can scare up some crackers and cheese, too," I said. "Did you even get any dinner?"

"I grabbed a gourmet fast food burger and super nutritious fries on my way over," he said. "Unbelievably wonderful."

"I have some very expensive—and by that, I mean at *least* eight dollars—white wine of unknown vintage and year, possibly inadequately chilled. Or cheap beer with no peanuts. And I may have a bottle of a mysterious red wine from a third world country."

"What are you having?"

"I will have the white wine of unknown origin."

"I'll have the white wine too, and I will fight you for the crackers and cheese."

"Oh," he said, when I handed him the bottle and opener. "I see the lady lies. Actually, quite a decent bottle she has in stock." I'm the one who turned more serious after I'd gotten cheese from the refrigerator, arranged a plate of crackers, and found some olives, cherry tomatoes and carrots to put out too. I'd guessed he might be as hungry as I was.

"Let's take these into the living room," I said. "More comfortable."

Marc settled himself on the couch and I shoved the ottoman in front of him so he could put his feet up. I slid my feet out of my shoes and tucked them beneath me, sitting sideways on the couch so I could face him.

"I like your place," Marc said. "Cozy, but not all fru fru. It's sort of rainforest colors, right?"

I laughed. "For sure. Not many people would recognize that. It's a little crowded, don't you think? Stuff from the big house and Mom's condo happened to work with the colors I loved from Africa, and then I had to take the piano, too, from Mom's condo—where she was after she couldn't handle the family house anymore, too big for one person."

I looked around. I'd not only kept the spinet piano, but her dining table and chairs, the good forest green couch we were sitting on, and the warm taupe easy chairs. Bright accent pillows—they'd been my additions, and the modern art on the walls, prints suggestive of nature, added more color. I'd chosen the apartment because it had a gas fireplace and a big enough balcony for two chairs, a little table, and tubs for flowers—though I hadn't planted any yet that spring. I got up and opened the drapes so Marc could see out the sliding glass doors.

"The fireplace, and this, out here, are why I chose this apartment," I said, flicking the switch that turned on the string of tiny white lights I'd fastened to the inside edge of the balcony railing. "In spite of the little kitchen."

"Oh, wow. That *is* nice. We have a yard. I don't do much except mow it. No fireplace but I'd love one."

"Does…your mother like to be outside, like to plant flowers, or vegetables?" I was curious about his situation, I admit.

"Mom is sort of freaky about leaving the house. It's a long story…goes way back."

"I can listen."

He shook his head. "Some other time."

I poured more wine into his glass and then my own. "Speaking of mothers, you were amazing. The response you got from her was completely different. I thought maybe she…it was like she understood something. Did you think so?"

"You'd know best. I'm glad if that's right, though."

"You were signing again when we left, right?"

"No, that wasn't ASL. I just made that sign up. The ASL for goodnight is this," Marc put his left arm parallel to the floor in front of him, bent at the elbow, touched his lip with his right hand and then made it do a sort of graceful little dive in front of his left arm, like it was tucking itself in. "It's not a sign that looks obvious, so I used another one I thought might be more of a…picture."

"That's so funny you say that. Did you see the big posters I've made with pictures cut out of magazines?"

"Yeah. That's what gave me the idea."

"Are you always so smart?" Tears prickled like nettles behind my eyes. Again. "I really can't thank you enough."

He must have sensed the emotion rising in me, because it only a simple act of caring when he leaned over and put first one arm around me, and then the other pulled me against his chest when I wiped beneath my eyes. "Hey, it's okay, it's fine," he said. "The first time it was an accident, just habit because you'd said she was mute, and the second time I'd seen the posters when I went to the bathroom and guessed that pictures might be an aphasia technique. At least for nouns. But if it gives us an idea of something new to try, that can only be good, right?"

"Maybe she just likes you better than me though."

"Well, of course. That would mean she has good taste." I pulled back and mock-punched his arm, and we both laughed. He was so easy to be with.

"I gotta get going," he said. "Linda said she'd go by tomorrow morning and spend some time playing the Lolly sounds I isolated for Eve, and maybe letting Eve get used to her presence. That way I won't leave so early. How would it be if we start moving your mom into the nursing unit at noon? You can stay with her and get her settled in. If you put your famous sticky notes on the stuff to go to the storage unit, give me the address and the key, I'll load it into the truck and get it over there. You said you were going to leave a few things in the apartment? We okay now on permission for that?"

"No, they refused. I was going to call Habitat for Humanity. There's room in the storage unit I rented, and they can meet me there when it's clear to me what to get rid of...permanently. But I'll help move the stuff. It's a two-person job."

"Are you calling me a wimp? You did it by yourself."

"Actually, I tipped a maintenance guy at Sycamore heavily to help me get the stuff up there."

"Huh. That makes sense. I'll take my tip in alcohol. And help with Eve."

I punched his arm.

"And you not leaving me disabled."

I punched him again just to see the funny face he'd make pretending it hurt, how his eyes held enjoyment and light. I wasn't thinking how he could be so right about my mother, but so wrong about zoos. No, I was just feeling the wonder of how he'd said *us*, how much I liked hearing the deep sound of his laughter with my higher notes rising over his like the white water that runs over rocks in a clear stream, and yes, how good his touch felt, that too, and that I wanted it again and more. His touch.

# Chapter 9

"HOW'S SHE DOING?" Marc said to Kate on Monday morning. On Saturday, he'd done his best to keep the move as uncomplicated and unconfusing as possible for Kate's mom, helping to get the room in the skilled nursing center set up with as many familiar objects as fit—pictures hung, the blue recliner Kate said her mother loved dragged in with the help of not one but two well-tipped maintenance men—all before Kate took her over. He could tell Kate was worried and he'd clowned to make her laugh so she'd not communicate upset to her mother. And because he liked making her laugh. There was that too.

"Dunno," Kate answered. "She hung on to my hand last night. Didn't want me to leave, and that's new, so I'm not sure if she's okay or not. I did get the curtain up—thank you for doing the rod—and I just put her quilt over their spread. I didn't ask their permission."

That lace curtain and the bed quilt were two of the things Kate was convinced her mother wanted, though Marc wasn't clear on why, guessed it was in the mysterious realm of stuff women knew. "Everyone over there is new to her. I think that would be disorienting for anyone. Anyway, if they bug you about what's in her room, screw them." Marc shrugged. "Just say you only made it to page five hundred seventy-two of their rule book before you dozed off."

"Right. That part must have started on page five hundred seventy-three. And I'm so, so desperately *sorry*." She held her hands out like a supplicant, while making a face, and they both laughed.

He did it then. Risked putting a hand on her back. No one else was in the primate keepers' area just then and they were standing near her desk, which wasn't particularly visible from the hallway. "Listen, I bet it's fine. You're paying plenty. Or she is, along with her insurance. Whatever. They want people to be as happy and comfortable as possible, I assume."

She didn't move away It was almost imperceptible, but she might have leaned into his hand, light as a bird landing on a branch, or maybe it was the weight of his hope. But she didn't move away, he was sure of that much. "You're probably right," she said. "I shouldn't borrow trouble. I know, I need to—"

Just then Christine Mead blew into the room, her unbuttoned lab coat flapping like white wings around black slacks. "Is Linda around?" She was clearly agitated, not paying attention to Marc's proximity to Kate and it was easy for him to drop his hand to his side without being noticed.

"Haven't seen her today," he said, at the same time Kate said, "No, isn't she in her office?"

Kate frowned. "Is something wrong?"

"I'd say so." Chris's face and tone signaled her impatience. "I really should talk to Linda first...Oh hell. Marc, you're in charge of Eve, yes?"

"What's wrong with Eve?" Marc's voice was sharp. "Yes, she's my responsibility."

"Did Linda mention any possibility that she was pregnant?"

"No way. Pregnant? She's only eleven. Not menstruating yet." Marc was the one to say that, while Kate interrupted with, "We were told she was always caged alone."

"Well, her blood work came back differently," Chris said, adamant.

"Could it be a mistake?" Marc was sifting through everything he remembered of her records.

"I don't see how that's possible." Kate said. "Unless they mixed up her results with a chimp from another zoo?"

"I double checked with the lab. They're Eve's results, no question."

"Isn't it weird that they even did a pregnancy test?" Kate asked, wrinkling her nose, her eyes narrowed down like mail slots.

"Not really. When I examined her—Marc, you remember?—I noted her abdomen was slightly rigid and distended. I had them test for the whole range of possibilities, in case any pathology showed up…just routine rule-out testing, it's what we do."

Marc and Kate stood silent for a couple of minutes. Then he scratched his head, and spoke thoughtfully, slowly. "Well, this isn't good. I guess either Linda or I need to contact the medical lab that had her and find out when she could have been impregnated, right? So we can calculate when she'd likely to have her baby. And…" he looked at Kate, "she'll have to stay longer in isolation? Can she be integrated into the group while she's pregnant?"

Kate put her hands up, like two white flags. "I don't see why not, but I've never integrated a pregnant female."

"How about I knock her down and examine her, tell how far along she is," Christine said. "Might be more reliable information." It bothered Marc that she'd want to do that without thinking of how it would affect the chimp, and he was quick to object.

"No. The last thing she needs is someone coming at her with a dart. She'd know exactly what that meant, and any tiny bit of trust I might have started to create would be shot."

Kate looked at him. "Literally."

Marc gave her a side eye under tented brows that said he had no idea what she meant.

"Shot. Trust would be *shot*…" she said, her tone the one they used when explaining something new to Bruce. Elaborate patience.

"Oh. Geez. I'm dealing with disaster and you're giving me shit." He'd not meant to sound annoyed, but he knew he had, when he heard her try to fix it.

"Chris, Marc is right," Kate said. "Not to want her knocked down, I mean. We'll have to get as much information as possible from the medical lab—obviously, there's something they managed not to tell us. But we need to let this pregnancy proceed naturally." Christine's eyebrows went up, but Kate pushed on. "She's already traumatized, that's why no darts. I think Linda will support Marc on that. I sure do."

"What I'm really thinking is, she should probably be sent on," Christine said.

Marc and Kate spoke at the same time. "What?" and "Huh?" On the same page.

"We're not a breeding program. This isn't our…thing. We don't really know—"

"And we're not ever going to breed," Kate cut in, adamant. "But she's been through enough. To send her on would mean knocking her down. Again. Traumatizing her. Again. She's already been damaged. We can't be the cause of more trauma."

"They are endangered," Chris argued.

That lit Kate's fire. "Really? Tell me about it, please."

Marc raised a hand. "Ultimately, it's Linda's call. I vote for keeping her, though. She's sweet-tempered as best I can tell, even with all she's been through. I think we can help her."

"Okay, you're right." Chris shrugged. "We go to Linda."

Kate had been correct about Linda's support. She'd flipped out, of course, at first. "What? This doesn't square at all with what I was told, that she'd always been isolated, not started her menses, the whole nine yards. Christine is sure about the results?"

"Said she double checked with the lab to make sure they hadn't sent the wrong results or something."

"I'll get on the phone right now. You want to stay? I can put it on speaker."

Marc was in Linda's small office, his chair wedged in next to one of the bookshelves that covered the two walls on either side of her desk. Behind her was a large window that looked onto one of the tree and flower-lined walkways between exhibits. In this case, it was the one between the elephant house and the primates, and, of course, the new great ape habitat currently under construction. There was an array of healthy plants on the wide ledge under the window, which Marc thought was just like Linda. Most living things thrived in her care. He was lucky to work for her.

"Sure, thanks. That's nice of you."

"Not at all. That way you'll hear first-hand."

But the call went nowhere. The two people who had been responsible for the chimpanzee care at the medical lab were no longer employed there—because the last chimp had been placed with a zoo. Linda and Marc rolled their eyes at each other, and Linda persisted, identifying herself a second time as the primate curator of the zoo at which their last chimp had been placed and explaining that she urgently needed to speak with the person who would have overseen the care of the female known as Eve, the last placed. Would the lab director kindly put her in touch with whomever had been in charge?

The director wouldn't give Linda contact information but said he would contact the former employee and ask that Linda be called.

"He didn't even ask if Eve was all right, or what I was concerned about," Linda said when she hung up. "Very guarded. Probably afraid they're going to be sued."

Marc drummed his fingers on his thigh. "Maybe they should be."

"That's Thurston's call." Linda replaced her glasses on top of her head. "Or Andrew's, I suppose. Or maybe Bryan's." Andrew was the zoo's chief financial officer, Bryan their legal counsel. She closed her eyes a moment as if calculating the likeliness, opened them, and looked at Marc. "No," she said with a head shake. "They'll get away with it." She pressed her lips together and slapped her hand on the desk. "I guess we wait now, see if I get a call."

"I'll head back to Eve." Marc stood to leave. From the doorway, he added, "She's looking at me more and more. Either she's thinking this *guy is weird as hell*, or she's deciding maybe I'm not going to hurt her."

"Or she really likes the fruit." Linda said.

"Or she really likes the fruit. However, since I am supplying the fruit, ahem—simple association, good thing with good thing." He was parroting a relationship building principle about which Linda was passionate, but it was one he'd already known well from his years training Goldie.

"Oh, all right." Linda smiled, her encouraging supervisor smile. "Good job. I'm proud of you. Go win her over. I'll tell you if I get anything. And, you know, we're going to have to tell Thurston."

"There's no *we* to that, Kemosabe. That one's in your Lone Ranger job description."

"Don't remind me."

Linda hadn't even brought it up. Marc almost didn't. Why stir that pot? But he knew Christine would, and best to deal with it off the top, he supposed. He took a breath and said, "I have to tell you, Chris is making noises. She thinks because we don't breed here that maybe we should a send Eve on to a place that does—because of the endangered status."

"How do you see it?"

"I think she's been through too much trauma already. A breeding program is going to start knocking her down for ultrasounds, and well, I think we can handle it and, you know, Kate. Kate wants her to have a chance to be with her own baby. She says Jasmine and Lolly will help, and…." He gave a small shrug embarrassed by the plea in his voice. "The troop. The way they do."

Linda's eyes went soft. She nodded. "I get that. Eve can stay. Christine can consult with Dr. Reagh, if that'll make her feel better. I'll deal with the medical budget later."

It was the next afternoon before Linda sought Marc out where he'd stationed himself just outside Eve's isolation enclosure after he'd done his part caring for Lolly, Jasmine, and the other chimps. He was still in coveralls, sitting cross-legged on the floor by the slot through which they put Eve's food, reading aloud a children's picture book about chimps in the rainforest. His back was to Eve. She was behind the partition but by only two feet and another foot to Marc's left. He was holding the book up to the side of that shoulder as he read, showing the bright pictures and pointing to story elements as he read. He had papaya and several bananas in a large stainless-steel dish next to him. When Linda came in, he hurriedly got to his feet.

"Just trying something different," he said, feeling himself flush and hating it.

"Huh. Interesting. Can you step out for a minute—I need to tell you something, and I'd like to hear about what you're doing." Linda looked at Eve, who was retreating back toward the wooden spools. "Hey pretty girl. It's me, you know me. Nothing to be afraid of, right?" She spoke softly, kindly. From the wooden spools, Eve stared at her.

"Well, she's not hiding behind them," Linda said as she went back into the hallway, Marc behind her. "What is it you're doing?"

Marc hadn't planned to talk about it yet, wished he could have put it off until he knew more. "Well, I thought I wouldn't seem dangerous if my back was to her, but I wanted her to keep hearing

LYNNE HUGO

my voice. And I thought maybe rainforest pictures might stir a faint memory. And that might be good. Each picture with a chimp eating, see, I'm putting some fruit in. She started to come get it while I'm right there, and I think just parking herself within a couple feet of my back. She wouldn't do that before. I've been playing the recording of Lolly too." Marc grinned as he read on her face that Linda was pleased. "I tried to make myself look sort of chimp like, show her I'm no threat," he ruffled his own hair the wrong way and hunched to show her, "but my knuckles started to bleed, and Kate said I just looked batshit crazy anyway. Especially when I let this go for two days." He rubbed his chin and cheeks where his beard was just emerging, heavy and dark, still shaved though he was.

Linda laughed. "She's right about that. But Eve's coming along. I like your creative thinking. You're good at using what you've got... you couldn't even think about turning your back if the partition wasn't glass," she mused. Then her smile faded, and she paused, sighed. "Listen, the employee—or former employee—from the research lab called me. He was pretty careful. I think he'd been warned about what to say. But anyway, yeah, she was caged with a male for a short time while they were moving chimps out, but he assured me she had definitely not had her first menses, so they were sure it was safe. Said the male was not aggressive at all. He doesn't see how she could have been ovulating."

Marc was confused. "But she *is* pregnant, so are they wrong about her age?"

"You're thinking about the next of kin thing, right? Our closest relatives. But it's the same with a pre-teen human girl. They can be fertile before actual menstruation starts—for god's sake, it's happening earlier and earlier. There's no way to know when she first ovulates. And since the chimps' copulation takes all of eleven seconds, unless they were watched twenty-four seven, they'd have no clue."

"Oh yeah. Wasn't considering that possibility, fertile before first menses."

86

"Obviously, they either didn't know and didn't care enough to find out. Or just didn't care."

"Have you told Thurston?"

"Not yet. Only Kate and you."

"I'm sure she took it well."

"Oh, absolutely. Thrilled that the research lab was so *responsible*."

"Well, me too. Big damn thing to figure in with integrating her. She won't have learned how to be a mother or had the babysitting practice that they get in the wild."

"Yeah. Well, one thing at a time. Kate can help about the baby. Pretty sure she had some field experience with that in Africa, the whole nine yards. I can't remember." She raised her eyebrows at him. As if he'd know. Marc shrugged and put his hand palm up, empty, and she said, "I'll ask her. The new habitat is behind schedule anyway. I'm going to go make an appointment with Thurston."

"Okay, good luck."

"I never know with him." Linda said. Rueful. She patted her hair down and straightened her shirt. "Okay, I'm off."

"Sometimes I don't think we really know anything. We just make our best guess and try."

"Amen."

# Chapter 10

I'D JUST OPENED my computer for a quick email check when Linda came looking for me a little before noon. I still needed to head to the new habitat construction and then see what Marc might need in the way of help before lunch. Before I even got to open my mail though, she was standing by my desk, her loose dark nest of hair in disarray and her face tight, worried.

"It's just that this pregnancy thing complicates it all," Linda said. "What's the chance that she'll know how to mother? Maybe thirty-seventy." She pinched the bridge of her nose between her thumb and forefinger, closed her eyes for a minute, which made me suspect she had a headache. "If we're lucky, fifty-fifty. So, the issues are, can we accelerate getting her socialized so maybe Jasmine could help her? Or do we keep her isolated, let her give birth and then watch twenty-four seven so we're ready to pull the baby out if she rejects or ignores, and either bottle feed, or…maybe see if Jasmine will be a surrogate mother again. Lord. I could throttle those morons at that test lab. How freaking stupid. Anyway, what do you think?"

"I think we just don't know Eve well enough to guess. When will the baby come?"

"Didn't Marc tell you? I got the dates she was caged with the male. December 24-28. Presuming they're telling us accurately, which may or may not be the case."

I'd gone to see my mother this morning and hadn't been in to see or help Marc, so hadn't talked to him and didn't know. I didn't particularly want Linda to be aware of that, so I didn't respond exactly truthfully when I shook my head once as I said, "I just haven't done the calculations. Just a sec…"

I quickly did them in my head. Two hundred forty-three days from December twenty-fourth to December twenty-eighth, providing the lab was telling Linda the truth, meant late August. Good lord. We didn't have a lot of time. She was already almost five months into gestation. Summer was not only our goal, it was our deadline.

"Let's shoot for a preliminary decision by the beginning of August," I said. "We ought to know a lot more about her by then. I want to integrate her. Gives the baby the best chance."

Linda straightened her shoulders. Again, I had a sense that she was overtired, even though her khakis were pressed into clean lines, and she wore a crisp white shirt with a bright bead and medallion necklace I thought was from the zoo's African jewelry collection in the gift shop. She gave me a half-smile. "Okay. Give Marc all the help you can. Not that he's not doing a good job, because he is. I just didn't expect this curve ball."

"At least you didn't call it a monkey wrench," I said.

"Sheesh. That was pathetic," she said on her way out. "I'll be in my office. Hey, will you keep an eye on Bruce, too? I'm picking up an edgy feeling with your crew. Not bad, just edgy."

In the new habitat construction area, I was thrilled. The crew had installed the enormous skylights, the equivalent of nearly three stories high, and in warm weather, they could be opened by remote control, the closest thing to completely real, natural light and air the chimps will have known since they were either snatched from their dead mothers' backs or chests back in Africa or born directly into a life of caged captivity.

"Oh wow, guys. You got that in *fast*." I shouted over the construction noise.

"In spite of the 'help' over there."

I formed a question with my face, raised shoulders, and hands rather than try to make myself heard.

The crew boss pointed with his graying chin, indicating Bruce, who was kneeling in front of something over in a corner of the work area. I kept missing chunks of what he said, but by catching, "… moving him out of the way … slows me down…too much equipment…" I got enough, and his arm swept toward the two men presently using power tools.

I walked over to see what Bruce was doing. It appeared he'd gathered up all the screwdrivers in the various toolboxes the crew had and was trying to organize them according to length but was frustrated because some were Phillips head. He looked up at me, his forehead wrinkled, eyes squinting, his thatch of pale hair askew. "Hey," I smiled. "You okay?"

He stuck his fingers in his ears by way of reply.

I motioned for him to follow me out of the area. When I looked back, I saw he was torn. He couldn't leave the screwdrivers unfinished, but he'd been told to follow me. "It's okay," I moved in close and said into his ear. "You can come right back, and finish that."

He followed me then, and once we were away from the noise, I said, "Bruce, is all that noise bothering you?"

"All that noise bothers me," he said.

"Would you like me to give you different work to do?"

"I would like you to give me different work to do."

"Okay, I can do that. Do you want to put the screwdrivers away first, or do you want someone else to do that?"

He hesitated and then closed his eyes. "In line," he said, flapping his hands.

"Would you feel better if I go into the noise and fix them for you?"

He wanted to say yes, but again, it troubled him, and although he'd struggled to get them down by his side, still, his hands were moving like motorized parts. I needed to take the decision away from him.

"Actually, I'll take care of those screwdrivers myself. Right now, I need you to do something else entirely, so I am going to assign you to work with Tom this afternoon. You have helped him before with checking all the water lines and feeding the gorillas, right?"

"I have helped Tom with the gorillas before."

"Well, let's walk down now and find Tom, and I'll let him know you'll be with him the rest of the day. He's been needing help lately."

That last wasn't entirely true, but Tom was kind and easy going, and he was good about teaching Bruce. I'd let him know what was going on, and he'd do it. I needed to talk with Linda about it, but it was obvious that being with the construction crew was not a great plan for anyone.

"I like gorillas," Bruce said.

"Well, they like you, too. Animals can tell who's a good person. That's why they like you. We all like you a lot."

Eve was sitting quite near the food slot when I went in to see if Marc was with her. He was talking to her as he put papaya into the tray. I stood back and watched. Now he just had to back a couple of feet away before she came and snatched up the fruit, and she only retreated to the middle.

"That's amazing," I whispered, not wanting to spook her by approaching. When he heard me, he turned, smiled, and signaled me to go out, that he'd follow.

"No coveralls?" I said when he caught up to me beyond the doorway. He was wearing regular clothes—navy slacks and a bright yellow polo shirt—which was unusual when we were around the animals.

"Well, Linda came in wearing a white blouse, and I was pretty sure Eve reacted. It occurred to me that maybe Eve thought it was a lab coat? And then I got wondering if at the lab, workers had worn coveralls, too, and…well, I thought, what if? I think she's been coming around a lot closer since I took them off. I've been trying the brightest shirts I have, so I look different than lab techs or the lab workers. Weird, huh? Just an idea, though."

"Huh." I didn't have to think about it long. "Damn good idea, really."

"How's your mom?"

"Not good. I think she's miserable over there."

"What makes you think that?"

"She just seems withdrawn. Worse than before even. I dunno. I hate this. I can't get a flicker of response."

"Do you think she'd feel like she had to try more with a visitor other than you?"

"Pfft." The question was annoying. "She doesn't have visitors other than me." He apparently didn't get that her friends had fallen away like petals dropping one by one off a dying flower until there was nothing but a stem and shriveled center.

"I'll go with you."

"I can't ask you to do that."

"I'd swear I just offered." He said it lightly.

I was embarrassed. "I know, and I appreciate your caring, but it's my job."

"Good grief, Kate. Friends help each other out. It's no big deal. Let's see if we can spark a response, huh?"

He smiled, all warm and encouraging, and I felt small as a kid. It was less embarrassing to retreat than to keep arguing, so I started mumbling ungraciously, as if I had a mouthful of pebbles my tongue had to find words in. "Um…if…you really want to…I mean…you don't need to…okay." I was not myself. Or maybe I was, and that was worse.

"Great. Might not make the least difference, of course," he said, matter of fact. "But you'll know something, and it might be useful. Right?"

I tried to regain some dignity, made myself stand up straighter and speak normally. "Right. It is a good idea. Thanks so much. Just let me know when it's convenient for you, and I'll play around with my schedule."

"You going on Saturday?"

I rolled my eyes. "Every Saturday. And Sunday. Pretty much every *day* now."

"Saturday works. Let me know what time. I'll meet you there. I can come be with Eve anytime. I'm not on the schedule."

I managed to come up with, "Thanks, Marc. That's really nice of you."

On Saturday, I was in my mother's room nearly a half-hour before two o'clock, the time I'd suggested to Marc. I don't know why that seemed important to me. It wasn't as if she grasped what I told her. I did give the staff a heads up, that my mother would be having another visitor, but that didn't prompt much response other than that I was reminded to have him sign in and out. The sign at the main entrance—along with the attendant there—made the instruction impossible to miss, anyway.

What else was impossible to miss: vacant-faced patients parked in wheelchairs, ashen skin blurring into thin gray hairlines, male and female alike, their lumpy bodies and faintly whiskered chins hardly distinguishable one from the other, like road and horizon in a fog, or life and death, the way they sometimes merge to confuse and terrify us. In the skilled nursing center, the old and infirm were treated to large bulletin boards in the hallway with pictures of flowers and cartoonish suns, and signs that informed them variously, *It is Springtime. The weather is sunny and warm. Flowers are blooming in gardens.*

Why were these adults at the very least not outdoors in the courtyard where the weather was, indeed, sunny and warm and yes, flowers were blooming? My mother should not be here. *I will never be here.* I wanted to scream it, sob it, rage against it.

"Hi Mom," I said, like some idiot blithe spirit. "How are you doing today? Isn't it a pretty day?"

She looked tinier, already diminished in her recliner in this too-small room. She didn't look at me. "Where are the picture posters I made?" I asked, pointless though the asking was. A search turned them up in her little closet, which infuriated me. I'd left them propped against her wall, so the staff would be encouraged to use them. It seemed wildly unlikely that my mother had moved them. In her apartment I always found them exactly where I'd last put them. It was as if over here, they weren't even going to try.

I was still stewing about it when Marc came. Maybe that was why I agreed to his suggestion later, no idea, of course, what we'd set in motion. He'd say that if the future were predictable, we'd all just buy crystal balls and save ourselves a truckload of pain. And he'd say the responsibility was his, though I know in the end there's not an action he'd change.

# Eve

THE SAME BIG ANIMAL, taller than Eve herself and with little hair like the others, brought fruit and never hurt her, came every day. His body was brighter than the others had been, like a parrot, and he made sounds that were friendly. Eve could hear another chimp often but could not see her. The other chimp was not sounding a warning, but no rainforest memories awakened in Eve, either; mating birds calling, insistent insects, rain on leaves, stealthy big cats prowling—those sounds were missing. Sometimes now when she heard an approaching animal and the sound was his, she was glad and did not hide.

# Chapter 11

MARC WAS RELIEVED he'd left early. First, the traffic was obscene, and then he'd messed up finding the right building, even though he'd been there before. But, of course, then he'd followed Kate through the retirement center campus maze of independent living cottages, assisted living apartment buildings, past the community center to the skilled nursing unit, all of which had required multiple turns around little ponds and mini parks.

White headed, over-dressed people bent over walkers and canes, their elbows held by middle-aged family, dotted the pathways here and there, some with small children orbiting like planets. Grandchildren or great grandchildren, Marc guessed, when he stopped to let first one, then another such group cross the drive. Then there were several wheelchairs he waited for, the seated figures in them wearing sweaters and hats, their gnarled hands resting on lap blankets, pushed by teenagers wearing some version of a T-shirt and angling their faces to the sun as they slowed their natural exuberant walk. A parent or two trailed behind them, probably issuing safety warnings. It was like trying to drive one of the service vehicles through the zoo, Marc thought, which was something he always wanted another keeper to get stuck doing.

If there was one thing he couldn't stand, it was to be late. Once he parked, he jogged the path to the door, signed in, and hurried to Mrs. McKinsey's room, checking his watch several times on the way. It was because he was harried, he thought, that he didn't pick up on Kate's sour mood right away.

"Mrs. McKinsey," he said, instead knocking on the open door, interested to see if she would respond to sound. She did glance over, but maybe she had seen him there in her peripheral vision. "I'm happy to see you again." Marc signed as he spoke and approached her chair. Then he stuck his hand out. She smiled and shook his hand.

He looked over at Kate to say hello and was taken aback by seeing her eyes widen as she looked at her mother holding on to his hand. "Hey, you all right?"

"Uh, yeah. Sure. Hi. What would you think about going outside? Like the courtyard? It's so nice out."

"Sure." Marc turned to Kate's mother, and said, "Kate's got a good idea, don't you think?" What he signed was, "We'll go outside," using the simplest, most obvious signs he knew, and then he walked to the window, pointed, and repeated the signs. Maybe she got it, maybe she didn't, but Mrs. McKinsey scooted forward, got out of her chair, and headed for the door of her room.

"She's either fallen in love with you, or…" Kate shook her head. "That's gotta be it. She's got a crush," she said as she rummaged through one of her mother's drawers looking for a light sweater. Her mother was already out waiting for them in the hallway.

"Yeah, I have that effect on women. If they're twice my age."

"Wait, don't forget chimps. Eve's only eleven."

"Oh yes, young chimps too, absolutely." He nodded. "Yep. And the girl gorillas say I'm hot."

"Well, see? They've got good taste."

Marc considered fishing for more but quit while he was ahead.

He'd stayed almost two hours, and thought the visit went well. They walked through the courtyard, then followed the tree-lined path that looped around a duck pond. Marc pointed at the swimming ducks, and then signed the word because it's an easy one to get, hand up at the mouth, opening and closing like a quacking duck's bill. No way to know, of course, if she got the idea, but she'd smiled and pointed at the duck. He didn't try the sign for water, three fingers of one hand up, signifying the letter W, lifted to the mouth, because it didn't look like water, to Marc's mind. Why confuse her?

Once Kate said, "That's amazing, Marc," after he'd signed about going back inside. He was grossly simplifying, shortcutting everything, but of course, Kate didn't know that. "Maybe I can show you…and her," he said.

"Do you think…?"

He didn't know crap about how to teach sign. Being fluent in it had nothing to do with teaching it. But maybe he could take a shot at it. Start with nouns, especially simple ones he could point to and then show Mrs. McKinsey the sign. Especially if the sign was one that looked like the object. Oh, he thought. Wait, that works with some verbs, too. But it would only mean something if Mrs. McKinsey caught on, and if Kate was right that pictures were the only thing that sometimes worked. A visual language… had that been tried with aphasia victims? It seemed so obvious, it must have been. But wouldn't Kate have investigated that?

When they were back in Mrs. McKinsey's room, Kate said, "Are you free later? Would you want to come over to talk about it? I could order in. I already have the wine."

Marc mimed tipping a glass as he said, "Sold to the cheapest bidder." She punched his arm. He pretended to stagger.

In her recliner, Dorothy McKinsey watched them intently, silently.

Before he went to Kate's, Marc showered and shaved for the second time that day, splashed his body with Royal Copenhagen. Before dressing, he inspected himself in the mirror, looking for carved lines that would please a woman, and finding fewer than he believed necessary, resolved to find time to lift some weights again. He hadn't gone dissolute, but he wasn't twenty anymore either. Dammit.

And who do you think you are, anyway? Kate asked you over because of her mother, not because she's hot for you. Get over yourself, he said aloud, and pulled on his pants. Still, Marc put on a shirt that Linda had complimented, then he stopped on the way to Kate's and bought a good bottle of wine, and then stopped again at a pastry shop and got hand-made eclairs for dessert. Why not?

The evening probably would have gone just as well if he hadn't tried so hard, because Kate opened the door as soon as he knocked and greeted him with a hug. He couldn't return it because, of course, he was holding wine and a box of two delicate eclairs, but she was, for Kate—normally guarded—almost effusive in her greeting.

It would be a mistake to ignore this new warmth from her, wouldn't it? He put his hand on her back while she got out glasses for the wine he'd opened, and then, when they headed to her living room carrying the glasses, he decided to push it one step farther: he sat in the middle of the couch rather than one end, and sure enough, instead of avoiding the couch altogether, which she could have easily done, Kate dropped onto the cushion next to him, exhaling comfortably as she kicked off the her flats and put her feet up on the coffee table.

"I can't believe all you've done," she said. "And I can't thank you enough."

Marc hoped all this coziness wasn't about gratitude. But then, she could have been grateful from across the room and without a hug, right? Right? This was where he'd really missed out not having a dad or an older brother to tell him about this stuff. When guys his age had been learning their way around girls in high school and college, Marc had been Mr. Responsible, taking care of his mother, certainly without the means to hire the help he did now.

And it had been awkward when he'd tried to bring friends home. He'd had to interpret for his mother, make up things she'd supposedly signed to his friends that made her sound like their mothers—who weren't afraid to leave their houses to go to their sons' games, their plays, their concerts. Then his friends had practically shouted to his mother, answering the questions and comments that Marc had pretended she'd signed. Why did people think they should talk loudly at deaf people when someone was standing there interpreting? Marc had no idea, only that pretty much everyone did. Loudly and slowly. Idiots. Well meaning, but still idiots.

His experience with women was largely limited to his fantasy life. Not entirely, but could he really count Peggy Benedetto, whose braces had cut his lip open when he was a sophomore in college? She hadn't even made him particularly horny. He'd thought something might be wrong with him until he identified the problem: he didn't like her.

No such problem with Kate. He liked her a lot. And now it was starting to feel like she might like him too. He didn't want to think he was using her mother to get to her, though. That wasn't what it was about when he brought it up again after they'd eaten the salads and pasta primavera and had just opened a second bottle of wine. It was more thinking how terrible it must be for Mrs. McKinsey, no way to communicate what she needed or wanted. Like having her will taken away or being locked up. How could he not help if it was in his power? If it brought him closer to Kate, well, then, that would be a welcome bonus, like hitting the lottery and then the powerball. Oh, for sure, and what a powerball.

"I was wondering if you've looked into whether there has been any research…has ASL been used with primary aphasia patients?" Marc asked. "I know you've said that pictures sometimes work, and I saw that."

"Honestly, I don't know. I don't know any sign. I've pointed and that's all. Used pictures, and she seems to get those sometimes. She responds to you better than anyone else. Is that you or the sign? Dunno."

Marc pulled out his phone and typed into the search engine. "Oh lord. There's a ton here. It's mainly about stroke and dementia patients, though, and it appears to have to do with which hemisphere of the brain was affected."

"Mom didn't have a stroke and the MRI shows—"

"No dementia. I remember."

"But we're getting some response...which is more than anyone else is pulling out of her."

"Would you like to learn some sign? I could try to teach both of you."

"Would you? Yes! We could at least try, right?" She said that, and then—he could hardly believe it was happening—she put her head on his shoulder. "It's so kind of you. I've been at my wits end, it all just seemed so...hopeless."

In a move that was at once awkward and weirdly natural, sort of couple-like, Marc momentarily dislodged her head as he worked his arm behind and around her, and pulling her in next to his body, let her settle her head into the space between his own neck and shoulder, where it could rest as if it had found a home. He kissed the top of her head.

"I hate that place," she said. "It's like a damn zoo, where they're all locked up. If she could just communicate."

"She's safe, though," Marc said. "That part is good, isn't it? Could she make it on her own? Outside?"

Kate sighed. "Don't get me going. Wait, do you think she could learn to sign that well?"

"Oh geez. I can't teach that much. Above my pay grade. Let's see what we get with simple signs. Then, we could look at other options—other than me."

"Okay. But I think she'll respond best to you."

"I'm not a teacher. Just being honest," he said, hoping that if he didn't make much progress with the mother that it wouldn't put a halt to his progress with the daughter.

Maybe it was just as well that it wasn't an option to stay the night at Kate's. Better to take it slower than to come off like a guy who expected sex on the first date—if this was even a date. He didn't know how to read this. It wasn't like he was fifteen and kept a lucky condom in his wallet.

Besides, he'd not arranged for one of his mother's helpers to stay over, and there'd be no one to wake her if there were some emergency. If he weren't so busy at work, he thought, he'd go ahead and adopt a dog now, one to take through the training to assist a deaf person. That would give him freedom, and his mother more companionship, another bonus. Maybe he'd take his vacation time in August and get started with that. If Eve had been transitioned to the troop by then.

Still, the thing was that maybe it had been an option to stay, and that was the important thing. Those last kisses had been real, and when his hand drifted to her breast, if her body had shifted at all, it had been toward his, not away. Had it been disappointment that edged the sympathy on her face when they were getting up from the couch? He'd said he needed to get home, that his mother had been alone for hours.

She'd taken his hand in hers. "She's really dependent, isn't she? I know what that's like. I didn't know that's what it's like for deaf people. It's weird, isn't it? I used to feel like I was the only one whose life revolved around taking care of my mother."

Marc thought of explaining, right then. He wanted to say, it's not like this for most deaf people. But it always has been for her, and it's the system, the history I was raised in. I don't think I can… And then what would he say? He'd have to explain all of it, wouldn't he? But why shouldn't he? Habit?

Not enough time to think. He'd ducked it. "It's okay. I hire a lot of help…audiology students who know sign. I just didn't arrange anyone to…stay…tonight." And to cover his dissembling, he'd put his arms around her and drawn her into a hug. Again, she'd leaned into it, and rested there until they both felt the moment pass and separated. "Okay, so let's figure up some times we're both free and I'll give it my best," Marc said, thinking of more than teaching Kate and her mother.

"Absolutely," Kate said. She was barefoot—her pink-polished toes when she'd taken off her shoes, like she'd walked through flower petals, had made her seem more vulnerable than he'd imagined her—and had to raise herself onto them to kiss his cheek then. "That's all we both can give."

# Chapter 12

"YOU'RE NOT GOING to believe this," Linda said, as she blew into the keepers' area Monday morning.

I'd come in early hoping to talk with Marc alone, but Linda had told me he was feeding the chimps and after that he'd be working with Eve. I'd found Tom picking up coffee in the cafeteria. He was taking over with Reece and Katari because Sandy was off, and before I asked, he'd guessed what I wanted and grinned, held up a hand to stop me from speaking, and said, *yes, sure,* he'd supervise Bruce today.

"You're a good guy," I'd said, and I wasn't being sarcastic.

"No problem. He's actually quite a good helper."

Since I wouldn't see Marc until the department meeting later that day, I'd started going through my inbox to clear it. Until Linda said, "Tell me what you think of this," and pulled the chair from Sandy's computer over to my desk. "Thurston is thrilled about Eve's pregnancy."

"What? I thought you said he was Not. Happy."

"That was then. Thrilled is now. I'm serious."

"And, exactly what changed? Still going to cost the department more money than in our budget. Still going to—"

"Oh yeah. I know. We were just stupid not to realize this was going to happen. Think about it. What does Thurston get off on more than anything?"

"You mean money?"

Linda rolled her eyes and sighed at me. "Yes. I mean money." Linda pushed her glasses back in place on the bridge of her nose. "What does he love second best?"

I hesitated a nanosecond, and was about to say more money, but she didn't wait.

"Come on! Easy question. It's publicity. Publicity attracts money," she said, her voice a knife cutting out the right answer and flipping it into the air where any fool could see it. This wasn't like Linda, usually patient and easy-going.

I did know what she meant, but she was moving too fast for me to grasp the implication.

"Don't you see?" She went on when I didn't fill in the blank and verbalize what was going to happen. "Thurston's brilliant idea is to publicize Eve's pregnancy and have a big contest…NAME EVE'S BABY…" She mimicked Thurston, making her voice deep and using her hands to magnify the words. "He says zoo babies are a huge draw and wants that baby on public display, with Eve, the devoted mother nursing her, the whole nine yards. Get prepared, honey, because—"

"Wait. We don't even know if we can integrate her, how soon. And there are all kinds of problems with—"

"Thurston wants a rush on the new habitat and on Eve integrated."

I was shaking my head. "What about what's right for her?"

"I told you you're not going to believe this."

I didn't do a great job of controlling my outrage. "You're the Primate Curator. You can say no."

"I get where you're coming from. You know I do. I can only say no to active harm to an animal." Her tone said she didn't like it, and I didn't get why she'd just roll over.

"A rush on integration will mean more medical intervention, probably knocking her down for exams. More trauma. You don't think that's harm?"

She sighed. "Not the way you mean harm. You know the power situation in the country. It'll probably already be too late regardless of what happens in the next election because right now when it's crucial—now they're rolling back environmental protections and the Amazon is being clearcut or burned to feed corporate greed, right?" She didn't wait for me to answer, just went on.

"Even their damn permits issued right and left for big game trophy hunting." Linda turned to bitter mockery, which I'd never heard from her before. "Sure, big man, big gun, big dick, bring it home, show it off. It's endangered? Great. Even better." Then she reined herself in. "*You know*, Kate. We're not exactly in a sympathetic political atmosphere for a crusade to save natural habitats, even though it's synonymous with saving the earth. That's not the fight we can wage here. As hard as it is to accept, we're the good outcome for our animals."

"The lesser of two evils argument. Like we should just give up on doing what's really right." I knew I sounded just as bitter as she had, but that was usual for me. I *was* angry, especially for our primates, but also for others, the ones that could have lived a natural life. "They don't deserve this. Eve doesn't deserve this. Look at what's she's already been through.

"I know, and I'm not arguing with you. But this is the hand we're dealt, and we have to see what's possible. I'll talk to Marc about how she's doing."

The department meeting that afternoon was routine, and I sucked hope from a twisty straw: Linda didn't bring up Thurston's plan, and maybe that meant she'd found a legitimate way to block it when she talked to Marc. She hurried out as soon as the meeting was over and as people scattered, I waylaid Marc.

"Nice shirt," I said. It was red, a color I'd not seen him wear before, but it did look good with his dark hair and brows and eyes.

He narrowed his eyes. "You making fun of me?"

"No, seriously. Red looks good on you."

"Oh. Thanks." The tension went out of his face, and he smiled. "I bought a few more in these bright colors. I'm sure of it, now, Eve is scared of lab coats and coveralls. So, when you go in there, please— "

"Got it. I'll remember. Hey, has Linda talked to you about Thurston's plan to push integrating her?"

He drew his head back, clearly surprised. "What?"

"I'll take that as a no."

"I'm supposed to see her in her office at three."

"Huh. She didn't tell me not to say anything."

"What's going on?"

I blew my hair back off my face and considered. It would not go over well with Linda if she knew I tried to influence Marc. But damn I was going to try.

I was considering how to explain it when Marc shrugged. "Never mind. I can wait an hour. She'll tell me." Then he grinned, his eyes softly creasing at the outer edges. "She's never asked me to do anything off the wall yet, so I'm not too worried. Listen, when do you want us to go see your mother?"

I wanted to blurt it out then, tell him it *was* off the walls, that it's not okay to display Eve's pregnancy and new baby to benefit the zoo, that she's been exploited and traumatized her whole life, it has to stop. *She owes nothing; she is owed.* I wanted to beat that drum again, but I didn't. Only because Sandy came back into the office and sat at her computer.

Marc said, "So would tomorrow work?" Meaning, of course, to visit my mother. I said yes. He went to his computer then, and although it all felt so unfinished, I couldn't strand there as if I were waiting for Godot or something. Hoping my frustration wasn't causing me to foam at the mouth, I went to my computer, too. I'd have to wait until after he'd met with Linda. Maybe he'd see what was right on his own and it would be me supporting him in the fight for Eve's privacy and peace. How much simpler—and better—it would be if he took the lead in this; after all, Linda had put him in charge of Eve. I had to remember that.

# Eve

NOW WHEN THE TALL animal came, the one who never hurt her and who looked more like a parrot than the other animals, Eve was not afraid. She was curious when he pointed at her and made the sound, which was not a pant, not a hoot, but most like a pleasure sound. His mouth stretched and he showed his teeth when he did it. Then he would touch his own chest and make a harder sound, but with the same pleasure around his eyes and mouth. Then he moved his two hands another way and gave her soft fruit that was good, very good. The juice would run on her hands and lips when she ate it. Eve let her face show her pleasure. Maybe he would give her more.

# Chapter 13

"IT'S GOING WELL, I think," Marc said.

Linda was backlit, the three o'clock sun coming in her office window behind her, and he felt at a distinct disadvantage. He squinted, held up one hand to block the worst of the glare. She didn't seem to notice, which he thought wasn't like her.

"I've realized that lab coats must have a really bad association for her—and coveralls, so, as you may have noticed, my wardrobe choices are quite colorful lately. She seems way less afraid."

"Huh. You've told the others about this, I assume?"

"Yeah, I've started to. I wanted to be sure. I bought a bunch of oversize colored T shirts at Goodwill and put them outside the door for people to put on over whatever they're wearing if it's a coverall or especially if it's white."

"Smart. Did you submit your receipt?"

"Nah. Didn't think it was reimbursable, and sheesh, it was Goodwill. Y'know. Two dollars each."

"Hell, you probably raised the sartorial standard for a few people."

"Well, Bruce wants no part of them. Not in the rule book." He gave a rueful smile and a one-shouldered shrug.

"I'm glad it's going well. I have to ask if you think you can push the timetable, presuming you even have a timetable. How soon do you think you can integrate her?"

"Why? I don't think she's ready for Lolly yet. And is she medically cleared to be with another chimp?"

"We'll have to work with Christine, and she'll have to get consultation. Thurston is wanting to do a publicity campaign around the baby, have a 'Name the Baby Contest.' Of course, tie in a membership drive and fundraising. The whole nine yards. I think he envisions having Eve and her baby available for the public to see pretty early."

"Woah." Marc raised his eyebrows. "That's a lot. Can we take it a step at a time? I just don't know."

"I'll do the best I can to push back, but…" She did not sound confident. The sun had finally shifted a couple degrees more to the southwest and the corner of the building blocked the glare now. Marc could see Linda's face clearly. Maybe makeup was smudged underneath her eyes, or she was just tired, and it had worn off. Her face just didn't have its usual color, but her hair spun around her head as lively as ever, so maybe it would be all right.

He tried to put it out of his mind, decided he'd just focus on his job. He couldn't control Eve's mind, whether she'd adjust and become part of the troop or never recover from the traumas she'd lived through. He was already doing the best he could. Linda was giving him more release time from his other tasks to work with Eve, and sure, maybe that would help, but maybe it wouldn't. Would more good attention packed into a couple months erase or even suppress years of isolation and pain? Wouldn't that depend on Eve's personality, and even her intelligence?

Marc hadn't told Linda that Eve had learned the sign for "more" because he wasn't a hundred percent sure that Eve got the meaning. Sure, she'd copied him in that moment, but would she remember and use it on her own? That, he was sure, would take many more repetitions before it stuck. If it stuck. He knew some chimps had learned to sign; it had been done. But Marc had no experience with those kinds of studies, he'd only read them. And those chimps were not traumatized and pregnant.

✿

"I hope you told her to go get fucked," Kate mumbled. At least that was what Marc thought she said. They were outside the entrance to Eve's isolation enclosure, and her voice was muffled because she was pulling one of the colored T-shirts over her head. It was, as he'd intended, huge on her, coming down below the top of her hips. Peacock blue, with a bright yellow logo for some drive-through beer place, one of Marc's second-hand buys from Goodwill.

"Well, you know how bosses are. A little dicey. I didn't exactly go there."

Her head emerged and she stood still a moment to say, "Well, where *did* you go," before jamming her arms through the short sleeves one at a time.

She was drilling him, as if she were still his supervisor. Without having to think about it, Marc resisted. "Ah, you know. Eve's the one in charge of how she does."

"But—"

"Let's go on in. She knows I'm here, and I don't want her getting anxious. I just want her to have time with another person in the room along with me while I play the Lolly recording. Look unthreatening, will you." He gave her a wide smile. "Like, smile at her! I'm going to give you some papaya." He lifted the cover of a cooler he had stationed at the doorway, and brought out two pieces, extended them to Kate. "You know the drill."

"Yep, I know," she said, but she didn't sound irritated. He liked that he was doing something Kate hadn't done and that he had the lead this time.

Eve did fairly well with Kate in the room. Marc had had Kate wait for thirty seconds while he went in first, pointed to Eve and said her name, and to himself and said Marc, then, just once, improvised a sign for fruit, thinking the ASL one, which used the finger sign for the letter F in a gesture by the mouth probably too difficult, because Eve's long tapered fingers extended so much farther than her thumb. He gave her a piece of papaya, then, and in a quiet voice, just said, "I have a friend coming. She's nice. She will give you more." He made the sign he was teaching Eve for more, and, right then, Kate came in.

Eve retreated, as she always did when anyone other than Marc came in, though not to the high platform where she'd made a sleeping nest, but behind the big wooden spools. She watched warily.

"Hello, Eve," Kate said. "I brought you some papaya. I hear you like that." Her voice was perfect, Marc noted, soft as cotton, no wheedling that might hint of duplicity. She put the first piece of papaya through the food tray and backed well away, so Eve wouldn't suspect danger if she came to claim it.

Marc stayed where he was, right in front of the glass, near the feed tray. He hoped she had enough trust in him now that she'd still come get the papaya even though Kate was present.

"It's okay, Eve, you can have it," he said gently, pointing to the papaya and smiling.

Eve was suspicious, looking at him and then looking at Kate, then staring at the papaya. She dropped to her knuckles and ventured a couple of feet closer. "Good girl. Go ahead," Marc said. "Don't be scared."

But she wasn't ready. He could see that. She wouldn't come that close, even for the fruit. Still, it was progress. "Let's try again tomorrow," he said to Kate. "If you wouldn't mind."

"Of course." Then to Eve, Kate said, "Bye, Eve. You did the right thing." Marc thought that a strange thing for Kate to say. On her way out, he asked, "We still on for Sycamore, tomorrow after work?"

"Thank you, that would be great."

After Kate was gone, Eve didn't hesitate. She was on that papaya as fast as she could get there. Marc laughed and made the sign, as he asked, "Do you want more?"

He only had to make the sign three times before Eve mimicked it. He gave her more.

# Chapter 14

I'D STARTED TO WORRY about the future. Yes, I was still busy with the new habitat, but when that was finished, would I be out of a job? Would I still be Linda's Assistant Primate Curator or would that job be shifted to Marc? In terms of professional interest, they were more aligned, and Linda probably appreciated his Master's thesis more than I did. The role of zoos in conservation of great ape species. The mere thought of it rankled. I know they both meant well, and I worked at the zoo too, so I was certainly complicit. Still. Since he'd finished everything and passed his comps, he had the academic qualifications, plus the experience, for the job. My doctorate wasn't necessary and wouldn't be likely to help. Marc was a certified vet tech, too and maybe that even gave him an edge. I wondered if the job was all but his.

Marc's whole approach to transitioning Eve was first to create a primary relationship with her. I'd never go that route. She deserved to bond with other chimps. Lolly was a good choice to be first so why couldn't Lolly have been the one to help her recover from trauma, if she was going to recover? It would have been putting faith in the apes' ability to maintain their own social structure. I didn't think Marc had reason to assume the troop wouldn't take Eve in, no matter how damaged she might be, and help her heal.

I wanted to argue, to take it on, to lay it on the line. Why didn't I? For the first time, I felt expendable. I couldn't leave the zoo because I couldn't move, not while my mother was in the nursing home.

And there was Marc. I didn't agree with him. But I did like him, too much already. And maybe I needed him. I skyped with Becky out in Seattle and laid it out. She listened intently, nodding a lot, asking questions here and there, sometimes running a hand through her short dark hair as she did, a gesture of hers familiar and dear to me. The point she kept raising in her loving way was clear: How can you find both joy and meaning in your life? You'll give the most if you're happy too.

The next day after work, Marc picked me up at my apartment, which he said was closer to Sycamore Center than his home, and we went directly to see Mom.

"I think we should keep it short today," he suggested, glancing away from the road to look at me. "Let's just see if we get anywhere. If we do, let's stop with a success. I want to use those picture boards you've made, okay?"

"Of course," I said.

He reached over and took my hand, which startled me a little.

"Your hand's really cold," he said. "Are you okay? You still want to do this?"

"Yeah, I do. Maybe I just want it to work too badly. Like if it doesn't, there's nothing else. And can I turn down the air conditioning on this side? It's blowing right on me."

He laughed and switched it off. "Oh, that's why your hand is a block of ice?"

"Could be."

We were in heavier traffic now and fell silent the rest of the way other than a couple of words here and there and once when he swore under his breath at a tailgater.

When we were finally in the building on my mother's floor, he said, "I'll do my best. Are you okay with trying it along with her, rather than just watching? I know it may be awkward."

"Sure. If you won't laugh at me if I'm bad at it."

"Huh? How will I have any fun if I can't laugh at you?" He draped his arm over my shoulder then and gave me a brief half hug before we got to her room. "I won't laugh," he whispered.

Later, I wasn't sure if anything had penetrated mom's awareness. Once words have meaning, how can we ever know what it feels like not to have them? I try to imagine. Would it be like my looking at the interior of a massive computer if I were plunked down in the middle of it without knowing where I was? But I'd still have words to describe some of what I saw—maybe words like metal, wheel, pieces, oh, I don't know, but I think I'd dissect areas and attach words as a way of trying to navigate that strange new world.

She has no words. But she sees me, and knows she's connected to me. I can tell that much. She sees Marc and I can tell she likes him, from the smile that reaches her eyes. He made a sign that looked something like a salute when he went in. As he did it, he said, "Hello, Mrs. McKinsey." Then, to me, "I just signed 'Hello,' I didn't sign her name. You do hello, and then go ahead and hug her like you usually do."

I did feel a little silly, but I did the salute, laying my thumb across my palm as I noticed Marc's was, and then I bent over her—she was in her recliner where I always found her lodged now, reminding me of an overturned turtle, blinking, confused, unable to right her world—and gave her the best hug I could manage from that angle. The small room felt crowded with the three of us and again, I had to hunt for the picture boards I'd made. The Monet print to the side of her bed was askew, and I straightened it.

Marc must have recognized that I was bothered by it all. "Stay calm," he said. "Look, this room is spotless. Her clothes are clean, and she is clean. Someone is checking on her constantly. Haven't you noticed how often an aide glances in the room?"

"But…"

"Let's work on that. Hand me the board. Okay, what here is her favorite food that you bring her?"

I rolled my eyes and pointed. "The chocolate kisses. I've got some in her drawer."

"Great. Can you grab some now?"

When I went to the drawer, the bag was empty. "Good lord. Mom!" Then, to Marc, "She's gone through a whole bag of them. I just brought them the day before yesterday."

"I should have thought this through better and asked you ahead. We could have brought them."

"I'd have told you she had plenty."

As we spoke, Mom was looking at the drawer. I pulled out the empty bag, shook it so she could see what I was doing, and put it in the wastebasket near the window. I thought a shadow of disappointment crossed her face, but it could have been the way twilight was rising off the ground outside, entering her window, a faint breeze stirring the curtain like an old sorrow.

Marc pointed to the bag and to the picture of the chocolate kisses on the board. He put his left-hand palm down flat in front of him, and then shaped his right hand into a C, and moved it in a circle directly over his left. He showed me, and said, "Sign for chocolate." He turned to Mom and did it several times. Then he pointed to the bag again and raised his eyebrows, as if he were asking a question. "Copy me," he said. "Use facial expressions a lot. I'm asking her if she wants chocolate. Is there a vending machine anywhere around?"

Mom didn't seem to be paying attention. "No, not that I know of."

"Can you ask?" Now he sounded impatient.

I checked with the nearest staff I came across at the nursing station, a ponytailed aide who looked way younger than I. She was sitting at a computer typing notes, being careful of her nails, she said, showing me, because she'd just had them done in fire engine red. I thought she'd be sympathetic when I asked about a vending machine, but she looked at me as if I'd inquired whether there was a free opiate dispenser on the floor. "No, ma'am, we have patients on restricted diets, you know," she said, as if speaking to someone with serious intellectual challenges in addition to being just dowdy.

Marc sighed when I told him. "Okay. Next time." But he got the bag out of the wastebasket and shook it, pointed at it, and made the chocolate sign again. He asked me to make the chocolate sign, and then he, so gently, picked up Mom's limp left hand and tried to stretch it out palm down in front of her. He was more successful forming her other hand into a C and moving it in a circle. He pointed to the picture of the chocolate kisses and did it again. Then he did it with his own hands and pointed at the picture.

This time, Mom held the C shape with her right hand. Did it mean anything?

"Whew. That's a definite maybe." Marc said. "Okay, now we'll do the goodbye. Easy. Watch." His right hand went up by his head and, palm facing forward, just opened and closed. I copied it. He did it again, as he got up to make it apparent we were leaving.

I couldn't resist words when I kissed her goodbye. "I love you, Mom. I'll be back," I said. Her face looked wistful, older than before, her body smaller. For the first time, I got a hint of an old person smell when my face was by her body. She was clean, but it was a kind of mustiness, like bread going moldy, that I suddenly remembered from my grandmother in her last years. My mother's hair used to be thick and blonde; silver had threaded in over years without my really noticing. Now, though, it was thinner, becoming whiter, too much like milkweed around her skull. And were her blue eyes getting rheumy, her skin more papery? I hadn't paid attention to that, but if I hadn't been kind, why had I thought time would be? I did the goodbye sign again, hoping. Always hoping, but not yet believing.

In the parking lot, Marc tapped my shoulder. "Hey," he said. "I think she might have made a start. That C, you know, chocolate. How about Saturday? With a bag of those kisses?"

"You really think? Maybe?"

"Maybe."

I might have been encouraged by his saying that or been plain attracted to him right then. Either way, I kissed him. It was impulsive but it was real. He was a good man who didn't have to be doing this. It was that simple and that complicated. I put one hand on each of his cheeks and kissed his lips like I'd considered it, considered him. Then I held his gaze for a moment, smiling at him, let go and got in the passenger side of his car.

He got in the driver's seat, fastened his seat belt, and just sat a moment before he turned to me. "You seem to have a gift for sign," he said. "As long as you know what your signs mean."

"I do. And also, thank you."

What *did* I mean, though? Maybe that I liked him, really liked him. Maybe that I appreciated what he was doing. Maybe that I was tired and didn't want to be alone. All of that could be equally true. And it was also true that we were committed to fundamentally different beliefs about one of the things that mattered most to both of us.

Marc had been so taken off guard by Kate's kiss that once he was home in his narrow bed replaying it, he wasn't sure he'd put the right feeling in his response.

What if that turned out to be his chance and he'd not managed to suggest warmth, let alone fire? He could have taken her in his arms. Nothing overwhelming. Or just kissed her, a second kiss, one that came from him. But maybe she'd have found that pushy. He'd been unprepared, that was the thing and now he couldn't tell if he'd disappointed her or gotten it right.

At the time, he'd been trying to hide what he was thinking about: how he was more heartened by Dorothy McKinsey's response than he'd wanted to let on. He wasn't sure, but he thought that her having formed that C, even if it was only a partial sign, was a glimmer of connecting the sign to the chocolate, the sign standing in for the word. Once she got the idea, would she learn more signs easily? Or would each sign require starting over?

He tried to figure out what he was asking himself: does memory require words? No, that doesn't make sense, he reasoned. When Goldie used to see him with the car keys, she'd get all excited and want to go with him, but he'd never taught her the word keys. It must be the same for human beings.

The communication between him and Goldie had been undeniable. She had learned to interpret his signals, what he meant her to understand. And she had let him know what she wanted and needed without either words or hands for sign. So what had been foundational for communication? If it was trust, how had he established it? How had she?

How to act with Kate and how not to let her down with her mother: these questions crowded his mind until sleep overtook them but were circling again on his way to work the next day. Excited and energized, he parked and walked the length of the path to the primate keepers' area through the arranged beauty of the zoo campus. It had rained the night before; the trees and flower beds bright and filling out now, along with hanging baskets of million bells and petunias, white, pink, purple, yellow, still watery as they cascaded from the lamp posts, all glittered in the sunlight.

Kate was already at her desk. "Hey," she said. "Good morning." Almost as if she were shy around him now.

"Good morning yourself. You got anything big going on today?"

When she answered, she was in her groove. "Well, let me tell you, it's a little weird being like the construction supervisor of the construction supervisor, or whatever I'm doing."

He made a face. He hadn't kept up with the latest snags. "That bad?"

"It's more a work in progress than I thought it would be at this point. I'm fighting all the time. I want it entirely naturalized. Thurston wants the public to enjoy...yadda. Anyway, I'm still working on the overhead area, and the trees, I want trees, but the problem is...oh don't get me going."

It crossed his mind that maybe Linda could advise him about Kate. On the other hand, that was probably crossing boundaries and totally inappropriate. "Lunch?" he said.

And still looking up at him because he was standing, she said, "Sounds great. Noon?"

"Did you bring yours?"

"Nope. Slept too late. Gotta buy."

"Okay, I've got mine. I'll get the table."

"Could you avoid...okay, let me think how to say this nicely. Don't sit near anyone to whom I report?"

He smiled. "How about I just bring a tranquilizer dart?"

"Oh, a creative idea. Excellent."

But even though Marc had grabbed an empty table out on the patio and put his lunch bag next to him to show the spot was taken, while Kate was going through the staff cafeteria line, Tom had seen him and plunked his tray down opposite Marc. That would have been fine. But Linda was with him. Marc saw the disappointment on Kate's face as she approached with her tray, and he gave a minuscule apologetic shrug that was imperceptible to anyone but Kate. She put her purse at the empty spot remaining on the patio table.

Really, it would have been fine. No one had pressed Kate about the new habitat. Marc had fielded a couple of supportive queries about Eve, and they'd talked politics, in their usual agreement about the outrage of the week, which was currently how the new Trump administration was now appeasing wealthy donors by allowing the trophy remains of endangered animals hunted in Africa to be brought home, even lauding the practice by claiming that the permits helped pay for conservation programs. As the staff listed the ways that was wrong, they were a troop as bonded as their great apes.

It was predictable that Thurston would show up halfway through their lunch with his own tray, and casting about for a place to sit, would see the one empty spot at their table—desirable because it was in the shade—would come and ask, "Is this seat taken? May I join you?"

Kate started to say, "Well, we're almost finished," which wasn't exactly true, at the same time, Linda, the diplomat, said, "No, it's not taken, of course you may." Kate moved her purse, and Thurston sat.

"I hope you're all pleased about the campaign," he said. "Nothing people like better than zoo babies. Well, except their own, I suppose." He chuckled heartily, his gaze circling the table Tom and Linda managed weak half-laughs. Marc smiled and busied himself with folding his sandwich wrapping.

Thurston turned to Kate, who was to his immediate right, and said, "So, Kate, what's your completion date now?" Marc could only see the back of her head when she looked at him to answer. He leaned over his sandwich ostensibly to take a bite, wanting to see Thurston's face. The director leaned slightly toward Kate, peering through the heavy black frames of his glasses. Maybe Thurston was just interested, but he sounded intense, and now Kate's back and shoulders were to him, and Marc thought he felt them gather and stiffen. *This is not going to go well*, he thought, and put his sandwich back down.

"I really can't say at this point," she started, "because— "

Marc watched disapproval—or maybe it was frustration—start on the director's face, although Thurston didn't interrupt her. But Marc did.

"Actually, if you'll excuse me for butting in, Kate, it wouldn't matter if the new habitat were ready right now, because in all honesty, we couldn't put Eve in it," he said to Thurston. "Do you mind?" he said to Kate.

"No, go ahead," she said, sliding back in her seat so that Thurston and Marc would have a clear view of each other. "We've got a severely traumatized chimp here; she's never been with other chimps, and she's still in medical isolation anyway," Marc said directly to Thurston, after wiping his lips with a napkin. "We're assessing her personality and—Linda's explained this, I'm sure—we have to make sure our other animals are safe. Linda's given me release time from other duties to work with her, and I'm trying to get her ready as quickly as possible. I know it's important." At the end, he'd switched to a conciliatory tone.

"I appreciate that," Thurston said. "Do the best you can. This can be a big fund raiser for the zoo. We have to get the publicity out ahead—"

"Of course." Then Marc said, to diffuse any tension, "I'll explain that to Eve this afternoon and maybe she'll help me out." He got away with it because there was no sarcasm in his tone; he'd somehow managed to make it self-deprecating, and Linda picked up on it.

"She's holding out to torment you, Marc."

"Way smarter than you," Tom added. "Smarter than all of us. Sometimes I really think that."

"Maybe as smart. Or differently smart," Linda said, swatting at an insect above her head. "Get away from my head, fly."

"That's it," Kate said. Other than that, she'd been quiet through the conversation. "And that's not a fly, that's a bee."

"Likes how you smell," Tom threw in. "Or thinks your hair is a hive."

Linda threw a wadded-up napkin at him. After that, Thurston talked on about the radio advertising the development director was planning, and some new signage. Marc could feel Kate beside him. He wondered if she'd been right that Thurston had a problem with her.

As soon as she decently could, Kate picked up her tray. "I need to get back to work. Have a good afternoon, everyone," and left the table. He waited through three or four more minutes of Thurston monologue, and when Thurston paused long enough so that it wouldn't be rude, Marc—who'd already closed his lunch bag—stood, and said, "Well, if you'll all excuse me, I need to head back in."

Although he wanted to go straight to Eve, Marc decided to check in with Kate first, make sure she wasn't upset. He wasn't responsible, yet here he was feeling responsible. And what could he do about it if she was upset?

He ducked into the new habitat area, but she wasn't there. Bruce was, although he wasn't exactly learning any constructions skills. The assignment hadn't been one of Linda's better ideas, but Bruce hadn't been reassigned yet, except the days when Tom could supervise him. Today Bruce had an enormous can of old screws and was sorting them according to length.

"Hey Bud—Bruce! How you doing, today," he asked.

Bruce, on his knees in the corner of the room farthest from the on-going work, looked up. "My name is Bruce. You mean *what* am I doing? I am putting these screws in order. Then I will put each group in a different plastic bag. Here are the bags." He lifted a pile of clear plastic bags with zipper tops to show Marc.

"Oh, that's interesting," Marc said, "Good job."

He stood to the side and out of the way waiting to get the attention of the crew boss. When he did, he inclined his head slightly toward Bruce, no longer paying any attention to Marc, and raised his eyebrows in a question. The crew boss shook his head slightly. It was enough.

"Do you need help?" Marc again gave a small nod toward Bruce.

"Nah. Okay for now. Thanks for the idea."

"You seen Kate?"

"Not since before lunch."

"Thanks. Hey, it's looking good."

"It'd look better if they didn't keep adjusting stuff. Skylight was a bitch. Dunno what they're gonna do about the overhead stuff. She's determined about getting that."

Marc smiled and shrugged. "A force of nature."

"You got that right."

He found Kate back in the office. "Thought you'd be at the new habitat," he said. "Hey, I did sit at an empty table. By the time you got there, they'd come and—"

"Yeah. I figured. Thank you for the bail out with Thurston. You didn't have to do that."

Marc sat at his desk. He might as well check his own email. "I didn't say anything that wasn't true."

"I don't know if he gets that. I'm so on his bad side."

"And he's so on yours."

Kate looked at him, surprised, maybe a little suspicious. "I'm on the right side. That would be the apes' side."

He'd gone too far. "Hey," he said softly. Hey, sweetheart, he wanted to say. "Me, too. I promise."

She studied his face a moment and then seemed to relax. "I know. Sorry. He puts me on edge." She brushed some stray hair off her face. "It's cold in here. I don't get why they start air conditioning the office when it's gorgeous outside." She took a sweater off the back of her chair and pulled her arms through the sleeves.

"Because the windows are sealed shut?"

"And the windows are sealed shut because it's great for the environment to use fossil fuels when you could use the sun, like, say, solar panels?"

"No, because otherwise upset primate keepers might jump out of the window."

"Huh. Suicide by jumping out of a ground floor window?"

"Well, primate keepers are known for grand gestures."

Finally, she cracked. Smiled, waved him away with one hand. "Oh, all right. You win. Go away. I know what you're doing, and it worked. But take me out to dinner when I get let go after the habitat's done and the chimps are moved in. The writing's on the wall."

"They'd be crazy to do that," he said, meaning it.

"Maybe, maybe not," she said, no longer joking.

"Whatever—you'll be fine, and I'll buy you dinner anyway." Keeping it light. He needed to get to Eve, and he was satisfied now that he and Kate were okay. It was strange how he could sense if something was off though she never told him. This was new terrain for Marc, accustomed to careful listening, watching hands, reading faces, this visceral sensing of the hidden, the unspoken, unsigned, un-signaled.

As he passed her desk on the way out, he resisted leaning over to hug her, but risked putting a hand on her shoulder, letting it linger just enough, a caress.

He was still thinking about it when he got to Eve's isolation enclosure. He went to the primate kitchen area and collected all the papaya—Eve's favorite—she'd be allotted that day. Outside the door beyond Eve's area, he went through the pile of shirts he'd stashed there and pulled on the most colorful T shirt he'd found yet in the local thrift shop—this one his favorite, from an LGBTQ Alliance, the entire shirt a brilliant neon rainbow.

He opened the door carefully, not wanting to startle her. "Hello again, Eve," he said. She didn't run behind the spools, which Marc considered a win, although he wondered if Thurston would realize how much progress that represented. And then, because the notion had been coming to him often, like a persistent caller saying, just try me, just try me, he did it. He hit his own chest. My name is Marc, he signed. And said the words at the same time. Then he pointed at Eve, saying, "You are Eve. Eve. Eve want fruit?" And he made the sign for fruit. He did this over and over, each time giving her some of the papaya she loved. Made the sign again, gave her another piece. He would do this all afternoon. He would wait between pieces, make the sign, give her a piece. "Eve want fruit," he would ask, make the sign, give her a piece. And Eve would watch intently, and Eve would eat the fruit.

Maybe he was doing this all wrong. But Eve watched and Eve did not hide and Eve ate the fruit.

# Eve

THE BIG PARROT-ANIMAL came again when the light returned. He brought the sweet fruit. Eve could see it and smell it, and she was hungry for it. After he pointed to her and made the soft sound, then touched his chest and made the harder sound, he put some of the fruit in where she could get it. She wasn't afraid now, and snatched it up and ate it, waiting close to the tray for more.

He didn't give her more. She could see it there, by him, and she wanted it.

He made sounds and pointed to the fruit. Then he took his hands and made them each into open circles, had the fingertips face one another and kiss, then back away and kiss again. He made the pleasure face, pointed to the fruit, and used his hands like that again. Over and over he did this.

When she put her knuckles down and came closer, staring at the fruit, he did it with his hands two more times, then fed himself a piece of the fruit. He kept making sounds, and they were not alarming or warning. Then one more time, he used his hands first, then fed himself a piece of the fruit.

He pointed at Eve. Confused, she touched her own hands together in front of her chest, then separated them. The big animal laughed and clapped his hands and making pleasure sounds, right away, he gave Eve more fruit. And she took it and ate it.

# Chapter 15

I WONDERED HOW LONG Marc would be able to hold Thurston off. The habitat even with the delays and snags—two different vendors had messed up material orders—was moving along finally, even if it was behind schedule. The greater issue would be Eve's readiness to be moved into it and whether we'd move in the other chimps first or wait until she was integrated. Marc was clinging to a medical isolation period to protect her and the other chimps. It was longer than usual, and I was sure he'd talked Christine into complicity about its necessity to get the extra time for his approach—his conviction that if Eve could first trust him, it would open the way to healing from the trauma humans had inflicted on her.

I was at my desk quite early one morning the next week when Thurston called. I contemplated not answering, but then thought, *get the hassle over with.* "Are you free?" He asked. "Can you come on down to my office? I'd like a word."

I thought he was going to fire me, that the habitat was so close to being finished he'd decided I was finally expendable now.

That's what I expected when I walked from our building to the administration center, my mind and feet as heavy as if the courtyard were filled with miasma and mud. I tried to force myself to hold my head up, to be dignified. There'd be no point in begging Thurston for time, no point in explaining the finances of a skilled nursing center and that I couldn't move. I knew what came first with him; everyone did. He half-stood when I knocked on the door of his stark office and pointed to the chair that was squared off to the side of his imposing desk where he wanted me to sit.

Pushing his black-framed glasses back into place on his nose, Thurston cleared his throat. "Uh, how have you been?"

I may have just caught myself from rolling my eyes. What a bizarre way to start a termination. "Uh. I'm all right."

"I'm aware that you've done a great deal of work to get the great ape habitat done, and that you didn't have the budget you hoped for, but you've accomplished a lot with what you have. It hasn't gone unnoticed."

That was weird. Thurston wasn't known for positive reinforcement.

"I've said right along that you're an excellent primatologist. The best. I'm coming to you for input. What I'm hearing is that the new chimp, Eve she's called, is nowhere near ready to be put on exhibit, even though the habitat nearly is. You're aware of the fund-raising campaign, of course," he paused, waiting for an acknowledgment, so I muttered yes, "and with her pregnancy, and the baby-naming contest, it would be best for the zoo to generate public interest in her as soon as possible. Not to the detriment of the animal, naturally." He paused again, waiting for me to say something, but I didn't know what he wanted.

"I understand," I lied.

"Good, good. What I want to know is about a faster way to get the chimp on exhibit. With the other chimps."

"You know that I'm not involved with her? Linda has assigned Marc Lopez to oversee socializing her. I think you might want to talk to Marc and Linda. Linda seems very happy with the job he's doing."

"Are you?"

"I'm not involved."

Thurston sighed. He ran his hand over his flattop hair and laid it palm down on his desk just hard enough to make a small noise. "Is he taking the approach you would take?"

"I think everyone takes a somewhat different approach, really." He was backing me into a corner.

"Let's try this differently. Exactly how would you do it? I'm aware that you favor the most natural possible environment for the animals, that, in fact, you do not think they belong in captivity at all. But given that they are, what would be the most natural approach?"

I closed my eyes a moment, choosing. "Let the chimps take care of her. She's not terrified of her own species; she's terrified of us. With good reason."

"Is she medically cleared?"

"I don't know. Christine and Dr. Reagh have the say on that. And she's pregnant so, there may be issues no one has told me about. As I said, my area is the habitat, and I haven't been involved." I couldn't have stretched the truth farther at a taffy pulling contest. Of course, Linda or Marc would have told me, but I had to undo some of the damage. Or try to.

"Thank you. I appreciate your time." He did his partial stand-up again and this time stuck out his hand, which I was supposed to shake, but I pretended I didn't realize that. I felt sick, used, ashamed. This hadn't taken more than three minutes.

"If I may add something?" I hadn't risen. I'd given a small shake of my head and I'm sure my face showed my consternation.

"Certainly," he said, and at least sat back down.

"I don't want Linda or Marc to think I've undermined them."

"This conversation is confidential. I asked for your opinion, and you gave it. That's all. I don't want you to feel responsible. I'd already decided—before speaking with you—that since the great ape habitat is nearing readiness, I'm going to ask Linda to have you join Marc integrating the chimp. I believe he will benefit from your field experience, and it will expedite the task."

I felt short of breath. How could this work? I started to protest, to say that Marc was doing a fine job and that I was confident he would have Eve ready soon. I thought, I'll warn Marc how impatient Thurston is. The monitor on Thurston's desk switched to sleep mode, and that side of his face was darker than the other when he went on before I could say anything.

"And one more thing," he said. "This information is not for dissemination at this time, but the Board has not filled the position of Research Director from the external candidates. We have decided to open it to internal candidates and invite you to resubmit an application. Now, how about I let you get back to work?" This time he stood up all the way and stepped to the side of my chair. He was going to escort me out, like a prisoner. And that was how I felt, trapped, reeling.

Was this a bribe? If so, all I had to do was what I believed in my heart was the right thing for Eve.

As I returned to the primate keepers' area, I walked under my own power while feeling I might crumple. On the path between buildings, I looked out and up, my old trick to keep back tears. The day sparkled, a cool spell brought in on last night's rain, and the leaves shimmered in the still-slanting sun. The zoo had opened, and now children's excited shouts ran ahead of them and their parents. I wondered why they weren't in school, then realized that the parents were chaperones with a field trip. The merry-go-round was not in my sight right now, it was over near the elephant house, but it whether or not I could see it made no difference, I knew it was there and it was turning, turning, turning.

By the time I got back to my desk, I'd decided I couldn't do it. Wouldn't do it. If I became Research Director, I'd always know it wasn't because of my research, my mission, or my qualifications.

I sat down, staring at the monitor as if I could see anything, shivering in the air conditioning, set, as always, too cold. Sandy came in briefly, tried to make small talk. I hoped I said something appropriate back but could not feel anything except waves breaking over my head, a sensation of falling. Sandy caught on that something was amiss because she said, "You okay? More habitat crap?" Her voice was soft, concerned, and I felt her blue eyes searching for mine. They didn't find them.

"Pushing to get it done," I said. True enough. "I'm okay. Really."

She felt the evasion and let it go. "It's going to be great," she said. She tucked her reddish hair, loose today, behind her ears. "It's a huge job. Better you than me. Well, especially since I'd have been terrible at it." She laughed. "Gotta go feed great apes, and at the moment I'm not referring to my kids. Hang in there, huh?"

"Will do," I forced a smile in her direction. "Thanks."

I really don't know how long I sat there, numb, answerless. Worse, I wasn't sure what question to ask. Was it about Eve? I thought I knew what was best for her. Was it Marc? Me? My job? The zoo? I thought if I could get the right question, or put the questions in order of importance, maybe I could start to answer them.

But then Linda came in. "Hey," she said. "I know you've got a full plate. But I forgot that two schools each have four classes on field trips today. Of course. Tom is off, so Sandy has no help, and I don't want to pull Marc, and I'm wondering if you can lend a hand. We'd marketed that we would discuss the habitat change, what we're doing, because they're all paying admission, yadda. Part of the drive to increase school traffic. Development office. This is my fault—I put the wrong date on the master calendar. I'm so sorry. The first bunch has already arrived. They're in the big cat area, but I can stall them and suggest reptiles next. Not much out of the way."

"Can't take them into construction. Haven't cleared inspection yet."

"Shit. Okay, yeah. You'll have to punt and be really descriptive from the current habitat about the changes they'll see when they come back. Emphasize how they should come back, how surprised they'll be." Linda looked frazzled. She felt the top of her head, and I knew she was checking that she hadn't left her glasses somewhere.

"Okay. I...was hoping we could talk." I hadn't planned what I'd say, or how, but I thought if anyone could help, maybe it would be Linda.

"Of course. Just not today. It's crazy. Check in with me tomorrow, okay?"

The rest of the day passed with wave after wave of elementary school children crowding in while I tried to talk to them about the chimps, how intelligent they are, and closely related to us, how they take care of their babies, live in families, use tools, build sleeping nests, protect each other. I saw awe in some eyes while more kids made faces at the chimps, pretended to knuckle walk or scratched their bellies and made grunting sounds at each other.

I talked to them about how the chimps' habitats in Africa are being destroyed, why we must stop that. When I got to that, I lost my audience. They do not believe their planet is small and fragile; they think it is vast, forever. They think the earth is indestructible, just like they are.

That evening, Marc and I had already planned to see Mom after work. Just a quick visit. He wanted to give her as many brief lessons as he could, he said. I saw how he lit with pleasure when he made the hello sign, and my mother raised her hand. Both of us thought she was mimicking it. Did it mean she was catching on? We'd brought some chocolate kisses because Marc says if he can get the connection between a sign and a meaning on a couple of things first, it may go better. She didn't do it on her own, but we did see her copy the C after we did it over and over, each time offering her a piece of the candy.

Marc had looked at his watch and said, "Oops, I've gotta get home. Mom's been…just gotta get home. That's enough for today anyway. Goodbye, Mrs. McKinsey," he said it, but made the sign as he got up, giving her his open smile, too, and leaning in to kiss her cheek. My mother grabbed his hand and brought it to her face.

We'd driven separately because we'd gone there straight from work. Our cars were parked side by side and he walked me to the driver's side of mine. "I was hoping maybe we could get a bite to eat," I said, facing him instead of opening the door. It was a soft dusk, the way long afternoon stretches into twilight in the summer, the air was clear and sweet, and the trees and flowers were not tired or thirsty or hopeless, not today, not yet, whatever might come.

"I'm really sorry. Mom's afternoon companion had to cancel and I…I'm just so sorry."

"I wish you wouldn't go…I…sort of need to talk to you." If he'd stayed, if we'd gone out, had a glass of wine or two, maybe I'd have told him everything. Or maybe I wanted to put the squeeze on him, a fraction of the way I was being pressured so someone else, even good, kind Marc—me standing there with these newborn feelings for him—would understand just a little.

He put his arms around me in a gentle way, not pulling me against him, but more inviting me. I accepted. I stepped in and let my body fit itself to his, my arms go around his waist, head slip into the nest between his neck and shoulder. We stood like that a few long moments. I felt him kiss my hair. Finally, I lifted my face and we kissed, a rose with no thorn, that tender.

"I'll see you in the morning," he said, then. I nodded, caressed his arm, and got into my car.

# Chapter 16

"WHAT'S THIS ABOUT?" Marc said to Kate before lunch the next day. He'd come in to check his email and to look for Kate, hoping to have lunch with her. Since Tom was on vacation, he'd helped Sandy with the hosing the indoor enclosure while the chimps were outside, and they'd hauled in more wood wool.

One of the chimps had taken apart a Lixit to play with it again, so he'd repaired the water line while Sandy checked the ventilation system. When they were bored or annoyed, the chimps could dismantle pretty much anything. The new habitat would be much more interesting for them—more arboreal space, more stimulating opportunities for the chimps to control their area. There was also much better environmental noise control and privacy when they wanted it. It really was brilliant, what Kate was accomplishing.

"What's what about?" she said, "and how was your morning? Mine was horrible, thank you for asking. Bruce had a meltdown. I got him out fast, and I think I covered so there won't be ramifications, but I do worry that…" She trailed off, tenting her eyebrows. "Wait. I'm sorry. What were you asking me?"

She really was so pretty. No, she was beautiful, Marc thought, the slant of window light almost spotlighting her as she sat at her desk, busy with he didn't know what, pale hair escaping her pony hair at her temples and neck. Her gaze was direct.

"Well?" she said again?

"Sorry. The email from Linda. To us."

"The primate department? I'm just starting on emails. What's it say?"

"Not the department. Just you and me. Wants to see us this afternoon."

"What for?"

"Doesn't say."

Kate looked upset. "Crap. I hope she didn't get wind of the Bruce thing. Damn those screws. Must be fifty thousand of them in that box. Why do they bring so many?"

Marc shook his head, put his palms in the air. "Dunno. We're supposed to email her a time we're both available."

Linda had never sent an email like this before. Kate seemed to think it was about Bruce, that maybe they weren't supervising him closely enough. "Well, I'm sorry if I haven't been on the ball enough with Bruce. He's a good kid. He can make it with the right support."

Kate nodded. "I know. Hey, you're doing your part. What time works for you? I can schedule around you."

"Just gotta help Sandy, gonna bring 'em in because of the storm coming tonight. Lolly, I think it is, anyway, one of them is bored, took apart the Lixit again."

Kate slapped her palm against her forehead. "Sheesh. I thought you patiently explained to them why that is so inconvenient and issued a cease-and-desist order."

"Their democratically elected spokeswoman said they don't take orders from a despot, and I had to submit a request in writing. A notarized copy for each of them. Then they'll take it under advisement, vote, and their decision will be to tell me to screw myself."

"Oh. Hmmm. So, then you got out before they threw their feces at you."

"Well, it seemed wise."

They both laughed. "Why risk it?" she said.

"How about I tell Linda one thirty, right after lunch, answer for both of us," Marc said. "Get it over with, so we're not wondering what she wants."

"Okay, that'll work."

He'd learned to read her. She was worried.

They walked to Linda's office together. Marc wished he could take Kate's hand, just touch any part of her for a minute, but he knew better. The last thing either of them needed was to grease the gears of the rumor machine. They hadn't discussed that, but he knew how that could go, would go, if someone saw him. He stepped back and let Kate precede him into Linda's office, manners not rank deciding that for him.

Linda had crammed an extra chair into the space and had tried to move her chair so that her desk wasn't fully between her and them. She'd partially closed the slats on the lowered window covering so they wouldn't be sun blinded as they faced her. On the wall to the left, the animals on zoo posters surrounded by bright primary colors looked ready to do a happy song and dance with delighted children. Marketing.

"You're probably wondering..." Linda said. She paused and looked at each of them.

"What gives?" Kate said, at the same moment Marc said, "Yes."

"I didn't mean to be cryptic. I just want to discuss this with you both in person."

"We're here, in the flesh." That was Kate.

"Okay. So, Thurston is pushing."

"I've just got to get through inspections, and then certification. Does he want me to pay bribes or what?" Kate sounded irritated.

Marc was quiet. He knew Kate was well ahead of him. Why did that have to matter so much? Sure ideally, the chimps would all move to the new habitat together, but it wasn't mandatory. Eve wasn't ready.

This was new. Linda, normally so confident, looked uncomfortable. "Look," she said. "Thurston is on a tear. He's all about the campaign, the great apes exhibit, and thinks the way to showcase it is Eve, her pregnancy, the baby naming contest. He wants them moved in, oh, say, last week, and Eve with them."

"Eve's not ready." Marc inhaled, then breathed out, reminded himself to stay calm, not to be defensive. "She's making steady progress, though. She's not hiding from me now, and when Kate comes in, she won't get fruit like she does with me, but she only runs about halfway back to the spools." He shrugged. "Still pretty mistrustful. Same with Sandy. Don't know about Tom, I'll see when he comes back." He didn't mention he was teaching her signs, saw no need to, and thought maybe Linda would think it was slowing him down.

Linda sighed and pulled her glasses off the top of her head and put them on. She immediately took them off and laid them on her desk. "I'm sorry, guys. I know this will throw a monkey wrench into your days. Thurston has directed me to have Kate work with Eve, too, Marc, to integrate Eve. He's thinking that she'll have a different approach that will move Eve along faster."

"Are you firing me?" Marc said. This was humiliating. He avoided looking at Kate, who was next to him, but he felt her movement. She was shaking her head.

"Good grief, no. Did you hear me?" Linda said, agitated. "Kate is to get in there and move things along faster."

"Linda, she's pregnant," Marc argued. Chris hasn't even cleared her medically yet. And—"

"I know, I know," Linda interrupted. "And Kate hasn't gotten inspections or certification. There's more to be done on the habitat first anyway. Arrange your schedules. Whatever you need."

Kate spoke up. "I don't see this working. I'd do it too differently." Marc couldn't quite tell if the soft underbelly he sensed in her tone was apology, and if so, was it to him or to Linda? He said, "Who's in charge?"

Linda sighed. "Marc, I'm not going to take the lead away from you unless I have to because it would look bad on your record. This all came down from on high, so you two are going to have to work it out. I'm confident you can."

Linda was dismissing them. It wasn't like her to play the boss role like this, like she'd given them their marching orders and there wasn't anything to discuss. But apparently there wasn't. Marc looked at Kate. She was staring at her hands. She must have felt his gaze because then she raised her head, glanced at him, nodded, and said, "Okay, then," and stood up. Marc did too, but he didn't say another word or look at Linda as he walked out ahead of Kate. Later he'd wonder if he'd been rude and would think maybe he should apologize, then think, hell no.

In the hallway, once they were a decent distance from Linda's door, he said, "I dunno. Can we?"

Kate mimed scales, raising one palm then the other. "Apples and oranges."

"I'm sorry, I don't mean to disrespect your approach," he said. "I just see it—"

"I know. And I think you're wrong. It's remarkable what you're doing, but you shouldn't try to humanize her. Let a chimp be a chimp. Let other chimps help her. They will."

"Humans hurt her. Let a human try to help her heal from that. And she's going to live among humans. 98% of the same DNA for god's sake. And the species is doomed if they don't."

"You mean in zoos." Her voice turned bitter on the last word. She picked up her pace, low heels clicking on the tile.

"There are some great ones, naturalized—"

"Let's not get into it now."

"Right." He waited a few seconds and then in a different tone asked, "You busy tonight?"

"No, why?"

"How about if I pick up some dinner and bring it over to your place? You supply the very expensive wine."

"Oh, I don't know if I want to use my nine dollar a bottle white or my nine fifty a bottle red in such a frivolous manner, but I'll consider it. Can you leave on time tonight?"

"I'll do my best. I'll call you when I'm on my way." Good, he thought. Everything wasn't blown up.

"I have habitat stuff on the agenda this afternoon," Kate said.

Marc nodded. Relieved.

On his way to Eve, he thought maybe he could buy time by having Christine stall. Eve was doing so well. Maybe Kate would give him a little breathing room, too. No, wait. He was still the lead. He would take more time, that was all. Kate was just going to have to stand back.

He pulled on one of the ridiculous neon shirts, this one lime green with some sorority's pink writing one it and went in to spend time with Eve.

Marc approached the enclosure talking softly, as he always did, signing hello, saying Eve as he did. He expected to entice her with food, but she climbed down from the platform she was on Marc and approached him right away. Marc repeated the hello sign, and started his usual, "My name is Marc, and you are Eve," routine, but she seemed to ignore that and did something different. At first Marc thought, well, she's just forgotten, and suddenly an overwhelming thrill: she was making the modified sign he'd devised for fruit. Oh my god, he thought. She's asking me for something good. We're going to make it. I just need more time.

Marc had called an excellent Italian restaurant and ordered pickup for two orders of lasagna with garlic bread, side salads, and tiramisu. After work, he stopped at a liquor store and bought a bottle of really good cabernet—he wanted this to be the equivalent of actually taking Kate out to dinner with more privacy. He texted her, "Yr job, and yr only job is light candles, set table. All else my job." Would the laughing emoji make a difference? He added it, with a P.S. "U do napkins too."

She'd have no idea he was celebrating, or what. He wanted her to understand. He needed her to understand. What he really wanted was for her to tell him she saw the value, even that she was impressed. Maybe proud, the way he was proud for her of what she was doing with the new habitat.

He carried two large bags with the food, the smaller one with the wine tucked into the one that held the salads and desserts, to Kate's condo. She opened the door immediately. "Oh wow. Something smells awfully good."

"Well thank you! I did shower today," he grinned, went in, put the bags on the kitchen counter, turned and opened his arms. It would have been embarrassing if she hadn't come forward into them, but she did, hugging him back.

"Someone's in a good mood," she said. "I thought you'd be upset…about Linda's—"

Marc kissed her. "I have good news," he said then. "Let's have some wine. You got any peanuts or something? I didn't think to pick up any pre-dinner snacks. But I've got everything else. Stuff'll stay warm if we put the oven on real low, won't it? Refrigerate the rest."

"This smells so good. Can we just eat now? I'm so hungry."

"Sure. I guess I am, too." Marc had wanted to talk to Kate undistracted by dinner and then let that be a celebration, but if she was too hungry and hurried him through what he had to say, that wouldn't be a promising idea. And she'd set a lovely table out on the balcony, a centerpiece of multiple candles which she lit now, while he warmed plates for the lasagna in the microwave, and Kate poured the wine after inspecting the label and taking a sip.

"I suspect you violated the nine-dollar rule with this one," she said. "Wow."

"Oh, I thought with reds the rule was nine fifty."

She gave him a sidelong look. "Also violated."

"I may have gotten confused. It happens. You carry these plates out, I've got these."

While they ate, neither of them brought up the meeting with Linda. Yet it wasn't as if they were picking their way around a potential landmine, either. They were easy with each other, just talking about everyday matters like how to help Bruce, summer heat, which season each liked best and why, the misery or enjoyment of long car trips. Marc wondered, realized it was that he hoped more than wondered, if they each wanted the other to know that yes, something was happening between them, and each wanted it to grow.

So when Kate said, "Oh my god, I almost forgot I was so hungry. You said you have good news—what is it?" Marc didn't want to risk a truthful answer. It would have led to telling her he needed more time and why. Not tonight. Tonight should be different, not about work. He saw that now.

After dinner, they went inside and curled up on the couch. Kate switched the music from the classical station she'd had on Pandora during dinner to one playing soft ballads. He wasn't sure of the era, but noticed they were pretty much all love songs. Each had another glass of wine, which emptied the bottle.

"I've got until midnight," he whispered. His hand went from her neck down to her breast. She nestled in closer, made no move to stop him, which he took as an assent. He felt himself hardening and moved his hand farther, to her rear, pulling her even closer. She lifted her face to be kissed. To kiss him back.

Marc had been with a couple of women. He'd been determined he wasn't going to be some pathetic guy in his thirties and still a virgin. He'd had sex. But that was exactly what it was. Oh, it wasn't like they were prostitutes; they were definitely dates with willing women who'd had feelings for him. The problem had been that he'd not had feeling for them, though he'd tried to. The upshot was that he'd still ended up—to his mind—a single man in his thirties, no virgin, but living alone with his mother, which made him, yes, pathetic. With nothing to be done about it.

"The bed would be more comfortable than the couch," she said. "Would you like…?"

"Definitely," he said, kissed her, and they got up. On the way, both of them starting to undress as they went.

Afterward, Marc wanted to tell her this was the first time he'd made love. He'd have had to explain he meant *made love*, not had sex, but made love, but it was too much. He was embarrassed by the depth of tenderness he felt, how tears had come to his eyes. Then he'd seen that Kate's eyes were wet, too. He kissed each of her cheeks, but only said, "Are you all right? Was that all right?"

She swallowed and nodded, cupped his chin with one hand, the other around his back, as she looked straight in his eyes above her, so close, so direct, and said, "Way better than all right," and Marc let it go at that.

They lay nestled together, her head in the hollow of his shoulder. He checked his watch but made no move to get up.

"Please don't say you have to go," she said.

"Nope. Still got an hour and a half. Remember when the afternoon companion cancelled a while ago? I got her to come tonight. It's dangerous for Mom to be alone at night. I really need to get another service dog, you know, to warn her. Goldie was so good about that. I could do the training, but I just don't have the time now."

"I wish you could stay the night. It seems like…you really can't leave her alone much at all. Like it's pretty confining for you. Aren't there services for deaf people?"

Marc was quiet a moment weighing honesty versus the long habit of shame. Would the truth make a difference to Kate? If they were closer before she knew, would she be less likely to react badly?

He started to dissemble. "Well, sure, but she doesn't drive and I'm at work, so…"

"But deaf people can get a license, can't they?"

She was going to push.

He sighed. "It's hard to understand, I know."

"Marc, honey, I can't understand until you tell me, right?" As she spoke, she used one hand to turn his face—which he'd had aimed at the ceiling—toward hers. She tilted her head, propping herself on the tripod of shoulder, elbow, palm. Lifted her brows in that way she had that wrinkled her forehead into a question demanding an answer. But that wasn't what made him respond. She'd called him honey, her voice like the substance itself, that golden and soft.

"It goes back a long way, and it probably won't make a lot of sense. She was raised in a situation that was…different. She had to be afraid of the outside world, and, well, I guess she doesn't believe that it could be better and different if she would…" Marc saw Kate's eyes react, confused by what he was telling her. Of course.

"Why did she have to be afraid of the outside world?" Kate said.

"Well, it was more taught by her parents. See, her dad was in hiding." Well, *that* sounded bad, obviously.

She picked up on it immediately. "Like he'd committed a crime?" A hint of shock or maybe disbelief in her voice that she tried to suppress.

Marc tried to laugh, which didn't work well either. "Now you see why I don't talk about it. No, he wasn't a criminal." He sighed. "None of it matters now, except it matters so much. I dunno. I'm named for him. Marco Adams Lopez. How's that for some ethnic confusion? See, my mom wanted me to have a name from her mother's side, too."

"Adams, from her, then. Right? And Marco?"

"My legal name. Marc's a nickname."

"Yeah, I sort of remember that. Why don't you go by Marco? I like it."

"Marc's just what they always called me at home. My grandfather was Marco."

"Anyway, it's off the subject. Your mom…"

He'd hoped maybe the name thing had diverted that conversation. Then again, why was it still such a big deal? "Right, sorry. Okay, see I'm a quarter Mexican, and that's my mother's father, the first Marco Lopez. He died when I was little, though." Kate gave a sympathetic murmur and put her free arm across his chest, her hand on his shoulder, where she let it rest, warm and still. Marc was lying on his back now, head on the pillow, thinking he couldn't look at her while he broke the taboo bred into him, the blood loyalty. "My grandfather came here, well, not here, but to California in the bracero program in the fifties," he said, a mixture of apology and defense in his tone, but then anger came out of nowhere and insisted on adding itself. Not at Kate, though. Surely not at Kate? "A farm worker paid thirty cents an hour then. My grandmother told me. Then he was sent up to the northwest to another camp. There weren't enough inspectors up there, and the conditions were bad. Sometimes they were penned up like animals. The pay got irregular and up there, strikes got going. My grandfather was one of the organizers.

"I remember studying something about that," Kate said quietly. "Didn't a lot of the braceros eventually get green cards and become citizens?"

*She's trying to offer me a way out, a way to get to how my grandfather must have been an upstanding American citizen. What's the point? Here comes the kicker, when her face changes,* Marc thought. He tried to put his voice through a sieve that would hold his thick emotion, let only the thin facts through. "Not my grandfather. He decided to take his chances in America rather than being sent back to Mexico after one of the strikes up near Portland. My grandmother is—was—an educated white, a teacher. She volunteered to help adults learning English as a second language. They met that way, but her family wouldn't accept it, and she chose him. They moved a couple times to areas they thought were safer and ended up here. They were always afraid he'd get picked up and deported. There was help they never got for my mom because of it—Gram home schooled her during the day and taught night school while...oh anyway, he never got caught. Because they were so careful."

"Like your mom learned to be afraid of the world because they were."

"Yeah. And she never learned the skills other deaf people do that let them function out there...she was never with other deaf people, never had that social life growing up."

Kate was quiet. "Is it too late, you think?"

"I don't know. Maybe just not motivated now. Or too stubborn. I know the world frightens her."

"Huh." She was silent for half a minute, and Marc wondered what she was thinking. "I really respect your loyalty," she said finally.

"But...?" he said, assuming there was one and mad at himself for telling her. A mistake.

"But nothing. Can't I just respect your loyalty?"

He was caught off guard. "Oh, okay."

Now she was annoyed, started to move her arm. "Well, I'm glad it's okay."

He caught her hand. "Hey, I'm sorry. Thank you. I appreciate that. I guess I expected a negative judgment."

"Why would you think that?"

"I suppose the political climate. It's hard, because I'm proud of my heritage, but you never know who's biased, y'know? Especially now."

"I guess I don't. But you know me."

"I know how you feel about a lot of things. But we haven't talked about the stuff at the border."

"Oh god. It never occurred to me that you'd think…" She inhaled deeply, pulled her hand away from him so she could use both hands, put fingers on each side of her own temples. She lay back on her pillow and said, "Come on, Marc. Do I seriously need to tell you I'm completely opposed to what's happened at the border? To the hate speech, to the inhumanity, the bigotry, the…but Marc, I don't get it. How it even pertains. Where was your mother born?"

"South Dakota."

"Where were you born?"

"Illinois." He knew where she was going, how stupid it would seem.

"So she's an American citizen, you're an American citizen. What am I missing here? Wait. Was it your father? You haven't said anything. Was he…?"

"No. He was Caucasian, an American." Marc stopped a moment, considered. Exhaled. He'd gone this far, might as well tell her the rest. "Christopher Tillis or Tilley or Tiller, something like that; Mom says she got confused, and I pretty much believe her. He didn't know sign, apparently just thought she was gorgeous and that he would learn…I don't know. Gram said it was over before it got started, the guy had no clue how to communicate with a deaf person, and to be fair, Mom hadn't been around anyone who didn't sign. Must have happened the first time they were alone. Mom didn't even get that she was pregnant for nearly four months, and he was long gone by then. Gram said the experience cemented Mom's resistance to the outside world. The danger of it."

"You've never met him…"

"Never. I really haven't a clue, y'know? Not particularly interested now, anyway. Gram says it was really her fault for not insisting on being there to interpret, but she was trying to be sensitive. She claimed they got me out of it, and he seemed like a good guy just in way over his head." Marc paused and then added, deadpan, "Oh, and he *was* extremely handsome."

"Pffft. I could have told you that much." Kate closed her eyes. Inhaled and then sighed out a long breath. "I think I get it now. Your mother grew up in hiding and then she had another reason to decide the world was dangerous and ended up depending on you for everything."

"Well, pretty close to everything. She doesn't have the skills other deaf people learn. Except signing, I mean. Gram took the classes to learn sign as soon as they knew Mom was deaf. She taught Mom."

"It must have been a lot for you to juggle. And no dad. I got along a lot better with my dad than my mom as a teenager. Oh course, now he's off with his child bride." She let her voice trail off, sad, edged with the bitterness that must have never really left. Still, she'd *had* a dad, more than he could say.

"Yeah," he said. "Yeah." Just as well that she was distracted, thinking about her own parents now. He wasn't going to ask; he knew it would be a deal breaker. What woman—especially one whose own mother was so needy—would want a man so tied to his mother? This time, though, damn. This time he really cared. This time he resented his mother as much as he felt protective of her, as much as he loved her. This time he wanted something for himself.

He pulled in close and caressed her. Kissed her with the tenderness and regret that was too close to the surface now, and even as the press of her breasts against his chest and his hand pulling her bottom against him began to arouse him again, he whispered, "I'm so sorry," into her hair and forced himself to separate, to get up, to move toward the bedroom door even as he was putting his arms through the sleeves of his shirt, half-hopping into his pants a leg at a time, walking out the door, walking to his car to go home. More angry with each step.

# Eve

EVE OFTEN HEARD the other chimp, but the pant-hoots were not alarms or warnings, they were good calls. She'd begun to look for the other chimp but never saw her. When the parrot-animal who never hurt her came, he always made his own sounds, the same ones each time, and his hands did the same things each time. She recognized them now, and there was one thing he did that meant fruit, and if Eve did the same thing with her hands, the parrot-animal gave her fruit. Eve learned that to get fruit she could do that, and so she did.

Something had been moving inside her. When it first happened, Eve looked at her stomach but there was nothing on it. It did not hurt and sometimes it stopped but then it started again.

When the parrot-animal came in, she put her hands the way he liked, and he gave her fruit. Her stomach moved a lot after that because her stomach liked the fruit.

# Chapter 17

WHEN MARC GOT UP and left so suddenly, I felt a stew of hurt, confusion and anger. Add in a soupcon of insult. Then I bounced to self-doubt. Had I said something wrong, disappointed him? I tried to reason with myself. He'd told me he had to go, that it was dangerous for his mother to be alone at night. He'd apologized. Still, he left so abruptly. And I remembered something else. When he'd first arrived, he'd told me he had good news. He'd been excited to tell me something and never had. What was that about?

I didn't know what face to wear the next day when I went to work. I wanted to see Marc, but wished I could avoid him, uneasy about where we stood.

It didn't matter what I wanted, though. I had to see him because of Eve. I couldn't come up with any new habitat-related issues requiring my immediate attention. My eyes were grainy from poor sleep, and I was edgy as I parked in the employee lot, ten minutes late and needing coffee. The day was oppressive, humid, a low-slung sky promising a storm. The apes would be inside. I decided to bypass the office area and go put on coveralls. Tom was off; I could be an extra pair of hands with the morning tasks and then be ready to help with Eve.

I barely made it in the door of our building when Linda waylaid me. "Oh good, you're here," she said, her nice way of letting me know she knew I was late. "There's a damn tornado watch. Not a warning, but—y'know. Can you get on it?" She meant we had to follow all the severe weather protocols for animal and visitor safety when there was a just a watch, no warning. We were used to it in Dayton where watches were common, even though Ohio isn't really part of the big tornado alley. The watches usually just mean unnecessary extra work—although we all knew about the F5 tornado that had destroyed Xenia, just twenty minutes from us straight down route 35. That was 1974. And again, in 2000, when an F4 hit the city again. Yes, it had been a while, but when disaster comes that close—twice—the memory and fear get passed down generation to generation.

"I was heading in now anyway, figured they could use extra help with Sandy gone, and then—"

She cut me off. "Good, thanks. I've got Bruce. Remember, don't say tornado around him, he flips out."

I knew. "Right."

I was embarrassed about being late especially because I could tell that Marc and Sandy had come in early. Did everyone watch the weather that closely? They already had the chimps in the more secure inner enclosure, which Jasmine never appreciated, although Lolly and the others didn't seem to mind all that much. The point was, of course, to have them where there was no glass. The zoo has good generators, of course, so losing electrical power isn't much of an issue, though, of course, the loss of visitor revenue is—as Thurston and Shultz regularly remind us.

"Do they need help over with Reece and Katari?" I asked. The western lowland gorillas were housed on the opposite of our complex, their separate environment was a section of the great apes' new habitat, too, although my specialty was the Pan troglodyte chimps.

"We got 'em," Sandy said, at the same moment Marc said, "S'okay." He looked at me straight on, and I didn't see anything off in his smile.

"I picked a terrible day to be late instead of early. I'm sorry you guys."

It was Sandy who answered. "It's just another watch. Not your job anyway. But thanks."

I helped them with the feeding—monkey chow and buckets of fresh vegetables and fruit from the kitchen. Marc had already separated out Eve's food. I saw that he'd saved extra papaya for her, along with bok choy, apples and bananas. He had a fix on her favorites.

He came into the kitchen just as I was going out with another armload, the first time we'd been in the same spot alone that morning. I tightened up, not knowing what to expect, tried to slip by.

"Hey," he said. "You okay?" He looked over my shoulder, checking the room, and then bent down and gave me a quick kiss, on the lips, one that required no decision on my part. "Don't worry. I'm out of camera range." He was trying to be funny—there were only a few cameras, and they were only in some large animal areas that were difficult to monitor for safety. I felt him searching my face. "I hope I didn't upset you last night. I know it's a lot to take in."

That answered one question right away, and I let down my guard. "No, I'm fine. I wish you hadn't left so fast is all. Were you okay?"

"I'm sorry," he said. "I know. I wanted to stay, and…"

From behind Marc, I heard more than saw Sandy approaching down the hall. I shifted my body and warned him with my eyes while Marc's body would still block Sandy's view of me, and at the same time, I started moving out the door with the monkey chow, saying, "I'll be in to help with Eve in a bit. Lovely outfit, by the way." He was already wearing one of the thrift shop shirts, this one a lemon yellow with a bright blue logo from a construction crew. The original owner must have been a triple X size, because it fit him like a muumuu.

"I'm okay with her by myself this morning," he said.

"Huh? But Linda…"

"I got her covered. Eve. But you if you've got time, if you could try to isolate Jasmine's calls, record some? That would be great. Definitely nothing alarmed, though."

"But they're inside; I can't separate her."

"Yeah, more of a challenge today, but we could use it this afternoon if you can get anything."

What the hell was he pulling, keeping me away from Eve? "Marc, I'm supposed to—"

"Yeah. And this is what I need you to do to hurry this along, like Linda said."

He must have known I wasn't going to argue with him in front of Sandy, who'd squeezed though into the kitchen, and anyway, I heard the subtext in his words: I'm still the lead. So this was how it was going to be. Of course, I was irritated. Was he taking advantage of having taken me to bed, acting like a dominant male chimp now, thinking he could tell me what to do?

As I carried pails of monkey chow to the chimps, I found myself—again—trying to be reasonable. He'd been put in the lead before we were involved. His approach was an educated one and he certainly had plenty of scientists backing it up; I just happened to completely disagree, and I had my backers too. Now, because Thurston needed me—and how like him to be utterly utilitarian when my philosophy could suddenly come in handy—I had a chance to not only keep my job but be promoted. I should tell Marc, I thought. Or maybe not.

I wanted to say, Over my cold dead body. What I said was, "Okay, I'll do the best I can," attempting a cooperative voice for Sandy's benefit.

"Great. Thanks so much. We can add it in to my Lolly recordings this afternoon."

Huh. My thought had been to introduce Eve to Lolly that afternoon. Like really move things along, the way Linda said. Use the glass partition, not the bars, to bypass Christine with what might well be unnecessary continued medical isolation. I still saw no reason to hold off on introducing Lolly.

The tornado watch was lifted as usual, nobody slipped up and mentioned it around Bruce, so all was well, although he was frightened during the thunderstorm, which had been close and loud, and he had hidden. Rhonda, a part-time college student intern stumbled on him, in the primate area kitchen. But he was fine, just scared by the noise and had slipped away from his supervisor of the day. He had his eyes closed, Rhonda told me, imitating how he'd had his hands clamped on the sides of his heads, earmuff style, and said she'd seen that he'd been crying and taken him to Linda. She said it had broken her own heart. "He did well in the aviary when he was assigned there," she said, "He liked the birds. His good days are so good."

I sighed. "I know. He's good when he's here, too. You did the right thing by taking him to Linda. Marc and Linda are the best with him. She'll settle him down and take him back where he was assigned today. I don't know where that was."

I'd been wrong about one thing though: Linda hadn't been able to settle Bruce down. She'd had to get Marc, who had the magic touch. Linda told me later, "Nothing I did worked this time. Once he gets beyond a certain point of terror," she shrugged. "But geez, I called Marc out of Eve's area, and he comes in, and puts Bruce in this bear hug—which I wouldn't have dared, y'know? Because of how he doesn't like to be touched, but there's Marc, gets him in a bear hug and he's talking to him in this low voice, and then gets him over in a corner and then they're on the floor together, and pretty soon Marc is telling me to just go, go get him all the broken pencils from his desk drawer, and damn if I don't find about fifty broken-off pencils in Marc's desk drawer in a rubber band, so I run back with them and two minutes later, Bruce is calm as cotton on the floor sorting the pencils according to their length."

"Calm?"

"Yeah. The whole nine yards."

I was thinking about that as I went to Eve's area that afternoon. Marc had skipped lunch—he'd left me a note telling me he was going to, that he'd be in with Eve. The note also said to knock lightly on the door and let him come out before I went in, that he wanted to show me something.

I pulled one of the bright shirts over my coveralls. They were in the little anteroom hall area where Marc had also stashed various extra fruit, including more than Eve's share of papaya.

I tapped my nails on the door to the place where Eve's isolation enclosure was. Marc came right away and stepped out. "Hey, thanks! Look, I'd like you to try this. I…am…Kate. Say it slowly while you do this." He pointed to his chest, and then made a sign with his hand that was like flicking his right ear. "That's a sign I made up for your name. Now here's the sign for fruit. No kidding, she knows this sign, she'll do it herself to ask for it—isn't that amazing? and just this morning she started letting me hand feed her. I'm going to go in first and tell her you're a friend. That's another sign I've been showing her. Like this." He extended his two forefingers, linked them first one way and then the other. "See, with a bunch of these I'm using what are called baby signs, not full ASL signs, because her fingers are too long, or the sign is too complex. And it's okay now if she can't give it back to me. Right now, I just want her to understand."

He realized I was staring at him, a cross between dumbfounded and alarmed. "Marc, I've said this before. You can't try to humanize her."

Marc's face as well as his voice showed frustration. I couldn't remember seeing him so reactive before. "But don't you see? This is huge. She's trusting me. She's understanding, we're evolving a language we can *use*. She's going to be living here, with human beings looking at her and taking care of her and she was terrified. If she starts with trusting one person, don't you see that—"

"What I know is that the chimps could and would take care of their own. They're not domestic animals." We'd argued our points too many times already.

Marc shifted his weight from one leg to the other and opened the door a crack, looked in, then interrupted me. "I can't do this right now. Eve's right there, waiting. She just asked me for fruit. I need to bring it in. Do you want to come or not?"

"This is wrong."

"This is the way I'm doing it. Are you coming or not?"

"I've been assigned to—"

"Fine. You take this papaya. It's her favorite. I'll take the apples. She likes those too, but not as much. Do you remember how to show her your name? Flick your ear with your right hand. And the sign for friend is—"

"I remember. Can't I say you're wrong without you thinking I'm stupid?"

"You are not sounding friendly. Like when you just said that. I get that you don't like what I'm doing. But you've got to sound and be friendly to her. Period."

He was right about that much. Animals, especially ones as intelligent as chimps, pick up on emotion quickly. I needed to clean it up. "Okay. Sorry. I can do that." I nodded, pulled up a smile and showed him the friend sign with my forefingers, locking them first one way then the other.

He relaxed visibly. "Good. Thanks. Let's go." He pointed to the papaya, which I picked up while he got two apples, and then Marc led the way through the door to Eve.

It was easy for Marc to make the love sign to Eve, even to sign "I am Marc, I am friend, You are Eve. Marc love Eve." It was as natural for him as loving Goldie had been. He could see the iceberg of terror that had frozen Eve's personality for so long slowly melting with the steady warmth of love and safety, and now she was starting to learn quickly, even show signs of playfulness. What would he have done without Christine's help, buying him this extra time? But Christine could see the value, or at least he'd been able to convince her it was there, and the pregnancy had been enough for her to use. Somehow, anyway, she'd manipulated just enough medical justification.

He'd used both the much simpler baby sign for I love you with Eve, pointing to himself, then crossing his arms over his chest signifying love, then pointing to her, and saying her name, as well as the American Sign Language, which he doubted she could do—the thumb, forefinger and pinkie finger in the air palm facing out, and a couple small shakes of the hand, the one he used with his mother.

Increasingly, though, he thought the baby signs were the better, easier choice for Eve, and that's the one he used with Eve, although Kate was behind him and didn't see it, only heard him say, "I'm back, Eve. This is Kate. She's a friend. See?" as he said, stepping to one side so that his body wasn't blocking Eve's view of Kate.

"Do it, now, Kate, give her the hello sign, your name and make the friend sign. Please."

It felt weird, much more so than the few times Kate had been in with Eve and him before. Was that because he had something to prove now? Or was it because of the easy love he'd grown for Eve, she with her sweetness intact somehow after everything she'd been through, and the trust and love he could see her growing for him? Could he raise his palm to Kate with thumb, forefinger and pinky up and shake the love sign in her direction? What about the words the sign signified? Could he whisper them, susurrant as small rainforest sounds she'd welcome, before he took her to bed again? Or say them aloud in the animal sounds of lovemaking?

When Kate saw Eve, she did it, made the hello sign and the friend sign. She didn't do it perfectly or easily, but she smiled and tried, and Marc knew she did it for him. After all, she cared passionately what happened to Eve's species. She'd fight endlessly to save the rainforest, the chimps' habitats, to stop poaching, the wanton killing, the selling of bushmeat. Was furious at the withdrawal from the Paris Accord and failure to use leverage to stop the deforestation.

Still, he needed Kate to *see* Eve. If she didn't, would she ever see him? Wasn't Eve, in her own way, a person too? Ninety eight percent of the same DNA as Marc himself. Her heart, her ability to love. And more than to love, to forgive human beings for what they had done to her, which Marc himself couldn't do. Surely Eve had a soul. Not a word Marc could exactly define, but there was a presence there, an awareness. She was so much more than what people called a dumb animal.

Eve looked at Kate and backed up. Not all the way to the spools, and she didn't climb to the nest she'd built the night before on the platform. Still, she retreated. Marc went all the way forward to the glass and signed fruit. Then he pointed to Kate while he flicked his ear and made the friend sign. "Her name is Kate," he said, "She's a friend. She brought you fruit."

Kate started to walk forward with the bucket of papaya she'd carried in. Marc said, "It's okay, girl, it's okay," softly, and made the friend sign again, but Eve turned and knuckle walked a couple of feet farther away, closer to where she could hide behind the spools. "She did better the last time I was in here," Kate said. "When you were reading to her."

"Yeah. She was distracted. I've lured her to eat from my hand through the feeding tray now, and I think it's made her feel more vulnerable again. The human hand's done a lot of damage to her, remember. But she's not hiding. That's good. If you don't mind, you could just tell her goodbye now. Maybe it's enough for today?"

"I'm supposed to…I was going to bring Lolly in on the other side."

"Not today. Too much. How about the Jasmine recording?"

Kate narrowed her eyes. "You're pushing it too far. Thurston—"

"Thurston knows nothing about chimps." He wasn't going to hear it.

"Lolly does."

"Let's not go there. I'm good with the Jasmine recording. You got it? "

"Did the best I could."

"Great. Right now, how about you sort of knuckle walk slowly toward her and show her the papaya? Then put it down. I'll feed it to her when you leave. Maybe start associating you with the good stuff."

"Pffft. You just want to see me knuckle walk, which you know I can't do carrying a pail."

"The effort might give you credibility with her though," he said, and winked. He was trying to paper over his worry with teasing. How could this work, the two of them with Eve—the two of them with each other?

Kate approached Eve, bending her knees to bring herself lower to the floor and hunching over slightly. "Stick your butt out," Marc stage whispered, but he was egging her on, and she knew it.

"Wouldn't you just love that view?" she whispered back.

Kate tipped the pail of papaya to show Eve but didn't get a response beyond an uneasy stare from the chimp. She put the pail down and backed away, showing her hands.

Marc made two signs to Eve that he didn't explain to Kate and said, "I'll be back," to Eve, and followed Kate into the anteroom.

I don't want to lose this woman, the thought came to him. I can't lose her. "How about we go see your mother after work?" he said. It was perhaps a hold he had on her, something she needed him for. While he figured this all out.

"Really? Do you have time? That would be great. She'd love that."

"I can maybe slip out fifteen or twenty minutes early. You?"

"Well—I wasn't exactly early getting in today and Linda knows it."

"Five, then?"

"Yeah, I better not try to leave early."

"That'll work. I'll meet you in the office at five. Can you start piping in both Lolly and Jasmine? Separately first, then together. Okay?"

"Sure. Give me a volume check, though."

"Yep. Thanks."

He went back to Eve, picking up the pail of papaya. Immediately, the chimp came forward all the way to the food slot, making the sign for Marc, which she'd only done once before. Then she made the sign for fruit.

"Oh, you want Marc to give you fruit?" he said, grinning at her. He took papaya and put his hand through the slot. Eve reached and took the fruit from him, and she ate it. He waited then, and sure enough, she remembered. There it was, the sign for more, the two hands facing each other, all their fingertips bunched up and brought together to touch, touch, and touch again. More, Eve was telling him. More fruit. Before he complied, Marc gave her the baby sign for I love you, pointing to himself, I, crossing his arms across his own chest, love, pointing to Eve, you, saying the words as he did it.

Marc remembered all the hand signals he'd taught Goldie, how perfect their communication had been when they'd worked together. But more, how she'd rescued him from his childhood stutter, how she'd taken care of his mother too, with patient, intelligent devotion. That was a two-way street; Goldie knew he wouldn't fail her, and he never had. Now, he hand-fed Eve more fruit, and the thought came to him for the second time that afternoon, but rearranged. I cannot let her be lost.

❋

By that afternoon, the air had cleared and taken on the crisp of a good apple, with a shining quality, like a reminder that summer would end, no matter that everything was lush and green. You can't keep anything, Marc thought and then shoved the thought down.

He followed Kate to her apartment where she dropped off her car. "Let's go to Sycamore first," he said. "Unless you're starving."

She opened her purse and drew out two packages of peanut butter crackers. "As a person of highly advanced skills, I have mastered the operation of the vending machines at work."

"Pure genius," he said, taking the one she held out.

When they got to her mother's room, Marc started signing right away. "Hello, Mrs. McKinley," he said at the same time. Her dinner tray was still there, so he pointed at it, made eating motions, and said, "food," aloud for Kate's benefit.

He asked Kate for the picture board she'd made and began pointing to the objects on it, showing wherever he could the simplified baby sign for it. A few times, he thought, oh, there's a glimmer. Kate's mother's hands would move, and he'd see an approximation of something he'd done. She had hello and chocolate. He showed Kate the baby sign for I love you, had her do it, then hug and kiss her mother, do it again. Maybe, maybe, maybe she connected the meaning to the sign.

After they left, Marc said, "You know what's the problem? I think maybe she could be taught sign as if she's deaf because she doesn't have words anymore, right? When my grandmother taught me, there were words attached. Sound. I don't know what I'm doing. But you know who I wish I could ask?"

"Who?"

"My grandmother. Obviously, both a teacher and fluent in sign. I'm just thinking out loud here—I wonder if my mother remembers how her mother taught her."

Kate shivered, rubbed her arms against the unseasonable chill. Marc put his arm around her shoulder to warm her. "I'll put the heat on in the car." He shrugged and opened the car door for her. "Where do you want to eat?"

"I want to pick up something and take it home. How about take out?"

"Fine with me," he said and closed the car door. As he walked to the driver's side, he thought, this is promising. We're going to her house. How long can I stretch out Mom being alone? Wendy, the afternoon companion, would have left by four-thirty. He wished he could ask Verna next door to check in on his mother. Stupid woman, she'd probably knock on the door again. A couple of times his mother had sat on their porch and Verna would call from hers, *Hi Honoria*, her mouth stuffed with a sandwich or while she was wiping her mouth on the back of her hand. Some people you simply could not educate about deafness, he'd learned that much.

Goldie had been so good about alerting his mother to anything happening, but Honoria wouldn't go to the door if Marc wasn't home now, so what difference would it make even if Verna were an option? *Don't worry about me*, his mother signed. As if that were possible. As if.

After they ate, carry-out Chinese in cartons on their laps in Kate's living room, Marc thought he'd been surreptitious about checking his watch, calculating how long Ria had been alone. He and Kate each had a just a bit of wine remaining in their glasses, and when they got back to the couch after carrying their leftovers to the kitchen, he brought the bottle with him intending to refill their glasses. She stopped him.

"When do you need to go?"

He hesitated. "I can stay a little bit more."

"You're worried, aren't you? I can tell. You've checked your watch at least twice."

At least she'd only seen him twice. "S'all right." He was dissembling. The truth would have been a simple yes. Instead, he pulled her to him so he could shape his hand into an eclipse of her breast while he reached the other hand across her body and lifted her hips toward him. She raised her face to his kiss, and her hand moved to feel his desire.

"No one would guess this about you," she whispered.

"Oh really? You think anyone would guess you have this wild side? I hope not." He pulled her shirt over her head when she pulled away from him long enough to get it most of the way off. She was in a hurry, unbuttoning his shirt while he unhooked her bra, let it fall. Took a breast in his mouth.

They didn't make it to the bed. The rest of their clothes quickly merged on the floor, bright and dark, lacy and tailored, male and female. Passionate and satisfied.

"Oh Katie...I don't want to leave you," Marc said. Thinking he had to. He was already so late. Kate was lying on top of him, both of them naked.

"I don't want you to leave either," she said, whispering into the hair on his chest where her head lay. Her hair, soft and faintly scented of orange and ginger, had covered his face a little while ago.

"I don't want to lose you."

She lifted her head. "What do you mean?"

"I just mean I don't want to leave," he said as if correcting himself. But it was a lie. He'd said exactly what he meant.

# Chapter 18

I WENT TO WORK the next day with two sets of feelings like equally matched boxers in a ring labeled Marc. I had nothing about which to be miffed. He'd lingered far longer than he should have. I knew that. And there was this: when he did sort his clothes from the tangled pile we'd heaped on the floor, he'd put them on as if they were stitched with sorrow and his shoes made not of leather but regret. He wanted to stay with me.

Then he wouldn't let me walk to his car with him. No farther than my apartment door. He circled his arms around me, and we kissed again. Then he nestled his face down into my hair and whispered, "Good night, love. Sleep well. I'll see you in the morning."

Love. He called me love.

Did I feel the same about him? Yes. Did he know? Well, not from anything I'd *said*.

Another part of me was uneasy. Warning myself to be careful. And then I thought of Eve, how she sensed danger when I approached, and how wrong she was. I, who would never hurt her. I, of all people. But it's Marc she trusts.

What would happen though if I lost my job? I can't let that be an option. And god knows, I'm right about letting the other chimps take care of Eve. Not only that. I'm proud of the new habitat. Short of what I really wanted to create if we'd had enough money, what the great apes will have is so much better than the old habitat. I want to be here to see them in it, to see the difference it makes to them to come a little closer to the lives they might have had. The lives they deserved to have, should and would have had. Except they hadn't. And they'd suffered. Because of my species.

⚜

When I saw Marc's face, I knew something was going on. For one thing, he wasn't already in with Eve. Although he had coveralls on, he was waiting for me in our office area.

"Got ten minutes for coffee?" he said. "I've got something to run by you."

"Sure." I started over to the coffee, which Sandy must have made. We had a small area where we kept the makings although half the time nobody got around to it, and we ended up buying it at the staff cafeteria.

"Not here. I need to talk to you. Let's go to the cafeteria."

The room was empty except for us, so I wasn't sure how much more privacy we'd need, but I shrugged. "Okay."

Marc didn't say anything on the way except small talk about it being a nice day and how Sandy and he already had the chimps outside. That explained the coveralls. He'd come in early. I surmised he had something to say about Eve, that he'd found a way to work around me. So, when we sat down at a table as far from the few others in the room as we could, each of us with a thick white china mug—the cafeteria coffee smelling slightly old, slightly burned even though it was scarcely eight-thirty—my voice was on the serrated edge of defensive, when I said, "So what do you want?"

He didn't miss it. "Whoa. Did I get you at a bad time?"

"No, go ahead."

"Seriously? Everything all right?"

He looked at me intently, tenting his brows into a concerned question, and even though it violated our agreement to keep our relationship private he touched my hand. I shook my head, ashamed. "I'm sorry. I'm okay. Distracted, I guess. What do we need to talk about?"

He relaxed. "My brilliant idea. Like the most brilliant in recent history. All I need is your okay."

I had to smile at his enthusiasm, even if he was about to screw me over with Eve. I smiled. "Lay it on me."

"Remember how I mentioned I wondered if my mother could teach your mother sign? I thought more about it. It would get my mother to experience being out of the house. And my mother doesn't have word-language like we do, so she'd be teaching someone a little more like a deaf person than a hearing person? Which is maybe where I am limited…because I have the words…. Are you dazzled?"

I scratched my cheek and scrunched my eyes and nose. It seemed such a long shot. "Do you think she would consider it?"

"I'm thinking I can work on her. That she's the only person who might be able to help. That sort of thing. And I'd need to bring you to meet her, so she gets the point that, uh, we're involved."

"Why haven't I met her yet? Is it because I don't sign?"

He closed his eyes a moment, then opened them but looked away. "It's always been hard. To be honest." Then he met my eyes. "When I was in high school, I'd try to bring friends home and I'd have to interpret, and then they'd talk extra loudly, as if that would help. And then I'd have to make up stuff when she signed so it would sound like stuff their parents might say, because it never did." He took a sip of his coffee. "God, this really is horrible, isn't it?"

"Well, my mother is crazy about you, we know that. If it involves you bringing your mother over to see her, she'll love it."

"I was thinking *maybe* we could work up to leaving them there alone together. Like company for one another. In the early evening, or something. Then I could pick her up. IF it works out, and they get along, of course. And my mother goes for it."

"Oh yes. I can pay extra and Mom can have a guest for a meal too."

"So, I can see if Mom is willing to try it?" There it was again, hope and enthusiasm blooming on his face. I wanted it to spread, let it spread.

"Of course. You're right. It is brilliant. Thank you so much. I don't even know what to say except thank you."

"Listen, it would help my mom too. I've been trying to find something to get her over her fear of leaving the house. I don't know if this'll work. But there's a chance." He looked at the clock on the wall. "Oh lord. I've gotta get going. Eve."

"What are we doing with her today? I'm thinking I'll bring Lolly—"

"Not today. But maybe tomorrow. Through the glass. We'll monitor, see if we can get a fix on whether she remembers. Today, let's keep the recordings going. She's come so far. And you should come in. Don't forget your neon shirt. And by the way, your knuckle walk is very sexy."

Did I know then that the next day he'd put me off about Lolly again? I could have guessed it. Christine's molasses act with medical clearance due to pregnancy concerns and psychological trauma let Marc drag his feet about adding Lolly to the mix, and what would be the point of even thinking about Jasmine when we'd not brought Lolly in? I pointed out that Eve was comfortable with the recordings, and even seemed to be looking for the source, didn't she? What would be the harm of letting her see Lolly? I knew Marc was working to build trust with her, to solidify the bond. I saw him signing, hand feeding now. He spent every minute he could with her.

Except. Except look at what he was offering me. All I had to do was let him work with Eve his way, no matter what I believed, while he was offering me himself, his mother—if she agreed—and a chance for my mother. How could I say no?

I did try, in a way. I kept trying. Marc knew what I thought and why. What I didn't do was go to Thurston. Or even to Linda. I made up stuff that had to be done for the new habitat, while I did whatever Marc asked me to do or let me do with Eve, and she did get used to me, although she had nowhere near the level of trust she had for Marc. He talked to her, he signed to her, he clearly loved her, all of which was both endearing and acutely uncomfortable for me.

Yes, chimps are highly intelligent, but they're not domestic animals. In the wild, chimps relate to their own well developed social groups, after all, not to humans. They communicate, they interact and raise their young, they share parenting, they build nests, they use tools.

With each other.

While we were in this holding pattern with Eve, Marc showed up beaming a few mornings later. He stood in the doorway of the primate keepers' area and motioned me into the hallway because both Tom and Sandy were at their desks. I nodded and got up, hoping neither had noticed him in the hall. It was poorly lit, and our attempts to cheer it up with zoo posters added color but didn't make it less dismal. I could hear shoes on the ceramic tile, the echo of approaching voices.

Marc stepped back against the wall so we'd both be out of sight from the office and whispered. "She'll do it," he said. "Mom'll do it. She's not sure she remembers much about how her mother taught her, but she'll try. And she'd be happy to sit with her, just to keep her company sometimes."

"Oh, Marc, that's great."

"So, how about I take you to meet Mom tonight, or tomorrow night, if you're already busy tonight. I don't want to overwhelm her with too much new at once. She's...she didn't say she had to, but I think..."

He was stammering. Not stuttering. Like he didn't know how to say it but apologizing that he thought it would be best. I interrupted him. "Of course. Tell you what—how about I pick up some dinner and bring it over?"

I saw what crossed his face. He stuck one hand in a pants pocket and pulled it out again. No idea what to do with himself. "Might be too much for the first time. Too hard to interpret and try to eat…"

"I'm going to need to learn some sign, aren't I? Um…for my mother, too, I mean." I didn't want him to think I was presuming.

He nodded, his face relaxing into a smile again. "That might help. I can show you some. Tonight we'll just have a glass of wine. Not Mom, though. She'll have tea. *We'll* have wine."

"Will that make her disapprove of me? I can drink tea." I pantomimed lifting a teacup, pinkie in the air.

He stifled a snort laugh. "Hell, I want her to disapprove of you some—otherwise she'll want you all to herself. She knows a good thing when she sees one."

Sandy came into the hall, looked the wrong way first, then swung her head toward us, her red ponytail flipping. "What's this secret meeting?" she teased. "Where are the donuts?"

"It's a conspiracy," I said. "You'll be the very last to know."

"Excellent," she said. "Just save me one with the jelly. And powdered sugar. Who is on poop scoop today is all I want to know."

"That would be you, babe," I said. "But I'm your helper. As usual, Marc has the easy stuff. Let's go. Anything else about Eve, Marc?" I was covering then, of course.

"Not for now. I'll update you tonight on the companionship situation."

"Okay, thanks," I said to him, and turned toward Sandy. "Who are you in the mood for first?"

"Gorillas?"

"Gorillas it is. Tell Tom he's on chimps. And as a bonus, he can have Bruce help him today."

"He'll be so pleased."

And it was so like Marc, the next thing he said, "Tell Tom if Bruce gets in his way to send him to me and I'll find something constructive for him to do. He's a good kid. He's learning."

Sandy smiled then. "Yeah, I know," she said. "You're right, he is."

Marc hadn't exactly lied to Kate, but he hadn't exactly told her the truth either. His mother had waited up for him while he was at Kate's that evening, which made him nuts each time she did it. Some corner of his mind knew she was, and damn if it didn't give him the creeps, like his mother was watching him make love to Kate.

When he got home, she was sitting at the kitchen table drinking chamomile tea, not even watching close captioned television. Not even reading. Just sitting there waiting, her few dishes neatly in the drainer, the blue dish towel folded on the oven handle. Good lord. Did she smell the sex on him?

"Mom, it would be safe for you to go to bed and read or something when I'm out. Or watch television," he signed. "I don't like it that you just sit and watch the door."

"I'm fine, son," she signed.

He decided to skip over the point he knew he'd lose, having argued it previously, and went directly to his new one. "I need your help with something," he signed.

"Of course," Honoria had signed back. "What do you want?"

"You know I told you about Kate. The woman I...like...so much. At work."

His mother studied his face. "Yes, what about your friend?"

"Her mother is sick." He'd tried to figure out how to sign that Dorothy wasn't deaf, but she'd lost words, that she didn't understand words anymore, and maybe it was like she was deaf. "I want you to try to teach her sign. But teach her the way your mother taught you, not the way she taught me. Because I could hear, you know?"

Ria looked at the ceiling and then at him. "Son. I do not remember how my mother taught me to sign. I was a baby." She used the rocking infant sign, although of course she'd been older and learned throughout her childhood.

Marc had sighed, and signed that he knew that, but he thought that a deaf person could teach sign to someone who didn't understand words a lot better than he could. And—Kate's mother was Honoria's age. And by herself. Maybe sometimes Ria was too? Marc deliberately used the sign for lonely, his forefinger to his lips, then moving it up, forward, down and around in two small, complete circles.

His mother signed back. "No. I have you. And Melanie and Angela." Those were the companions Marc paid, to keep her safe. He'd just found another one he hoped could start soon, too, because she was Ria's age, a huge plus. Not a graduate student who would be moving on. Barbara was fluent in sign, though she wasn't deaf; her brother was. Perfect.

"You stay in this house, that's no good," he signed now. He hadn't stated that flatly before. "No good." Surprised himself by repeating the same thumb down sign. "You need to get out, see other people. You can help Kate's mother."

Ria shook her head, dealing with her son as she always had. He'd never been trenchant with her. Marc knew she wasn't prepared to deal with him wanting something of her. Demanding something of her. He hesitated, felt something like shame for a moment, thought of the rest of his life, and pressed on, pushy, insistent, like something had set root inside the earth of him and grown, hell bent now on breaking out to breathe free air.

It had been an uneven match, and his mother had conceded. Because she needed him. She would try. It was enough. Marc could make it work. He had enough will for the two of them. For all of them, and for Eve, too. He could make it work, make it all work. He would make everything work.

# Eve

THE SMALLER PARROT-ANIMAL that made different sounds came more and didn't hurt her, but Eve stayed farther back and didn't eat from that parrot-animal's hand. But when the first one, the bigger parrot-animal was there, Eve used her hands to greet him and pant-hooted back in happiness when he made his sounds. Her hands could tell him she wanted fruit, and he gave it to her. He brought her something new sometimes, for Eve to chase around until she was tired or something different to take apart if she was full and wanted something to do. There were ways to move her hands to say she wanted the thing to chase or take apart, and she learned them.

Sometimes the parrot-animal would reach to touch her, and she let him because he never hurt her, and it felt good. She tilted her head and closed her eyes, but she didn't remember why. He always gave her fruit, and it was ripe and good. Juice ran down her arm and chin and chest. She knew how to ask for more, and when she did, the animal gave it to her. Her stomach moved by itself still, but Eve was used to it now, and it did not hurt.

She heard others like her calling each other but did not see them. But where she was, with the big parrot-animal there, was the best place she remembered. Nothing was hurting her, and she built her own sleeping nest up, in the place she could climb to, and she was not afraid.

# Chapter 19

MARC WANTED TO PICK ME up to visit his mother that night. I told him not to be ridiculous, the nineteen fifties were over, and not only did I have my very own driver's license but also my very own car that had navigation, and he just had to give me the address and tell me when to be there.

"Mom will say I'm not being a gentleman."

"It's obvious how long it's been since she got out."

"Oh, god, you're so right," he said, with a deep sigh.

"Well, she'll have to get used to me."

He rolled his eyes toward the sky. "I can't wait to see the show."

We were walking out of work to the employee parking lot, one of the rare nights we left at the same time. The summer flowers—reds, oranges, yellows, dots of blue here and there, pinks and purples—spilled from hanging baskets and lined the walkways. Salvia, zinnias, dusty miller, marigold, alyssum, ageratum. I could name them, and more; my mother had planted flowers that I'd never appreciated when I'd grown up, back when we were a family in the big house. So much I'd let go by without notice, and no way to tell her thank you now that I did.

Marc was talking to me while I was looking at the flowers. I dragged my attention back to him.

"...okay? We won't really talk about that tonight."

"Oh? What will we talk about?"

He gave an exasperated huff. "What I just said. Weren't you listening?"

"Sorry. I'm just tired."

"Hey, would you rather put this off? It's okay. I didn't mean to press—"

"No, I want to come over. Tell me what you were saying. Really." He slowed down and looked at me, searching my face to see if I meant it. "Honestly, I was looking at the flowers and feeling guilty about not being a good daughter, that's the truth."

He shook his head and waited until my eyes met his. "You're a really good daughter." He said softly, seriously, as if he knew all of me. Which, of course, he didn't.

I showed up at Marc's house, or his mother's, at seven, as he'd told me. I brought her an assortment of herbal teas. I would have brought Marc a bottle of wine but thought it might make a bad impression on his mother, and we were asking her for a favor. A giant favor.

I parked on the street, by the curb, and was glad I hadn't ever described the house I'd grown up in because their house could have fit into it at least twice. Probably more. But this was where Marc had grown up, the house his mother was afraid to leave. Theirs had no garage, a yard like a Post-it note, with a little covered porch and three steps from the front down to a short walk, sidewalk, street. Neighbors close enough to eavesdrop. Marc could have moved; I knew his salary. But he was loyal, and abandonment wasn't his style.

"It's such a pleasure to meet you, Ms. Lopez," I said, giving the hello sign that Marc had taught me to use with my mother. "I'm Kate." His mother looked delighted. She signed something, and Marc looked at me and said, "I'm very happy to meet you too, Kate. My son speaks very well of you."

I realized that I needed to look at her, not Marc, when I spoke to his mother, although during the first couple of exchanges after my initial success, I'd looked at him. He cued me with a small head gesture. He was smooth, an experienced translator and although it was awkward, I was determined not to do the stupid things he'd told me his high school friends had done.

*Breathe*, I reminded myself. She's a regular person. Just look at her and talk. When she asks a question, answer it. Smile at her. Give Marc a chance to translate. I tried to find the rhythm. "I want to learn to sign," I blurted, surprising myself. I didn't think Marc translated that. I never knew, of course, exactly what he was translating.

"What did you tell her?" I said to him.

He didn't answer.

I took another sip of the chardonnay he'd poured me, and Ms. Lopez drank her tea. We sat in their small, cozy living room in a triangle configuration, me in the middle of a green couch, she in a beige wingback chair, and Marc in an uncomfortable-looking wooden one. There was a hand-knit afghan folded behind me, on the back of the couch, and a patterned area rug on the wood floor. Several framed pictures of Marc at various graduations were on lamp tables. One had a faded picture of young, blonde Ms. Lopez hugging a dark-haired man (her father? I wondered) both wide-smiling. I could see a resemblance between Marc and the man. There was another picture of a young Marc, a golden retriever, and elderly frail-looking woman. Marc was holding a trophy.

Ms. Lopez asked if I'd met Eve, from which I guessed that Marc hadn't told her much about our roles at work. I said yes, she was a beautiful chimp, and I was excited about getting her into the new habitat. That opened the subject. I told her what I'd been working on, why it was much better, the naturalized environment, and why that was so important. I was putting my slant on the topic, but she seemed quite interested.

What are you telling her?" I said to Marc as he signed.

"What you're saying," he said. "Are we feeling paranoid?"

"I have to learn to sign."

"Hmmm. So you can check up on me?"

"Darn right."

"I'm telling her that you're not sure I'm translating right," he said as he signed to his mother.

Ms. Lopez laughed, rough, hoarse, almost soundless, and signed something in Marc's direction.

"Now Kate knows how I feel," Marc translated what his mother had said to him. Then he added, an aside, not translating. "It's always an issue. How can she know what people are really saying?"

I left after a little more than an hour. Teaching my mother never came up until I was at the front door. Marc said, "We're thinking that this weekend, we'll come meet your mother. Maybe Saturday afternoon after lunch. How does that sound?"

I noticed he wasn't signing it, though, so I wasn't sure if he really meant *we*. I said, "That would be great." What he did then was louder than shouting in any language. He left the front door open so his mother could—and would, I was sure—watch. He walked me to my car and kissed me goodnight.

It had seemed we were in a sort of limbo, my impatience to integrate Eve stuffed aside, while Marc had the vet—who presumably had the consulting vet, the primate specialist, somehow backing her up—holding off on Eve's medical clearance because of her pregnancy. Or something. Christine hadn't talked to me about it because I wasn't the lead. I'd managed to avoid Thurston, and Linda hadn't said anything to me. Each day, I thought *tomorrow. I have to push it tomorrow.* And then, as each day came there was somehow a reason to let it go one more day.

It was inevitable: an email from Thurston, or a drop by chat. Or his finding me in the cafeteria. I knew it was going to happen. So how could I have been so unprepared? But I was.

"Kate!" There he was, with that slightly-off gait of his. But it was his flat-top and the thick black frames on his glasses that most people noticed about him first, as if he'd been put in the wrong decade of his grandmother's photo album and just liked it there.

I'd come out of the primate keepers' area on my way to meet Marc for lunch. I'd told him I'd join them if I got my email caught up. Sandy and Tom, and probably Linda would be there too, so we wouldn't have any time alone, but it would be nice to sit next to him. I waved to Thurston and tried to look like I was in a great hurry.

Thurston was coming down the hall toward me and motioned in my direction. "I need to speak with you."

Shit, I muttered under my breath. "Of course," I called to him, and turned to take a few steps toward him as if speaking with him made it onto my list of desirable ways to die that day.

He caught up to me, holding his paisley tie in place to keep it from flapping like a flag caught in a breeze—he'd picked up his pace that much to prevent my escape.

"We need to discuss exactly how the new chimp is progressing," he said. He knew. I could feel it like weather. He knew damn well.

"I was just on my way to meet with Marc and Linda," I said. "To discuss that."

"Really." His eyebrows went up just slightly, and it didn't sound exactly like a question, but as if he were saying, bullshit. It made me queasy, especially since I was lying. Then he said, "Then perhaps you can fill me in later this afternoon."

"Definitely," I said.

"How would three o'clock be? In my office."

"I'll be there."

"I'll look forward to it."

He reversed direction then, presumably returning to his office. I felt sick. There was nothing to do but insist that Marc let me bring in Lolly. Now. It would buy time with Thurston. I was sure there wasn't a medical issue—but I'd cover that. I'd leave the glass partition in place, not slide it away and just let them get acquainted through a metal cage wall, so preferable, letting them safely smell and touch each other. That would have to wait.

Then it came to me: what if I just did it? Like now. While Marc and the others were in at lunch? I'd get a couple of the assistant keepers to help me bring Lolly in, ones who wouldn't question what I was doing because I'd been their boss for a long time. It could just be a short first time, but it would be something. And I had to do *something*.

So, I did.

Lolly is a sweet-natured chimp, born at the San Diego Zoo and raised by her own mother, always a plus, so she'd had a good start in life, and we'd found her a calming influence in the social group. I'd thought she'd be the best for Eve to meet first, too, because she's small in stature, an unintimidating ninety-eight pounds, agile, but not heavily muscled. She has a somewhat flat face, and almond-shaped deep brown eyes that seem wise and thoughtful. I've never seen her be aggressive—in fact, I've heard her pant-grunting now and then, a sound chimps make when then are being submissive. I hoped she might help Eve learn to play with other chimps, because Lolly had that side too.

We'd just about gotten Lolly into the glass enclosure adjacent to Eve. Lolly was approaching, as I'd expect her to, given her friendly nature. It was true that Eve retreated. She was frightened, screaming. But she hadn't had time to realize there was no danger. I was on the keeper side of Eve's enclosure where she could hear and see me, and I'd had the assistants play the recording of Lolly's pant-hoots and the few pant-grunts I'd been able to capture, thinking that Eve would make the connection with the chimp she could now see and those friendly sounds she was accustomed to. It would have worked, I was sure.

Except.

Except I didn't know that Marc had gone to lunch early. That he'd come back early.

I heard the door open behind me and jumped, the way one does when caught doing something wrong. I flushed, guilty as a child, though what I was doing wasn't wrong. Eve had to be integrated.

I turned to face Marc. "Thurston insisted," I said. I didn't want to sound defensive, but I did.

He set his jaw, pulled his neon shirt—turquoise with lime green and yellow—further down over his khaki pants and signed to Eve as he walked around me to put his body between mine and where Eve had scurried, the area of the enclosure farthest from Lolly—and me. He signed as he spoke. "It's okay, it's okay. I'm here. No hurt. No hurt. Friend. No hurt Eve."

Then he spoke to me, without looking over his shoulder or signing anything. "Go get Lolly out of there. Do it now. Eve is terrified. That's more trauma."

"Can't you let her—"

"Move her out. Now."

# Chapter 20

HE'D LEAPFROGGED OVER his own emotions. Eve was all that mattered. She was huddled into herself, rocking and screeching. She wouldn't come to him to get the papaya he offered, wasn't looking at him as he signed, didn't seem to hear him when he spoke.

She did, though, appear to look at Lolly when Kate and the assistant keepers coaxed her out of the adjacent enclosure with treats. Marc wasn't sure of that, though.

He was able to calm her by reverting to sitting with his back to her and reading aloud in a soothing tone, holding the book so she could see the bright illustrations of scenes from the rainforest. He threaded papaya through the food tray, then, and signed to her as he spoke. "Sorry, sorry Eve scared. That was a nice chimp, like you. Lolly. Friend." He had to make up a sign for Lolly's name, of course, so he used the baby sign for dessert, thinking of lollypop, which would suit Eve's long fingers; all she'd have to do was brush her chin with them, but of course, she didn't imitate that. Not now. She wasn't learning now.

All of this distracted him for the better part of the afternoon. He left long enough to find Tom, to beg off helping with moving and feeding the gorillas, to buy himself some extra time. He knew he was pushing it, spending more time than Linda had authorized with Eve, presuming on the other keepers' willingness to pick up extra work so he could. All he'd said to Tom was that Eve had a setback, and Tom said, "Got you covered."

He didn't say anything to Kate when he went in later to help with the other chimps. She was directing Bruce, and Sandy was working the area, too. But seeing her, not in the pink, green, and blue tie-dye shirt anymore, but in regular coveralls, still managing to be so pretty and sexy but now worse than a stranger to him. The feelings he shut off when he walked into Eve's area, feelings in concert with Eve's—shock, betrayal, fear—roiled up. But then he added what was human: he was angry. So angry.

He felt her seek his eyes when the others were intent on their work.

What kind of patsy did she think he was?

When the feeding was done, the Lixit checked, wood wool replenished, and the area secure, he resolved to leave directly for his car without even changing from his coveralls. He'd just bring them back tomorrow. Or burn them. He didn't care.

He didn't go to the office to check email. He didn't care if there were messages there saying he'd won the lottery. He was sure Kate would be in there and try to wait out the rest of the staff to talk to him, but he had nothing to say to her, and there was nothing he wanted to hear.

As he drove home, Marc worked to settle himself down. His mother was expert at reading facial and body language, like most deaf people. The absolute last thing he wanted, even less than he wanted to talk to Kate, was to discuss any of this with his mother, who knew zero about great apes or their needs. He stopped and bought himself an iced tea, then detoured to the small park near their house, parked and sat on a bench under a maple that let the small breeze turn its leaves palms up, the late sun silvering them while he listened to an oldies station on his phone and let the ice melt in his mouth. He put his thoughts away on a high shelf above his head, distracted by the music from his high school and college days, not that he'd been at the parties, but he could always blast music in the house, because why not? He knew all the words and now he let them lighten his mood.

When he was ready, he drove home. Marc pulled up to the curb in front of their house and parked. Verna The Useless was parked on her porch polishing off the family size bag of corn chips she was cradling on her lap. "Nice night," she called through a mouthful as she waved, clutching a fistful. "You oughta mow the grass."

He pasted on a fake-friendly smile and gave a half-wave back. "Yep," he said, and quickened his pace.

As always, the front door was double locked, the deadbolt and the doorknob. He unlocked both and let himself in. His mother often sat in the living room facing the entryway when she expected him so she'd see the door open and wouldn't be startled, even though she was good at sensing the small disturbance of approaching movement.

Marc stomped on the hardwood several times so she'd feel the vibration and know he'd come in. He stood and waited. When she didn't appear, and he could see that she wasn't in the kitchen, he walked back toward the bedrooms. She was in hers, and when she sensed him at the open door, she looked up from the bed where she had some of her clothes laid out as if waiting for a body on a cream-colored afghan his grandmother had knit.

"What are you doing?" he signed, raising his eyebrows to form the question.

"Trying to make a nice outfit," Ria signed back, and pointed. "What do you like best?"

"Why?" Marc had never known his mother to do anything remotely like this. Most of her clothes were ones that his grandmother bought for her before she died. And Ria had kept her mother's clothes. They wore the same size, and once she had that stash, Ria was set for life.

Ria's closed fist went up in front of her chest and the rotated in a single circle out and around and back.

LYNNE HUGO

"Saturday?" Marc repeated the sign to her as a question. He had no idea what she meant.

"Saturday. We go visit Kate's mother." Ria signed. "I want to look good. Which one?"

She'd turned back to the laid-out outfits. Her only dress, blue with a subtle print. Black pants, a white top, and she'd put out a pink silk scarf that had been his grandmother's. Then an alternative, her khaki pants and her black top. She'd even set long colored beads on the shirt. His *mother* had done this. Marc wasn't sure he'd recognize her in any of these get-ups. He didn't even know why she had them; she never dressed up. He hadn't realized that she'd been thinking about this, worked herself up to anticipating it. That she could have crossed that bridge.

"I've gotta use the bathroom," he signed when she looked over to him. "They all look good." He ducked into the hallway and escaped.

Hamartia. The word he'd learned in high school when the honors English teacher had been drilling the class on vocabulary, preparing for the SAT. It meant a critical flaw or shortcoming. Different from hubris, because it's not necessarily excessive pride, although that might be someone's hamartia, she'd explained, and added her advice. "We all have a hamartia. Just know what yours is, or it leads to failure. Control for it, be self-aware, that's the trick."

His grandmother used to say, "Don't be so quick to judge, Marco."

But Kate had gone behind his back. After he'd trusted her, made himself bare to her, and let himself love her. It wasn't as if he hadn't seen with his own eyes what she'd done.

He'd been quick to love Kate, or maybe it hadn't been as quick as it seemed given how long he'd adored her from a distance, like a tourist admires a place—wonderful, beautiful, exotic—that he never thought he could live. Was being needy his hamartia? But to help her, he'd tried a key that might unlock her mother's isolation

186

and stumbled on the one that might unlock his own mother's: the notion she could help a woman more isolated than herself. For Kate, he'd tried it, and *click, click, click*, the tumblers turned. His mother—Honoria Lopez—who wouldn't consider technology, who wouldn't consider the life skills or social programs for the deaf, the culture available to her, or try to overcome her ingrained fear of the outside world despite his exhortations, was ready to try for a stranger in need. He didn't know whether to be pissed off or overcome with joy.

Would he turn the key back the other way? Now? Ridiculous.

He'd go on and open the door now for his mother. Because it was exactly what she needed. But it wouldn't be to help Kate. Or himself.

I'd had no opportunity to talk to Marc—and suspected he was keeping it that way—so of course he had no idea about either my first or my second encounter with Thurston that day.

When I went to the director's office at three-thirty as commanded, Thurston had been, as usual, sitting behind his desk, but he dispensed with his usual courtesy of standing up when I appeared in his doorway. Instead, he just gestured to the defendant's chair on the other side.

"So," he'd said, chin in hands which he propped on his elbows and narrowing his eyes in my direction. "I've not been made aware of progress toward the goal. What gives?"

Behind him I saw the western sky, darker than it had been, distracting me into a worry about Bruce. "Excuse me, Thurston. Would you mind if I just check the radar on my phone? I notice the sky changing, and if the apes need to be brought in unexpectedly—"

"If they do, the keepers will handle that, I presume?" His tone made the question rhetorical. "Eve isn't outside, as we know, unfortunately, since to my knowledge, she's not integrated into the troop, and weather isn't an issue with the new habitat. Since it's not being used. Since we're waiting until Eve is integrated. Which hasn't happened. Correct?"

I picked my way back through that maze and landed on his first question. It ought to be safe to respond to that. "We all pitch in when it's a weather issue."

Thurston looked over his shoulder to personally assess the sky. "I don't see anything particularly menacing. Now, regarding Eve and the other apes."

He had no idea how long it took to batten down for a storm, why we always watched weather closely. "Well, this morning, I introduced Lolly to Eve," I said, infusing some fake enthusiasm into it.

He perked up. "And?" Finally, I'd said something he wanted to hear.

I should have known it wouldn't be enough. I had to tell him. "I wish I could say Eve reacted well. She was very frightened. I believe Christine and the great ape specialist—Dr. Reagh—are most concerned about dealing with her trauma history and protecting the pregnancy, which is now fairly advanced."

Thurston smoothed his tie, lined it up so it hung straight. The papers on his desk were perfectly squared. "There have been no pregnancy-related problems that I've been apprised of," he said. "As I understand everything you have wanted to do, the whole point is to—"

"Right." I tried to appease him. "The goal has been to keep the pregnancy as stress-free as possible, though, and of course, not to take risks. She's very young, as you know."

"Did anything happen? Was the other ape aggressive in any way?"

"No, no she wasn't." Lolly was an unlikely candidate for that, but she couldn't have hurt Eve, anyway. I didn't mention the glass barrier. Thurston's relative ignorance about our department worked to my advantage as long as he didn't stumble on the right questions to ask. He wouldn't like that I'd used the glass barrier, but he wouldn't expect that of me, either.

"Aren't you the one who's for replicating nature?"

I hesitated. "Nature can't really be replicated, but in principle and as much as possible in practice, yes."

"Let me make sure I understand. For example, in a sanctuary, say, for example Chimp Haven, once Eve was deemed free of infectious disease, she would be introduced to the other chimps, maybe one or two initially, but rather quickly to the remainder, and they would be the ones to socialize her. Many of those chimps that have been retired to sanctuaries have been previously traumatized by humans in laboratories, circuses, and the like, have they not?"

Of course, he was correct. "That's right," I said.

"And yet they do well with each other in those sanctuaries."

"For the most part, very well."

"You believe chimps don't belong in zoos?"

I squirmed through possible words. This was a trap, damn him. "Ideally. But zoos are a reality, and the goal is to—"

He interrupted. "—to replicate as closely as possible what would happen in a natural habitat. Is that your belief?"

"Yes. As best we can."

"Excellent. I'm discussing this with you, because you're the expert on this approach and all I want you to do is what you already think is best. I expect you'll put them together again tomorrow?"

"I'll certainly talk with Marc and Christine about that." I said, trying to meet his eyes and largely failing. I knew exactly how it would go with Marc. It would be like trying to put out a house fire with a thimble full of water. Thurston didn't know that, and I wouldn't throw Marc under the bus. But I also didn't see how he— or we—were ever going to integrate Eve. Or how I'd keep my job, forget becoming Research Director.

"Although I don't like to interfere in personnel matters… generally, our curators do a fine job with those…" He'd let that trail off. In my experience, he didn't have any problem at all interfering in personnel matters.

Thurston had been right about one thing, though. The distant storm outside hadn't advanced. The air wasn't heavy or ominous, no breeze raising the leaves like warning hands. Maybe it would bypass us.

But the storm within the zoo had been a direct hit.

That night felt like an empty jar of time. It shouldn't have felt different from the nights before I'd been seeing Marc, but it did. The phone quiet as a memory. It was three hours earlier on the west coast; Becky was still at work and couldn't Skype. A microwave dinner, white wine in a juice glass while I curled on the couch to read, only now I couldn't follow the timeline or who was who among the characters.

I worked myself up to call him, telling myself to be brave, but courage proved unnecessary; he didn't answer. I left a message.

He didn't call back.

The next day the rain that had held off the previous afternoon moved in like a lumbering bear. Our indoor exhibits were crowded with visitors using a discount coupon that had been in an advertising flyer and staff were swamped. There wasn't an opportunity to talk with Marc alone, and even if there had been, and he'd agreed, there was no time that day to pull Lolly aside and bring her in again. We couldn't spare the help.

I did what I could: I sent Marc an email telling him Thurston was insistent that Eve be integrated, that he'd confronted me. I wrote that I was sorry, that I should have told him first, and that I missed him.

The next morning a reply was waiting for me. He understood that I'd convinced Thurston that my approach was the correct one. If Saturday afternoon at one would be acceptable, he and his mother would meet me at my mother's building entrance then.

What?

What did this mean? I was flummoxed, not daring to hope he'd accepted my apology, or even understood, because there was an almost palpable chill coming from him when we were with others by necessity. And he was ensuring we were never alone. That he would still bring his mother to help mine? It would be more than awkward.

That evening after work, I stood next to the driver's side of his car in the employee lot so he couldn't leave without my having a chance to talk to him. At least to try.

We were dragging into late summer, then. It was humid twilight, shadows lying down as if exhausted by the heat, the air heavy. Sweat beaded on my forehead and temples and ran between my breasts. I was tired and leaned back against his car, a gray sedan that was definitely not new. The metal had absorbed the heat of the day and it went through my clothes like an iron.

Marc finally approached, weaving a shortcut through the thinned-out lines of employee cars. My heartbeat was too fast and loud. Then he looked up and saw me. His face was set, hard then. "What do you want?" he said, when he got to the car.

"Marc, please. Be fair. You've got to know I wasn't behind it. Thurston agrees with *you*. He's a zoos-will-save-the planet guy. He's pressuring me to go around you now because it works for his fundraising timeline. That's what he cares about."

I didn't tell him the carrot Thurston had dangled, the research director job that would let me stay here, keep my mother where she was and pay her bills. He wouldn't believe I hadn't thrown him under the bus to get it.

What he did think was obviously bad enough. He didn't give any ground. "Whatever," he said. "It's what you wanted anyway so you let him use you. Bypass Linda. Forget me. Forget *Eve*."

"No! I didn't do that, Marc, I swear—"

He put his hand up like a stop sign almost in my face and talked over me. "So, we move on," he said. "How's Saturday?" As if he knew it was too much, his hand went down right away.

"Are you serious? You still want to come? Wouldn't that be… difficult? If we can't talk?"

His expression softened. He shook his head slightly once and shrugged. Almost smiled, a little rueful. "I don't need to let your mother down—or mine—because I feel let down. Let's give it a shot."

"That's really kind of you." I wanted to ask him why he would do this, but this was like dealing with a new animal, one I didn't know at all, and I know not to push with a new animal. "Thank you," I said. "Would you maybe want to get a drink?"

"I don't think so. I'm too tired. If you don't mind, I'll just get in my car." He gestured with his hand and head, raising his eyebrows, as if to ask me to move out of his way.

"Yeah, okay."

*What about Eve?* was on my tongue, trying to push its way out from behind my lips. But I held the words in, even though the subject was the great divide between us. They needed to be said but I couldn't. I didn't want to alienate him further, not now. If I had lost him for myself, I still wanted his help for my mother.

I had no idea what to expect on Saturday. I'd slept badly, woke, drank too much coffee which then upset my stomach and twanged my nerves. Got dressed, checked myself in the mirror and changed. Brushed my hair out, studied it, then put it up. I was a wreck.

I went over to the facility almost an hour early. I wanted to make sure the posters with the pictures were where I'd left them, and to at least try—knowing it would make no difference—to tell her Marc was coming with his mother. And I thought then how much effort I spent on things that made no difference, except that I always convinced myself that I had to try, that this was the time that would count.

I found a big smile somewhere inside myself, put it on, and gave my mother the hello sign as I came into her room. She had eaten about half of her lunch and then apparently lost interest in it, but she seemed glad I was there. Her hand went to the back of my head when I bent down to kiss her, in what she could manage of an embrace. When I stood again, I didn't let her see the tears in my eyes.

The picture posters were not where I'd left them, and I found them in the back of Mom's closet again, which meant the staff still weren't even trying to communicate with her. I'd brought a bag of kisses and made the sign for chocolate, the way Marc had taught, hoping I remembered it right. I showed her my hands, raising my eyebrows, trying to make my whole face into a question mark to ask her if she wanted chocolate. Hesitant, she looked at what I was doing, and I saw her process it: *she remembered*. She made the sign, and I produced a kiss.

I had no idea how to communicate that Marc and his mother were coming, but at least I'd primed her with the chocolate sign. I carried out her tray, tidied the room, and suddenly thought of borrowing more chairs, which we'd need anyway, as she had only one extra. She might get the idea from that that other people were coming. Once that was done, I could only wait with her, each of us silent islands in a lonely sea.

Marc was often early, so at twelve fifty, I went downstairs to wait on a bench by the sidewalk. I couldn't have been there a minute and a half when I saw him park. How quickly I'd grown to know his ways.

I could tell he shortened his usual strides so his mother could keep up with him as they walked from the parking lot. Ms. Lopez had gotten dressed up and I kicked myself mentally that I hadn't thought of fixing Mom's hair and putting some makeup on her.

"Ms. Lopez, you look beautiful!" I said to her. "I can't thank you enough for coming, for doing this." In that moment, I'd managed to forget she was deaf, only accidentally doing the right thing by looking right at her when I spoke. I'd also gestured at her outfit, again a lucky accident. She looked at Marc, and he signed what I'd said.

She broke out a wide smile. Her teeth were slightly crooked but quite white. She was more fair than Marc, lighter eyes. Her hair looked as if a brush of silver paint had been lightly whisked over it. She had pinned the sides with barrettes. While Marc was watching her sign, I studied them both, wondering if Marc looked like his father, or if his were the genes from his grandfather, the earthy dark of his eyes and hair, the thickness of his eyebrows. He'd worn pressed khakis and a green and tan button-down shirt, scrubbed and handsome. His hair was looked damp from his shower. Or maybe it was gel.

"I'm happy to be here and to meet your mother, Kate," Marc translated what his mother had just signed. "I don't know if I can help, but I will try to show her."

I remembered the sign for thank you. Flat fingers to my lips, then tip them down and toward her. Smile. Thank you!

That delighted Ms. Lopez. Even Marc looked pleased.

"Shall we go upstairs?" I said it to Marc, and he nodded, so I turned to lead the way. When we got inside, we had to wait a moment for the elevator. Ms. Lopez was signing to Marc, her face animated, agitated, even.

"Is something the matter, Ms. Lopez? Do you need anything?"

"She's all right," Marc said to me.

Ms. Lopez's hands looked like a whole flock of birds taking off, her eyes intent on Marc.

Marc put up both his hand toward his mother. Then he stepped over to me, leaned in and gave me a quick kiss on the lips, pulled me in and put his cheek next to mine as if he were nuzzling me in affection. His back to his mother, he spoke quietly into my ear, "She wants to know what's going on, said I'm being rude to you, that I hadn't greeted you. She does not need to be involved in my personal life, okay?"

"Got it," I said.

He stepped back and we both gave his mother bright, fake smiles. I had no idea if she was fooled. The elevator opened and the three of us went down the hall to my mother's room.

When I got back to my apartment late that afternoon, I tried to sort out what had happened. First, my mother noticeably lit up when she saw Marc, more so than when I'd come in. Just by gesturing and with a few signs—or maybe it was evident by her age, how would I know? —he seemed to get it across that the older woman with him who was wearing the pretty scarf and had barrettes in her hair was his mother. Ms. Lopez signed hello, and I couldn't believe it, my mother returned the greeting. I hung back, staying out of the way. Every little while there was a bit of magic when the drawbridge, long raised, turning my mother into an isolated island, went down. An idea could flow across. It was the idea that was needed; it could be wordless, as it was for a child born deaf learning to communicate. *The idea was enough*. My mother made a connection, picture to sign, person to sign.

When they were ready to leave, Marc said to me, "Well, I was right. Mom knows what to do. I think we can make progress." He signed to his mother without translating for me.

"She's willing to keep going," he said after Ms. Lopez responded. His mother looked at me and nodded. I signed thank you to her and, impulsive, gave her a quick hug, before I signed thank you again.

"Did I sign that right?" I asked Marc.

"It was fine," he said, a non-answer, which made me wonder if I'd messed it up, said something like take out the trash. How was this going to work if I didn't learn too?

"I'll bring Mom over maybe tomorrow after work. It would be good for your mom to have a short review session soon, keep it fresh in her mind and make sure she remembers Mom. But she seemed comfortable, so I'm not worried about that."

"Um…okay. I can do that."

"Okay, if you're free. If not, it's all right, I'll still bring her if I can get away a little early."

"You don't need me?"

"Not absolutely necessary."

I'm sure my eyes got bigger. "I thought I needed to learn with her."

"You can catch up. And I can also find you some tutorials online if you miss visits."

"But…"

He interrupted. "You have the advantage of words. For you it's memorizing and practice. Mom's using a lot of the baby signs now. Just signs for nouns. Essential actions. Your mom needs to catch on. You already do. I've got Mom into it, and I want to—"

"Okay," I said, sensing his impatience. Or irritation. "I appreciate what you're doing so much. If you could try to let me know when you're coming, I'll likely be here."

He hesitated. I thought he wanted to say not necessary, again, but he said, "Sure."

I realized his mother was looking at us, left out, and that this was rude. "Tell her I'm sorry. I didn't mean to leave her out of a conversation," I said, looking at Ms. Lopez.

Marc looked surprised. "You're getting it," he said. And then he did translate. Not that I could tell what he signed.

Ms. Lopez smiled, and I signed thank you again. "You don't need to walk us out," Marc said. "I'll see you tomorrow at work," and moved toward the door, signing to my mother as he said goodbye, Ms. Lopez in tow, signing also. Ms. Lopez bent and gave my mother a kiss on the cheek too.

After they left, my mother looked in my direction, almost as if she could ask a question. *What now?* I had nothing to offer; the worry and confusion rattling in my mind like lost pennies in a clothes dryer was useless to either of us.

The animation on my mother's face had faded into a blank screen again by the time I'd returned the borrowed chairs and picked up my purse to leave. At home, I did try. I wish I could say that I came up with an idea about how to make it work with Marc, our mothers, Eve, Thurston, my job—that my thinking time and analysis resulted in a plan. I came up with nothing because I couldn't accept that I'd have to sacrifice something, anything, truly important to me.

And then, in a way, it was all taken out of my hands. Out of all our hands.

# Eve

THE DARK CREPT IN slowly and the parrot-animal was not there. None of the animals she saw when it was light were there and that was good. Eve could hear the calls of two other chimps. She heard them often now. Restless, she did not climb to her sleeping nest, though she had made one. She wanted to be alone, to hide. Her stomach moved in a long slow wave, which hurt but not the way the big hairless animals used to hurt her when they came pointing their small sticks. Still, Eve wanted it to stop.

She crept behind the wooden spools. She couldn't see the others, but she could hear them and now she wanted to hide. Had to hide. She crouched for a long time in the corner behind the spools, where she'd brought some wood wool, until something wet and round started out of her. Eve was confused but felt she should grab hold of what was coming out of her, faster now. She reached to grasp it by a piece that was moving. A rope tied it to something else wet that came out. Eve ignored all that while she first put the wet thing that moved down on the wood wool. That did not feel right. She picked it back up and moved it onto her stomach, where it had come from. Tired, hungry, she lay down. The wet thing moved, then was still.

# Chapter 21

HE'D BEEN MORE THAN pleased about how the visit had gone with Mrs. McKinsey. Marc hadn't seen his mother as a separate person that way, well, not ever that he could remember. It was as if some vital part frozen inside her, inside the house, had thawed. She'd dressed up, gone on the visit, worked at teaching sign to a wordless woman and forgotten to be afraid. Marc wondered if it was because his grandmother wasn't there to step in and fill the need? And she'd known that he couldn't.

He was still congratulating himself on his own brilliance when he got to work the next morning. He'd been entirely right that it would help his mother, and fair enough, it seemed to be helping Mrs. McKinsey, too, fine by him. He'd have to come to terms with Kate was all. He was just so disappointed, so let down that she'd gone behind his back. He and Kate didn't agree on fundamentals, but he thought she valued him, saw him as an equal. Respected him. Thought he could trust that much. Love was a ridiculous idea without respect and trust. What sand had he had his head stuck in?

He hadn't slept well, too keyed up from contemplating how to proceed with getting his mother back to Mrs. McKinsey to keep this good thing going. The first thing he did once he got in the building was pour himself a large coffee, his second, before a quick email check while only Tom was in the office area, and then he went to the primate department kitchen to collect apples, melon, and papaya. He pulled an eye-popping orange and lime green basketball camp shirt leftover from some summer program—he couldn't imagine any adolescent male willing to wear this one, it was that bad—and, carrying the food bucket, headed in to start work with Eve.

She wasn't up on her platform as she often was when he arrived in the morning, the first place his gaze went now. He scanned the rest of the enclosure. No sign of her.

He closed his eyes for a second, opened them again. This had never happened, not since she'd been first been there. She'd always been in sight. There was an emergency phone on the wall. Not yet. He'd give it a few more minutes. No one would know he'd waited if he didn't let the security camera make a liar out of him. He banged on the glass, called her name.

"Eve. Eve. It's Marc. I have fruit." He called it several times and rattled the food slot as loudly as he could, stuck a piece of papaya in the tray. "Fruit," he called, careful to keep agitation from his voice. Don't sound frightened, he warned himself.

Then he saw the top of her head rising like a dark sun from behind the big wooden construction spools. "Come and get it, girl," he coaxed and made the sign for fruit.

Slowly, slowly she emerged. She was holding something against her body. Marc couldn't see what it was and didn't recognize it. Something hung from it, too, maybe wood wool? It looked as if she'd soiled it, and he wondered if she'd had diarrhea. Was she ill?

But then she dropped one hand to her side still holding the thing.

*Oh god, please no.* Eve came closer, wanting the fruit, and Marc realized he was right. *Oh no, oh shit.* He moved to the phone. "Connect me to Christine Mead, please. Stat."

"Chris," he said, when he heard her voice on the line. "You better get down here. Eve's had her baby."

"Just now?"

"No idea. During the night, I suppose. That's what they do in the wild. Kate said."

"Alive?"

"Don't know. Can't see. She's holding it by an arm, dangling it at her side. Not nursing that I can see right now." As he spoke into the phone Marc watch Eve approach the papaya more slowly than usual, pick up the piece he'd put through, into the food tray, with her free hand and eat it. She wasn't herself, though. Usually she'd stay there and sign *more*, *more* until he produced it, but now, when she saw none, she retreated, the tiny baby swinging loosely from her other hand. Marc couldn't tell if any of the movement he saw was the baby's own or from Eve.

"On my way," Christine said and broke the connection.

He went close to the glass and tried to show Eve what to do. Made a cradling motion. Told her, "Eve, good Eve. Like this," and picked up the food bucket, held it to his chest with both arms, not that it looked anything like a baby, but it was all he had, and hadn't Eve shown she could imitate him? He felt prickling behind his nose, his eyes growing wet.

Christine blew into the enclosure area wearing a lab coat. She hadn't knocked to signal her arrival. Marc tried to block her from approaching the enclosure.

"The whites...please. Take it off," he said, gesturing at her coat. "The last thing we need is to freak her out." He shook his head. "She's not herself."

She sighed. "Marc. If she's not nursing...look, that baby is likely premature. If it's alive, we have to knock Eve down and get it out. You get that, don't you?"

Marc saw it: The oversize pocket of her lab coat held a tranquilizer dart.

"No. No, give her a chance. She doesn't know. Let her figure it out." He was half commanding, half pleading.

Christine brushed by him and went to the glass. She peered in. "I've got to call for backup here. Consultation. I'm obligated."

"Just ten minutes. I think she was sleeping when I came in. She had the baby against her chest when I got here, and I startled her."

Christine turned to examine his face, narrowed her eyes. Usually she was a reliable ally, but he felt her support eroding, his cause resting on quicksand. She wasn't going to risk herself, not this time. "Hasn't been long," she said. "Cord's still on the baby and placenta's attached."

"Yep. Probably just happened." Marc had read that chimp mothers usually ignored those at birth. Embarrassed that he'd forgotten, Marc was relieved he'd not asked.

Marc took an apple and more papaya out of the bucket and put it into the food tray. He signed fruit, although he didn't think Eve was watching now, and said, "Hey, Eve, here's some more fruit. Don't worry. This is Chris. She's a friend." And he made the sign for friend, and pointed at Christine, a short distance away, hoping it wasn't so much bullshit, that she wasn't going to cause Eve fear or pain. Not again. Not after what she'd been through.

Marc knew there was something very wrong in it but still he realized he was hoping that the baby was dead, and in a few minutes they'd know that for sure. Eve would abandon the little body and be spared then. She deserved to be spared.

Eve approached the food tray, the baby still suspended by a fragile-looking arm and swaying like a pendulum as Eve moved on two legs instead of knuckle walking. Chris got even closer to the glass, and Marc went over and behind her to whisper, "Let me get the lab coat." She didn't answer, but when Marc tugged at it from the back of her neckline to get it off as much out of Eve's sight as he could, she cooperated, moving her hand to take the dart gun out of her pocket as he pulled down on the shoulder.

"Don't let Eve see that!" Marc hissed and Chris half turned and said, "You put it right on top of the coat, hear me? You're responsible." Her face was hard as she handed him the dart.

Marc folded the coat roughly, stashed it behind some bales of wood wool, the tranquilizer dart set on top of it like a warning of failure.

Chris was wearing some light blue sleeveless top, but he saw she had on multicolored beads, and thought, *that'll help, that's not scary*, and for a moment he had hope—the baby had been stillborn, Eve would be all right, the whole baby-naming contest and the inane push to integrate her on Thurston's fund-raising timetable could be dropped, and it wouldn't even have to be an issue between him and Kate.

"I haven't seen the baby move," Marc said quietly to Chris. "Have you? Wouldn't she be nursing if the baby were alive?"

"Maybe. Or she's rejecting it. Or doesn't know what to do. I'm only giving this three more minutes, Marc. Could be any of those."

Eve went to the food tray and retrieved the additional fruit Marc had put through. Marc left Christine's side and went to the glass near the food tray. He asked Eve if her baby was okay. Tried the cradling motion again, which was the same as the sign for baby, though there wasn't a rewarding connection he could make for her, the way there was with fruit. He should have started this with a doll, weeks ago. *Oh god, why hadn't he thought of that?*

As he made the sign, though, Eve lifted the baby, still trailing the umbilical cord and remains of the placenta and seemed to copy him. Or she did it instinctively, putting the baby against her chest. But Marc saw two things and knew Chris saw them too: one of the baby's twiggy legs moved independently. And Eve was holding it exactly wrong, its bottom and legs against her chest, and its head under her elbow.

That was the moment it no longer mattered that Marc was the lead. He felt the difference that quickly, his role already gone as far as the vet was concerned. Nothing he said would make a difference.

"Have you called Linda and Kate?" Chris demanded. She took a rubber thing off her wrist and pulled her dark hair back into a ponytail, getting ready, Marc realized, needing to make sure nothing got in her line of sight.

Marc shook his head.

"Do it. Now. She's getting knocked down. She has no idea what she's doing. We're getting that baby out of there before she kills it. I'm calling Reagh for the baby." She shook her head. "I'm not comfortable with assessing a premature chimp birth. And while she's out, Eve can be examined, too. Just as well."

"Can we just give her a little more—"

"No," Christine said. "Absolutely not." She picked up the emergency phone and made her call. Then, pointedly, she did not wait for Marc. She asked the switchboard to page Linda, and when Linda picked up, asked Linda to get Kate. "Come, hurry," Marc heard her say. "Eve's had her baby. Yeah, it's early, or she was farther along that we thought, or both. But doesn't look like she's got a clue, and we're going to need to take it."

How long did he have now? Three minutes? Christine didn't interfere as Marc talked to Eve, signed, modeled what she should do. Still, Eve held the baby backward. To Marc, she seemed dazed, her eyes not holding their usual bright curiosity. She turned and lumbered back toward the spools. "Eve!" he called. "Stay with me, girl." But she kept going.

There was a quick knock at the door before it opened. Kate. Marc's heart went soft. She'd put on one of the wild shirts. He gestured her in. Thank you, he mouthed silently, it coming to him suddenly: *Kate won't want her knocked down, either.*

"Baby?" she said, keeping her voice quiet.

Marc pointed.

Kate approached the glass but didn't get too close. "Where?" she said.

"Behind the spools, just now."

"Shit. Not nursing?"

"Not entirely sure."

"Not nursing and holding it backward when she's not letting it hang by one arm," Christine interjected. "We're getting the baby out. I called for you and Linda because you need to get a bottle ready and warming lights. Might need an incubator, don't know. Got to assess its condition." As she was telling this to Kate, Linda came in, and Christine repeated her first sentence, which Linda hadn't heard.

Marc came into the circle of women. "I'd like to give Eve a little time to figure it out."

Kate erupted. "If she'd been integrated with the troop the way she should have been, Lolly or Jasmine would likely be already helping her. Jasmine's had experience, raised by her own mother and Loll—"

Linda put a hand on Kate's arm. "That's not going to do us any good now. We do have an obligation to make sure the baby has a chance. If she's holding it upside down or dangling it by an arm, well, she doesn't know. She wasn't with her mother enough to learn—and she never got the practice with babies that they do in the wild."

"She's really smart," Marc started. "We can show her with—" he was going to say dolls, but Linda interrupted him.

"Marc, it's not a matter of whether she's smart, it's—"

"We don't have the time." Christine butted in. "We don't know how premature the baby might be. Zoo policy is to prioritize the physical safety and well-being of any animal, and this time I have to insist we do that."

Marc got it, that she was aiming that last part at him, that she'd not knocked Eve down and done an ultrasound while she was pregnant, and now she held them both responsible.

"It will traumatize her again," Kate objected.

"Choosing between two problems, which is greater," Christine countered.

Linda closed her eyes. Technically, as primate curator, she had the final say, but nobody thought for a minute she'd overrule the zoo vet.

"Go ahead," she said to Christine. Her glasses were on top of her head, and she pulled them off and as she spoke to Marc they served as a pointer in her hand when she gestured in his direction. "You're a tech. You'll need to assist. I'm sorry." Then she added, "Kate, I'll need your help with nursery preparations."

Chris reached back and pulled her ponytail apart to tighten it without saying anything. She went over to the wood wool bales and retrieved her lab coat, put it on and slipped the tranquilizer dart back in her pocket. From her other pocket she drew a surgical mask. "My son's got a cold," she said apologizing when she saw Marc react to it. "Can't risk any human viruses."

*Well, she's getting to do what she wanted and planned from the minute she heard*, Marc thought. *Never mattered in the end what I was doing.*

"I'm going use the barred access window in the back, obviously. I want you to get her to the food tray. That way, her back will be turned. She won't see it coming. I'll shoot for the rump or the thigh."

*Maybe. Maybe. Maybe Eve won't get what's about to happen and we can recover. At least Christine is trying.*

"I'll go out now and get around to the back side," Christine said. "I'll watch through the one-way and wait for you to get her out with food before I open the covering, so she doesn't see me. I'm doing my best here, Marc."

He couldn't say anything, didn't say anything. Just nodded, picked up the food bucket and waited for her to leave. When she did, he began calling Eve and rattling the food tray, telling her fruit! Fruit! She had to be hungry. She'd not had any monkey chow that morning, nor her usual ration of fruit. More, more fruit he called, and when her head emerged above the spools, he signed to her with the words. Marc love Eve, he signed. Fruit. Friend, he signed and again, fruit. Tears rose and spilled. He put papaya in the food tray and pushed it through.

Eve emerged. The baby was clasped to her chest with both hands now. Its scrawny legs were at Eve's chin, its head down on her abdomen. *Oh my god, she's getting it, but they won't give her the time.* He didn't see the baby move, but still, she was holding it with two hands now and on her chest. She made her way toward the food tray when from behind Eve, Christine uncovered the window into the enclosure, her face masked and lab coat buttoned, dart in hand. Marc saw her, elbows on the ledge, leaning heavily to his right trying to get a shot at Eve's upper left thigh. Marc tried not to let his eyes go to Christine so he couldn't see exactly what happened. Had one arm slipped from the ledge as she leaned into the awkward angle of the aim? He only knew there was a sudden noise. If they'd thought to play the recording of Lolly's calls, Eve might not have heard it. But the enclosure had been silent as a cloud, and she did hear it, and she looked. And when she looked, she saw Christine's mask and lab coat and she knew, and she panicked.

Eve spun around and saw Marc. There was not one thing he could do to help her, and he would have done anything. Was that that shock her eyes held? Or only terror? Eve must think he'd tricked her, betrayed her. She cowered now, facing Christine as the vet aimed, too late for any plan to work. Marc knew that all Chris could do was try to hit a safe spot. Hit her. Wait for it to take effect. Deal with it all then.

✱

The eight or ten minutes after the dart hit Eve were agonizing. Part of me was furious at Marc. None of this had to happen. She could have been with the other chimps already and they would have helped. Jasmine had raised a baby, and she'd know what to do. Chimps shouldn't be raised by humans, but now it might well happen, and we'd have another whole set of problems. The part of me that loved Marc, though, oh my heart hurt seeing him swipe his cheek with the back of his hand, talking to her gently, signing, too, while she was still conscious and whimpering in pain, confusion, and, yes, probably, betrayal.

"I'm sorry, Eve, I'm so sorry. Marc sorry," he said and signed. "Marc love Eve." I realized that the sign for sorry was his closed fist rubbed in a circle over the center of his chest, as he said and did it over and over. He was trying to connect with her, and for a moment I thought he did, but then I saw how she wasn't behind her eyes anymore, not the Eve I'd seen with Marc. She was hurting, shocked, and Linda was hissing at Marc, "She needs to put the baby down."

"Marc sorry," Marc said and signed again. "Put baby down," he said and mimed rocking with his arms and then gently laying the imaginary baby he held on the floor. "Can you get me a doll?" He said over his shoulder to Linda. "Like a monkey one, from the gift shop? Anything?"

"I'll send Sandy in with something. I've got to get an incubator ready, and make sure we've got a bottle and formula waiting, the whole nine yards. Gotta talk to Chris, too."

Christine came back in then, and Linda went over to her, near the door. She blew her nest of curls back off her forehead where they'd spilled. "Chris, we've got a chimp doll, right? Anyway, we need formula mixed right away...and Dr. Reagh?"

"Yeah, I've called him," Christine said. "You want me to run and get the doll?"

"No, I'll have Sandy bring one. Need the specialist and the formula priority. I'll get on that and set up because you have to retrieve the baby. You need to stay suited up and back there ready to go in. Everyone okay?"

"You want me to go with you now?" I asked Linda.

"No, not yet. You stay here to back up Christine going in for the baby. Kate, suit up in coat, face mask and gloves. Till we know if the baby's healthy. If it is, I'll need your help in the nursery."

"Okay," Christine and I had taken it in simultaneously, and she nodded and left in a hurry, Linda right behind her.

Marc stayed at the glass, talking to Eve softly and signing. He'd picked up a kitchen towel we used to dry our hands, folded it, and now held it as if it were a baby, rocking it and then over and over mimed putting it down, trying to attract Eve's attention before she collapsed.

A few minutes later, Sandy knocked once, signaling, and came in with a stuffed monkey from the gift shop, the price tag still attached. Linda must have called, and a volunteer must have brought it to Sandy at a dead run. Marc grabbed it and to show Eve what to do, but it was too late. She started to bend over to put the baby down, I thought, but the drug was overcoming her. She swayed, and her hind legs crumpled beneath her. She went down on top of her baby.

Marc moaned, near collapse himself. I couldn't say anything. I wanted to put my arms around him and say, it's not your fault, but was that true? And there was no time. I touched his shoulder with my hand and whispered I'm sorry as I rushed out the door, diverting to pick out a clean lab coat, gloves, and face mask from a supply closet between the kitchen and the back door that would get me into the temporary enclosure.

Christine was already inside, but not approaching Eve yet. Sometimes a tranquilizing drug hasn't fully taken effect, an animal isn't unconscious and will muster the strength to attack. Chris was waiting. She held a folded white cloth that she must have brought from medical supply. I went in next to her, ready, and raised my eyebrows into a question.

She shrugged in answer, held up a finger telling me one more minute. There was no movement from under Eve, but she'd not fallen entirely on the newborn. Because its head had been upside down, it was the lower part of the body that was underneath Eve. So, if the baby was alive, it could—possibly—breathe.

From this side of the glass, I could see Marc, his head down. He used the towel that had served as a baby to wipe his face. I knew he was despairing.

Chris, ghostly looking in the whites and face mask—as I must have been, too—pointed toward Eve, and made a show of looking at her watch. Took several deep breaths herself to let me know she was trying to count Eve's respirations. Then she was ready. Motioning me forward, we advanced.

Slowly, carefully, she lifted Eve's arm. Now she started to speak very softly, hardly above a whisper, evidently feeling it was safe. "Get behind and pull her shoulder and torso. I'll try to slide the baby free."

Marc stood up and came back to the glass. I knew it was hard for him, that we were in there touching Eve, moving her, taking the baby, and he was stuck on the other side of the glass. When I moved her, I was gentle, and then—although Eve would never know—for Marc I stroked her head and patted her shoulder while Chris lifted the baby onto the clean cloth, the afterbirth and umbilical cord still attached.

Christine put her head down onto the baby in her arms. Still whispering, she said, "Breathing. Shallow. Let's go. Stay in front of me and head directly to the infirmary. Let Linda know we're on the way. Tell her the baby's alive and breathing, doesn't appear terribly underweight. I may only need warming lights. Oh, and it's a girl!"

Chris wrapped the cloth lightly around the little body, covering it entirely, and we left, moving as fast as we safely could after I called Linda. We were a third of the way there when I realized that neither of us had thought to signal Marc that the baby was alive. He had been left alone, unable to see with us blocking his view, not knowing what was going on.

As soon as we cleared the enclosure, Marc would have put on clean coveralls, shoe coverings and a face mask—to protect Eve from being exposed to a virus. Before any vet went in there to examine her, he'd be there to check her, to touch her, to comfort her unconscious body as best he could. To tell her again that he was sorry. I was sorry too. But he and I were sorry for different reasons, even though his pain hurt me too.

The baby in Chris' arms was quiet on the way, not a good sign. When we got to the infirmary, Linda had the warming lights set up and the incubator out, but it wasn't ready. "Dr. Reagh said it'll be at least ninety minutes unless you say it's emergency," she told Chris.

"I don't think it is," Chris said, laying the baby down under the warming lights and, without unwrapping her yet, checking her carotid pulse and her airway, although she was obviously breathing. Still, the vet went ahead and tried to suction the newborn's mouth. The baby started to resist that. Good, I thought. And her eyes were open, although I couldn't tell if she was seeing anything.

Chris cut the umbilical cord, tied it off, and then set it and the placenta, no longer moist and glistening like dew on a bruised rose, on a steel table to the side.

"She needs to nurse right away, doesn't she?" I whispered. I knew the answer, but I wasn't sure she did. Chris was a vet but not a primate specialist. What this baby really needed was a mother chimp. "Can I give her a bottle?"

"Yeah, let's see if she'll nurse but I need to get her weight first. We'll have to know if she's gaining. I must have been off on how far along she was. We would have known if she'd had regular ultrasounds. But…" she trailed off, implying that the keepers—

backed up by the curator—had blocked knocking her down even once for that, and it was true.

Linda was preparing formula. I pulled a couple of the smallest flannel blankets from the stack near the lights and stuck them by the baby to warm them while Chris unwrapped and examined the baby. She had a honey-colored face, heart-shaped at the top, a small flat nose, and dark ears. Her eyes, open wider now, were big, the color of expresso. She'd started to cry, high-pitched and scratchy. I draped warm blankets over my shoulders and chest just before Christine finished by putting a tiny diaper on her. "Sheesh. Where'd you get that?" I said.

Christine shrugged. "Leftover. In my file cabinet. Remember I brought Colson in every now and then when my sitter wasn't available? I kept a supply here. He outgrew the newborn size right away and I never took them home."

"Get together a list of supplies we need," Linda said.

I reached to take the baby and sat. Linda brought me a small bottle of formula and, rather than cradle the infant like a human, I tried to simulate the position in which a mother chimp would nurse. I was holding out hope that we might transition this baby to Eve soon, that she'd nurse. I was almost sure Jasmine would do a lot of nurturing, too. Human touch is confusing to chimps; we don't set boundaries effectively or in the right ways to socialize them for a troop. Chimp mothers use different vocalizations and bite to discipline when they must. I wanted to move Eve soon enough for her to have a chance to learn to mother her daughter. We didn't have a big window of time.

The baby took the nipple and sucked. Christine grinned. Only part of me was glad. This baby had a right be raised by her own species. The infant's hand felt around and grabbed the blanket over my shoulder. I wrapped my hand around hers, trying to remember what I'd seen the chimp mothers in the wild do with their babies. When I'd been in Africa, I'd believed there wasn't a detail that could ever lose its distinct edges in the haze of time, but now, I found, they had. Did a chimp mother cover her newborn's hand? Hold it like a human mother? I didn't remember. Maybe Becky or one of the others from my cohort would.

"We need a chimp shirt, right away," I said, aiming what was part request, part demand at Linda. The North Carolina Zoo had one we could borrow, I thought, and they could overnight it: a vest made of fake chimpanzee hair that fits over a keeper like a sandwich board; the baby can cling to it without hurting the keeper while she learns what a mother chimp feels like. "And let's start playing the recordings of Lolly and Jasmine in here. Oh, and make sure Eve and the others see her every day, and let's have Marc record Eve. I should have thought of that right away."

Linda caught on right away. "You're probably not being realistic," she muttered privately, leaning over and speaking into my ear. "Two steps are missing. At least."

Tears came to my eyes. I shook my head. "Not giving up," I said. "Not ready to give up."

She sighed. "Up to you."

Later I'd remember that exchange and wonder what part of my life I'd been talking about. Maybe all of them.

# Chapter 22

.

Marc didn't know what was happening in the nursery for over an hour because he'd stayed in Eve's enclosure, his regret, sadness, worry and guilt mixing in the salty stew of tears that he tried to contain as he sat next to her still body. He stroked her lightly now and then and spoke to her. He knew that if she stirred, even slightly, he had to leave, but she hadn't and so he stayed.

He wasn't sure how much time had passed—only because he'd not thought to look—when Linda came in, not to Eve's enclosure but to the keeper's area, on the other side of the glass. "Marc," she said. "Is something wrong with Eve?"

He looked up, hoped she couldn't see his eyes well though he thought she probably could. He didn't wipe them though, to avoid the tell. "Not that I know of," he said. "She's still out."

"Right. You'd best get out of there anyway."

"I was going to wait until she starts to— "

"No, I want you out now. She's going to be down a while longer." She said it in her Primate Curator tone, the one that said Don't Argue. She didn't use it often.

Marc inhaled and sighed it out through the face mask he wore. He stood up slowly, stiff from sitting on the floor with his legs bent beneath him.

When he'd come around through the hall and entered the keeper's area outside Eve's enclosure, Linda put her arm around his shoulders in a half-hug. "I know you're upset," she said. "I know you're really attached to her. I want you to take a breather now. Go home. Come back tomorrow. I don't want you working when you're this upset. You know, they pick it up. Tom and Sandy and I will take shifts, plus I'll pull a couple of the assistants to do the housekeeping stuff. Kate's with the baby right now, and she's staying during the day. I'm taking the night. Someone will look in on Eve regularly, make sure she's fed and play Lolly and Jasmine recordings. Also, Kate wants to bring the baby in for her to see—and show the baby to Lolly and Jasmine. Once Dr. Reagh has cleared the baby, everyone will mask up and pitch in with taking—"

"The baby's good? Is it a boy or girl?"

"It's a girl and based on her weight and condition, Chris thinks she didn't come all that early. She's taken a bottle, and she seems alert and healthy."

"I have to be here with Eve."

"No, you don't. Other people can take care of her today."

"But she'll think— "

"And she'll see you tomorrow and know you didn't leave her."

"Please, I will be okay." And damn if his eyes weren't filling again. It was just so wrong. All of this was so wrong. Now someone in a lab coat wearing a mask would come in with Eve's baby—isn't that what would happen? He'd seen how she cowered when she saw Chris in her enclosure dressed like that. And he wouldn't even be there to sign and talk to her?"

"No," he said. "I'm the lead, and— "

"Marc, I'll remove you from that position if..." Linda didn't finish that sentence. "Don't fight me. Your love is your great strength. Don't let it become your blind spot."

Marc started to protest, and Linda held up one hand, warning him. He closed his lips and briefly his eyes, pressed his upper and lower jaws together. Inhaled and huffed out, unnecessarily hard. Turned then, without speaking, and left the enclosure. Linda followed him out, but she didn't follow him down the hall; rather, she took scrubs out of the supply closet.

After he closed his computer in the office area, he cracked the door to look in at Eve before he left. Yes, Linda was masked and in scrubs and in Eve's enclosure checking on her. Even through his frustration, Marc recognized the kindness, and that Linda was protecting him and would protect Eve too.

When he got home, he was full of restless energy. His mother didn't seem to notice his agitation, and he didn't tell her the truth about why he was home so early, only signed, "We had our schedules changed."

Ria beamed. "We can go to see Dorothy," she signed. "More learning time for her. Shall we go? I can change quickly." She looked down at her everyday khaki slacks, and faded blouse and then back at him. "Don't worry, I won't look like this and embarrass you." Her face was bright as a child's.

It hadn't occurred to Marc to do anything but flop on the couch for a while and then maybe try to fix the screen door that wouldn't latch right. Maybe one beer. Maybe there would be a game on TV. He couldn't remember the last time the Reds had won a game, but it was the only team Marc followed and only because his grandmother—who had no connection to Cincinnati whatsoever—had been an irrationally loyal fan. But here was his mother volunteering to leave the house. Wanting—no, eager—to leave the house. Some solid barrier in her mind suddenly had a significant crack in it and daylight was sneaking in like hope. How could he say no?

But how could he say yes? Today? Kate was at work, and there was this rift between them. It was harder to hedge in sign than verbally, but Marc did his best. "Mom, Kate is at work."

"You said schedules changed."

"Not Kate's schedule. My schedule changed." Not strictly speaking true, but he'd deal with that tomorrow when his normal schedule resumed. At least she hadn't asked him to explain.

"Kate doesn't need to be there. I teach Dorothy, you teach Kate. There's no restriction on visiting hours. Dorothy knows us."

"Not really." That wasn't true. Kate's mother's face had showed she was happy to see him each time after the first.

Ria rolled her eyes. "Send Kate a message to say we are going to see her mother if you want to. I will go get ready." She signed and then, not waiting for him to agree, headed for her room.

This was a different side of his mother, one Marc had thought he wanted to see. He sighed.

# Eve

EVE WOKE SLOWLY to a sound like big cats roaring in her head. She tried to open her eyes but couldn't for a time. Bit by bit she felt the ground beneath her, hard. Her body hurt. On the other side of her eyes, she sensed light, but she lay still, confused. She tried opening them to see where she was.

Somewhere near, chimps were calling each other, pant-hoots: now she made out these sounds through a circling insect-buzz inside her head. Eve was afraid, although the chimps were not sounding an alarm. But they weren't showing themselves either. The ground under her was wet and her chest pained her, too. One muscle at a time, she risked moving. First an arm, then the other. Each leg responded. Should she try to lift her head?

She did, and though she was unsteady, if she could knuckle walk, she could find a place to hide. Her stomach wanted fruit, her mouth wanted water, but more she needed to hide because memory was making its way back to her: there'd been a pale animal with a pointed stick. Again.

That was why she was hurt.

# Chapter 23

EVEN THOUGH, WE WEREN'T supposed to use personal devices while we were at work, I kept mine on but silenced because of my mother. Staff with children did it, too. So, when Marc texted me, I felt my phone vibrate against my backside, but I couldn't reach into the pocket of my khakis because I was giving the baby—still nameless of course, Thurston's baby naming contest to be rolled out in quick high gear tomorrow—her second bottle. Dr. Reagh had examined her, said we had a fit and healthy newborn female chimp, and that while she was a "little small," he guessed she wasn't more than three weeks early, if that. Christine rolled her eyes and muttered, "Yeah, we shoulda had ultrasounds."

Dr. Reagh, bless his curly head, spoke up. He stepped away from the baby, took off his face mask, and said, "Well, no harm done. This little one is fine. Go ahead and give her more formula." Chris shut up then and took him down to Eve's enclosure to have him look at her.

I'd heard her say, "I made sure she'd be out..." as they left the nursery area and realized it meant that Chris had given Eve a heavy dose of sedative. She'd be out longer than would have been necessary just to take the baby away safely and she'd feel the effect when she woke. I hoped Marc would be there when she did. Chris was going to keep her own ass covered now, for sure, although I didn't know what that would entail.

Linda was working up a schedule for us to take shifts with the baby. We'd have to use all our assistant keepers, and she'd said we might need more help from outside the department, which would mean training them. Unless, of course, we could jump the hurdle Marc had put in the way, get Eve integrated into the troop, and see if she could raise her own daughter. We didn't know that she was rejecting the baby. Eve was young, too young. What if it had been a difficult birth and had happened right before Marc arrived? She'd had no time to figure it all out. That wasn't helpful intervention; that was harmful intrusion.

When the baby finished, her greedy sucking slowing as she gave in to sleep, I lay her down in the little plexiglass bed—knowing that what we were doing was far too like how we'd care for a human baby—and checked my phone to make sure the Sycamore's nursing home wasn't calling about Mom.

It wasn't even a call. It was a text from Marc that read,

"Baby ok? "

Had nobody told him yet? He must just want an update. But Dr. Reagh was down there right now. Marc could've asked him and Chris.

"Baby strong/fine," I texted back.

Then his next message came. "Mom wants to visit yr mother for lesson today. OK with U?"

To say it took me off guard is way understating it. I thought he was furious with me, for one.

Various responses went through my mind, ranging from a simply stated hell no, to an outright and transparent lie like my mother doesn't want to continue lessons, to the truth, I can't handle being around you. I don't want to feel the way I still do about you. I can't choose between you and doing what's best for the chimps. For Eve. I just can't.

But—my mother. Mom. That lamp that seemed to switch on and shine from someplace inside her, lighting her eyes and a smile, when Marc came. The way she seemed to enjoy his mother and to be catching on to the idea of signing. Just bypassing the whole verbal processing that had shut down. I couldn't put a stop to that.

I texted back. "OK. 6:30? Likely late here. U too?" Christine and Dr. Reagh must be in with Eve, and he'd probably slipped into a private spot for a moment.

"After lunch ok?" The words appeared on my phone screen.

I looked at my watch, and then at the clock on the wall. It was a little after eleven-thirty in the morning. "Aren't you with Eve?" My thumbs moved rapidly, and I had to backspace to correct two mistakes. I thought he meant dinner, not lunch, but I'd confirm.

"Linda sent me home."

"R U sick?"

"No."

"What the hell?"

"B back tomorrow. Ok I take Mom after lunch?"

Shit. He wasn't going to tell me. Why would Linda send the lead home today of all days? "OK"

"Thx"

And the texting ended. I was flummoxed. There was nothing to do but wait. I was on baby duty and had to stay in the nursery. Linda would come to relieve me, or she'd have the whole schedule worked out, and more likely, and someone else would show up. The chimp suit would be here tomorrow, and we'd settle into a newborn care routine.

I had to find out Marc's status. If Linda was relieving him of his lead position, maybe I could have it. I'd be the logical person. And my approach would move Eve in with the troop as soon as possible. And to get her acquainted with her baby girl.

An hour later, Linda came in with a schedule. She looked harried, her blouse coming untucked on one side of her black slacks, and some of her curls stuck, damp on her neck. "I'll relieve you here while you go get some lunch," she said. "Take the schedule with you and make sure I haven't overlooked anything. I think it'll work fine."

"I'm okay," I said. "It's warm in here and you look like you're already hot. Isn't your air conditioning working?"

"I was helping with the feeding," she said. "Gorillas." She grinned. "Reece tried to convince me it had been a month since anyone last fed them. Anyway, we're going to have to swap people around, so I wanted to free up some staff time."

"You shouldn't have to do that..." I muttered as I stood up. Then I motioned toward the sleeping baby. "She's had the second bottle and she's putting out urine. You can just sit for a few minutes. Chris said she'd be back to check her vitals. I bet she'd stay with the baby, and you could come to the lunchroom. It would be good for—"

She cut me off. "S'okay. Just bring me a Caesar salad, will you? Charge my account. I'll take it to my office when you come back."

"You sure?"

Linda stretched her legs out in front of the rocking chair. "Yes."

"Can I ask what's the deal with Marc?"

"He'll be back tomorrow."

"Yeah, he said that." She didn't volunteer anything more, and though we'd always had a close working relationship, I sensed a line I shouldn't cross. I changed course. "What's the plan with Eve now?"

"I think we'll stick to what we were doing. We need to accelerate her integration into the troop, as you were working to do, but not do it precipitously. Work it out with Marc."

"Have her see the baby, though, right? I know you think it's not realistic, but I'd like to have Eve raising her own daughter part of the goal?"

Linda sighed. Behind her, the stainless-steel vaccine refrigerator glinted under the overhead lights. She wiped her forehead with her hand. "It's a good goal. Sure, let her and the other chimps see the baby. Play their calls for the baby and for Eve. Be prepared for it to go either way. If it doesn't work, we'll have to punt."

This wasn't what I wanted to hear.

At the end of a long afternoon shift doing baby care, I checked on Eve, who was awake but still groggy. I put a yellow post it on the door to her enclosure area reminding anyone who came in to put on one of Marc's crazy bright oversized T shirts and to please not wear scrubs or a lab coat if they were within Eve's sight. He'd see that when he came in, and maybe it would mollify him. I put a T shirt on and brought in papaya.

"Eve, remember me? I'm Kate, and I am your friend. Here is some fruit." I signed the words I remembered. She appeared dazed and didn't come to the food tray to get the papaya but stayed with most of her body hunched behind the first spool. The recordings of the other chimps were playing but she didn't appear to be listening. "Tom will be around tonight," I said. "He's your friend too. I will see you tomorrow."

I sounded like Marc, for god's sake, as if I was talking to an injured human being. It made me wonder if some point of no return had already been reached. Where would this end, then?

The sun was spreading out like butter, melting its way down the western sky when I finally left the employee lot, and though I put the visor down, it still poured into my vision. I was tired, confused, and hungry. I wanted to put my feet up on my couch, microwave a dinner, have a glass of wine, and untangle my worries, but I felt I should go check on Mom. I wanted to know something about Marc having been there. How I expected to find that out, I have no idea. Traffic was bad because I was running late already. I should have just gone home, but I didn't.

It wasn't long after her supper time that I arrived, but my mother was asleep, the picture boards I'd made her propped against the walls. Some had diagrams added beneath them showing hand signs. Someone—it must have been Ria—had used a sharpie to draw them on. It seemed too early for Mom to be sleeping, so I asked at the nursing station if she was all right.

"Oh wow, she's plain wore out from the excitement," an impossibly young aide with a jaunty ponytail said. "She had friends come see her today, and they were laughing like mad in there! It was way cool."

"Good to know," I said. Good to know.

And I left. My mother wouldn't be aware I'd come. But I should be glad knowing something had made her laugh, and I supposed I was. Yes, glad was mixed in with frustrated and irritated, that irrational stew bubbling away in the August heat.

# Chapter 24

MARC HADN'T REMEMBERED that his mother could draw. She hadn't since his grandmother died, as far as he knew. When he was a child, they'd done elaborate art projects at home, drawing and painting detailed scenes to illustrate stories that Marc wrote with his grandmother. But she'd been good, able to capture perspective, expression, and mood. Those books they'd created must be still in the house somewhere.

In Dorothy's room, today, Ria had sent him to the nurse's station to ask for a marker, and he'd come back with a black Sharpie. "That's what I want," she'd signed when he showed it to her, and then added, when he sat in the extra chair, "You don't need to stay, if you want to wait somewhere else."

"You want me to leave," he signed, making it a question with his raised eyebrows and shoulders. The notion hadn't occurred to him.

"You can go," his mother said, dismissing him while Dorothy sat in her recliner, waiting, quiet as a piece of blank paper. Ria had dressed up again—she wore a bright African beaded necklace she'd never put on since he'd given it to her for Christmas three years ago. He'd ordered it online, Linda's suggestion, because it supported a small, Kenyan business that was environmentally friendly. Not only that, she'd worn her good slacks and white blouse and had done something different to her hair. And she had lipstick on.

He hesitated. He was looking at a stranger.

She put her palms up, as if to say, "Well?"

"I don't know if I should. I'm supposed to teach Kate what you teach her mother."

"Write down the pictures on these." She pointed to the boards Kate had made. "I'm going to start by teaching her these signs. Because I've got the pictures to work with. I think she already gets what this is about. After basic names, we'll see… But you can just teach Kate these signs."

Sure. Simple. If we're speaking to each other, he thought, and didn't move.

Ria jerked her thumb toward the door. Marc's eyes had gotten round, wide open with his mother's thumb gesture.

"Huh," he muttered, leaving the room, and lacking anywhere to wait on Dorothy's floor, took the elevator down to the lobby where there was a television and he discovered again that he hadn't even gnat-sized interest in daytime television, so he read the news on his phone. Every twenty minutes he took the elevator back up to Dorothy's floor and snuck down the hallway on big cat feet as if to eavesdrop, which, of course, should have been useless; there should have been nothing to hear. Except twice, he heard the treble music of women laughing.

He was so surprised, he'd turned and gone right back to the elevator.

Ria had been with Dorothy nearly two and a half hours. Marc was tired and bored in the lobby, his eyes closed, head back against the wall, legs stuck out like fallen tree trunks propped on the rigid chair.

Ria poked him, and he startled. "Let's go," she signed.

"You ready?" He was stiff, sliding his butt back underneath him and unlocking his knees. He stood.

"I'll come back tomorrow."

"What? I can't do that," Marc signed. "I have to go to work."

"Okay. After work."

Marc fell into step beside Ria as they left the building through the automatic glass doors.

He waited until they got to the car so he could turn in his seat and sign to her again. "We need to discuss this. I can't take you every day."

"Why? She is learning. I can help."

He wasn't going to explain. "That's good. Just not every day. Maybe we can work it out for once a week."

Ria's mouth set into a straight line. Right then, it didn't matter she was mute; Marc could tell from her face that she wouldn't have spoken to him anyway. She dropped her hands to her lap, always a dead giveaway she was pissed off. He sighed and started the car.

After dinner that night, he watched a baseball game, still irritated, like one of the grumpy elderly cats or dogs back in Dr. Duff's animal clinic. Only Marc was still young. But his mother was so used to having him around, she had the idea that he had no life—other than doing her bidding after work.

Now he thought again about getting another dog. Not a puppy, he couldn't expect his mother to deal with housebreaking, but what about a guide dog flunk-out? They were on the expensive side, as much as a dog from a breeder—and Marc preferred shelter rescues— but the dog would be already trained, and the temperament likely sweet and reliable. And smart. With Marc's training skills, he could teach a Lab, which was what guide dogs generally were now, to assist his mother and to watch out for her. That would give him more freedom. And even though he and Kate hadn't worked out, he needed to have a life of his own.

He was musing about this, half paying attention to the game, when his phone dinged with a text message. Kate again. "Did your mother say how it went today?"

"I guess went well. She wants to go back tomorrow. LOL"

"She was asleep! when I got there, aide said they laughed a lot. Really?"

"No idea"

"Weren't you there?"

"Mom threw me out. Waited in lobby."

"Wow. Ok, thx much for going."

"U ok with mom going back?"

"Sure. Thx again."

"News about baby or Eve."

"Both fine now. Linda says we plan together."

Marc sighed. Considered what to text back. Decided on "?" because now, Eve had been set back. He'd seen her terror. He'd need time to let her heal. She'd be around humans the rest of her life. It wasn't as simple as turning her over to the troop.

"Dunno."

"Talk in morning?"

"OK."

Restless didn't even describe it. If my mother saw me now—and could speak—she'd have said, Kate, you've got ants in your pants. Settle down.

But I couldn't. After that frustrating exchange with Marc, I had two glasses of wine and not enough dinner which gave me a headache. Then I didn't do my laundry, didn't replace the burned-out lightbulb in the kitchen, didn't pay the three bills that would be overdue if I didn't get them in the mail by Friday, didn't succeed at reading, couldn't find anything worth watching, and slept fitfully, fighting an unmoored sheet and fragmented dreams.

In the morning, my eyes were grainy. I was going to have to fight for Eve and for the baby to be with her mother, and I would have really liked to have felt at least halfway decent. I looked terrible when I would have liked to look alluring. I was still a woman, and if Eve was going to come between us, it would be satisfying to have Marc think he was missing something good.

The air was already heating up, too early. I kept the windows rolled up and put on the air conditioning, something I rarely did on the way to work in the mornings. When I was in the rainforest, I'd adapted and stopped being particularly reactive to the heat and humidity. Now I didn't want to lose any more of all I learned there, to be persuaded to see with European eyes what was "best" because it was expedient for westernized industrial societies, but today would be a steamer and just the walk from employee parking to our building would make me sticky.

Once inside, I stopped in the cafeteria for a coffee. I was going to need energy. Breathe, I reminded myself while I walked to the primate keepers' office area. Stay calm and stay strong.

"Good morning," Marc said when I went into our office.

Did he have to look so crisp, so put-together? I noticed he was wearing the blue and white checked shirt I'd told him was my favorite. A coincidence or for my benefit?

"Hi," I said, then thought to add. "Thanks again for visiting Mom yesterday." I could be nice, I thought. In case.

"Well, my mother is hot to go back. I had to tell her I just can't take her every day."

I wasn't sure how to respond to that. "Did she…think my mother was catching on?"

A slight up and back down of dark eyebrows. "Apparently."

Wasn't he just a fountain of information? I went to my desk and sat down but didn't turn on my computer. No one else was in the room yet, and I decided to find out what I could before anyone came in.

"Um, I was wondering how am I going to know what Mom knows?"

"Yeah. Mom drew diagrams on the picture board of the signs. I know some are hard to follow. You can ask on google for the ASL sign and it will take you to a video demonstration. If there's a baby sign for the word, Mom'll be teaching her that one, for sure. If your mom was ever to get beyond simple nouns, you'd have to take a class."

Oh. He wasn't planning to teach me himself. That let me know where I stood, so I plunged ahead. "I'd like to bring the baby in for Eve to see her right after feeding this morning."

"I don't think there's a problem with that. I need time to see how she reacts to me, first, though. I was just about to go to her. You're headed to the baby, right? Can you check with me in an hour, and we'll compare notes?"

"Sure," I said. I swung my legs under my desk and turned my computer on. "Linda gave me a hard copy of the revised schedule, and said she'd also email it. I don't remember her accounting for Bruce. Did she mention that to you?"

"You'll see when you get your email," he said. "She'd forgotten. He's on the revised schedule. She got some help from other departments, but he's with us some days. He's pretty good with hosing down enclosures now."

"I wish he'd clean the Lixits," I said.

"I wouldn't mind that either. Or put them back together when Lolly dismantles one because she's bored."

"Bruce is smart. Can you show him how to do that?"

"Probably. But I think he's about ready to clean an enclosure by himself. He likes messing with anything mechanical and he's precise about how he puts things away. When things get back to normal, one of us can teach him. You're right. He'd be good with the Lixit, and he'd like it."

"I hope that'll happen, that things will go back, I mean. The way they were." Maybe I meant the way we were: the anticipation that was like the aroma of something delicious coming that I'd felt with Marc that had infused excitement into time and work that was what I wanted again. Not this dull worry and dread. But I needed to get over wishing.

"I don't have him today, do I?" I typed in my password to check.

"I don't remember. I don't think so." He shook his head. "Oh, no, wait, you can't have Bruce today. You've got the baby this morning."

"Oh, right.

Except Marc was wrong. Linda had made a mistake. She'd put me with the baby this morning and also put Bruce under my supervision. "Whew." I said. "This is going to be cute."

"I'll ask Tom to relieve you. He's feeding now. Bruce can practice hosing the enclosure when Tom moves Reece and Katari outside. You go ahead to the nursery. I'll take care of it and let Linda know."

Marc slid his chair under his desk, looked at his monitor, and began to type. Then he looked back up and me, managed a smile, and said, "Don't worry, I'll follow up with Tom and make sure Bruce gets with him. You go now. Linda borrowed JoAnn Pryce from small mammals and she's been with the baby, so she's probably beat. And oh god, Thurston's big contest roll out is today. Wonder what name the public will come up with? Good thing it's not Thurston naming the poor little girl!"

Grateful that we were agreeing now, I pretended to gag on the idea of a Thurston name. "Who's judging the contest anyway?"

"No idea. We really should pay attention to this crap," Marc said, shaking his head with a laugh.

"Aren't you the lead? I can't believe you weren't informed." I let bit of sarcasm dribble into my tone, a mistake. I saw his face change as if crossed by a shadow, and the smile died.

But then he responded, and cheerfully. "Not with the baby, I'm not. Maybe she's your charge."

I didn't know if he was being generous, collegial, or shaming me for being a bitch. I had nothing to say except a weak, "Not that I know of. But you're right, I've got to report for babysitting duty. I'll check with you in an hour or so."

I felt petty and out of kilter as I went to the nursery. JoAnn, a middle-aged Asian woman with glossy hair and a hearty laugh, was rocking the baby, holding a bottle in her free hand. It looked as if she was mid-feeding. "Oh, good. Christine gave you a crash course, huh?" I said by way of greeting.

Over her face mask, Jo's eyes smiled at me. "That she did. But she forgets I've raised my own babies. This isn't very different."

"Excellent. You wanna change her diaper for me, then?"

"Sure. It won't be my first."

JoAnn is probably the best natured person on the entire zoo staff. "I'm kidding," I said. "I'm here to relieve you. Overtime's over."

"Suit up. Chris was clear about that."

"Yep. Just checking in. I actually wanted to see if the chimp shirt is here yet."

"Not yet. I heard delivery around noon by FedEx. She's trying to grab my hair."

"That'll hurt. Chris should've mentioned you could put a cap on. If you're back, it'll be better with the chimp shirt. I'll go suit up."

"Great," she said. "I really have to pee."

When I came back in scrubs, I took the baby out of JoAnn's arms. She must have been sitting for a long time. She limped for a couple of steps when she first stood. "My knees," she said. "That baby is precious, though. Almost scary how like a human baby."

"I know. I think that's why people think they can raise them as part of their families. It never works; by the time they're adolescent—sooner, really—they're way stronger than humans and when they get bored—which is often—they get destructive. One of my friends describes them as hyped-up toddlers on steroids, and yep, pretty damn accurate.

"Oh, you're preaching to the choir, honey."

"I know. Sorry. I'll get off my soapbox," I said. "I do it all the time. I get mad. The babies *are* adorable, and…okay, I won't start. Go home, dammit."

I could tell she was smiling as she moved away from me and the baby. She'd handed me the bottle before she got out of the chair herself, and now I lowered myself into the rocker, the baby in one arm. "I need to work on my abs, apparently," I said. "Sheesh."

"Do some squats, too, work those quads," she said, pulling off her mask. "Ah, I can breathe." And she was gone.

The baby was easy duty, really. She fell asleep after she finished the bottle Jo had been giving her, and I set her in the bed. I called Marc when about an hour and a quarter had passed since I'd left the primate keepers office area. Finding Tom to ask him to supervise Bruce might have put him behind with Eve.

"How's it going?" I asked.

"Not great," he said. "We lost a lot of ground. She's still hiding. I'm just now getting her to look at me. I put papaya in the food tray, talked to her, and then left the room. Then she came and got it.

"Well, that's good, right?"

"It's miles from where we were."

"Can I bring the baby down?"

"Maybe later."

"Marc, even if Eve doesn't need to see her baby, the baby needs to see her mother. To imprint, to see a chimp, not just humans, and it should be her mother." I knew my voice was rising in pitch and urgency, and I tried to slow and lower it. "Please, I think it's important."

His side of the phone was silent then. "Kate…" He sighed. "Linda said…Never mind. All right. But not until mid-afternoon. And no scrubs—you've got to wear one of the shirts. I'll have the lab sterilize a big one for you. We'll use markers to color the mask or something. If you're wearing one with the baby. We are not going to do that to Eve."

I got it. He didn't want anyone in scrubs and white mask to approach Eve again.

"Yes, yes, ok. Thank you."

How easily he stepped up to being in charge, and oh, how it frustrated me to have to step down.

It was the second time that day Marc been out maneuvered, and he was mightily annoyed. First, he'd clearly told Kate mid-afternoon. She'd showed up at one-thirty, not exactly mid-afternoon, in one of the oversized colored T shirts and wearing a brilliantly colored face mask. Marc had suggested to Tom that Bruce color one for her during the morning. Tom told him that Bruce had borrowed the brightest markers from the summer day camp that the zoo operated for elementary school kids, and he'd drawn intricate neon designs on a number of masks. That the last part—coloring multiple masks—had been Kate's idea. To make sure somebody could always bring the baby in.

Leave it to Kate, Marc thought. Her way or the highway. He felt crowded. It wasn't that he didn't want Eve to be with her baby or to be integrated with the other chimps. Of course he did. If it was possible. What he needed now was time to do repair work with her first.

He just wanted time. Time to regain Eve's trust—if he could. Time to see if she'd remember the sign he'd taught her, time to see if she'd risk using it if she did remember. Did she still trust at least one human?

Kate showed up with the baby at one thirty, and when he objected, she said she'd thought he said *this* afternoon, not *mid*afternoon. "I'm suited up, now, can we just go ahead for a couple minutes? Just see if they react to each other? It's already been over twenty-four hours."

Marc was irritated with himself for caving, but he hadn't had a good clear reason to say no. So far Eve hadn't used the sign for fruit or the one for more, though Marc had repeatedly tried both. He'd reminded her of his name and told her friend, friend, friend, in word and sign even as his eyes filled, friend, and Marc is friend. Marc love Eve. She hadn't gone back behind the spools, but she'd not come close nor responded either.

"I was thinking I should wear the chimp shirt, instead of this," Kate whispered once he'd relented about the timing, and she was in with the baby. It's underneath the shirt if you want me—"

Something else he hadn't had time to think through. He shook his head reflexively. "No, stick to the plan for now. She's not used to seeing other chimps."

"But I might be a transitional object," she argued.

"Not now."

"Maybe you could try it while the baby is sleeping—"

"I don't think so." He knew it was a good idea, and he'd circle around to it later. If the zoo had owned one, he'd have been using it from the beginning. "Okay, here's what we should do. I'll go up ahead of you with the doll and talk. You come behind me and to one side and show the baby. Let's go."

Marc picked up the doll and approached the glass. Holding the stuffed monkey to his chest, he pretended to groom it, and said, "Look Eve. Here's a baby. And see, Kate there? She's a friend, and she has *your* baby."

Kate did her part, tried to face the baby toward Eve so that she would see her mother, though neither of them knew how early their eyes focused or at what distance. Likewise, Eve wouldn't come in close although she did seem to look rather intently in their direction.

After ten minutes or so of gentle, steady encouragement to both chimps, with Marc putting papaya in the food tray and Eve not coming to get it, he said "Okay, that's enough for now."

Kate didn't argue the point then, just said, "Maybe then we can bring them together again before we leave work today?"

"Let me see if I'm getting anywhere with her."

"Yeah. We...you know we need to talk about when to bring in Lolly or Jasmine. Did you play the recordings?"

"Yes, I played the recordings. Today. Do you have them going in the nursery?"

"Marc, don't be like that. You know I do."

He was taken aback by her direct plea, and looked at her, considering an apology, but then couldn't suppress a smile. That face mask was ridiculous. "Sorry. You sort of look like a refugee from a Halloween party."

Marc saw her narrow-eyed reaction slowly relax. "Hmm. Have you looked in a mirror lately," she muttered, now mock-irritated. Her change in tone sent an ache through his chest. He wished they could pick up where they'd left off and go on together. He wished he could trust her.

Linda had given him the latitude to work with Eve all day. Marc knew it wouldn't last, that the whole business of bringing the other chimps at separate times to the outside of Eve's glass wasn't going to be avoidable anymore. The new habitat was ready, Thurston had rolled out his baby-naming contest to the public, and the Development office was whipping up autumn fund raising around it. Most zoo baby events were in the early spring, so Eve's baby was unique—and especially appealing. The photographer was chomping at the bit. Of course, it would be so much better to have pictures of the baby with her mother, so Marc was under pressure to get the job done for a different reason than Kate's. It was coming down from Thurston.

Frustrated, Marc asked Linda if Thurston even understood that Eve had arrived severely traumatized by her previous life, that she'd been set back, terrified, when Christine had come in to tranquilize her. Linda said, "Well, somewhat. That's why I'm able to buy us a little time. He's looking out for the overall well-being of the zoo, with publicity, fundraising, how many animals can we help, yadda. Ah, you know, the whole nine…" And she'd trained off with a head shake.

"Yards," Marc finished with a half-smile.

That afternoon, Marc did see progress. Eve became increasingly Eve-like. She was still quiet but came closer to the tray. He tried reading to her again, his back against the glass and holding the colored rainforest illustrations high over his shoulder so she could see them. He put apples, a banana, and papaya in her food tray along with monkey biscuits and left the room for two minutes so she'd feel comfortable advancing to get them.

The enormous triumph of the day came when he returned after that. It was a little after three o'clock then, and she'd only retreated part way back from the food tray, as if she were waiting for him. Expecting no response, Marc said, "Was that good, Eve? You like fruit." Automatically, he gave the sign for fruit. Then he said, "Do you want more?" while inflicting his voice into a question and giving the sign he'd taught her for more.

Eve made the sign for more.

"Good girl, good girl," Marc whispered. "Marc friend, Marc love Eve," he said aloud then, signing it, and "more fruit," as he signed that too, and refilled the tray.

He stayed at work late on his own time, and drove home happy, relieved, hopeful. If Linda would just get him another day to consolidate the ground he'd gained back today, maybe he could repair the damage.

The baby was another issue. The goal was to see if Eve would accept her own baby while she was still lactating, to integrate her with the troop soon enough that they could help her with raising the baby. A tall order in his view. Very tall, and damn wide, too. For Marc's part, he didn't see it happening.

He was musing about options for the baby when he got home. His mother was waiting for him in their living room. Dressed up.

Literally. In a dress. Well, a navy-blue skirt Marc didn't remember, a print blouse, long white beads, and some sort of fancy sandals with heels that he thought had been his grandmother's. And, her hair was fixed with that barrette thing, and she had makeup on. "Um, hi, you look nice," he signed.

"I'm ready to go," she signed.

"Where?" But he knew what was coming even as he signed the question. He'd told her no the previous night, hadn't he? This was just nifty. Marc could smell a pleasant cologne on her. On himself? The sweaty fatigue of the workday.

"You can take me and then come get me. Go on a date."

Marc shook his head. "No. It's too much. Not today."

Ria gestured toward the door, agitated now. "You tell me to do things outside. When I do, you say no."

"That's not true." It sounded weak, even to him. When had she wanted to go out before? "Why does it have to be Kate's mother all of a sudden?"

Her head moved back, as if she was shocked. Maybe she was, or maybe it was put on. "I want to help. You like Kate. I can help someone. What's wrong with that?"

Marc sighed, a long exhalation, and retreated to the bathroom to try to figure her angle. He didn't know if she was sincere about helping or had an agenda about his dating life. Stalling, he put cold water on his face after he flushed the toilet and washed his hands, then brushed his teeth. Did she realize that she was breaking out of her own prison, though? That she was venturing out willingly? Would she come to see that if she could do this, she could do more? Venture elsewhere in the world?

Marc came down the hall from the bathroom and back into the living room, picked up his keys from the side table where he'd laid them. "Okay, let's go," he signed.

He'd have sworn there was triumph on her face when she picked up her purse from the kitchen table.

"She might be asleep," Marc signed as he parked the car in the nursing center lot. Already the sun was down, the birds had hushed, and the crickets had taken over to call in the evening. He hadn't even had time to eat, to say nothing of how tired he was. "I'll go up with you to make sure you can stay. Not long, ok?"

"Fine."

When they got to Dorothy's room, Ria cut ahead of him and went in on her own. Before he cleared the door, he heard Kate's voice. "Oh, Ms. Lopez. How nice of you to come." She sounded surprised. Then, as Marc rounded into the door, she continued, "I was just trying to practice these signs with Mom. Automatically, Marc translated what Kate had just said. She palm-slapped herself lightly, and said, "I'm sorry, Marc. That was so dumb of me."

Kate sat in a straight chair next to her mother's recliner using own her lap as an easel for a poster board of pictures of everyday objects. Ria stood next to Kate, looking extremely pleased with herself. Now she set her purse on the floor by Mrs. McKinsey's bed as if she'd been coming to visit for years, pulled up the second chair, and plunked herself down. "Hello," she signed. "I'm glad to see you."

Marc was damned if Mrs. McKinsey didn't sign hello back, her face lit with an immediate happy smile. Marc signed hello to her, and she signed it back to him then, too.

Ria turned to Marc and signed, "You can go now. You should take Kate, too. Dorothy and I will practice alone. You show Kate. It's easier that way."

Marc put his palms up in irritation, then signed back. "What if I don't want to?"

"Easier for Kate's mother without too many people watching." She had started just using a K for Kate rather than finger spell her whole name, which Marc was finding overly familiar.

Marc looked at Kate. She was backlit because of the western window so it was hard to read her expression.

"My mother wants us to leave. She says it's easier for your mother if people aren't watching."

"Seriously?"

"Seriously."

"Um, okay." She sounded dubious, but retrieved her purse from the floor, went to her mother, kissed her, and told her she loved her and to sleep well. Then she pointed to herself and to the door. Mrs. McKinsey didn't seem at all perturbed by those indications that her daughter was leaving for the evening. She looked back right away to Marc's mother.

Marc gave his mother a stink eye from the doorway, when he was sure Mrs. McKinsey couldn't see him. He signed, "I'll be back in an hour or so to pick you up."

"Take your time," she signed back. "Have fun."

Kate had already started toward the elevator. When he caught up, she pushed the button. "What's that about?" she said.

"She did the same thing yesterday. I waited in the lobby. Remember, I told you."

"Yeah, you did."

The elevator doors swished open. "You headed home?" Kate asked. Then, without waiting for an answer, she went on as they were lowered toward the ground floor, "Listen, the least I can do with your mother helping mine is wait and bring your mother home."

"Thanks. That's really nice, but it's okay. I stayed late at work and then she was all fancied up wanting to leave the minute I walked in the door." The elevator doors swooshed open then and they walked into the deserted lobby area where two exhausted-looking people sprawled in chairs, carry-out food containers on the floor and side tables. "I'm starving, so I'll just grab something to eat and come back and get her." Then, because it was only polite, he added an afterthought. "Did you get dinner?"

"No," she said. "I came right from work. I'll find something at home."

He hesitated but went on, not wanting to be rude. "Do you want to come?"

Now they were out in the twilight. He felt as much as saw her try to see his face. "Really?"

"Sure. We can grab a beer and a burger, at least."

She laughed and mock punched his arm the way she used to. "Or a glass of wine and a salad."

"Whatever. Why don't you follow me in your car so you can go home afterward?"

"If you're sure you don't want to switch up and have me bring your mom home. I can still do that."

Wouldn't Ria just love that? Marc thought. She'd completely misread it. "No. But thanks. Think about it. She wouldn't even get why you were there, and it's not like you know the ASL to tell her— "

"Yeah, well—"

He thought she was going to bring up his not teaching her, but she nodded and said, "I see. Right."

"How about Demos Bar and Grill," he said. "You can get your wine and salad and I can get something good. With extra fries."

"Good idea, that's close. I'm parked over there," she said, pointing to the other side of the lot and veering off in that direction. Marc resisted his inclination to walk her to his car, as he'd been taught was always the right thing to do, telling himself it wasn't really night yet, though darkness was rising from the ground to overtake the light lingering above the tree line on the horizon. But then he waited in his car until he saw that she'd turned on her headlights and her car was moving.

During dinner, they'd avoided mentioning the elephant—or, more accurately, the chimpanzee named Eve—in the room, sticking to easier topics, like the baby. It started with both of them proposing appropriate names. Kate was strongly in favor of an African name, while he thought that the American public might relate better to something more familiar. "I just hope we can end up keeping her," he said. "If Eve won't mother her, we'll have to hand-raise her until she's four or five months old, right? I don't know if we have the staff to do that, or if Thurston will want to find her a surrogate mother at a bigger zoo. That twenty-four-seven care takes a lot of people."

"How are you at grooming and pant hooting? We should probably practice, in case." Kate said. "But remember, Jasmine is our ace. She's done it before."

"I know. But we just can't throw a newborn in there. Eve would have to be there." Marc immediately recognized his mistake, that he'd stumbled toward the familiar precipice. Kate would argue for getting Eve in with the other chimps right away so that if she were having trouble mothering, probably Jasmine would step in and assist her, and they wouldn't have to take the baby away again, so he excused himself to use the restroom. He'd come back and start a new topic.

But he hadn't needed to change the subject. When he returned to their table, the server had already brought their checks, and Kate had put them both on her credit card. "Thank you for bringing your mother," she said when he protested. "Really, just thank you."

They walked out of the restaurant together. Later, he'd ask himself if it was the beer, or the warmth with which she'd thanked him, or a bit of shame or embarrassment because although he hadn't acknowledged it, he had seen her point about the baby being with Eve and Jasmine—even though in his mind it would never outweigh the need to repair the damage and pain that had been inflicted on Eve.

No, he didn't know why he'd done it, and he was sure it'd been a mistake. He couldn't remember any decision he'd made more unlike his usually rational, planned-out behavior. When Kate turned around to say something before she got in her car, with no thought at all he'd leaned in and kissed her. Not a peck like someone might give a casual female friend, either, but a kiss that left him floundering, all coherent thought pulled away and lost as oversize boots in mud. Deep mud. Oh yeah, he thought later, nothing half-way about it: First a soft, easy kiss, then, like sleeping passion startled awake, a long, tongue-involved kiss. And then, as if that wasn't confusing enough, he'd taken her in his arms and they'd rested, each leaning on the comfort of the other, before they both whispered goodnight without meeting the other's eyes, gotten in their respective cars, and driven away in different directions.

As he drove to pick up his mother, Marc berated himself. "Things weren't difficult enough? Not adequately complicated?"

# Chapter 25

I COULD HAVE PULLED AWAY when Marc kissed me, and later I couldn't give myself a single good reason why I hadn't. Except that I'd missed him. But why did he do it? Did he miss me too or was it something more? Was he trying to manipulate me? Get me to back off pushing for Eve's integration with the other chimps? It was easy to see that Marc was committed to the zoo, wanting it to continue, even to grow, while I'd prefer to eliminate any perceived necessity for it, particularly for large animals that live in herds or social groups. It pained my heart to see our apes confined, gawked at, taunted or teased as every now and then I caught a visitor doing. Marc and I were oil and water in our beliefs, and we both knew that. And it wasn't as if our work was tangential to who we were, for either one of us. So, overnight, I'd warned myself into thinking the worst and in the morning, I went in loaded for bear. I was determined that Jasmine was going to be introduced to Eve that day, as well as to her baby. I'd switched my preference from Lolly to Jasmine because of the baby's birth and because I hadn't had the chance for Lolly and Eve to form a relationship first, so I figured, let's go right to Jasmine, the chimp with the mothering experience.

As I walked from the employee lot to our building, I saw the first kiosk with a poster about Eve's baby and the naming contest. A close-up photo of the baby's face, wide-eyed, irresistible. The voting had opened, a choice between four names. The primate staff had come up with three appropriately African names—Marc had inexplicably proposed Tammy, but he couldn't get the rest of us on board—and Thurston and administrative staff had picked the fourth option, Mathilde, which they apparently thought seemed both slightly familiar and slightly exotic. The public vote would determine the final decision.

Now Thurston was hot for us to give him a date when he could bring in the trustees, most of whom also happened to be significant donors, for a reception and to view the baby. "Sure, it can be through a glass," he said, brushing off the obvious objection. "That'll show them how careful we are. Linda can talk about the twenty-four-seven care a newborn chimp has to have if the mother isn't available, what the costs of that are. And Kate can show off the new habitat before the public sees it."

I resented the pressure from Thurston. Managing the animals was supposed to be up to the curators and keepers and based on the animals' well-being. But there was no getting around that Thurston's hurry-up agenda once again matched mine—for entirely different reasons. I believed it was in the best interest of the animals, and even though I was sure that wasn't Thurston's driving motivation, I wondered if that mattered. I tried to tell myself it didn't, but I felt tainted. I knew how Marc would see it, too. A sell-out.

I was going to have to be strong and let him think whatever he chose to think. Jasmine was coming in today.

But when I got to the office, there was an email waiting for me from Linda. "Come see me when you get in," it read. At least I wasn't late that day.

"On my way. Shall I bring you coffee?" I emailed, to get a time stamp on it to show that I was in the office a full minute early, because I was going to detour to the cafeteria.

"No thanks, already had too much," came the reply. There was no sign of Marc, but I noticed he'd already responded to a group email from Linda that had gone out a half-hour earlier, which meant he had arrived early. He must be in with Eve because it wasn't feeding time for the other chimps yet. I had baby duty again, but my shift with her didn't start until nine. I had other duties before then. Meeting with Linda now included on that list.

She looked tired, frazzled, rumpled as late afternoon. "Hey, what can I do to help?" I said. It was unusual for her to call me to come to her office; usually, she'd come by the group office when she had something to say, or just wait for a team meeting.

She moved her glasses from on her nose to the top of her head, and leaned forward in her chair, motioning me to sit. When I had, she said, "I've given Marc one more day to work with Eve. I'm holding Thurston off. No Jasmine or Lolly today. I want you to back him up. It's okay to bring the baby in a couple times. And go ahead and show the baby to the other chimps, especially Jasmine. Let her hear and see them, and vice versa. Just use the mesh, no glass. Wear the chimp shirt, no neon. The only thing I told Marc is he might want to try the chimp shirt when the baby is sleeping."

"May I ask—"

She interrupted. "Because he thinks he made real progress yesterday afternoon and that she was coming back from the last trauma. We have to remember the life she's going to have, for god's sake. She's going to be around humans, not living back in the rainforest. If she can heal and not be so reactive, that's a good thing, Kate. I know you have a point, but we're in this thing."

There was no arguing, I could see that. Marc had won, at least for today.

"Okay. Well, I'll get the baby ready, and after I feed her, I'll take her in to the other chimps first. Maybe Marc will be okay with my bringing her in to see Eve mid-morning. I'll check with him."

Linda's face relaxed. She must have been expecting me to give her grief. "Good. Yeah, that sounds good." She moved her glasses back down onto her face and opened a manila file. "I'm sorry I don't have time to catch up now. I've got to check the kitchen orders and get it out this morning, and I'm behind. We do not want angry, hungry gorillas."

"Definitely not," I said, and got up and out. "Hope the day gets better. Let me know if I can help."

"You are helping," she said, finally producing a smile, but I thought it looked as if she'd dragged that smile up from the bottom of the zoo's August-tired lake .

So, the rest of my day had been determined. On my way to the nursery, I passed Sandy and Bruce on their way to the gorillas both dangling a bucket of fruit from each hand.

"Hey, Sandy," I said. "I see you've got our helper today." I already knew Bruce was with Sandy, but I was trying to make him feel good.

"My name is Bruce," he said.

"Yes," she said, giving me a warning look along with the emphasis. "*Bruce* is helping me carry fruit to the gorillas."

That actually was helpful because Sandy would have fewer trips to make. Bruce was strong and willing, and the buckets were heavy. "Hey, thanks, Bruce. You do a good job."

"They eat a lot," he said in his ultra-serious way. Even in the lesser light of the hallway, his eyes were an unusual light blue, the color of some spring wildflower my mother used to show me in the woods. She'd wanted me to learn the names—was it bluebell? Blue-eyed Mary? Or damn the irony, maybe it was forget-me-not, those little blooms recalling someone once loved, now gone. I wished I'd paid attention.

"You're right they eat a lot," I said. "After you're done feeding, if you have time and you can get into clean scrubs, I can show you Eve's baby. Would you like that?"

"I don't know."

"She's very cute."

"I don't know any babies."

"That's all right. If you don't want to, you don't have to. But you don't need to be afraid."

"I am afraid. Is the baby in a cage?"

"No, she is just a tiny baby. She can't do anything on her own. You know, like a human baby can't. Maybe we can help you not be afraid."

He looked uncomfortable so I dropped it, then. "Well, have a good day. If you decide you want to see the baby, tell Sandy."

Sandy nodded at me, and I knew she would encourage him. Her ponytail was high and perky. How did she manage to both be *and* look cheerful all the time?

It went fine taking the baby in to see Jasmine. The chimps were definitely interested in her, and as best I could tell, she noticed them, as much as a two-day old baby notices anything other than its mother or the nipple of a bottle. The adults vocalized, and I thought some of the baby's small sounds might have been reactive to that.

I thought Eve showed more interest in her daughter than she had the day before. Marc had given her a monkey doll—he must have gotten another one from the gift shop—identical to the first. It was on the ground, in the wood wool. Marc was encouraged, though. He'd kept the first doll, the one he'd used right after the baby was born, and during the morning, he'd been showing Eve how to hold the doll, pretending to groom the one he held, even holding it to his chest the way she would if she were nursing. *That* was above and beyond, I told him.

"Every now and then, she gets it," he said.

"What about in between?"

He grimaced. "Drops it on its head."

This was right after lunch. The awkwardness of our initial contact in the morning—which I'd felt—was easing, and realizing that he was skipping lunch, I'd picked up a tuna sandwich and iced tea and brought it to him. "No need to do that," he'd said, but then remembered himself and thanked me. "I *am* hungry," he said, unwrapping it, taking a bite, and wiping his mouth. "Linda only gave me today, so...well, I don't want to waste any time."

"I've got an idea. How about if I try bringing the baby down when she's hungry?"

"Because...?" He gave me a look that asked if I had lost my mind.

"Because she'll cry. And Eve will hear her baby crying. Maybe her milk will let down, you know? Maybe some instinct kick in? She's only seen the baby after one of us has fed her—because we didn't want the baby unhappy. But it won't hurt her to be hungry for a little bit. We could let Eve hear her cry—then I'll feed her."

"Huh. Yeah. That's worth a try." He nodded. "Thanks. Good idea."

"I occasionally have one," I said. He was wolfing down the sandwich, so I was quiet a minute then, turning my back to let him eat, pretending to busy myself by messing with the fruit he'd brought in from the kitchen. When I heard him crumpling the sandwich paper, I moved a few steps back closer to him. "What about the chimp shirt?"

"Yeah. Wear it when you bring her. I need to wear it when the baby is sleeping this afternoon. Maybe you could run it down?" Then he was talking to me over his shoulder moving toward Eve again, his oversize T-shirt a bright turquoise with an ad in yellow and orange for a tiki bar.

"That's a good idea." I didn't tell him I knew Linda had told him he should do that. "Where in god's name did you get that shirt?"

"I have a very active social life," he said, rolling his eyes. He picked up an apple and deposited it in the food tray. Sliding it forward, he stood so she could see his hands clearly. "Eve, come see Marc. Marc loves Eve. Marc is your friend."

I wondered how many times that day he'd already said and signed his love for that chimp.

# Eve

THE PARROT-ANIMAL gave her a lot of fruit because now Eve knew what to do to get more. She heard familiar calls from somewhere near and though they were not alarms, she was still careful. But he did not come with any sticks, and his sounds were good. He put a small, soft thing where the fruit should have been, and Eve took it out and walked around with it. It did not smell like anything she knew. Her chest hurt.

Another animal came that was something like a parrot, too. Eve did not know what it was because a very small, hairy animal that cried was with the parrot, and the crying made Eve's chest wet. And she felt something strange that was not like wanting fruit, but Eve did not know what she wanted then.

# Chapter 26

MARC WAS SPENT, dragging, sloth-like moving from his car up the steps to his front door after work. The day had sucked him dry. Cicadas had already started up, like a September song. He'd hardly noticed the summer and now it was already turning its back. He sensed the first cooler evening coming on soon. What had he done with the months except for the evenings he'd spent with Kate? He wondered sometimes what life he was missing. It was a thought he'd had before when he came home from work, settling into his old man routine, eating food his mother cooked, stretching out on the couch, falling asleep early.

Tonight, yes, he might be drained, but at least he was convinced he'd squeezed the time Linda had given him for every drop of progress possible with Eve. If only, he kept thinking, if only there weren't so many if onlys, like if only he had more time to help her heal. He couldn't help how much he hated what had been done to her, the hurt and confusion imposed on her, or how he'd come to love her.

He unlocked the front door after waving wordlessly to Verna next door, lodged in her porch chair stuffing her mouth with the contents of whole bags of bright orange genetically modified crap while ironically drinking liters of diet soda. As usual. What had Verna done with her life? At what point has someone wandered onto a course that, practically speaking, won't be altered? Had he already?

In the kitchen, though, he was suddenly grateful. Something smelled delicious. A Dutch oven sat on the stove, and the oven was on, too. He went looking for his mother.

She was in the living room, watching the news on close captioned TV. "Hi," he signed. "What smells so good? I'm hungry."

"Chicken and dumplings. Remember I had you buy that whole chicken. Your grandmother's recipe."

"Ohhh. Excellent. I love that."

She nodded. Marc squinted a little to make her out better in the dim light and saw that she wore her good black slacks and a pink short-sleeved top. No jewelry, but she combed her hair nicely with a silver barrette on one side. Definitely not an outfit to cook in. Something was up. "And I also made chicken soup with the rest of it to take to Kate's mother."

"Huh? She gets her meals there."

"Yesterday she was just starting with a cold, and when I pointed to her dinner tray, she pushed it away and held her nose. She doesn't like it. Chicken soup is best for a cold."

"I am not going there again tonight." Marc signed while shaking his head to show that he had no intention of changing his mind.

"Her eyes didn't look right, and she sneezed more than once. I know when something is starting." Ria wasn't going to give up.

"No. Not tonight."

"No visit. Just soup," his mother countered.

"No."

"Then you take it tomorrow morning before work. Ask them to give it to her warm, lunch and dinner. Say please. Or we take it tonight. And you take me to visit on your day off."

"Mom, you are a piece of work," Marc signed. "How about you get a driver's license and a car and start taking yourself."

He'd said it in frustration, to get her to back off, never expecting what came next. Not then, not ever. Not after his whole life's experience with her.

"I think I should do that," she signed. "I don't like you telling me what I can do."

His mother's new companion, Barbara, the one that was her age, had started, and he wondered exactly what they talked about. She had stellar references, though, he knew that much.

"Look in on her for me," Ria instructed Marc in the morning. She'd gotten up, heated some of the soup in case Dorothy hadn't eaten breakfast "because it made her hold her nose," and packaged four meals of it, labeled Dorothy McKinsey on the Tupperware lid in black marker, and the instruction "Heat in microwave two and a half minutes. Homemade chicken soup from her friend Honoria Lopez." Then she signed, "Show Dorothy what you've brought so she'll know it's from me. She likes you. Could you quick go over some signs with her? I can go with you if you can just bring me home before you go to work?"

"It's already out of my way, Mom. I don't have time." Marc was irritated. He'd already have to call in that he'd be twenty minutes late, more if he hit traffic. As it was, he was leaving the house forty-five minutes early.

He did it though. Took the damn soup, as he referred to it on the way there, but he had to admit, it turned out to be a good thing he did, because the charge nurse was there. He stopped at the nursing station to make sure they would be willing to heat up the soup before he left the extra containers, which she said they'd be happy to do, and then she asked him if there was a chance that his mother might be available to visit with deaf residents and nursing home patients who were lonely and needed a visitor. They could find money in the budget for a small stipend if she were interested in something just part time. They had no one on staff who knew American Sign Language, and they thought an older person such as Marc's mother could relate to their clientele. Aides had noted that Ms. Lopez had gotten Dorothy laughing for the first time.

Marc said he'd discuss it with her. He didn't mention that she didn't drive and hadn't been willing to even leave the house until she'd visited Dorothy. He took the warm container of soup to Kate's mother, who was still in bed, and damn if his own mother hadn't guessed right: her breakfast tray was still in the room, a bowl of congealed oatmeal appearing untouched, along with toast and half a cup of black coffee. He signed hello and opened the one container that Ria had wrapped in kitchen towels to keep it hot.

He pretended to sneeze, pulled a tissue from the box by her bed, wiped his nose and eyes. Then he motioned to her and to the soup, pretended to sneeze again. He saw the understanding bloom on her face. The rich aroma of the soup floated up and out.

Dorothy tried to raise herself up to a sitting position in the bed. Marc, seeing that she was struggling, leaned in to lift and scoot her more upright. Then, bending close, he reached behind her, supporting her back with one hand while he propped the pillows against the headboard. Then he took her oatmeal tray off the bedside table her meals were served on and wheeled the warm soup and the toast from breakfast in to where she could reach it. With a smile, he handed her the spoon.

Mrs. McKinsey lifted the container and breathed in the scent. She looked at Marc and smiled, put it down and signed *hello*. Hello. Marc thought she's trying to say thank you, but those are words. Gratitude is a feeling we've attached words to. What happens when we don't have words?

He bent in again, this time to kiss her check gently. Hello, he signed back. And then he had to leave.

Being late hadn't helped. Kate was way ahead of him—she must have come in early. *It's not a competition*, he reminded himself. But when he saw her in Eve's area with the baby in her arms, and right up near the glass—wearing the chimp shirt again, no less, and one of the ridiculous parrot-colored face masks—he couldn't suppress the feeling that she was trying to get the jump on him today. Seeing that she'd brought in a bucket of papaya even though she knew that he'd been making a point of being Eve's primary food source had the effect of highlighting the feeling with a bright yellow marker.

When she heard him come in behind her, Kate turned and chirped, "Good morning," with too much enthusiasm for Marc. "Guess what? I think Eve recognized the baby."

"What did she do?" Intrigued despite himself.

"Well, she advanced a couple of feet toward us, for one, and sort of stared. Didn't exactly call, but sort of did, and baby looked back at her."

"Huh."

"Come on, that's a lot."

"Maybe." He was pissed off he hadn't seen it so he could judge for himself. "Hey, you know your mom's sick, right?"

"She might have been starting…Wait. What are you talking about? How do you…?"

"That's why I'm late. My mother made her soup and made me take it over to her before I came to work. Not exactly on the way here, obviously. She says your mother doesn't like the food there. She was pretty happy to get that soup." From the door, Marc went to the back of the area where he'd stashed extra monkey biscuits. He wanted something to give Eve when he greeted her. Not exactly Eve's favorite, but Kate had commandeered the papaya.

Kate's eyebrows had gone up, her eyes widened. Off guard now.

"She didn't seem like she was sick when…and they haven't called me."

"My mom got a bead on it, anyway, and noticed she wasn't eating much of their food. I could see that when I got there this morning." Saying it felt a little like revenge, even if the satisfaction of evening the score was lightly threaded with shame. Still, he hoped she'd tell Linda she had to leave, that her mother was sick. It would give him one more day, and he hadn't said anything that wasn't true.

When she didn't say anything about that, the hope was too strong to abandon. "I think she might be running a fever, actually," he said. "I had a chance to feel her face when I lifted her so she could eat some soup. She was just lying in bed, and she'd ignored her breakfast," he said, picking up some monkey biscuits and advancing toward Kate who was by the feeding tray with the baby. "Eve..." Marc started to call.

Kate's eyes narrowed, worried and more upset. "Marc. Stop. I need you to back up right now. Like ten feet. Do it. Back up." Her voice was urgent, so he did. "Now, before anything else, I need you to go out to the supply closet, right now, and get a face mask. Put it on, and don't come back in without it. And, even if you've already done it, after you put it on, scrub your hands for a minimum of thirty seconds, before you come back in."

"Jesus, Kate, I'm not sick, your mother is, and I haven't touched the baby or been near enough to breathe on her."

"I don't give a rat's ass, this is my watch and unless you've bathed in an antiviral and wear a mask, I don't want you anywhere near this baby." She'd suddenly adopted a boss voice. Marc heard it through her mask but realized he didn't need to hear anything. It was all in her eyes and brows. As much as he'd thought he knew her face, he hadn't gotten before how mobile and expressive those were, which he saw was the real distinction of her greenish eyes, heavy lashes and curved brows, those much darker than her hair. But now, when they were all he had to go on, he'd have gotten the message without a word.

Of course, she was right. He knew it, and Marc's usual way of responding to his own mistakes was to own up, apologize and immediately do whatever he could to fix it. What was called for was to tell her she was right and do what she said. But she'd already overstepped. He was the lead with Eve, and here she was, hadn't even checked with him.

"Aren't you overreacting just a bit here?" He let his eyes go toward the ceiling to show annoyance even while he kept his tone light.

"You know better, Marc."

Indeed. He did. The vulnerability of great apes to human viruses is frightening to curators and keepers.

"Fine. Have it your way. Again." As he said it, his tone bitter, he walked around her, giving a deliberately wide berth, and went to the door. He'd not connected with Eve, but it was too late now.

"What's that supposed to mean?"

He didn't look back as he answered. "Exactly what it sounds like." He let the door close on his frustration.

With no idea what to do with himself right then, he started toward the cafeteria and then abruptly reversed. It was feeding time. He could help with the other chimps and then, if Kate pulled another fast one and tried to bring in Jasmine without his help, or even his knowledge, he could intervene. Did nobody get what he'd been doing all this time? That it was important?

It took him most of the morning to calm down. When he replayed it in his mind the first couple of times, he got himself into a snit of righteousness. Bruce was with Tom, helping with flushing the water lines, bringing in fresh bedding material while the chimps were outside, and Tom had a relaxed way with Bruce. "Sandy showed me the baby chimpanzee," he heard Bruce announce at one point.

"So, did you like the baby?" Tom said as he opened a bale of wood wool. Marc moved closer as he spread his own supply so he could hear the answer.

"She introduced us. The baby doesn't have a name. My name is Bruce. I wasn't scared because it's a baby. I'm scared of the big ones. They're not in here now."

"That's good you weren't scared."

"I scared the baby."

"Oh? How did you scare the baby?"

"I had on a mask. Masks are scary."

Tom chuckled his easy baritone. "Everyone has to wear a mask around the baby, right? It's so she doesn't get sick."

Bruce gave a solemn nod. "So she doesn't get sick."

Marc wanted to back Tom up. "Sounds like you did a good job, Bruce."

"I did a good job," Bruce repeated, and nodded again.

"He's been great, really helping out," Tom said, and Marc checked Tom's face looking for another message to him that Bruce wouldn't decode, but there was none.

Damn. A cloud of shame and embarrassment again edged into the bright indignation he'd worked up. Marc did not want to wonder if or why he'd been an ass with Kate. He shook his head to dismiss the thought. "Want me to do the Lixit?" he said to Tom. Cleaning that required concentration.

He was in the middle of the job when his cell phone dinged. He pulled it from his back pocket. A text from Kate, who showed that she wasn't above breaking rules herself by texting.   Where r you? Can we pls try a glimpse of Jasmine?

He sighed. Didn't respond immediately.

Finishing the Lixit as quickly as he responsibly could, Marc went back to Eve's area, mentally cleaning up his act on the way. Outside the door, he pulled on one of the oversize bright T-shirts over the coveralls he'd worn helping in the indoor chimp enclosure and looked in, holding one of the masks in case she was in there with the baby again. But luck was with him; no Kate, no baby. A bit of time with Eve. He ducked back out and went to the kitchen for fruit.

"Hello Eve," he said, and put down the pail so he could sign. "Eve want fruit?"

The chimp made the sign for fruit. Marc grinned at her, put an apple and some papaya in the tray, pushed it through to her and waited. She approached and took it. This time she didn't retreat. "Oh good girl, good friend Eve," he signed.

Eve made the sign for more. "You want more fruit?" Marc signed as he spoke, and Eve made the sign for more again. She understood, he was sure. "Yes," Marc signed. "More." After he gave it to her, he tried something else. He cradled his arms around empty air and said, "Eve, where is your baby?"

He was sure of it: Eve looked at the door. It was where she'd last seen her baby, that morning, in Kate's arms. Then she looked around her enclosure, and he watched her locate the doll with her eyes, but she didn't go get it. She seemed confused then.

They were all signs she didn't know. Yet. Still, Marc tried. "That's right. That's a toy baby," he said, pointing, and signing the word toy, which Eve did know. Then he pointed to the door. "Friend Kate has your baby. She'll bring her back."

As smart as Eve was, how much of that could she grasp?

Now, he couldn't shove aside the shame. Here was this beautiful animal to whom so much harm had been done, and here she was trying, risking herself again and again. Had he really needed to be petty ass with Kate because she'd skipped over that he was taking care of her mother this morning? And Ria had made him, so did it even count?

He took out his phone and texted Kate. Might as well go for broke. "Let's do it. Jasmine. I'm here to help."

# Chapter 27

THE PERSON I WOULD have told before this morning was Marc. The nursing center called me right before lunch to say that my mother was running a fever. Do I need to come, I asked right away, and the head nurse said no, they were just notifying me. Marc had been right. I was worried. I wanted to tell him how torn I was. I needed to be at work to take care of the baby and to introduce Eve to Jasmine—we had so little time left before a door would close and the baby would have no chance to be raised by her own mother. But there was this, too: despite what the nurse said, would a good daughter, an attentive one, leave work and go to check her mother personally? It's not as if she can tell the staff how she feels. How had Ms. Lopez realized she was sick when I hadn't? I wished I could ask Marc's advice.

This morning, though, he'd been cold. Or angry. I wasn't sure, but neither made sense to me. I thought he'd be so pleased that Eve had seemed interested in her baby, but he wasn't. I considered discussing it with Linda, but she was meeting with the development office and Thurston—probably trying to hold back the tsunami of pressure to move the chimps into the new habitat—and the last thing Linda needed was the hint of a delay while I took an afternoon off. She needed to be able to report concrete progress. Administrators and the Board were salivating over the fundraising opportunity.

I'd finally texted Marc about Jasmine, keeping it brief and careful. He didn't answer. It would be a mess to proceed without him, but I was getting ready to call in the department's senior staff to help me because it had to happen today. I fed the baby a bottle and turned the chimp shirt over to Christine, who put it on over her white lab coat and pants, wanting a turn with the baby. "I'm not wearing one of Bruce's masks, though," she said.

"Baby won't think you're as pretty as me," I teased.

"Or as crazy," she said, looking at me askance as she sat in the rocker with the baby, who was still awake but ready for a nap.

I shrugged at the exact moment my phone dinged signaling a text. Chris raised her eyebrows, silently asking why my phone was on. "My mother…" I said, hoping it wasn't the nursing home.

She nodded. "Gotcha."

It wasn't. It was Marc, ready to bring Jasmine in to see Eve, his tone was entirely different.

"Meet you at Eve's in 5," I texted back and then said to Chris, "Well, if you don't need me here, I'm going to go help out with Eve. It's introduce Jasmine day."

"Your mother okay?"

"Yeah. Just—well, probably a cold."

A concerned look. "Be vigilant about the protocols, huh?"

I nodded. "No worries. I'm aware."

"Good." And Christine turned her gaze on the baby whose eyes were now at half-mast as she lay in Chris's arms. Chris's own eyes softened into a smile, then. "Good luck with Jasmine. I hope this little one has a name and her mama soon. She's such a sweetheart, isn't she?" There were dust motes in the light around them, a shaft of afternoon sun from the far window, wonder dust, I used to call it when I was a child believed it meant there really was magic. At that moment, Christine and the baby looked like they could be from a story that would have a happy ending, like an unspoiled Eden, and I wanted it to be so. I willed it to be so.

"That she is. They're good, you know? The chimps are just good souls."

It had only taken me, Tom, and Marc—all of us in the neon-bright shirts, Tom good-naturedly going along although he commented that Jasmine was going to think we'd all been smoking crack and want some—to isolate her while the other chimps were outside. "She's a sucker for both apples and monkey biscuits," he said, "so I put them together, like this, see, and use it as a lure—"

We got her to the other side of Eve's isolation unit. Marc had started the recording of the chimps calling to each other, and Jasmine's pant-hoot was distinctive. She heard herself and reacted wonderfully, by laughing. Tom had put a new red ball that he knew Jasmine loved—because she'd destroyed several of them—in there too, so she'd be excited to enter. She went in happily.

Marc hurried around and went in to be with Eve, on the side of the glass where she was used to seeing him. The rest of us stayed out of sight initially, watching Jasmine through the window in the door to her side of the enclosure. I could barely see Marc, but I knew he'd be talking to Eve, encouraging her. From what I saw, either it worked, or it wasn't necessary. Eve wasn't scared this time, she was curious. Jasmine called to her and Eve—yes, she called back. She went up to the glass on her side and called back. Right after that, Jasmine got busy playing with the ball, which was predictable, but she'd looked at Eve easily. No big deal.

"Do we dare slide the glass back and just have the metal screen between them now?" I said to Tom, "What do you think?"

"Geez. That would be your call. Or Linda's. I dunno."

"It's not introduction protocol. Okay. I think we'll go for that tomorrow. Make sure the recording is off, so all they can hear is each other."

"Do you believe how well that went?' I said to Marc later. "I feel sort of high. Everything's been such a mess, I can't believe something was that good. I mean, Jasmine was great, really relaxed, and Eve was just curious. I didn't see any fear, she went right up to the glass."

I was pulling off the brilliant turquoise T shirt I had on over my normal work clothes—today tan slacks and a black top with gold jewelry—and wasn't looking at his face as I was pouring my enthusiasm on him like maple syrup. I realized what I was doing and cut myself off abruptly. The shirt had caught in my ponytail anyway. I extricated myself from the cloth and changed course. "Sorry, I didn't mean to go on and on…what did you think?"

"You're right, they did great," he said. His smile looked sincere.

"You mean that? I know you wanted more time."

"Yeah, I did want more time, but that doesn't mean it didn't go surprisingly well. I'm relieved." His face looked tired to me, and he had some five o'clock shadow, although it was only four; I'd not seen that start much before six.

I searched for eye contact. "Marc, thank you so much for taking my mother that soup. Please tell your mom how grateful I am. And please tell her she was right. And you were right, too. The nursing home called me before lunch to tell me that she was running a fever."

"Oh shit," he said, closing his eyes. "Damn," he added, exhaling into a slump. He looked so disheartened I didn't know what to say. It wasn't his fault.

"I'm going over now."

"Want me to—"

"No, you've done enough today. But thank you so much."

"My mother will want to visit."

"It's really kind of her. Let me get the lay of the land first."

"Yeah, okay. Listen. You were right about the mask and the scrub down. I'm sorry."

"Oh Marc, it's okay, don't worry about it."

He put on a wan smile, like something wilted. He felt bad, I could tell. We were in the hall, outside of Eve's area, not someplace I could touch him. I wanted to at least put my arms around him, a quick it's okay hug, but neither of us needed the rumor that might start if some random staff happened to see me do it. Whatever had gotten into him this morning seemed to have passed, though I'd seen another side of him, one that wasn't as reasonable as the Marc I'd thought I knew.

When I finished at work, I decided to go straight to the nursing center. I was still pumped from our success with bringing Jasmine in, excited about sliding the glass away tomorrow—that would let them have contact through the wide-holed metal screen, smell and touch each other. It was the standard protocol for introducing a new chimp to a troop at the zoo. What it meant was the beginning of Eve being treated like the others.

The new habitat was naturalized, the closest I could come with the budget I'd been given to providing a normal life for these beautiful, intelligent relatives of ours, one that would give them a modicum of dignity and privacy—and even something akin to making their own decisions. It didn't make it right to lock them up and it certainly wasn't as good as their home in a western African rainforest, but it was an improvement over a cage. So, as I said, I was feeling good.

I sang with the radio as I drove, window open for the early twilight air. Already the sun was setting earlier, and the summer flowers looked bedraggled here and there as if they were growing tired, getting ready to hand off being colorful to chrysanthemums, pumpkins, and scarlet maples. I wasn't ready for summer to end. Was there still time to get away for a weekend, maybe a lakeside cottage where there'd be hiking, maybe with Marc? I decided I'd call to suggest it when I got home from visiting Mom. We could do it soon, when Mom got over her cold—he'd need time to arrange helpers to be with and spend a couple of nights with his mother anyway.

The upbeat feeling didn't last, and I never did bring it up to Marc, though I did call him when I got home. To tell him.

When I got to Mom's floor, I asked at the nurse's station for a mask and scrubs, because of the baby. There was an LPN on duty, and she looked startled. "Oh, certainly, ma'am," she said. "I didn't think you knew. Did Charlotte reach you this evening?" She spoke with a Southern accent, but I couldn't place it better than that.

"Know what?" I said. "That my mom has a cold?"

Her ID badge, pinned to navy scrubs, said her name was Doreen, and Doreen looked really confused then. "About Mrs. McKinsey... Um, why'd you ask for the mask and scrubs?"

She wore glasses with rhinestones set into the temples that she shoved up the bridge of her nose with a neon pink forefinger. I wondered if she'd gotten the glasses to go with the rhinestone cross that hung from a silver chain below the hollow of her throat. Doreen didn't know it, but she should've been glad that Mom couldn't talk because there were few fashion statements my mother hated more than rhinestones.

I tried to focus. "I work in a zoo, and we have a ... no, wait. What's going on with my mother?"

"I'm real sorry. Charlotte meant to call you before she left. Your mother has a fever, and—"

"Yes, I know that. She called me before lunch."

"Yuh. This morning it was just under a hundred, but this afternoon it spiked up. Not like a simple upper respiratory infection. You know, see, that's a cold. We're watching her real carefully, and the doctor will be in to see her in the morning."

"I know what a URI is," I said, irritated by her condescension but really angry about something else entirely. "I don't understand why I wasn't called when her fever went up."

"Um, I don't know about that," she drawled. I tried to breathe normally, check my temper. None of this was her fault.

"May I see her chart please?"

Doreen got a look of consternation. "Uh, well, I'd have to get, I mean, I'm not sure—"

I cut her off. "She can't communicate how she's feeling as you might be aware. I'm her power of attorney legally and for all health care. Copies are with her chart. You'll also find the HIPAA forms signed by the court when I was designated her guardian. I have the same right to see it that she would have if she were able to process words, which she is not." Now I put a significant pause between each word and used the voice that I'd mastered when I used to be a supervisor. "Let. Me. See. Her. Chart."

Doreen's eyes widened a bit, and her head went back on the stem of her neck. Good, I thought.

Without saying anything, the nurse turned to her computer and typed. When the screen changed, she silently pointed at it, and said, "Here you go," without inviting me to come around the desk and enter the nursing station where I'd be able to read it. She possibly figured I'd do it without that courtesy. She was correct.

"Holy shit." Yes, I said it out loud when I scrolled down to vital signs. My mother's temperature had been 103.6 at three o'clock that afternoon. They'd given her acetaminophen, called the physician and requested that she be seen. Mom had been served dinner but hadn't eaten it. There was no mention in the chart of the soup from Ms. Lopez in the notes. "Was my mother given the chicken soup that her friend sent in early this morning?" I asked a couple of minutes later, letting my voice have an edge. "I don't see any reference."

"Uh, I wouldn't be sure, um, maybe."

"Let's go check the refrigerator."

Of course, it was all still there, neatly labeled. "So, my mother hasn't eaten all day, except the soup a friend brought her this morning. When there was food she would have eaten right here, labeled, and he was told it would be heated and given to her. Where's the microwave?" I pulled one of the containers of soup out as I spoke. Doreen pointed, mouth clamped. I'd been too worked up to notice the microwave on the counter, two feet away from the refrigerator.

"I'll be reporting this to the director tomorrow," I said as I put the soup in to heat. "If you'd be kind enough to find me a spoon, I'll take it from here."

"I'm sorry, ma'am. Sometimes we get busy, and something doesn't get into the chart unless it's vital. We missed gettin' that soup from her friend in the notes."

"And missed calling me about her fever."

"But you were called." Beginning to get her back up, I could tell but I didn't care. Her hair was bleached, an unlikely icy champagne. I added the shade to Doreen's rhinestones in the catalog of what must drive my mother silently crazy.

"Not when it spiked," I shot back.

"Oh. Right. We'll do better."

"Good. I'll appreciate that. Now, if you would please get me a mask and scrubs? I work in the Dayton Zoo and am handling a newborn chimp who has no immunities to human viruses." I tacked on the thanks and an explanation because I'd already given her a hard time. I didn't want her taking it out on my mother.

I took the heated soup and the spoon Doreen gave me to my mother's room after I suited up in the kitchen. She was in bed, lying flat, covered with a single sheet. "It's me, Mom. Don't be scared by the mask, I have to wear it because of the apes, you know." Of course, she didn't know. She couldn't understand a thing, but she could still get a warm reassuring tone of voice. I smiled, put the soup on her bed tray, thought to sign hello, and smoothed her forehead. Despite the acetaminophen, her skin was warm enough to frighten me.

I pulled up a chair and sat, took the lid off and showed Mom the soup, brought it close enough so she could smell it. I raised my brows into a question above the mask, mined eating it. She gave a wan smile and a hint of a nod. Oh bless Ms. Lopez, I thought. Bless her for seeing what I hadn't.

I raised Mom's bed, but she still needed to be scooted up and her pillows adjusted. I did the best I could, remembering that Marc had said he'd lifted her. I needed not to have my face right next to hers, so I used the call button to ask for help. If I wanted to be fair, I'd have to admit Doreen was quick to respond and thank her for that on the way out. I sponged Mom's face and neck with a cool cloth when she was upright.

Mom ate the soup, almost all of it, and drank some water. When I got ready to leave, I left a note myself: I wanted to talk with the doctor after she was seen in the morning. I wanted to know exactly what was wrong, and whatever my mother needed, I'd make sure she got it. And I should remind them regularly to please, please, give her soup. There were two more servings in the refrigerator, and I'd make more myself.

I scrubbed my hands, shed the mask and scrubs, and made myself stop to say a sincere thank you to Doreen. Back when my mother had words, she used to say, "Be kind, Katie. You don't know what other people might be dealing with. And besides, you catch more flies with honey than vinegar." Even if I couldn't recall wildflower names she'd wanted me to learn, I'd retained some of her words…and I didn't wear rhinestones, either. That would please her.

It was already past dark, and Marc was stretched out on the couch after dinner when Kate called him from a grocery store. "Can you read me your mother's recipe for that soup?" she said. He figured out she was in the store from the background noise.

"She needs more?" He hedged. "Mom doesn't use recipes that I know of. She just...knows. What's going on?"

"Too much, too much. Mom spiked a high fever this afternoon, they didn't give her the soup, I got there after work and gave her a container full, the doctor's coming in the morning. If you can't give me the recipe, I don't know what to do. I don't know how—"

She'd spoken at a high clip, but he'd gotten the gist of it. "Whoa. Slow down. I'll ask Mom to make more. She can vary it, too."

"Marc, I can't ask—"

"You're not. She'll want to. And she'll want to visit. Besides, there's something I haven't had a chance to tell you, it's really good. So...does she have anything left now? You said they didn't give it to her?"

"Right, she's got two containers of it in their refrigerator. If they manage to—"

"Okay, I'll talk to Mom, and I bet we can get food over to her tomorrow evening. How's that?" He glanced at Ria, who sat across from him in the living room. She knew he was on his cell and was looking mildly curious. Often that annoyed him, a grown man questioned by his mother about who he was talking to and about what. This time, though he wished it had occurred to him to use the speaker and translate the conversation as it happened. Well, he'd explain as soon as he hung up. "Do you need to take tomorrow off?" He hesitated to ask, knowing it would be a problem, but on the other hand, this would be considered an emergency.

"I don't think so. I just need to be able to answer the phone. I'll come in early, we'll start with bringing Jasmine in, if that's okay. I'll get my shifts with the baby covered and be available to get to the nursing center if I need to. The doctor is supposed to call me. They can't tell me when the doctor will show up anyway. I don't think I need to—" Her voice faltered, her inflection hinting at a question.

"That sounds just fine," Marc said, not that he had any idea if it was or wasn't. "Try not to worry. Get some sleep, okay? Knowing you, the fear of god is in them now. They'll call you if—I mean, they'll call you now."

"Pffft. I'll be calling them on the hour for a while. Not sure I trust them," she said.

That couldn't be good. "Hey, I'm really glad you called." Should he say I love you? Too much maybe, though the thought was there. Something else, like I'll be thinking of you?

"Good night," she said, filling the space. "And thank you so much. Sleep well. I'll see you in the morning."

"You too. Sleep well, I mean. Good night."

The question was on his mother's face. Marc took a breath and signed the story. She'd been right. Kate said her mother was worse, that it seemed to be more than a cold, maybe Ria wouldn't mind making some more soup?

He'd known how she would respond. Ria loved to be needed. She was signing yes and that he had to take her over, too, while she got up and went to check the refrigerator and cabinet. Marc sighed. He could guess exactly what was coming next, could practically count down how long it would be before she came back from the kitchen with the list of ingredients she wanted him to go get. Now. And it didn't matter that he'd like to relax.

Odd how a stranger, a woman who'd lost her words, could elicit a whole different side of his mother. How long had he wanted her to have her own life so he could have his? This halfway business, though, it was damned inconvenient. He could ask Barbara, Ria's new companion, to shop on her way tomorrow, this one time. Marc signed the idea as a question to Ria, who quickly shot it down. The soup had to simmer for hours. And hours. No, she must have the groceries tonight, not tomorrow.

Of course, he went. Brought back the chicken, brown rice, yellow onion, carrots, and celery, bok choy, fresh greens. Ria had garlic, and peas in the freezer, she said.

"Practically all the way there," Marc signed, but sarcasm

gets lost in sign sometimes, and Ria smiled and answered that yes, she had everything now. "I need to get to work," he told her preemptively. "She has two servings left, Kate told me. I'll take you over after work. I can't go before work again."

"Why does she have two servings? That should be gone."

"I don't know. I wasn't there. I had to go to work, remember?" Calm down, he admonished himself. She doesn't know what it is to hold a job. He needed to tell her that the nursing home might be interested in hiring her part time. He hadn't yet. There were so many hurdles between here and there. And he'd have to get her over each of them. Taking her to driver's ed. Taking her for the test. Helping her buy a car. Taking her for the interview so he could interpret. Making sure she could go places alone. Maybe it was easier to leave it all the way it was? Then he couldn't believe he had that thought after wishing she were independent for as long as he could remember.

He excused himself and went to bed. The rich cooking scent made its way through the house to his bedroom late into the night. Ria believed in bone broth, too, and she'd simmer it for hours. By tomorrow mid-afternoon, the soup would be thick with diced chicken, vegetables, rice, chopped fresh greens, possibly a few white beans, and the broth seasoned so well that a teaspoon more or less of anything would be wrong. That was the thing about soup, Ria said once. Everything must be carefully balanced, or it all goes wrong, all wrong. That's what he was afraid of—the sudden fragility of balance, the shifting odds of success.

In the morning. Marc left for work early and Ria was still asleep, which was unusual for his mother. It was a relief; he'd thought she might start in on him to take the soup over before work and he didn't want to argue.

The sky was holding a grudge, threatening and dark, and Marc thought how much easier it would be to separate Jasmine if the chimps could be outside, but if an electrical storm was on the way, there was no chance of that. Normally, Marc was all over the weather forecast, but he'd missed it last night, and it had been chance-of-this and chance-of-that predictions the day before yesterday. None he could sink his teeth into and believe in. There hadn't been much of that lately, weather or otherwise.

He was nervous about sliding the glass between Eve and Jasmine away, leaving only the wide-holed metal mesh between them. Of course, Jasmine couldn't harm Eve, not physically, but she could act like an alpha female, frighten Eve—and how would Eve even know what Jasmine's behavior meant, know how to respond, know she didn't need to be terrified? Eve's emergence, her trust, was fragile, wasn't it?

He had to remind himself to exhale, to be calm when he was on Eve's side while from Jasmine's side, Ben, one of the maintenance staff who was both genial and burly, slid the glass wall back from the screening. This time, they didn't give Jasmine the red ball, wanting her undistracted, though they used apples and monkey biscuits to encourage her into the separation area. She went to the screen, again inquisitive, not appearing threatened or aggressive—not that aggression would have been in Jasmine's character even though she was the dominant female, and if Eve's baby hadn't surprised them by showing up, their first choice for introductions had always been the exceptionally easy-going Lolly. But now, here was Jasmine doing them proud, pant-hooting a greeting, and Eve cautiously answering, approaching the screen staying low, knowing somehow that she needed to appear submissive, but not retreating to hide. Had he underestimated her resilience all along?

They could, this time smell as well as see and hear each other, a significant difference.

It had been huge, the kind of triumph Linda, he, and Kate—with Sandy or Tom, whoever was available from the department—might have gone out for a beer to celebrate, because it meant they'd do it a few more times, too, when they introduced Lolly, and then moved them all into the new habitat. They had the ball on the two-yard line, first down, Kate said, surprising Marc with the analogy. When he looked askance at her, she shrugged and said, "So I like football."

"Huh. Who knew? Excellent." Then he cocked his head, snuck it in, sotto voce. "Baseball's better."

Tonight, though, instead of arranging someone to check on his mother because he wouldn't be going home but instead going out with colleagues—including and especially Kate, next to whom he surely could have angled to sit—he had to pick up his mother and her vat of homemade soup to drive over to a nursing home again, where he'd doubtless spend the evening in the lobby. Quite the exciting life for a single guy. Not that he'd ever minded being a good guy, which he supposed was what she was asking of him. He hoped Kate would be there, and that maybe Dorothy would be at least better enough that his mother would banish Kate to the lobby, too, so she could give Dorothy another lesson. Now that would be a half-decent outcome.

Ria was, of course, ready. Again, she'd dressed up, done something different with her hair, sweeping back one whole side of it into a silver barrette, a long silver necklace that had been Gram's over a bright pink shirt.

"Do I look cheerful?" she'd signed when he signed that she looked nice. He hadn't seen her this animated—well, when had he ever seen her this animated? Not for years. In the parking lot, she walked ahead of him toward the glassed entrance, knowing the way now, another moment when he hardly recognized his own mother.

She didn't wait for him to push the elevator button and went directly to her friend's room. Marc stopped her from entering.

"You need to keep distance." Marc was carrying all the separately packaged and labeled containers of soup which put him at a distinct disadvantage for signing, and he'd already mentioned contagion earlier.

She raised her brow, as if she didn't know what he meant.

He put the bag down. "You know. Stay back. Not to catch it."

She brushed him off. "I'm fine," she signed, making the motions slow, as if he were.

"Just give me the one that's hot," she pointed to the bag, "and give them the rest to refrigerate," she signed.

Marc sighed and pulled the top container out of the bag.

"This is very kind," the aide at the nursing station said, adding in a lowered voice. "Mrs. McKinsey hasn't had an appetite. All she ate was some soup."

When he got to Dorothy's room, Ria was sitting in the room but not next to her, signing about the soup. Kate, in navy scrubs and mask was trying to imitate the signs—not very successfully, he noticed—and how would she know what Ria was signing? Not that Dorothy would. What sense did this make? He signaled with his eyes in Kate's direction, shook his head, and pulled up a chair. To his mother, he signed, "Slow down. A lot. I'm going to translate for Kate and try to teach her some."

He caught the flash of victory on his mother's face.

"You think I should suit up?" Marc said quietly to Kate. Dorothy appeared pallid to him. Wan was the word, really, as if she were fading into the sheets, her eyes with an unnatural sheen. But she did seem to be trying to pay attention, so maybe the stimulation was beneficial.

"You're not on baby duty. But I don't know. I guess it can't hurt. Whatever this virus is, we need you healthy. If you don't mind?"

Marc grimaced. "I've already been exposed, and now Mom is," he said as he stood to go out and ask for scrubs and a mask. "But I'm healthy, so…"

"Yeah. Thanks," she said, looking up at him. "I moved Ria's chair back, so she's got distance from Mom's bed. She didn't like it, but it's for safety." It must have been the light, Marc thought, that made Kate's eyes so noticeably green—bluish green—above the mask. Could someone actually have aqua eyes? He hadn't seen before that she had the faintest start of crow's feet that spread from the outside corners when she smiled.

As he left the room, he saw his mother now signing very slowly, repeating the signs they'd already worked on, hello, more, me, you, eat. The picture board that Kate had made was propped up against the near wall, but for now, between signs, his mother was urging Dorothy to take just a spoonful of the soup, using the signs for eat and more.

Marc spent the better part of an hour teaching basic signs to Kate, the same ones his mother was repeating with Dorothy, acting out word significance and pointing if a nearby object was involved. The simplest building blocks of connection between two people. His mother had a knack, he could see that.

Dorothy seemed to rally briefly, but soon it was apparent that whatever energy she'd mustered was leaking away. "I think we need to go," he said to Kate, nodding in Dorothy's direction.

"I was just thinking the same thing," she said. "Even though this is good for her mentally. Can you tell your mother?"

He did, and she nodded. "I go now," she signed to Dorothy, and pointed to the door.

Dorothy reached her right hand toward Ria, and before Kate or Marc could stop her, Ria leaned in and took it in her own and held it against her heart before she released it and stood to go.

"Tell her not to touch her face," Kate hissed to Marc. "Get her to wash her hands right now."

Marc signed the instruction to his mother, then signed goodbye and blew a kiss to Mrs. McKinsey, putting his arm around his mother then and speeding her toward the door. He walked her directly to the restroom. She wasn't pleased at what she called his bossing her, but she complied. Marc thought: I should have at least done this myself when I first brought her the soup. Stupid.

Well, he felt fine, so it was probably okay.

On the way home, Ria fell asleep. He knew the nurse and the aides on duty had taken note of his mother's presence again. He needed to tell her of the interest in her working there. He suspected she'd want to do it. He felt the table beneath the careful domino construct of his life start to tilt when he considered what that would require. He had Eve to think about, especially the enormous shift that was coming tomorrow. He wished the weather weren't so volatile lately, fall coming on, bringing the storms of change. He wanted the chimps as relaxed and unbothered as possible when they were moved into their new habitat. Presuming there was no problem moving out the screening between Jasmine and Eve, and then using the same two-step process to bring Lolly and Eve together, it would be soon.

# Chapter 28

AFTER ALL THE OTHER planning we'd done, how had we not nailed down the exact space we were going to use to bring Jasmine and Eve together with no barrier for the first time? When something hasn't been done before, of course, we punt. We'd never added a chimp with a trauma history to the troop, and certainly not a lactating female that we hoped would accept her newborn. That called for an impromptu morning meeting in the keepers' office area, the primate staff drawing chairs into a ragged circle to brainstorm, trying to bake something new with random ingredients we'd read about or heard by calling around to primatologists, curators, and keepers we'd met at one time or another.

Finally, Linda said we needed to put together a list of possibilities based on what we knew of the personalities of the main players in the small chimp troop: Eve, Jasmine, Lolly, and Adam, our fixed male.

I admit, I'd been only half-there so far. I'd slept badly, worried by signs of deterioration in Mom. How her energy had failed last night even though I could see she'd really tried to be present, wanted to be. It wasn't just energy, I realized. It was physical strength, the exertion required to lift her hands to imitate the signs. And last night I hadn't been able to tell if she understood, when before I'd thought she did.

Linda gave me a penetrating look that held a question: *where are you?* And I knew I had to participate. I was needed here now, so

I gathered up the scattered scraps of my attention into coherence and started to contribute. Linda already looked bedraggled in a wrinkled blue shirt, and I wondered if, like me, she'd run out of clean laundry and was pulling stuff out of the back of her closet. I'd taken the shirt I was wearing today out of a bag I'd designated for Goodwill because it was old, an unflattering grayish beige from some neurotic fashion trend. All of us were showing the strain, from baby care and overtime, I thought as I looked around our scraggly staff. Even Marc needed a haircut. Only Sandy still looked perky, but she was congenitally incapable of anything else.

Linda had said one option was to put Eve and Jasmine in a neutral temporary enclosure, new to each of them. Marc, coughing every now and then, voted to have Jasmine brought into Eve's space, arguing that Eve had already shown she'd be submissive so there was no need to worry that she'd see Jasmine as an invader.

Finally weighing in, I said that the best option was to simply remove the screen between the two enclosures we'd used. Eve was in her familiar space and being moved wouldn't be a possible upset, and Jas wouldn't be in an entirely unfamiliar area.

The discussion dragged on longer than it needed to. We huddled over coffee and kept adding variations on our themes. Maybe all of us, now that the time was here, were nervous, willing to postpone it another hour. The air was electric with the possibility of failure as it banged against an exhilarating hope, and maybe we didn't want to know which way it was going to go for a little while longer.

I was able to persuade the others to my notion. I hoped it was right. Marc pointed out that introductions of a new chimp to a troop are supposed to be gradual, gradual, gradual and he was right that when a zoo adds a great ape, that's the way it's done. We all knew he'd used up a lot of the grace period we'd been given. Now we would be taking shortcuts and crossing our fingers.

We all wanted Eve and her baby to stay together, even if Jasmine ended up largely raising the little one. Of course, it was an option for us to bottle feed the baby for the next five months—although a huge strain on the primate staff, but doable with help from other departments—and then perhaps a sanctuary would take her if it didn't work to integrate her into the troop, the way a chimp hand-raised by humans sometimes just won't adjust. But none of us wanted that, although our reasons were wildly different. Thurston and the development office had theirs, and the primate staff had ours. As usual.

Thurston wanted to announce the winner of the naming contest on the same day the apes were moved into the new habitat. We didn't want it opened to the public until the apes had at least some time to explore it and make it theirs. Linda sighed. "Okay, we can allow the photographer to get a half hour of pictures when they're in," she said. "Those can be released to the media." She used her glasses like a headband to get her hair off her face, left them on top of her head, and then rubbed her eyes, already tired, already reddened.

"Wouldn't it be best for us to know if the baby is going to be in the habitat before we do that, so Thurston knows one way or the other?" Tom asked this quietly.

"I think I can satisfy him by suggesting a series of pictures. First the adults in the new habitat, and then a second reveal of Eve with her baby if she accepts it. We can make the habitat the big thing first, and explain it'll stretch out the publicity," Linda sighed. "Anyone got a better idea?"

Naturally, no one in their right mind wanted to volunteer to take Thurston on. Linda got a series of slow nods and murmured "That's good," and "That ought to work," responses.

"Okay, then, we'll go with that plan. So, before this rowdy well-rested group explodes from all the energy in the room, let's divide up the tasks and get this done. Marc, we'll want you over with Eve to talk her through, right? Sandy or Tom? Which one of you want to keep talking to Jasmine?"

Like that, Linda worked us through how we were going to get the screen aside, what our emergency response would be if there was any hostility or problem (I was put in charge of that), how long we'd allow them to stay together, how we'd re-separate them, and what our assessment criteria would be. We'd film their interaction so we could analyze it later and make sure we'd missed nothing that could be a safety issue.

It was time. Despite how long as I'd wanted this, anticipated it, I wasn't ready at all. It was exactly the way I'd been with most things I wanted in my life. Even Marc.

# Eve

THE PARROT-ANIMAL came with fruit and more fruit, and Eve heard the pant-hoots that she'd grown used to. The parrot-animal made his sounds that were not pant-hoots but were soothing and not alarms, and Eve ate the fruit and showed him that she wanted more. Then she saw the new animal that was like herself come, and she heard that animal call and she could smell her again too, and the animal made her remember something faintly, but she did not know what.

She went closer, staying low, and gave a quiet answer call. The other came closer to her and touched the metal mesh. Hooted. Eve knuckle walked the rest of the way. Waited. Then she touched the hand that was on the screen. Through the wide holes, then she was hand to hand with the other.

Later, the parrot-animal made good sounds. Something started to move, a rumbling noise like weather, and hands weren't touching anymore. But the space was big, open, and now Eve was by the other.

And the other came close and touched Eve: her head, her shoulder, her chest, and it combed through her hair, and then Eve felt what she hadn't remembered, mother.

Mother.

# Chapter 29

I COULDN'T REMEMBER when I last cried. Maybe it was when I left Uganda. It had become too dangerous to stay, even in the sanctuary, the poachers finally unbeatable in their numbers, their determination born of either ignorance or desperation. Human life was as easily ended as that of any animal that could be used or sold for bushmeat. Researchers, scholars, foreigners, all of us had to get out when the government couldn't provide any help or protection for us or the animals, let alone its own people.

I cried then, oh, how I cried then. Maybe I have a bit here or there since, but no real tears like those.

Not until today, when Eve and Jasmine first touched their hands, and then Jasmine started grooming Eve. Today, I couldn't hold tears back. I didn't know if all Marc had done with Eve had gotten her ready for this, or if I'd been right all along and that she needed to be with other apes to heal, but then it didn't matter. We'd saved her.

All of us were quiet, letting it happen. Marc had stopped talking Eve through it, stopped encouraging her from his place on his side of her original enclosure. Eve was moving into a different world now, and he was letting it happen. I knew what he'd established with Eve would never be the same for him and wondered if he was happy for her and sad for himself too, if there were tears on his face. I wanted to be with him. I wanted to say, "Let's go out, let's celebrate, let's drink and make love, because look what's happened! It's going to be all right! It's going to be all right."

We had to monitor them, of course, but we left the two together for most of the rest of the day. Jasmine did some exploring of Eve's temporary enclosure and checked out her toys. We were thrilled when she picked up the doll and held it to her chest, Eve watching intently. Later, when Jasmine put the doll down, Eve picked it up on her own and held it the way Jasmine had. It was far more than we'd hoped. We gave them fruit, cramming enough into the food tray at once that there'd be plenty for each to avoid any potential rivalry over food, the way they'd be fed when the troop was together. Papaya for Eve, apples for Jasmine, bananas for both.

It was tempting to bring Lolly in, to skip a step, but we all decided not to press our luck. We'd give Eve and Jasmine another day together and then repeat the entire process with Lolly.

"When do you think we can try Eve with her baby?" I said to Linda in the mid-afternoon, when she and I were doing the monitoring. The rest of the staff were variously caring for the other chimps, the gorillas, and relieving Christine and the volunteer who'd been on nursery duty.

Linda looked into the middle distance, mulling it over. "What're you thinking?" she finally asked.

"I'm thinking maybe tomorrow...we first give Jasmine another try with the doll in front of Eve. Then we slide the glass in briefly, put the baby in the other side, let Jas have a look-see, and then we get out and open the glass. I know we have to get out. But I'm thinking Jas will go over and pick that baby up. You know she's nurtured before."

"There's a risk," Linda said, the worry of it closing her eyes for a moment, like she couldn't stand the image of what could happen.

"Yeah. Okay, what if we cover the floor with wood wool. Cushioning." I rubbed at the headache that was climbing from the back of my neck. Afternoon light was waning, and I hadn't even had a minute to talk to Marc alone, to see how he felt, to ask if we could just get a drink by ourselves after work. My Marc I wanted to call him. He might find that bizarre, but I felt so connected to him by what had happened that it seemed right.

"Maybe that would work," she said slowly, tilting her head, thinking about it, half skeptical, half buying in. "Let's not make a final decision until we see if things are going as well tomorrow as they did today. But we'll put the wood wool down on Jasmine's side before we bring her in and open the screen between them, yes?"

"Great." Really, I couldn't push for more than that.

"Let's get Jasmine back with the others. I'm exhausted and I still have to report to Thurston," she said.

I gave her a side eye. "Lucky you." We still had to get Jasmine into her side of the enclosure without Eve so we could return her to the troop for the night. It took us a while, but we managed with Tom's help and some trickery involving a couple of apples. Marc distracted Eve for us from his side.

When we finished, I went to Marc's side of Eve's enclosure, pulled on one of the parrot shirts, and went in. I put up my hand to give him a high five. "She did great," I said, and just this once, not caring if someone walked in, I started to put my arms around him, but he abruptly pulled away.

"Don't!" he said.

"Okay—sorry. I didn't mean anything except—" I was about to lie, to say it was just professional excitement. I'd hide the hurt of that rejection from him, pick at the hurt of it later in private.

"No. It's not—I've… listen, I think I've got a fever."

"Oh. Oh no. Shit." My stomach jangled, the way it does with when I hear something sudden and it's bad. I looked at him more closely and saw that his hairline was edged with sweat.

"I haven't been near the baby, I've kept clear distance from all the apes, and while you all were working on the other side, I was in here alone. I just want you to stay away. I'd like nothing more than to—but I don't dare." As he was saying this, he backed up three or four steps.

"Okay, I get it. Damn." I made my voice sound calm, which was a lie.

"You should get out of here, now. I'll put things away and go home. Maybe I'll be fine tomorrow." He said that, and then he coughed, swinging his elbow up to catch it. Behind him, in her enclosure, Eve checked her food tray, rattling it. Marc saw me look at her and then back at him and knew. "Don't worry. I keep washing my hands and I haven't given her any food without putting on surgical gloves first," he said.

"You sure you don't want me to do it?"

"Just go. I'll be okay."

He didn't look okay, but rather than argue with him, I did what he asked after saying, "Please call me when you get home. I'll be with Mom."

"I know. Yes, I'll call you. Stay well, babe," he said with a wan smile. He'd never used an endearment with me before. If babe was an endearment, which I thought it was. Well, not true. Once he'd called me love.

"You get well," I said, and closed the door behind me. *Get well, sweetheart.*

Marc did call me while I was with Mom that evening, claiming he thought he felt a little better, and not to worry. His fever was just a hundred, he said, nothing to be upset about. "I'm trying to get Mom to leave me alone. Meanwhile, she's fussing because she doesn't have all the ingredients for another industrial-sized vat of soup. How's your mother?"

"The doctor says she hears lung congestion, probably some pneumonia. I guess the inactivity? Oh Marc, I dunno. She looks bad. Really listless. She's supposed to blow into this thingie, but I can't get her to do it." I cradled the phone between my shoulder and ear and right then tried to coax Mom to use the device again, but she closed her eyes and turned her head away. I deliberately didn't mention that Mom was also hooked up to an IV. She'd been started on an antibiotic because the doctor couldn't determine whether it might be bacterial pneumonia as opposed to viral.

"Is she eating?"

"Not much. And yes, tell your mother, she has plenty of soup still, thank her again because it's really all Mom wants."

"I will. And I'll load myself up with acetaminophen and come in to do Eve in the morning, even if I don't stay all day."

"Marc, you shouldn't—"

"I won't do anything but Eve. I can stay on her side, and that'll keep me isolated behind the glass from staff and her. I'll wear gloves. You know. We've got too much to do that can't wait."

I sighed. Under the surgical mask I wore, my cheek itched. The room was too warm, the scrubs binding over my work clothes, my shoes uncomfortable, my stomach rumbling hunger. I wanted to go home. "Oh Marc, honey. You shouldn't have to do that," is what I said.

"I'll be fine." His voice came through the phone strong and reassuring then. I wanted to be reassured and I let myself be. I should have argued, said absolutely not, and I'll have to tell Linda if you come in when you know you're sick. I knew in my heart that whatever he had, he'd caught from my mother, and careful as he'd be, anything can happen.

On the other hand. Always, the other hand holding out something of equal value, also too precious to lose, so I didn't know what to think, like a heavy sky that would neither rain its sadness nor let the clouds break and scatter.

That night, though, I didn't even have a premonition. I was worried about Mom, sure, and concerned about Marc too, though not about him in a serious way, just that he'd be out sick, and we'd be shorthanded when what we needed was extra staff right now. When I got home, I was tired and not in the mood to watch the evening news and weather that recorded automatically. Instead, I put on music, had a glass of wine and a salad out on the balcony where a temporary break in cloud cover let starlight lie again about what endures, then took a shower and went to bed with a novel Becky sent me weeks ago.

I fell asleep with the light on and the book sprawled, spilling the unknown story onto my sheet. I slept hard and deep until the phone startled me awake a little after six in the morning. The doctor was making rounds at the nursing home and the charge nurse was letting me know that my mother was being started on oxygen.

I swung my legs over the bed. "Should I come now?" My feet hit the floor.

"Not necessarily," she said. "It's just protocol to let you know."

I took a breath. "Are you sure? I'd be coming right after work, but if I need to…" It would be a terrible day to call off, but on the other hand, if I had to be with my mother, then, well, I had to.

"She's already back to sleep. A fever will do that."

"I'll try to leave work early," I said. "I can probably work that out."

# Chapter 30

MARC HAD A FEVER in the morning, but it was only a hundred point one. Acetaminophen would bring it down to normal and he'd take three of them to be sure. He made himself eggs and toast even though his stomach was a little off, but he needed to make sure it wasn't empty so he could handle the pills. The cough wasn't bad, and he wasn't sneezing much. Just an inconvenient virus he could push through to do his job. He'd be extra careful to keep his distance today.

Storms were crawling across the country from the west, giants capriciously exhaling destruction. Staff would have to start getting the animals in early, but relieved, Marc thought it would be fine until at least mid-afternoon before even the first rain would arrive, and a full morning was all they needed.

Hello Eve. Marc started signing as he spoke, as soon as he entered his side of her enclosure. Marc is friend. Eve want fruit?

Fruit, Eve signed.

Friend, Marc signed, persisting.

Friend. Fruit. More. She tried all three signs. Triumphant, Marc who'd scrubbed and put on gloves, handled her fruit, loaded her food tray.

"Where's your baby doll?" Marc said, rocking the monkey doll he had on his side of the glass to show her. He'd timed that badly because she was busy with the papaya, so he waited before repeating the question while showing her what he hoped she'd do.

This time she turned around and found the doll where it lay on top of one of the wooden spools. She knuckle walked to get it, picked it up—more carefully than Marc had ever seen her handle it—and held it against her chest one-handed. It wasn't what Marc had done, but it was close to what Jasmine had. Was Eve really glomming on to another chimp's behavior this way? Marc didn't quite know how to sort that out before it was time for the primate staff to roll their three dice: Jasmine, Eve and Eve's baby together.

The staff moved quickly, having verbally rehearsed their parts in advance except for Marc, whose job was to stay in place and talk Eve through it. Linda had had Bruce lay wood wool inches deep on the floor in the hope of cushioning a clumsy move by Eve. Or Jasmine, whose baby-nurturing experience had, after all, not been recent.

First Chris, wearing a parrot shirt and Bruce-designed mask so as not to alarm Eve with a memory of her with the tranquilizer dart, brought in the baby and gently laid her down on the wood wool, then left through the regular door out into the hall. The entrance for Jasmine was entirely separate, through a short tunnel from the current indoor primate area. She'd have to be lured again, Tom's job, with apples and monkey biscuits, while Sandy and a couple of assistants distracted Lolly and the others.

Jasmine saw the baby right away and approached her. From behind another screen, Tom talked to her. "It's all right, Jas. It's Eve's baby. You can pick her up if you want." The important thing was his tone of voice. Easy and steady as arriving daylight, a safe sound Jasmine knew. Jasmine touched the baby tentatively like a slow arriving memory. Eve watched.

"That's your baby, Eve," Marc said. "Eve's baby. Jasmine will show you." It was too many words that Eve didn't know. He'd have to back off. *Think*, he told himself. *Dial it back.* "Baby love Eve. Jasmine friend." Then he decided to shut up and let her watch for a couple minutes.

Jasmine seemed to be considering what to do with the baby. She touched her, then touched her again, moving closer, hunching over, examining. Marc couldn't see well enough, but she might have been grooming the little body. He saw the baby's arms wave briefly. It seemed as if the entire earth didn't breathe, didn't blink, suspended itself equally in fear and hope then, waiting. Waiting motionless.

Jasmine picked the baby up. She held her against her chest and looked around as if to say, "Anyone gonna try to do something about this?"

No one was.

Jasmine leaned back on her haunches and examined the baby, seemed satisfied.

Marc started talking again. "Eve, now you go see your baby with Jasmine." That was the cue. Ben, the maintenance worker, would start sliding the mesh screen out of the way. It was possible that Jasmine would lay some exclusive claim to the baby herself—another problem—but chimps share parenting, so he, Linda and Kate hadn't thought that was likely.

Eve knuckle-walked toward Jasmine. Now her back was to Marc and his view of the baby was blocked, but there was no commotion. He saw that Eve reached forward when she was in front of Jasmine. Oh, was she grooming? Jasmine? The baby?

Some inspired keeper—must have been Tom, as he knew Jasmine best—used the vents nearest Jasmine and started dropping monkey biscuits in. They weren't a favorite of Eve's, but Jasmine particularly loved them. It was chancy, really anyone's guess what she'd do with the baby, but Tom must have had faith in her. She took the baby with her and went to retrieve a biscuit, but then there were more, and oh, it was enticing, and she did exactly what Tom wanted her to do. She gently laid the baby down and busied herself with two handed biscuit retrieval.

And yes, yes. Eve, who already had a belly full of fruit and wasn't a great fan of biscuits anyway made her way over to where the baby lay and did exactly what Jasmine had done a little while earlier. She picked the baby up, and the baby did what baby chimps do: she latched on, hanging tight, this time to her own mother while a silent collective cheer rose from the staff, all of them secretly giving either credit or thanks to whatever they believed in, whatever love was holy to them.

They were patient. Bonding takes time, and the staff was going to extend the longest legs of it they could give the two adults and infant today.

Later Marc would think that was their mistake, that they'd taken too long. Linda would take the blame and say she should have gone ahead and told Thurston what they were doing today, rather than just hoping she'd be able to, for once, spring good news on him at the end of the day. Then he wouldn't have assumed she knew and was having the staff prepare according to the emergency directive.

Kate would shake her head and marvel aloud that they'd all been so caught up in the magic that no one was looking out the windows, checking their muted cell phones, or paying attention to the outside world. None of them had an inkling until the wail of the sirens, which weren't even on the zoo's campus, but close enough in the city that there was nowhere isolated from the sound on the property.

Tornado warning.

The sound was piercing. How'd they all managed to miss that a watch was in effect? They were so shocked that at first no one reacted. It had to be a mistake. A drill? But the sirens were tested weekly, briefly, as a noon whistle on Mondays. It was Thursday and one o'clock in the afternoon.

The noise cut the air like a chain saw first paralyzing them all. Some made wide, unbelieving eye contact with the nearest person. Can this be real? Some instantly remembered how the weather report had included the storms moving across the country, that there had been a tornado three states southwest yesterday. All knew the emergency procedures and as adrenaline spurred them, they began to shout to each other who would do what, dividing the tasks.

Now they had everything to do in reverse. Lure Jasmine back out. Get Eve to put the baby down so Christine could retrieve her. She hadn't had her full course of vaccinations yet, and Chris needed to study the film of what had happened to make sure that Eve was nursing, not just holding the baby. That would mean she still had enough milk, and the supply would increase.

And there were Lolly and the other chimps to secure. And Reece and Katari, the gorillas. *Move, move, move.* Marc had to leave Eve alone to go help, but at least she was in one of the very safest areas, although she was in a corner trying to cover her ears. The sirens screamed relentlessly. Marc didn't know if he would hear a tornado over them. Suddenly, then he thought—oh god, has Barbara already left Mom alone? What are her hours today? Shit! He had to call his mother's companion, had to. He pulled out his cell phone as he was running through the hall heading out to join the others, paused to hit a number on his contact list, and got *we are unable to complete this call, please try again later.* Barbara wouldn't leave, would she? He swore again and ran on. Right now, he'd have to rescue what he could rescue.

# Eve

PARROT-ANIMAL GONE. Other like Eve gone. Little Eve gone. Loud bad hurt.

# Chapter 31

THE SOUTHWESTERN SKY changed to a color I wouldn't have thought possible, a greenish brown like the wind-churned earth was throwing up, right before Marc made it to the chimps' indoor enclosure and helped us secure it. The pitch of the nearby sirens was deafening. I was grateful for his capable hands and to see that he was safe—at least as temporarily safe as the rest of us, which really wasn't safe at all. The gorillas were in, and now the chimps were, too. Loudspeakers repeated over and over for any stragglers who hadn't cleared earlier and zoo personnel to take shelter immediately in the designated emergency sites.

We did, huddling together, protecting our heads. Marc put his arms around me as a shield, but I knew no rumors would start because Tom, bless him, did the same thing, his big wing over Sandy. Ben was with us, and he and Linda cocooned together with us in one of the windowless indoor tunnels between areas, Ben's balding head shining faintly in the dim light. Marc's fingers dug into my arm.

Normally outdoor sounds were lost in there and we were people who heard lions and never flinched, but the roar we heard was like the earth had sucked up all its breath, held it and then let it out in a long rage. There were some shattering and splintering sounds either above our heads or nearby, and we gasped, not knowing if the animals we loved were still safe. The walls and ceiling surrounding us held.

When it was quieter, Linda raised her head. "Everyone okay?"

She got a chorus of "Okay here," and "Yes, thank god. You all right?"

Then she said. "Anybody know who Bruce was with today?"

Oh god, I thought. Bruce who is terrified of a simple thunderstorm. Who did have Bruce today? "Ben? Do you know?"

Bruce was doing a turn for a couple of days in the maintenance department, and Ben was having him learn from other workers now. Ben thought for a minute and then lit on the answer. "Oh, yeah," he said, nodding relief. "He's with Sam. They were sweeping, cleaning up that wood wool you guys spilled, in fact." He nodded again. "Sam would watch out for him."

Sam *was* a good guy. "Does he know about Bruce and storms?" I asked.

"Geez. Sorry. I dunno."

I looked at Marc, to read his expression about the likelihood that Bruce was okay, but instead I was struck by how sweaty and pale his face was. Marc knew why I looked at him though. He shook his head and shrugged slightly.

"We better try to get out of here and assess," Linda said then. "Our animals first. Then help other staff if ours are secure and all right. Do a rough facility damage assessment, just what you can see, if there anything we have to deal with on an emergency basis. Marc, you go to Eve. Kate, back him up if he needs it, then help Tom with the other chimps, then both of you head over to Reece and Katari. Sandy, go to the gorillas first. Got it? We'll reconvene back in the keepers' area and compare notes. And everybody keep an eye out for Bruce. And for god's sake, be careful. Everyone has a cell phone, right? Stay in touch. Let's aim to gather in a half hour with reports. Reasonable?"

I didn't know if it was or wasn't reasonable. None of us knew what we'd find out there. Some of us gave each other quick side glances as Linda tossed aside the no texting, no personal phones rule. Without even needing to explain, both Sandy and I handed Ben our unlocked phones—his was the only number that wasn't programmed in mine, and apparently not hers, either. Big as his fingers were, he keyed it in quickly on each, and we got to our feet to make our way out to see if our world was whole.

'I'll go straight to Eve," Marc whispered to me. "Before you come, check Jasmine and the others with Tom. There's four of them and only one Eve. Linda didn't calculate the order of operations right. If they're okay, come see if I need a hand."

"Got it," I said. Because it made sense at the time.

I was only delayed by a few minutes. We'd sustained damage, even more than we saw then, and a sudden sun mocked us and the grotesque brokenness of trees, signs. Impossible, how air sifted down on us now, quiet and cool. We heard people shouting inquiries here and there, random animal complaining. Still, the chimp's indoor enclosure was secure, so Tom went to get some monkey biscuits and fruit—presuming access to the kitchen wasn't blocked—to distract and calm them.

I went on to Eve's area.

# Eve

THE PARROT-ANIMAL did not come, but another animal did and when that animal came there was noise, noise, like when the many animals came once, and Eve's mother and Eve fell out of the tree. This animal now had a long stick, a stick, and Eve remembered the long stick with the noise and her mother falling, Eve holding on, and how Eve screamed then and tried to run. Now this animal with the stick screamed and ran around and ran over the doll that was like the baby, and Eve liked the doll now and wanted it, so she went to get it, but the animal made noise and was going to hurt Eve and Eve did not want to be hurt.

# Chapter 32

FIRST HAD BEEN THE wash of relief. Eve was all right. Of course, she was agitated, of course she was terrified, but it must have been the noise because there, in a protected inner area of the building, the temporary isolation enclosure was intact. She was pacing wildly and shrieking alarm which he'd never seen or heard her do, and Marc's first thought was that he needed to get her attention, to sign and talk to her and that she'd settle down.

As he approached the glass and Eve advanced in an erratic way toward the spools, he thought oh no, there is damage, something is broken. There was a long stick protruding toward Eve. When the stick moved as if to hit her, Marc couldn't make his mind wrap around the possibility. No. No. He dashed to one end to get a better view. It couldn't be, but it was. Marc backed up, starting to call instructions in the calmest voice he could, which came out like a scratchy blanket.

"Eve. Eve. Marc here. Friend. Look at me, Eve. Marc love Eve."

He reached for the emergency phone. It seemed a miracle that it worked. "Code red, code red. Primate temporary isolation enclosure." It was too much to hope for that the public address system was working, but there'd be a text alert. Seconds later he felt his own phone vibrate in his pants pocket.

Kate was just coming in the door, pulling her phone from her back pocket as she did. "Hey, there's an emerg—"

"It's here. Bruce is in there with Eve and he's swinging a broom at her and she's losing it. Get me fruit, quick."

He barely saw her reaction, panic enter her eyes and widen them, the whip of her ponytail onto her cheek as she instantly turned and was out the door. He was grateful she was the sort who knew when it wasn't the time for questions.

"Eve. Eve. Marc friend. You want fruit? Fruit, Eve," he tried it again and again. How seconds can stretch to the feel of hours. "Bruce, it's me, Marc. You need to put down the broom. She thinks you're going to hurt her. Put it down, and back out slowly. You'll need to go backward and to the right to get to the door. Do you hear me, Bruce? Put the broom down."

But Bruce, his straw-colored hair sticking up, and dammit, wearing coveralls that would set Eve off, was yelling, out of his mind terrified, brandishing the broom like he thought he was going to beat back a great ape.

Kate appeared without fruit. "Stuff's broken in the kitchen. Could be glass in the fruit." She went to the storage area in the rear of the area and rushed to him with two handfuls of monkey biscuits.

Marc shook his head. "Won't want those."

"Try anyway."

Marc jammed them in the food tray talking steadily to Eve who was swaying, screaming alarm as Bruce poked the broom toward her, when Linda appeared with Thurston and two security guards behind him.

"The disabled boy is in there?"

Marc resisted the urge to correct Thurston's terminology. "Yes."

Thurston listened for a moment as Marc kept trying to get either Eve or Bruce to respond. "If she could see me, I could sign. She knows me—and she's gentle," he said to Thurston. Begging.

"Tranquilizer?" Thurston said to Linda, not responding to Marc.

"It takes a good ten or fifteen minutes to take effect. She could become more aggressive, from fear. She's got the history." Linda meant trauma history, Marc knew, but thought Thurston would misinterpret, so he started to clarify.

"Not aggression, traum—"

"Shoot the ape," Thurston said to the second guard. "You'll have to remove the vent cover over there. And then Marc saw what he'd managed to miss: the second guard held a rifle half behind him. "Can you do it okay?"

The guard—Mark didn't know his name but recognized him, older than his baby-face made him look because his beard was so light—nodded once and said, "Yeah. Monkey's far enough away from the boy."

"No! No, I can get Bruce out, just let me," Marc said. "Linda?"

Linda closed her eyes for two seconds, opened them and met Marc's, which were pleading with her. "Human life first."

Kate was wiping tears with the back of one hand. "Let him try, for god's sake," she whispered.

"Now," Thurston said to the guard, ignoring her.

There was a protocol because there was liability, danger to human life. Linda looked at the floor then looked at Marc and mouthed, "I'm sorry." She, too, had tears now. The guard started to move, lifting his rifle, checking it. The vent Thurston meant was on the other side of the area, and it would take at least a minute to remove it.

Kate approached the glass, trying. "Eve. Kate friend. It's okay. No one will hurt you." Eve couldn't have heard her anyway, not over the racket she was making and over Bruce's inarticulate shouting. Marc wheeled, pulled open the door to leave the room, and when Linda tried to stop him, Kate said, "He can't see this, don't make him."

A moment later, the back-access door into Eve's enclosure opened, the door Bruce mistook for a safe place, a closet to hide in when the sirens went off, taking the broom he'd been using to sweep up their spilled wood wool with him.

Suddenly, there was Marc, still wearing the flashy-bright green and yellow shirt he'd worn during the great triumph of Jasmine, Eve and the baby together inside the enclosure with Eve, putting himself between Bruce and her, forcing the handle of the broom to the floor with his foot. This was what no staff was ever, ever to do, enter an animal enclosure. But now Marc approached Eve, signing, talking. The doll was on the floor two feet to his right, and he edged himself that way.

"Would you like your doll?" he said softly, then he signed. "Eve love baby." And he slowly squatted to pick up the doll.

Once Marc had disabled the broom by forcing it down with his foot, Bruce had continued his babbled crying. "Hey buddy, I'm needing you to be very quiet now," he said deliberately, testing. Bruce got quieter.

"My name is Bruce."

"Right, good, okay Bruce." As he spoke, Marc slowly extended the doll to Eve, whose screaming and pacing had subsided when Marc entered. She looked at it for five long seconds, and then took it from his hand and held it to her chest. Marc signed, "Marc love Eve." He started backing up slowly, glancing over his shoulder once to calculate distance.

"Bruce, stay behind me and slowly move toward the same door you came in. Leave the broom down!" He added, his tone sharpening as in his peripheral vision he caught Bruce starting to reach to pick it up. "Good, now move slowly. Now."

Marc continued backing up, signing, speaking in soft tones. He promised fruit, the papaya Eve loved. He never took his eyes off Eve, who had quieted, retreating to a pile of wood wool to hold the doll, rocking slightly in the aftermath of terror. Bruce got out the door, and Marc said, "Good Eve. Good, good Eve," and then he, too, was out.

Once he had him out in the hall, Bruce had immediately sunk to a sitting position, his arms wrapped around his upraised knees and his head down on top of them. Marc sat next to him, legs extended into the hallway, making himself slow his breathing and put ease and reassurance in his tone, though his own heart was thudding, and he wanted nothing as much as he wanted to go to where he could speak to Eve, sign to her, somehow get her the fruit he'd promised. He would, as soon as another staff member showed to take over with Bruce.

He should have expected what did come, could have anticipated it. Yet it felt like as great a blow as the tornado itself. He kept looking down the hall, and when he saw Thurston leave the keeper's area of Eve's temporary isolation enclosure, he was relieved, though he'd have rather it be someone else to comfort the boy, but Thurston would do in a pinch. The rest of them were needed to tend to the animals and facilities, anyway.

As Thurston got within quiet speaking range, Marc got to his feet and gestured toward Bruce, saying, "It's best not to touch him, he—"

"You're relieved of your duties, Marc. Suspended. Linda will be in touch with you, but you should leave the premises now. It doesn't appear that vehicles in the employee lot have sustained damage."

Marc realized that he'd opened his mouth, but words weren't coming. He found one.

"What? But—"

"It's automatic. You know that. It will be reviewed."

"Eve—"

"It will be reviewed. You are suspended."

Marc felt lightheaded, disbelieving. Eve needed him. Linda would be shorthanded. "Can't you make an exception. It's an emergency situation. I can take the suspension as soon as we…"

"An issue of accreditation. To say nothing of liability. No. Do I have to have Nick escort you out?"

Marc closed his eyes, breathed in and exhaled, and finally looked at Thurston. "No," he said, controlling his voice. "Can I go in to see Eve before I leave?"

"I'm sorry, Marc. That's a no."

Marc said nothing then, clamping his lips together, turning away from Thurston. He stopped in front of Bruce and said to the boy's folded-up body, "Hey, Buddy, you're gonna be fine, okay, big guy?"

Bruce raised his head from his knees. "My name is Bruce." His pale eyes were water-filled.

Marc smiled at him. "That's right. See what I mean? You're Bruce. You're always Bruce and that's a good thing to be. You're fine, okay? You're fine. Remember that."

"Okay. Bruce is fine."

"Good. You remember now."

And having elicited that much, Marc walked out of the building. On his way, he pulled his cell phone out, texted Kate, and tried again to reach his mother's companion, Barbara. When the line didn't work, he texted her. He didn't allow himself to take in the damage around him, now drenched in sun and where scattered cleanup crews were already busy assessing, lifting, moving. And he refused to pick through his anger, hurt, sorrow, worry, defensive righteousness, all fever-heated and too ready to roil loose and spill humiliation down his face. Not until he was alone in his parked car.

Even though my first reaction was almost euphoric relief, right after Marc got Bruce out of Eve's enclosure, I knew there more trouble was coming. Worse trouble. Of course, Thurston had the security guard, an ex-marine, *stand down*, as he put it, to show off that he'd been in the military too, probably never having left a desk chair.

That wasn't what started me coming down to earth, though I couldn't help privately rolling my eyes. It was hearing Thurston grill Linda about how in hell Bruce could have had access, who exactly had violated protocol. Any questions he asked were rhetorical; it was a rant about how furious he was about liability, accreditation safety standards, and how *he* was the one who had to deal with damage, and how *he* had to deal with the breach. Linda never had a chance to explain what we'd been doing when the warning sounded. But it *was* a lapse, however brief. The door should have been secured immediately, so maybe she didn't want to take that issue on.

"Do you want me to—" I didn't hear the rest of what Linda said because they moved, conferring, and Thurston dismissed one of the guards, who opened the door at the same time. Also, right then I was trying to soothe Eve, continuing to talk to her. Marc had been right; she really wasn't going to be tempted with monkey biscuits. I'd looked quickly around the back and found a leftover apple, and showed it to her, signed fruit, friend and love, the signs I knew for sure. She did look at the apple, and I thought she was starting to come around, to be interested, so I kept talking. I'd thought to grab one of the bright shirts, too, from the box Marc had outside the door, and though, of course, Linda and Thurston weren't wearing them, nor the guards, which wasn't helping, I pulled one on and tried to put myself between them and Eve's line of sight.

"I'll handle it," Thurston said, cutting off whatever Linda was saying. "You said your primate team is gathering in—" he must have checked the time, because he stopped for a couple of seconds, "about fifteen minutes? Just do your job with them and report to me later. Godammit anyway."

I'd never heard Thurston swear. Ever. The rest of us did regularly when an occasion warranted, but not him. That, as much as anything, was a clue.

My cell phone vibrated in my pocket. A text message. I dared to check it then only because Linda had said we were to text the group if we ran into a problem. Still, I tried to do it surreptitiously, but it was unnecessary because just then Thurston left, and Linda turned to me.

"As soon as you think she's settled, check on the others, all right? See if anyone needs help."

Startled by that, I turned, cell phone still in my hand, and said, "I'll wait for Marc and then—"

"No, just go. Don't wait. Marc's been suspended."

"What?"

"Think about it, Kate. You were a supervisor. You *know*." She sounded angry.

Of course. But wasn't this different? A tornado? When we were in the middle of moving animals? Yes, there's been a breach, and yes, Marc had broken the cardinal rule, but it had already been broken and he'd saved both Bruce and our chimp. Didn't that count? I started to stammer that argument, and Linda held up her hand. "Don't, Kate. Just don't. Whether I agree with you or not, I have no power in this. I'm a curator, not the damn director." Her eyes watered, and she shook her head as if to make that stop as she walked away and opened the door to leave.

I felt sick. What would we do? Then I remembered my phone in my hand and looked. It was Marc. *I'm suspended. Look after Eve for me.*

I don't know what made me think of it then. There was another problem that as far as I knew neither Linda nor Thurston was aware of. I wasn't going to bring it up. Maybe it would be all right. Something had to be.

I stayed with Eve, finally getting her to the food tray where she ignored the monkey biscuits and took the apple. As soon as I thought she was calm, I slipped out and went to the primate kitchen when I found Sandy looking for fruit for the other chimps, exactly what I wanted. Neither of us knew if the nursery area was all right; we hadn't heard and there wasn't time to go find out. She did say that the damage she'd seen wasn't too bad, but she didn't know about the rest of the property. A window was broken in the kitchen—a tree branch had come through it—but no food was contaminated.

I found Eve some papaya and brought it in to her, trying to act as much like Marc as I could. She wasn't herself, I could see that, but she didn't seem to have regressed nearly as much as she had after Chris had gone in with the tranquilizer dart.

If only Marc was here.

I don't know how I'd thought I could protect Marc, keep it to myself. We were only ten minutes into the primate staff meeting when it all came over me, how stupidly thoughtless I'd been and how obvious it was that I had to say what I did. Linda had matter-of-factly said that Marc would be unavailable for an indeterminate amount of time and that we all had a lot of work to do. She turned to me and said, "Tom tells me that Jasmine and Eve did extremely well together today, and that Jasmine took to the baby beautifully, so although I know there's some risk, we'll go ahead and let Eve join the troop now. With her baby. We'll have Chris monitor to make sure she's nursing, but the likelihood is that she'll have enough milk. That'll take pressure off staff that's been doing baby care, and—"

I raised my hand to indicate I wanted to insert something, and she paused to let me speak. I had to try for delay "It would be best if we could at least bring Lolly in with Eve first, make sure that works well. With the glass. Like we did with Jas."

Linda shook her head, impatient. "Of course, it would be best. But as I said at the beginning, we have some damage to the gorillas' outdoor space. What I was about to say is that we're going to go ahead and have you move the chimps to the new habitat first thing tomorrow morning. Not the fanfare we'd planned for the day, but we've got to use the current chimp enclosure for the gorillas. Maintenance needs access for repairs. I know it's not ideal, and if we have a problem, we'll deal with it."

I blew the hair that had fallen loose around my face out of my eyes and shook my head.

"What's the problem?" Linda demanded.

"I think it'll be fine," Tom chimed in, his voice deep and sounding as if he were the one in charge. "Jas pretty much calls the shots with the others. She went for the baby right away."

I didn't mean to sound annoyed, but I'm sure I did. "I know. I was there. It's not that. Guys…" I sighed, and I felt the tingle behind my nose and eyes that meant incipient but entirely unacceptable tears. I sniffed, clenched my teeth, breathed in, and said, "Marc came to work sick today. It would have been fine except for the goddamn tornado. But he exposed Eve, so I don't think—"

Linda interrupted me. "What does he have?" A mixture of anger in her voice and alarm on her face. She looked wilted, exhausted, bedraggled. We all did, and I'd just given her a shot of frantic.

I put my palms up. "He had a fever, all I know really. Some cough? Didn't feel well."

Linda put her face down into the cradle of her open hands. "Oh Jesus," she said. "No. No."

"I'm sorry," I half-whispered it.

"You aren't his supervisor," Linda said, letting me off the hook, probably thinking ahead to how she'd keep me from being suspended too, because that would leave her hopelessly short-handed. She assumed I was apologizing for not intervening when Marc came in with a fever, which none of us are supposed to do; great apes are so close to us in DNA and without whatever immunities we have. I let her believe that was the basis of my apology but that was my smaller guilt.

Marc was sick because he'd helped with my mother. And helped and helped and helped.

And then unbelievably I felt another sickening guilt: I'd not even thought to call the nursing home. Had it been hit? Was my mother all right? How many hours had elapsed since I'd checked on

LYNNE HUGO

her? But they'd call me, wouldn't they? She must be all right. How much could go wrong in a day?

Right then Linda was giving instructions, and everyone else pitching in to divide up assignments. I was distracted, worrying about Mom then, and I almost managed to miss it when she said, "Kate, I'll need you to start calling external sanctuaries. Find one—try Chimp Haven first, of course—to take the baby."

"But Eve was—" I started to argue, but it was only my heart. My head knew that it was hopeless.

Linda just stood and waited, looking at me, her eyes steady as a schoolteacher staring down a wrongheaded student. This was why she was the curator and I would never be, the way she could take her own fear, grief, panic and by some alchemy spin it into reasoned control, step up on a dime and lead. Even after I shut up, she waited, underscoring the futility of argument. She put her hands in her pants pockets. "You ready now?" she said finally.

"Sorry. Yes."

"Good. Find a place for the baby. Then we'll make transfer arrangements. Eve's in quarantine as of right now. We'll need medical consultation regarding how long, and Kate you'll be in charge of her care." She took in a big breath and exhaled, rubbed her forehead like she had a headache, then straightened her stance. "All right. It looks as if we may have been lucky. The largest structures on property appear only somewhat damaged, which protected our animals. I'm told there's damaged fencing, the landscaping's torn up, and branches all over the place. Outdoor enclosures have sustained worse damage. We're going to have to work around maintenance and construction workers—try to stay out of their way while putting the animals first. Do the best you can tonight, make sure they all have food, water, and are safe. Let Chris know if you see any other needs. And for god's sake, get a good night's sleep."

When she stopped talking, we all stayed where we were, most of us having expected a short check-in meeting were leaning against our desks or letting a wall prop us up. Now we variously stared at the floor, each other, or middle space, stunned, trying to absorb what our saturated minds were rejecting: Marc suspended? Eve quarantined? We weren't going to keep the baby?

Linda tolerated our inaction for almost fifteen seconds and then somehow found the right note. She clapped her hands once and barked "Hey!" Startled, we all looked at her. Then she went on, making her tone into soft bandage to staunch our bleeding. "I know you're struggling, and I'm with you in that. We have to keep it together, gang. Please, go, do your jobs."

And we did.

I'd decided to hurry through my work, let Linda know I had to check on my mother, and just go directly to the nursing home. I'd feed Eve early and talk to her more, make sure she was okay, leave the recordings of Jasmine, Lolly, and the other chimps, too, going softly for the next couple of hours so she wouldn't forget. I'd just pushed play to start the soundtrack when my phone vibrated in my back pocket.

Dammit, dammit. The nursing home. As long as my mother had lived in any part of Sycamore Community, no one had ever called me with good news. This time was no exception. "Kate McKinsey," I said into the phone.

"This is Angela at Sycamore. I'm sorry to be calling you."

"Is my mother all right? I was heading over there now." Not strictly true, but close. I was so frightened at that moment that I reached to use the back of a chair for support.

"Well, no, but it wasn't the tornado. Our facilities were extremely fortunate. Mainly downed trees, some cottages with broken windows. But your mother, her condition does seem to be deteriorating, and we want to keep you apprised. The physician has her on oxygen, as you know. She's not eating, and now we're concerned about dehydration, too."

"Okay." I took a breath. "Okay. I'll be there as soon as I can."

✳

Bless Barbara, she had seen and heard the weather forecast, kept the television on, and hadn't left Ria. "No big deal," she said, "I'm single, and besides, you have a basement and I don't. I was safer here watching out for Ria than at my own apartment. I should pay you today."

She was a gray-haired gem who signed as she spoke, so Ria was never left out. It was the first time Marc had found a companion for his mother who was middle-aged, available to work full time, knew ASL, and even had a sense of humor. Perfect.

"We were fine," Ria signed. "Went to the basement when Barbara said there were sirens, but then it was all right."

"Missed us," Barbara said.

"I tried to call, but couldn't get through," Marc said. "I'm…really…thank you." He was fighting tears. All of it, what was lost, what was saved, all of it, too much to hold in his mind. He headed for the bathroom, embarrassed. He shut the door and ran the water to mask the sound he made until he got control of himself, took cough medicine and Tylenol. Flushed the toilet.

When he came out, the women had the television on, Barbara making no move to leave. "Forsythe Road has wires down," she said, signing it, too. "I guess it's a mess, my neighbor said. She'll take my dog out and feed him—I can't get to my apartment until a crew can clear the street. Ria said I can stay here. I hope that's okay with you."

"Of course," Marc said. He coughed into his elbow and cleared his throat. "You stay as long as you like. You're always welcome." He hoped his face looked normal.

"You're home early." Ria signed it as a statement, but he knew she wanted to know why. "Something wrong?" There was the question, on her face. Normally something wrong at the zoo would make him late, not early. She knew that.

He shook his head. "Fine. Just tired," he lied. She wouldn't push him in front of Barbara. "I'm going to lie down. Got a headache with all the commotion." Well, that last part was true anyway.

He did lie down, which lasted for all of ten minutes. He'd not turned off his phone, thinking Kate might update him on Eve, but telling himself she wouldn't be able to do it right away. When his ringer sounded, he was startled. Kate.

"Where are you?" he said, skipping a greeting.

"Eve's okay. I got her papaya right away and I think she settled down. I made sure she's fed, and the recordings are on, too. But Marc, I couldn't stay. I'm on my way to Mom's. They called me. She's worse."

"Can you get through? Barbara just said Forsythe is closed. Wires down. You'd best check where roads are closed before you leave."

"Uh…What if I go farther north, maybe on 48, and then drop down? Sandy got through to her mom who told her the worst of the damage is south, a swath. We were lucky."

"Just not far enough south."

"Yeah."

"Is it urgent, your mom?" Marc shifted the cell phone to his other ear and sat up on his bed, swinging his feet to the floor.

"It wasn't one of the ones I know that called—she didn't say."

"Let me get off, I'll try to check what roads are open. We have power."

"Okay, that would be great. Thank you. I don't know if GPS is updated in real time yet, for closures. I didn't even think of that."

"I'll call you." He disconnected abruptly, in a hurry to get to his laptop, check the news sites and the state police.

Damn. Tractor trailer overturned on I-75, traffic lights on route 48 were out. It was going to take her forever on a peeling-paint commercial strip of used car lots, bars, nail salons, liquor, fast food and drugstore chains. He checked the roads from his house, on the east side, which had been minimally affected. He could get through easily.

"Barbara, since you're here, would you mind if I leave? I'm... needed." He'd just as soon not outright lie, but he'd rather his mother assume he meant he was needed back at work. When he signed about being needed, he pointed to his cell phone, to intimate that he'd been called in.

"Go right ahead," she said. Such a good woman, he thought, grateful.

"I'll save you dinner," his mother signed.

"Don't know when I'll be back." Then, to Barbara, "Use my room. I'll sleep on the couch."

He didn't wait for an answer.

It took me an impossible amount of time to get to Sycamore. Trees had been snapped at the knees, taken down fast and hard, like third string quarterbacks, and they'd toppled over power lines, ineffective blockers, on the way down. Chain saws and police sirens grated and whined through the stilled air as I skirted the area of most damage according to local news I got from the radio. Without working traffic lights, and apparently not enough police to cover all intersections, drivers were either taking idiotic chances or being so cautious that nothing moved. My nerves were in tatters. Upset, worry, fatigue, and now hunger. I wanted just a day of normal life, which I hardly remembered, time stretching like a piece of stuck-on gum that wouldn't break off, though I was willing it to collapse down into some welcome dreamless sleep. But it wouldn't, it didn't. It just stretched farther, sticky with expectations.

As soon as I was upstairs, I commandeered scrubs and a mask from the supply closet without asking—no one was at the desk— and went into Mom's room. Marc was there, suited up, seated at Mom's feet when I got there. He had one hand on one of her ankles, his cell phone playing some soft classical string music, which seemed exceptionally right to me, like an antidote to the soft whirring of the running oxygen, tubes taped to keep them in her nostrils. Her eyes were closed, and my first thought was that this was how she was going to look right after she died. Hollowed out, nothing left. I was immediately upset and started to go over to try to rouse her, to tell her I was there, talk some life back into her.

Marc saw my intention, got up and as he did, held out an arm to half-block me. "She's better when she's sleeping," he whispered. "She was really uncomfortable when I first got here. You might want to let her be." I strained to make out what he was telling me, the mask muffling it into the hiss of the machine.

I nodded. He waited a couple of seconds then went and grabbed the extra straight chair we'd borrowed when we were last here from where it was crowded in next to Mom's unused recliner and set it near the head of her bed. He pointed to me, then to the chair.

I pulled the mask aside, mouthed thank you, and let my knees fold me to the seat. Before I replaced the mask, I whispered, "Do you know if she's eaten anything."

He shook his head.

"Meaning no she didn't eat anything?"

This time he shook his head yes. That meant he'd been there a fair amount of time.

"Not even your mom's soup?"

Again, he shook his head and gestured that I should put the mask up. I did.

After an hour, Mom hadn't even fluttered her eyes. Marc gestured toward the hallway and I followed him. "Stand back," he said when we were out there. "Keep your mask on. The last thing we can afford is for you to get sick, right?" Behind his mask, he coughed.

"You shouldn't be here," I said. "I'm all right."

"Listen, I'm okay, too, and as long as I stay on acetaminophen, I don't feel terrible, and the fever stays down. It's no big deal. I'll get a throat swab tomorrow. But you've got the baby at work, and now they're shorthanded, and it's a mess…you go home. I'll stay a while longer, and I can help by coming tomorrow. Tell them at the desk I'm the family rep, and they should tell me about any changes immediately. I'll keep you apprised. You'll have to sign the HIPAA form, or they won't talk to me."

I felt like I shouldn't accept this. At the same time, I needed the help desperately. I'm sure he saw me wavering.

"It's a trade," he said. "I want you to take care of Eve for me. Please." His eyes, already red-edged, began to water as he said it, and I saw how much he was hurting.

I nodded. "Okay," I said. "I'll tell her you'll be back."

Marc shook his head. "They're going to fire me."

I turned away, my own eyes suddenly teary, because I wasn't at all sure he was wrong.

From behind me I felt his hand on my shoulder. "Hey, Katie. It's okay, love. I'd do it again."

We ran things that way for the next two days. I was already assigned to Eve, with stints of baby care, and filling in, of course, with the other chimps. We accomplished moving Jasmine, Lolly and the other two into the new habitat without much difficulty and they were actively exploring it. It should have been such a fanfare day for us, but it passed like a relief sigh instead, because then a flurry of flustered cleaning and re-preparation had to be done to move the gorillas into their side.

I let Marc know everything about Eve, Marc updated me regularly about Mom, and I saw her at night. She hadn't improved, and the doctor confirmed that she had pneumonia. Marc hadn't heard anything about his status, but I didn't take much hope from that. Administrators were too pressured, dealing with damaged areas and approving plans for rearranged exhibits to deal with personnel issues.

Then when we thought we couldn't bear any more, there was more. I went to work in the morning and found Eve lethargic.

She didn't respond to her name, and when I called that I had fruit, she didn't hurry to the food tray, although she did come. She took some papaya, ate a tiny bit, and left the rest. She knuckle walked in the unsteady gait of indecision veering toward the trunk she could climb to a sleeping platform, but then stopped where she must have gathered some extra wood wool. She lay down and curled into herself.

This was not normal. Not at all. I had a guess what was wrong, and even if it had nothing to do with Marc, if Eve was sick, he'd be blamed. Alarmed, I called for Chris. All the while I waited for her to come, I thought, *if she were in the wild, she'd forage for medicinal plants. That's what they know to do. If she were with the other chimps, they'd be keeping her company, giving her comfort. But she's not in the wild, and she's not even in with the other chimps here. After all she's been through. What have we done?*

And, of course, my phone dinged. It would be a text message from Marc with an update about Mom. I couldn't tell him Eve was sick. I just couldn't.

I was only going to read the message about Mom and thank him. I'd text him that I was on baby duty, and I'd be in with Eve later. Until I read Marc's text:

*She woke up briefly. Wouldn't drink anything. Signed goodbye and love. Pretty sure she tried the sign she uses for you. The doctor wants to speak with you about comfort care. They think she's trying to go, or the doctor said, "wants to go." You need to tell them no way. We can save her.*

Linda didn't answer when I called, but I left a voice mail telling her to call me immediately, that I had an emergency, but I wouldn't leave until I heard from her. I couldn't leave, not with Eve appearing sick and with department short-handed already. I texted *okay, thank you*, to Marc, and added a question. *Did you go to the clinic for a throat swab?*

*Yes*, he texted back. *Rapid strep test. Negative. Just viral.*

If he knew about Eve, he would be in a panic that it was viral. If it was bacterial, Chris could treat it with an antibiotic. Viral? Not a damn thing she can do. Not a damn thing except hope that Eve will fight it back.

While I waited for Chris, I got right up to the glass. Eve wasn't looking at me—I couldn't even see if her eyes were open or closed, and I didn't know what signs to use anyway. I talked to her, though I should have been with my mother, who needed her daughter. "Eve. Listen to me. Your daughter needs you. You have to stay strong and get well. Marc will be back, all right? I have to go for a while, but I'll be back too. Marc loves you. Your baby, your baby loves you, and I know you love your baby, so you get well and you can be with your baby girl. You need to eat and drink water, Eve. Please."

I went on and on blathering like that, for my sake I'm sure, not hers, half pleading, half praying, grieving our losses and hoping for salvation somewhere, somehow, or for a way to accept our failures. And then Chris arrived. She wore a lab coat closed over her navy pants, but at least Eve wasn't paying attention, so I didn't react.

"She's sick," I said, though I'd already said on the phone that I'd thought she was. Now, though, I was sure.

"You sure? How can you tell?" She had a dubious look on her face that said, I hate when unqualified staff think they are vets.

"Not herself. Wouldn't take food. I heard her cough." Now Chris started to look more interested. She gestured to Eve with her chin.

"Does she always sleep there?"

"No. She climbs to that platform." I pointed. "And she wouldn't be sleeping now, typically."

Chris sighed. "How's Marc?"

I didn't want to answer that. Of course, Chris's mind had jumped right to the obvious conclusion, right to where Linda's and Thurston's would, too: Marc had exposed Eve, and now inevitably her life would be at risk. No immunities. "He's doing okay," I said.

"Well, that's irritatingly vague." Chris said, her tone sharp, uncharacteristic. "What's the deal?" She drilled me with her eyes.

"He had a strep test. Negative. He's got a cough and sore throat. No fever as long as he takes Tylenol."

"So you're telling me it's viral."

"Yeah, likely." In spite of my intention not to, I shrugged. Then we both heard it: Eve coughed. Raspy, bronchial-sounding.

"Shit. I can try something in her drinking water," Chris said. "But if I make it taste funny, she won't drink it and we need to keep her hydrated. All I can do without knocking her down, but…"

I shook my head. "No! Not unless—"

"Well, there's no point. Not right now anyway, which is the reason not to." Her voice was like a warning. *I will if I need to.* But she'd not brought a tranquilizing dart with her, and her hair spilled loose. She didn't even have a mask down around her neck, so she hadn't prepared even though I'd said on the phone that I thought Eve was sick.

*Good.*

"Is it okay to just let her rest?" I said it hesitantly, even knowing it really wasn't an option for me to stay and monitor her. "My mother has taken a turn for the worse, and I need to get to the nursing home." I added this when she didn't answer right away.

"I'll put a camera on her and monitor from the infirmary," Chris said, kind, now that she knew.

"I still have to clear it with Linda," I said.

"She'll be fine, she'll get it," Chris said. "It's not under your control." She said it confidently, as if there were still things in her world that she could predict, be sure of. I was envious. She looked like she'd showered and found fresh clothes today, too, and she could leave her hair down because it was clean. Way more than I'd managed.

"That's exactly the problem. Nothing is anymore. Nothing."

# Chapter 33

MARC COULDN'T WRAP his head around her thinking. Right after Kate had been in to see her mother—with him sitting down by the foot of the bed the whole time, close enough to see her face crumple, the times she used the back of one hand to swipe an eye—she'd asked if he could stay in the room while she left to read her mother's chart. She'd asked how he was feeling, and when he said he was better today, Kate asked if he'd be able to stay longer because she wanted to try to talk with the doctor on the phone.

He asked her about Eve, but only once, because she'd said I'm sorry, I can't think about anything but Mom now. He felt like he shouldn't intrude on the craziness at the zoo, knowing all the extra they had to contend with. But still. Still. How was Eve? How were the other chimps? He loved them too. He didn't ask her about his job status, on the chance that she knew. It wasn't fair to put her in that position, though surely she could find a way to let him know. Surely she would if she knew.

His uncertainty had started when she returned to her mother's room, crossing behind him to pull the window shade against the spilling afternoon sunlight that Marc found so welcome. She dragged her straight-backed chair closer to his, pulled her mask in place over her nose and mouth, and said, "The doctor says it appears she's not responding to the antibiotic, that the pneumonia is likely viral, and that she needs a ventilator. Breathing is more difficult for her, and the oxygen isn't doing it. He says she doesn't appear to be fighting, and do I know what she wants? She says I should think ahead about what I'd be willing to—"

Marc shook his head, interrupting. "People come off ventilators. She's been…"

"And the next step is a feeding tube."

"You don't know that. You can still save her. And then—I can help. She was catching on to the—"

Kate cut him off. "I do know about the feeding tube. The doctor mentioned the possibility. I don't know what saving her means." She used one arm to gesture, a motion that quickly circled the room, following it with her gaze. "You know what this already looks like? And then…add a tether? A chain?"

"So, you mean…?" He thought he understood her analogy, but could she really mean that she'd rather their animals be dead than in a zoo? And was that the comparison she meant to draw to saving her mother's life now?

But rather than explain, Kate looked away, took a long breath in. Then she exhaled and stood. "Thank you so much for being here. I'd kiss you—but the masks might make that less satisfying." She made her eyes smile at him. "I can stay with her now—I know you don't want Ria alone this long."

"Serious stroke of luck. Barbara can't get home. Power lines down, road closed. She actually asked me if she could stay. If I weren't in love with you, I might marry her."

He said it teasingly, but there, he'd said it.

And she laughed and said, "Over my cold dead body," but as soon as she said it, she clamped her hand over her masked mouth, horrified that she'd said something so inappropriate to the time and place.

Marc saw her reaction and reached over to take her hand down. "Hey. It's just an expression," he said softly. Then he broke out his best teasing look. "And it's so good to know you're jealous."

It was going to be days, they heard from an aide who was listening to local news, before power was restored to much of the city. The zoo had generators, and Sycamore had power. It seemed miraculous fortune that both Kate and Marc's homes, each more to northeast, had electricity. Barbara, who lived south had none.

As soon as he got home and the news confirmed that major thoroughfares were open, Marc took Barbara on an emergency run to get her dog. How had he not known she had one? He'd have told her she could bring him with her any time. She'd adopted the smallish mixed breed from a shelter and clearly adored him. "He's really smart too." Barbara rubbed her cheek into Bear's tan and black face. "He's my special buddy." No wonder she'd been concerned about not being able to get home.

"Pack a bag," Marc said. "Mom won't have it if you don't stay with us until your power is back on."

Barbara protested, but did, and loaded her small stash of perishables and frozen food into a bag, "...to contribute," she insisted.

"You're doing me a favor," Marc said.

That first night, he slept on the couch, but after that, he stayed at Kate's. She went to work for a few hours when she was most needed at the zoo, and he filled in for her with Dorothy.

Kate was evasive when he questioned her about Eve and if she'd heard anything about his job, but her answers had been as insubstantial as clouds when he tried to get a grasp on their actual meaning. She'd held out another full day before he articulated to himself that it was her way to be confrontational, not his, and if he was serious about knowing something, he was going to have to adapt. He persisted with direct questions when they were down in the lobby while two aides were bathing Dorothy and changing her catheter bag.

She hadn't met his eyes. "Okay," she said finally, like she'd decided something. She looked up and spoke a matter-of fact sentence that came at his head like a club. "Eve is sick."

"Oh god, no. No." He recoiled. She didn't have to explain. He'd done this. "How bad?"

"Not good. She's not moving much, getting dehydrated. Not taking in enough water."

"Eating?"

"A little."

"Papaya? She loves—"

"Yeah. Don't worry. We know." When she said that, he knew he was on the outside now.

"They're firing me, aren't they?"

Kate shrugged, closing her eyes and shaking her head, half-raised both palms flat out. But Marc didn't miss the slight wetness that leaked from beneath her lids. Two women entered the lobby, crossing it on the way to the elevator and she was silent until its door whooshed softly closing the strangers inside, and it dinged and gurgled the news that it was headed upstairs to the Kingdom of Loneliness and Other Sufferings. That was what Kate called it.

"I'm not included, or I could fight," she said when the lobby was empty again except for the two of them. "I'm guessing yes." Her eyes looked like he imagined the Caribbean Sea, that swimmy green-blue when she whispered, "I'm sorry. I'm so sorry."

It was all so ironic to him, how his life could be unraveling at the exact time his mother was coming to life, like a straggly plant moved into the sun and given water. And all he'd done was hire Barbara and—after the head nurse inquired again, so he knew they were serious—tell Ria that Sycamore would like to talk to her about part time work teaching some rudimentary sign to very hard of hearing residents. And an introductory class for staff. They'd supply an interpreter for that, unless of course, Ms. Lopez had one she preferred they hire.

Of course, it helped that Barbara lit up and told Ria she'd be wonderful at that and mentioned that Ria had told her about her friend Dorothy, how she was teaching her sign. "When do they want to talk to Ria?" Barbara signed it as she spoke to Marc. "I can take her and interpret if it's during the day."

"You wouldn't mind? That would be terrific. Mom, you know if you do this, you're going to have to get a driver's license."

"That would be exciting," Barbara injected. She had a friendly cat-like face, active, curious, that didn't quite go with her larger body—small nose and penetrating eyes. He couldn't guess what color her hair used to be, or if she'd always been the thirty pounds overweight she was now. He imagined she came from a big, enthusiastic family because she was a natural cheerleader, exactly what Ria needed.

"I can help with that too," she said. "Bear loves to ride in cars." At the sound of his name, and the word car, the dog jumped up, tail wagging, ready to go. "See what I mean?" Barbara pointed at him, and she and Ria laughed. His mother was laughing. His mother. Unafraid. Laughing. Barbara still didn't have electricity, thank heaven for that. Staying at Kate's made it easier to hide his suspension from his mother, and he didn't even try to pretend to himself that sleeping in her bed wasn't his first choice.

They felt the strain, though. It never really went away, even in their lovemaking, he felt it. She'd said yes to the ventilator, but she was resolved she'd not agree to more. Marc agonized over Eve's condition, sure he could get her to eat and drink if only he were allowed back.

It seemed forever that nothing changed. Until, far too fast, everything changed.

# Chapter 34

IT WASN'T LIKE it was the first time the gulf had opened between us. We had different visions, but we'd imagined those as just our professional approaches to saving the great apes.

It's strange to think of it—I'd not even told Marc that Thurston had suggested I might become Research Director, his bait in a trap for a gullible animal. I'd thought it could work; I'd come at the goal that way while Marc came at it from the other side, both of us loving the animals and each other, and so much could remain unspoken.

But it wasn't only saving the apes that we clashed about. Marc was never going to understand, though he'd been there with me when Mom was briefly awake yesterday afternoon, and she signed goodbye. I cried, and signed back, goodbye and I love you. Marc put his arms around me. When she was sleeping again, I told Marc, "She's telling me, just like they said. She wants to go."

"Not necessarily. She confuses hello and goodbye all the time. It's the baby sign, and babies confuse that too. They use it interchangeably a lot. Don't give up."

I was glad he wasn't there when Mom's doctor told me it was time for a feeding tube because I said no. She asked me if I'd like her to certify my mother for hospice care and I said yes. She nodded again, and extended one hand to my shoulder, a gentle kindness I could hardly bear. She waited for me to wipe my eyes and nose with the too-used tissue I scrounged out of my pocket and said, "We'll see that she doesn't suffer."

"Thank you. Thank you very much," I said, and it was all I could get out.

I remember thinking Marc won't understand; he'll argue. He'll argue out of love for me and passion for life, the hope of it. But I won't change my mind. I could see the rift ahead and that we would try anyway. We wanted to love each other, and we would make love out of grief for what we were losing, but we would make love because we would try.

I thought all this, and then I thought, but what if I'm the one who's wrong?

# Eve

HER HEAD HURT, and her mouth. She wanted to drink but too tired to drink. Just lie down, listen. No parrot-animal. Only doll, keep doll. Maybe animal like Eve come back with baby. But they not come. Maybe parrot-animal come, Eve get up then.

# Chapter 35

TIME BLURRED AS DECISIONS either fit together or didn't, like a series of numbers to a combination lock. Marc believed I was wrong, as I'd known he would. I didn't change my mind, but it did hurt. And then there was another, separate mourning, anticipated yet still a shock, when Thurston notified him that a decision had been reached "regretfully" to give him an opportunity to resign considering the circumstances of the breach, but if he chose not to do so, his employment would be terminated.

Eve languished, seeming not to improve at all, but not worse in that she was drinking "enough," Chris said, and every now and then, she'd eat. At the same time, she said, "we can't let this go on indefinitely." That was infuriatingly vague. I tried every Marc trick I knew, but I also knew I wasn't Marc, and that was the problem.

I'd been making calls when I was at work and found a good sanctuary in Louisiana willing to take the baby, and one in Oregon that I liked better, but they wouldn't send someone to get her, and couldn't take her until she was able to eat on her own. Linda said no to that. There aren't that many great ape sanctuaries in the country, and I had some contact in each of them, either professionally or personally, so I kept at it.

Jackpot in Tennessee. Yes, they'd take the baby now—and how about her mother? Could they have her too? They knew she'd probably lost her milk, but that needn't prevent bonding entirely, since I'd said she seemed to recognize her daughter before she got sick. Was Eve well enough for transport? They had a strong preference to keep families and social groups together. No, they couldn't send staff, but they could raise money if we could do the transport.

I closed my eyes and lied. "Maybe we have someone," I said, knowing that was a stopper with Linda, that we had no staff to spare. "Let me talk to our curator and get back to you later today or tomorrow for sure. And thank you so much. Eve is sweet and gentle and smart, and she's been through...I'll email her history as soon as we hang up." I had to stop talking for a moment because my voice was wavering then. I changed the subject once I had control. "She did really well when we first introduced her to our alpha female. With her baby too."

Before Linda could say no, I put up my hand to stop her. "We're short staffed without Marc anyway, and we'd not even introduced Lolly and Eve. It's best for Eve and the baby—we never even named the baby, for heaven's sake—to be together. Think of the ethics of separating them now. They'll take them both. It's the right thing."

Linda sighed and laid her glasses on her desk, rubbed her eyes with one hand. "Kate. First, I'd have to get it by Thurston. Second, let's say it's fine to send Eve, too. They want *us* to get them there. I. Have. No. One. What don't you get about that?" The walls of her small office, stuffed with books, plants, and framed zoo posters pressed in then, less friendly than chaotic, like a mirror of my mind.

"Wait," I said, grabbing a lifeline. "They'll pay. How about Marc? You've fired him. Let them pay. We treat him as if he's their employee, help load her. I think he can drive straight through. Tiring, but possible."

"Oh my god. Please try to remember that *I* didn't fire him. Don't tell me you've tried to arrange this on your own." She was getting on her high horse. "And get your hand down, please."

I put my right hand in my lap, set the left on top of it like a rock to hold it down. "Sorry, I was trying to tell you, no, I haven't said anything. It's just that Marc's been saying that he thinks he could get through to Eve if he was allowed to work. Maybe it would be good for her to see him, and if he were the one transporting her…"

Linda wasn't listening, I could tell, so I stopped mid-sentence. She half turned and looked down where her hands had fallen, restless on her wrinkled black pants. All of us were rumpled and tired, and I'd been stealing time from my mother to be at work, and from work to be with my mother. If Marc hadn't been sitting with her while I was at work, I think I would have lost my mind, even though I had no idea if my mother knew when I was there. Since hospice had been in the picture, and the ventilator removed, she'd been sedated to keep her comfortable. The doctor was surprised she was breathing on her own, though it was shallow and labored. Occasionally she'd open her eyes. I'd hold her hand, and try to connect with eye contact, to let her know I loved her. Did she know? I couldn't tell. Here I was, though, making a suggestion that, if Linda agreed, would mean I had no backup at all.

"I take it he's recovered from the…illness?" Linda said finally.

"Lord yes. Days ago."

"So you've talked to him."

I answered no more than specifically what she asked, now, being more careful. "Yes."

"They'd pay for the transport?" she said.

"It'd be cheaper for them if he could use our van. Then it's just a round trip."

"Instead of sending him down to get theirs and then returning it," she mused. It was as if we were negotiating terms when nothing had been agreed to, and I had no idea if Marc would do it. Or could. What about Ria?

I shut up then and let her think. She was likely to decide I was right about the ethics of keeping Eve and her baby together if it was possible, but she was the one who'd get the fallout from Thurston, how he'd have to spin the zoo baby angle, the naming contest results, fund raising.

"We could probably get the sanctuary to let us announce the baby's name and maybe a news story about the tornado damage making it necessary to place her? Use that for a different fundraising slant? At least with known donors." I ventured the thought tentatively, after a period of silence.

"Probably already doing some..." Linda lapsed back into thought, ignoring me, until she looked up and said, "All right. I think it's best. I have to get Thurston's approval first. Then I call Marc, not you."

"Understood. Thank you." And I got out of there.

Linda moved on it more quickly than I imagined. She must have gone straight to Thurston. The strain on the primate staff was obvious, though, so it made sense that she would. Eve was requiring extra care and attention and still not integrated with the other chimps, and the baby was a drain on staff time and resources right when both were strained. The zoo was struggling to complete cleanup and repairs so we could reopen; it was a no-brainer, in a way, to take advantage of placing Eve and her daughter.

I was with Marc when Linda called him, as it happened. I'd only been in my mother's room for about fifteen minutes, and Marc was getting ready to leave. Looking shocked, he silently flashed his phone screen in my direction to show me it was Linda calling and left the room as he said hello. It was almost fifteen minutes before he came to the door and motioned me into the hallway.

"You're not going to believe this."

"Actually, I am," I said. "I met with Linda this morning, after I talked with the sanctuary. Can you work it out with Ria?"

"I already called Barbara. She'll stay with Mom. Remember— Mom's interview here too? That's the day after tomorrow. Barbara was already going to interpret."

"I remember. Marc that's terrific. You can…"

"Yes. Linda's going to see if the university could send at least one graduate student with me to take care of the baby. You…"

"I wish I could—"

"I know." He looked both disheveled and handsome standing there needing a shave and a haircut, his good eyes earnest and honest. I'd never know a more generous heart.

When he left, we told each other and ourselves that he'd be back quickly, that I'd help him hunt for a job in the field that wasn't too far away because I was the one with the most connections. We put up lovely gauzy curtains to obscure a clear view.

# Eve

THE PARROT-ANIMAL came again. He brought fruit and then came again and the little Eve baby too. Eve knew the parrot-animal and the little Eve baby, and she felt good. It was good.

# CHAPTER 36

HE HAD EVERY INTENTION of going back home. What he hadn't factored in was how much more he'd accomplished with Eve than even he'd realized. She'd obviously been sick with the virus—he wasn't shirking his responsibility for that—but his disappearance during and after that illness had made her react in a way that made her appear sick for longer than she was. It had been another, different trauma, and Eve had no resilience for either.

He and a veterinary student had caravanned down, Marc driving Eve, caged, in the back of the transport, lightly sedated but not knocked down, he wouldn't hear of it. The student had the baby, in a bed and caged, in the back of a rented SUV. They drove straight through, arriving in just over nine hours, tired and hungry, since they only stopped once to feed and change the baby, using the most remote section of a highway rest stop they could find. Eve had slept through that stop, been quiet the whole way.

The student left the next morning in the zoo's van, but it was clear to Marc and the caregivers at the sanctuary that he needed to stay to ease Eve into the transition.

There was the process of introducing her into the troop that lived on the grounds and exploring how much mothering Eve might do. Might she still have some milk? If the baby started to nurse and Eve had enough hormones in her body, the nursing would stimulate the production of more and more. In that case, the most important objective was to reunite mother and baby right away.

"You'll stay on a while." He knew the executive director meant it as a question, but like everything she said, it was worded as an order. Still, her tone was warm. Helen Harper was an energetic woman Marc figured to be ex-military. She had shoulder-length straight gray hair, washed-out coloring, and no makeup. All her color came from her animated personality. And she adored the chimps. "Do I need to clear it with your boss?"

"No, that won't be necessary." Marc didn't explain further. "But I do need to make arrangements for my mother. She's…disabled." It was easier to say that than the lengthy version, though Marc knew the deaf community fought to be viewed to be as fully able as the hearing. What he meant was he'd need to check whether Barbara was available.

The sanctuary was over a hundred acres of tree-filled space for climbing and foraging, in process of being divided into separate areas as chimps were added, indoor "bedrooms" that the chimps could access at will, another two acres for a big house for staff who lived on the grounds—not all did—a kitchen building for the chimps, and storage buildings, one of which held toys for the chimps' enrichment and mental stimulation. There was a vet there twice a week and always on call. But it was the space, the lack of confinement—nothing but tree branches and sky over the chimps' heads—that Marc grasped. *Oh yes.* Yes.

Not only could Barbara stay, she seemed exceptionally pleased about it. Ria's interview had gone extremely well. She signed to Marc over Skype that she'd gotten the job. It didn't pay a lot, but Sycamore planned to increase her hours by having her teach some basic sign to staff, too. And next year's budget would for this would increase. They saw the benefit. And, when she needed an interpreter, Sycamore would pay Barbara. Both women were delighted by that, and Barbara told Marc she was genuinely excited to work alongside Ria in a new context.

And Ria couldn't wait to tell Marc that Barbara had taken her for her first driving lesson afterward. They'd used an empty elementary school parking lot, and Ria was proud to point at Barbara and tell her son that Barbara hadn't had a nervous breakdown, and they were both still alive. Barbara spoke up and said, "We went to the motor vehicle department, and got the rules book too. So she can take the written test."

"Is my car still in one piece?"

"It doesn't really need a mirror on both sides, anyway," Barbara said and signed. "I wouldn't worry."

"Very funny."

"We used Barbara's. And I didn't hit—" Ria signed, defensive. Marc would have sighed and launched into an explanation, but Barbara elbowed Ria and signed that they were teasing. Marc felt it again, how good Barbara was for his mother.

"Thank you so much," he said, hoping Barbara knew he meant for more than staying longer.

"It's a pleasure for me, honestly. I get very lonely by myself," she said. As they disconnected, he saw Barbara and his mother shoulder to shoulder, now both facing the camera, grinning at him.

There'd been that, a feel-good moment, and the camaraderie at the staff house over dinner, half-burned candles standing next to beer bottles on the plank table under the high wooden beams, and then the cool-night sleep near an open window. He'd been ready to help introduce Eve and her baby to Dembe, a dominant female in the troop, when Kate called.

"She's gone," Kate said, her voice breaking. "I wanted you to know."

"Oh god, I'm sorry. I'm so sorry. I should be there."

"No, I'll be all right. It was very quiet, the end I mean. She just slipped away. I think she wanted…"

Marc closed his eyes and willed himself to be quiet. If that was what Kate needed to believe, then he shouldn't say anything. It was too late now anyway.

"…it wasn't good." Marc tuned in to hear the end of what Kate was saying. He'd seen Dorothy catching on, starting to connect before she got sick. It hadn't had to end this way.

"I hear you." It was the most he could manage. "It must have been so hard."

She wasn't fooled. "You don't agree, do you." It wasn't a question.

"That's not important. I'm just so sorry. I'll miss her too."

"Thank you for all you did." It sounded formal. Or maybe it was just that she wanted to get off the phone right then. He couldn't tell, not when he couldn't see her face.

"I'll talk to you later?" he said. "We're just getting ready to introduce Eve…"

"She'll be fine. It's what she's needed."

"Okay, good, but—"

"Bye," she said.

After he finally replaced the phone in his pocket, at first not believing that she'd hung up, he was pulled into the life that still was, the life that needed his attention right then, and Marc liked being needed. Later, he'd think about calling her again, but wasn't sure what he'd say so he didn't.

This is how words fail, again and again, he thought, how our aim is off over and over although we try. We try. But it's not enough. It would be a long time before he'd tell himself that it may not be enough, but language is what we have and if we give up and let it fail, there is nothing left.

Helen Harper offered him a position on the staff, thinking she was stealing him away from the zoo. Barbara and Ria were both delighted with the notion of Barbara moving in with Ria as a full-time companion and interpreter in return for free room and board, a stipend, and free time when Ria went to work alone and to her deaf community classes and social events. What? Marc had tried not to wear shock on his face that because *Barbara* suggested that Ria become involved with the deaf community, Ria had agreed. When had life upended itself this way?

Marc was grateful Barbara had the sensitivity to leave Ria by herself for a while so Marc could Skype with his mother in private after the three had discussed his taking the job, the major changes they'd all undergo. "You sure about this, Mom? I'd only be able to talk with you this way and come back to visit every other month or so. It's a big change."

"Time you live your own life, son. Time for me to be more on my own. I have Barbara. We get along great. What about Kate? You have many feelings for her. Is she moving too?"

He shook his head.

Her face formed the question he knew how to read from all their years together.

Marc shook his head again, signed, "I don't know."

Marc made the trip back north to hand in his resignation, return the rented SUV, pack, and pick up his car. Ria was talking about buying a car for herself once she had her license. It was while he was back that Marc learned that the baby's name had been chosen in the contest, which the sanctuary had agreed could be completed. Masiko. A Ugandan name. That must have pleased Kate, as it had been her suggestion, and Marc remembered she'd said the name meant hope. He hoped she'd taken it as a sign. But when he and Ria attended Dororthy's memorial service, he didn't see much of it.

They sat in the last row so Marc could interpret. That was just as well; it was uncomfortable to be around the zoo staff now, though they knew why he'd been fired, and Marc was still getting frequent texts saying how much he was missed and that he'd done the right thing. Bruce was there, sitting with Tom, and Marc was relieved to see he was doing well. Linda had told him that she and Tom were seeing that blame wasn't put on the teenager's shoulders, and Tom was stepping in to support and mentor him. And he'd taken Marc's suggestion that he retrieve the collection of broken pencils for Bruce to put in order if Bruce got anxious.

Ria and Kate hugged fiercely, Ria signing to Marc to tell Kate that she'd loved Dorothy and would miss her, that Kate had been such a good daughter. Kate signed thank you to Ria and hugged her again. When it was his turn, Marc hugged Kate and whispered, "I'm so sorry. So sorry." He'd pulled her close and held her for as long as he dared. "Can we get together later? We need to talk—"

"Thank you," she said, a strange non-answer, as if she were answering someone else's condolences by rote. She turned to the next person without lingering.

He left to go back to Tennessee the next morning. She'd not answered her phone when he called the night after the funeral, and as it was, he was taking time off he'd not accrued yet. But she didn't call and didn't call back either time he called again. He surmised that she held him responsible. For their losing Eve and her baby. For causing hurt. And he was.

After Mom died, my relief that she wasn't suffering turned on me as if a choir that had sung a benediction became a mob shouting accusations. I was guilty and bereft. And alone. Marc was gone, as large an absence as Mom's, although that made me feel guilty too. How could I be so disloyal to her as to feel that way? And why hadn't I been a better daughter when she would have heard my words and taken them in?

I wished I could talk to Marc. But I knew his judgment, his conviction I should have said no to hospice care, held out for a chance to communicate with her, even if it was differently. I just couldn't make her live tethered, helpless. I'd made the decision I could live with if I were in her place. I'd never know if it was right for her. How could I tell him how guilty I felt? That now I had no idea if I'd done the right thing.

I barely made it through the funeral. Whatever people said to me was so much white noise whirring in my head. I just kept saying thank you over and over. I figured that would be right. He was there, with Ria, and he hugged me, I remembered that. But he'd taken a job at the sanctuary in Tennessee. The sanctuary that had taken Eve and her baby. I understood that. He'd want to be away from here, from me.

I poured out all this to Becky and while she was sympathetic, she told me to call Marc. I wanted to. I wanted to beg. But for what? There was nothing I could do over. And maybe I wouldn't anyway.

How had everything been lost so completely, so suddenly? I was aware of the emptiness by day when I tried to work, and by night when I tried to sleep. Autumn was crisping the air, and the sun slanted down on the walkways, filtered through gradually thinning scarlet and gold branches. Zoo repairs finished, we reopened quickly and the new habitat for the great apes became a popular feature.

Thurston thought he was being magnanimous when he called me to his inner sanctum to offer me the position of Research Director. Tie straight and flat-top hand-flattened, he laid it out. "I know you did your best with the situation," he said solemnly. "I need to keep my end, and let you have a shot. We'll make it an Interim appointment, and let you see what you can do."

My reward for selling Marc out. Had I done that?

Perhaps I'd wanted it for so long that getting it was a let-down. Everything had fallen apart. My familiar life had collapsed like an abandoned building around me, and there was no way to reassemble it. So much had happened that getting the job I wanted couldn't begin to fill the hole left by the losses. I should have been thrilled and enthusiastic, but I would miss being around the animals, and when I thought about the habitat destruction and poaching continuing in Africa, I circled back to my dream of returning. Good people still worked there, trying to put out a forest fire with a garden hose, yet they couldn't, didn't give up. It seemed that now was finally my time to return.

I applied for a post doc fellowship when a month of working under Thurston's thumb had gotten to me. A project in Uganda would put new structure around my free time, let me dive deep looking for solutions. Maybe I hoped to distract myself from loneliness, fill the evening hours that I wasted thinking about Marc, my mind always picking at everything that had happened, worrying it back and forth like a hangnail. I had been right, I had been wrong, did it matter?

Thurston approved a leave of absence, probably thrilled about the budget relief, saying there would be a job for me upon my return. He couldn't guarantee it would be for the research job, though he'd do his level best, he said. Linda would want me back in the primate department for sure, though I didn't know if I could bear it. I'd found a new project that showed promise and I couldn't wait to return to the lush beauty of Uganda.

It was work associated with a Lake Victoria island sanctuary, and the mission was to save the habitat of the over six hundred wild chimps in an area of the rainforest where they came into regular conflict with subsistence farmers. The chimps raided the farmers' crops looking for food, and to save their livelihood, the farmers killed the chimps.

The project—a new one for the sanctuary—formed and trained groups of community farmers to work like co-ops to raise different crops, ones that would sell well at market but that the chimps found unpalatable. Banding together, the farmers could build community financial resources. We distributed seed for ginger, soybeans, onions, potatoes; none are on a chimp menu.

I lived in a remote field camp, an area where we knew the farmers raged a particularly fierce battle against chimps, one the chimp population was losing. Our conditions were primitive, though I was grateful we had a cook. At first it was strange and disorienting to be cut off from the world, without the internet. Finally, I let the silence be more liberating than painful.

The weeks lengthened their shadows into months. The long rains came, leaving the road to the camp impassable for a while, the mud thick and slippery. We were doing some good, yes, the project made a difference, but it couldn't begin to compensate for the habitat destruction, as the rainforest steadily gave way to the giant machines clearcutting for palm oil and sugar plantations, industrial agriculture, firewood, and now, oil extraction.

The deforestation meant there wasn't enough rain, too, so while the population and poverty exploded and land was grabbed by international conglomerates, drought killed like a silent stalker. Politicians on the take and corporate executives intent on profits and increasing shareholder value held all the power and ignored all the warnings research scientists, primatologists, zoologists, and biologists gave. We struggled to make a difference, struggled to be heard, to address the dangerous climate change that would kill animals and humans alike. Our warnings were discounted, studies and projects either dismissed or actively undermined. Still, we tried.

One day when a few of us were out in the forest to assess how much fruit the trees were bearing, whether the chimps would have an adequate natural food supply, we stumbled on the decaying bodies of three chimps. Their deaths weren't recent, only heart crushing. As best we could tell, they'd been shot. From the amount of broken undergrowth, some of us thought it had been a nursing party, poachers after babies. If so, there'd have been more adult mothers here too. Had they been taken, their bodies sold as bushmeat, their babies sold to middlemen, like Eve? Had our farmers been involved?

After we returned to the camp, I slipped off to be by myself, to sob my hopelessness into a towel, alone under the glorious canopy of trees that suddenly seemed so desolate. If there were words for this despair, I did not search them out then. To whom would I have spoken them anyway?

As a British anthropologist said one night when we joined some of the Ugandans for a group meal, "We scientists have the will, but we don't have the power." That was more true than I'd been able to bear. Or admit.

But it was something my tent mate said once that got to me. Vanessa was older than I by ten or fifteen years, a university professor from a small eastern college on a sabbatical. She reminded me so much of my mother as she was before her first move to Sycamore, hair threaded with early gray, her waist with that light padding, her earnest trying. Being around her made me teary, which, of course, I hid. Vanessa kept trying to be friends, and why wouldn't she? There weren't ten feet between our cots. Over the weeks, she'd dropped various details about her family, her ex-husband. I hadn't reciprocated. She was kind and cheerful, but I knew she felt put off. I had enough decency to feel guilty, but not enough to do something about it.

One night, she asked me a couple of questions about my family, and whether I had "someone special" back home. My brief responses must have been abrupt; she sighed into the silence after one of them, a silence starry with the small sounds of the night alive between the tents and beyond the camp. She reached for the lantern on the small table next to her and shut down the amber circle of light. "I'm sorry," she said. "I was just trying to talk with you. Good night." I didn't confuse what edged her voice with annoyance. It was the gently frayed hem of loneliness.

I hadn't talked with my mother when she could have understood. Why would I talk to Vanessa now? How could I?

I lay in silence for a few minutes, knowing from her breathing that Vanessa was not sleeping any more than I was. She wouldn't press me. I could go on exactly as I had, and it would be an okay life. I could be a productive person. Alone but productive. Was that a bad thing?

"I'm sorry, Nessie, I'm really sorry," I said into the unlit space between us, using the nickname she'd told me her colleagues back home had given her. I turned on my side, tried to make out the shape of her body on her cot. I had to do better. "It's not your fault. You're good. I had some big losses recently, right before I came here, I mean, my mother died, and a man… I guess I'm not handling it as well as I…But I don't mean to shut you out. We can talk. I'm really sorry."

Her voice turned warm, soft as a cotton blanket then. "Thanks for telling me. Don't worry, honey. You and me, we're fine. I understand. It would be good to talk more."

Before exhaustion wrapped me in its gauze that night, I wondered to whom else I'd apologized, who'd answered me, forgiven me. It was too much to hope.

# Chapter 37

EVE AND MASIKO THRIVED in the sanctuary. Eve had never forgotten the signs for fruit and more, which touched Marc, and he still signed Marc love Eve to her when he saw her, but he'd not tried to teach her more. She was fully integrated into the troop at the sanctuary now, and though he felt a special tie to her, the right thing was to let her go.

She'd learned to mother. Nursing had been a struggle at first, so much of her milk had dried up, but the baby was persistent, latching on, and working at it hungrily, and the sanctuary staff had been willing to wait it out. Marc shook his head; it wouldn't have happened at the zoo where they'd have been in a hurry to intervene. But it had worked. And Dembe, an experienced chimp mother was acting like a devoted aunt, babysitting when Eve learned to forage. Dembe, particularly popular among the males at the sanctuary because she continued to cycle despite the birth control implant she, like all the females, had received had only recently stopped nursing her four-year-old baby boy. Akiki—a softie, although he sure loved to display—was presumed to be the father based on the interest he showed in the infant.

It was Akiki that Eve copied, learning to use a stick as a tool to look for bugs in the ground. Now she presented her head and back to him as well as Dembe to groom, as if she'd done it all her life, and Marc grinned, more satisfied than he'd imagined he could be. Yes, he said to himself sometimes. Kate was right about what's best for them.

And Ria, well, his mother was happier than Marc remembered her ever having been. Even over Skype, that was apparent. Sycamore was welcoming more deaf residents as staff grew more comfortable and Ria was there every day now to communicate, and, for those deafened by advanced age or disease, teach them new skills. She'd gotten her driver's license and Barbara had helped her buy a second-hand car. "We already *negotiated*," Ria had bragged to Marc when he offered to come home to help her with that, and he hadn't quite known whether to be thrilled or sad at not being needed.

When he went home to visit Ria and Barbara, it had taken quite a while before Marc was ready to visit with his old colleagues at the zoo. Finally, enough time had passed that the sting of being let go had eased and what he'd learned from the zoo coalesced into gratitude, aided by the dignity of a significant promotion at the sanctuary.

Had he hoped to see Kate? That, too. So much he wanted to tell her. He'd start with the sanctuary and watch her face to see what more he could risk, if he could just say how much he missed her.

That wasn't to be. It was Linda who told him she'd returned to Africa for research. Uganda again. And Marc said, "I'm not surprised, actually," though he was, though it felt like a body blow. "She loved it there."

Linda said, "I can give you her contact information."

"That's ok, I was just hoping to say hello." He felt himself start to redden, but said, made himself go on, "Well, if you don't mind, maybe you'd give me her email?"

"She's still got her email here, she's just on leave. I wrote her one snail mail care of the project, myself. I suspect field delivery is pretty sporadic, but I'll give you that, too," Linda opened her desk and pulled out a lengthy address in Uganda, copied it on a yellow

Post-it note that brought back a host of memories. She handed it to Marc who thanked her and stuck it in his shirt pocket.

As he was leaving her office, Linda hugged him in the doorway. "Marc, you saved that chimp. Broke every rule. Amen. I sure wouldn't want you making a habit of it—love is one thing, and a savior complex is another—but between you and me, I'll recommend you and write you references for the rest of your life, anytime for anything. Thank you for what you did."

Replaying Linda's words in his head, Marc returned to the sanctuary at the end of that long, Indian summer weekend. It was Tennessee hot, but the sanctuary had deep forest shade and the tree breeze for which to give thanks, and the chimps didn't seem in the least bothered by the heat. Staff slathered on sunscreen and bug repellent.

He did email Kate at her zoo address, only hinting at his longing, how sorry he was, how much he missed her, cloaked it in saying he wanted her to know how Eve and Masiko were living, and he saw how good what she'd wanted for their zoo chimps was. He signed it *With love, Marc*, so much more he wanted to say, yet being careful, careful. He left it in drafts and redid it over four days. Finally, impulsively, he added a P.S. *I wish more than anything you would talk to me. I hurt you by not understanding your decision and I want to tell you I'm really sorry. I was trying to save your ability to communicate with your mother but instead I wrecked ours. I know now that there's so much I/we can't save —but can I save that? Or, rather, can we?*

Before he let himself spend another four days second guessing, he pushed send.

By then, Marc was Director of Education and was working with a University of Tennessee group on a project on which he'd base his doctoral dissertation. He'd made friends on the staff, turned out to be a decent cook himself, joining the lively pot-luck dinners three or four times a week in the big staff gathering room, and the other nights choosing quiet music in his small quarters, using his galley kitchen, opening a bottle of beer or wine, and putting his feet up.

It was a good life. He knew when various women from the university flirted with him, but he pretended not to get it. And he knew Samantha, who managed interns and volunteers at the sanctuary, was interested in him. He pretended not to get that too. He vaguely knew that his non-participation in any liaison—of course they happened all the time as staff and interns got involved and gossip spread like soft butter on warm bread—was the subject of speculation. Something else he ignored.

The staff dinner went extra late one night. Pete had a new guitar and Kim—the most creative among them—improvised a couple of drums, and they'd all sat around in candlelight drinking wine and calling out song requests. If Pete had forgotten some of the words, well, the ones he made up were way more funny than the originals. By the time Marc left for his own quarters, he was tired and inclined to omit his routine email check, the one he always did just in case. Even though his good sense told him there was no point. Not anymore, not after this long.

He shouldn't have looked. Finding nothing in his inbox but a note from his dissertation advisor made him think about what he'd lost, rehearse in his mind what he could have done differently. Those thoughts made sleep so elusive that nothing helped, not even reading an article loaded with statistics by a primate veterinarian, so boring and dry the pages should have crumbled in his fingers as he turned them. He gave up, turned out the bedside light and lay awake for a long time. He kept playing it out in his mind, what it would be like to see her again. To be with her. To make everything right. *Marc, you can't save everything.* He heard the voices of his mentors.

The small night sounds of the Tennessee woods came through his open window. Crickets, branch against branch, one primate that might be Eve calling, another answering, calling and answering in the language of kin, giving the comfort of kin. *Are you there? Yes, I am here.* Was that their meaning? He had to acknowledge he couldn't know now, and although the antiphon was mysterious, still, hearing it was deeply satisfying.

A month later, Marc lifted two buckets of fruit to carry out to distribute. It wasn't his job—but he'd hoped to spot Eve and the baby, Masiko, because he could say he loved her and it would take him back, but not all the way, to the place that was too sad. It was ironic, in a way. He'd thought that taking care of his mother would be the reason he couldn't have what he wanted for himself. That secret frustration seemed ridiculous now.

As he walked outside and down the path, he saw someone standing outside the gate, though it wasn't a day when Board members or any visitors should have been coming, so Marc walked toward the distant figure. Helen Harper was ahead of him, already on her way out from the office. She'd be polite but pointed as a dart, letting the stranger know this was not a proper day or time.

Squinting, Marc picked up his pace, then disbelieving, he put down the buckets and broke into a run. "Wait. Wait Helen. It's okay. I got it." The director swung around toward him, stopped to see what was happening. Marc didn't explain, because he was close enough now to see the familiar face, the blonde hair, the shape of her.

"Kate? It's really you? Are you here? Oh my god. Kate!" And then Marc was there, and his arms were around her. "I can't believe it," he said into her hair as he held her to him, one hand caressing the back of her head.

"I'm here," she said, and he felt her nod against his chest, and her voice broke with emotion as she said, "Can we talk?"

I'd imagined it on the trip back from Uganda. First, he'd take me to see Eve and Masiko. Then he'd want to show me all around, though I'd been there and knew Helen well. "But you haven't seen the changes we're making. The improvements," he'd say. He'd be right about that, but really, he'd be wanting me to know that watching how the chimps lived in the sanctuary had changed him, too. But later, after dinner when we could be alone, uninterrupted, we'd go to his quarters and finally, we'd talk. Could we sort out what needed to be sorted, pan for each other's gold, save it?

If we could, I'd stay. Marc would arrange with Helen for me to stay with him while we made decisions. If I stayed, when he opened his arms again, I'd lean into them. I'd press my face to his neck, and his hands would be tender on me. When we kissed, tears would mingle on our faces the way streams that flow from separate headwaters merge in a river that carries life on.

# Eve

THE PARROT-ANIMAL came only sometimes and was not the same, not like a parrot anymore. But Eve knew him. He made the same sounds as before and moved hands the same way, and Eve still knew how to get more fruit from him. Now Eve was not alone, she was with ones like her all the time, and the little Eve was hers and theirs too, all with each other, and it was very good. There were some animals who were not like Eve, but they did not hurt her and she did not fear them because the others who were like her were not afraid. Another animal Eve knew came again after a long time, and Eve gave a pleasure greeting of short breaths and hoots so the others would know too.

Eve liked to climb high in many different trees to see that in each one, above her were only birds and smaller branches, green playing with breeze, breeze playing with green, like it was all there to play with Eve in the great open.

# Discussion Questions

1.      What do you understand to be Marc's argument for the importance and necessity of zoos?

2.      What do you understand to be Kate's reason for arguing that zoos are immoral and unethical especially with regard to primates?

3.      Did either argument surprise you? Is this an issue about which you already had feelings? If so, what were they?

4.      Did reading this book change any feelings you had about zoos in either direction, especially as regards great apes in zoos?

5.      Do you have a favorite character? What particularly appealed to you about him/her?

6.      Have you been familiar with any deaf people personally? Do you know any American Sign Language? Did you find Honoria relatable?

7.      How about autistic people? Do you know any? Were you comfortable with the depiction of Bruce? Did you feel the zoo staff understood him and did you feel you were able to?

8.      Were you previously familiar with primary aphasia? Do you feel you have a reasonable layperson's understanding of it now?

9.      Were you able to understand both Kate's and the Sycamore Retirement Center's point of view when at the care meeting the Director insisted that she move her mother out of

assisted living and into the nursing facility. Did you find yourself "siding" with either one?

10.     Have you cared for a dependent elderly parent or relative yourself, or perhaps taken part or been a direct observer? Is this something you expect to take on in the future? How does either Kate's or Marc's experience compare?

11.     How did you feel toward Eve? Did you like the way the sections of her story were presented? Were you already aware of the backgrounds of many of the great apes now in America? What did you think of Marc's approach to working with her? What about Kate's? Were you inclined to believe more in one or the other?

12.     How did you react to Kate and Marc's relationship? Did you find yourself annoyed with either or wanting either to be or do something different? Was how each acted consistent with his or her character as you understood it?

13.     Did you think what Vanessa (Kate's tentmate in Uganda) said to Kate was pivotal, or was Kate emotionally recovering, seeing things differently, and "ready" to work things out?

14.     If you were writing a movie script for this novel, would you take the ending farther? By how much? Hours? Days? A year into the future? How would you end it? What do you think happens between Kate and Marc and what do you think they do in the future?

15.     Did any of your views or feelings change or become reinforced by reading this book? Did you find the story engrossing?

# Acknowledgements

I'M TYPICALLY BOTH EAGER and terrified to write the all-important Acknowledgments; I want the people who have been so much help with a book to know how grateful I am, and I'm afraid I'm going to overlook someone I couldn't have done it without. So, I plunge into it, hoping an episode of being dumb doesn't overcome me, and I apologize in advance if it does.

My agent, Stacy Testa, was nothing short of abundantly generous with her time and help with this novel. I am so grateful for her ability and her faith, backed by the wonderful team at Writers House. My editor, Kristina Makansi, is responsive, skillful, and kind. She caught mistakes I didn't realize I even knew how to make. *And* she has a sense of humor. Jackpot. The team at Amphorae Publishing Group, especially Lisa Miller and Laura Robinson, has been supportive and hard-working. I appreciate them all beyond words.

The novel wouldn't have ever made it to a first draft stage without an enormous amount of research, particularly because in-person visits were not exactly considered welcome during the covid pandemic. Dr. Linda Marchant, a biological anthropologist with a specialty in primatology, who has done a great deal of field study with wild chimpanzees in Uganda and several other African nations, provided a large stack of research books, articles, videos, and helpful website links. She was extremely patient, answered questions, and put me in touch with colleagues. I had lunch at Dr. Marchant's home with Linda Koebner, M.A., who has worked with captive chimps in laboratories and sanctuaries, including doing behavioral rehabilitation with them. Dr. Marchant also put me in contact with Dr. Samantha Russak, who, like Dr. Marchant is a biological anthropologist with a specialty in primatology. Dr. Russak studied wild chimpanzees in Tanzania and has over eleven years of experience working in the zoo industry across the U.S. She is currently the Manager of Research and Welfare of a zoological facility in Kansas. Dr. Russak read a final draft of the manuscript and provided consultation to ensure its accuracy regarding chimps, including their care (and rehabilitation) in zoos. There aren't adequate words to thank these professionals enough for helping me grasp the genuine dilemmas involved. Finally, Dr. Kathy McMahon-Klosterman gave me helpful information and directed me to websites and sources of accurate education regarding American Sign Language and deaf culture. I am so grateful for her kindness and interest.

First readers are crucial to an author because they give feedback about what's working and what's not in the story. In addition to, of course, Stacy Testa, I had Tara Gavin, who truly devoted herself to making the manuscript the very best it could be in the most loving way imaginable. I lost count of how many times she read it. Additionally, authors Donna Everhart, Randy Susan Meyers, and A.C. Burch, and my very literary sister, Janice Rockwell, and extremely well-read husband, Alan deCourcy, all read *The Language of Kin*, either in an early draft form or a later version and gave encouraging feedback.

I'd be remiss if I didn't mention the importance of the online writing community. Now here's where I know I'm leaving somebody important out, as I try and fail to list all the caring and helpful book club moderators and recommenders on Facebook who make such a difference: Sue Peterson, Linda Zagon, Kristy Barrett,

Tonni Callan, Jennifer Bryan Vawser, Denise Birt, Linda Milito Martin, Andrea Peskind Katz, Dawny Ruby, and the on-top-of everything Suzanne Leopold. And so many thanks to those special Instagram reviewers like the Tarheel Reader, the Bookish Mama, the Mary Reader, the Good Book Fairy… here's where I get myself into trouble because this acknowledgments page will become a chapter if I go on with the bookstagrammers and online book people (Susan Roberts! Carla Suto!) who support authors, and I hope the rest of you will forgive me for leaving you unnamed—you're never unappreciated. Thank you, thank you all for the way you share your love of books and help promote the work into which we authors invest our minds, hearts, and time—because you do, too. And thank you from my heart to each reader who's read one or all of my previous books. I hope you'll love this one and will let me know your thoughts.

I also want to thank the community of authors who support each other, knowing it's sometimes hard, sometimes discouraging. Caroline Leavitt and Jenna Blum started A Mighty Blaze to showcase authors' new work during the pandemic when no live events were held and steadily expanded it since. Writers reach out to one another regularly to empathize, agonize, and celebrate, affirming that although we do the work in solitude, we are not alone.

It's a privilege to work with Ann-Marie Nieves of Get Red PR, whose enthusiasm for this novel and sheer professional skill are the wind beneath its wings. And a life preserver for many years have been my web designers at Nodebud Authors, whose listening skills and creative work are always equally excellent.

Lastly, thank you to my husband, Alan deCourcy, always interested, always willing, always supportive of this crazy work I do; I love him for that and so much else.

# About the Author

LYNNE HUGO IS A National Endowment for the Arts Fellowship recipient who has also received repeat grants from the Ohio Arts Council and the Kentucky Foundation for Women. *The Language of Kin* is her tenth novel and thirteenth book. Her memoir, *Where The Trail Grows Faint*, won the Riverteeth Literary Nonfiction Book Prize and her novel, *A Matter of Mercy*, received the 2015 Independent Publishers Silver Medal for Best North-East Fiction. Another novel, *Swimming Lessons*, became a Lifetime Original Movie of the Month. More recently, *The Testament of Harold's Wife* was a Buzz Books Fall/Winter 2018 selection. Through the Ohio Arts Council's renowned Arts in Education program, Lynne has taught creative writing to hundreds of schoolchildren.

Born and educated in New England, Lynne and her photographer husband live in Ohio. They are grateful parents who have three grandchildren and large, rowdy extended families. Their yellow Lab, Scout, insists that you be aware he is the terror of squirrels in a three-state area, most excellent at barking and rolling in anything gross and stinky on the hiking trails.